# the further adventures of

# SHERLOCK HOLMES

## THE ANGEL OF THE OPERA

the further adventures of

# SHERLOCK HOLMES

## THE ANGEL OF THE OPERA

### SAM SICILIANO

TITAN BOOKS

THE FURTHER ADVENTURES OF SHERLOCK HOLMES:
THE ANGEL OF THE OPERA
ISBN: 9781848568617

Published by
Titan Books
A division of Titan Publishing Group Ltd
144 Southwark St
London
SE1 0UP

First edition: March 2011
10 9 8 7 6 5 4 3 2 1

Visit our website:
**www.titanbooks.com**

What did you think of this book? We love to hear from our
readers. Please email us at: readerfeedback@titanemail.com,
or write to us at the above address. To receive advance information,
news, competitions, and exclusive Titan offers online, please register
as a member by clicking the 'sign up' button on our website:
www.titanbooks.com

A CIP catalogue record for this title is available from the British Library.

Printed in the USA.

To my mother, for introducing me to Sherlock Holmes, Tarzan of the Apes, and the Land of Oz. She tolerated my youthful vampire novel, but this is the book she would have been proud of.

*Dear Reader,*

The following manuscript was written in the summer of 1891, shortly after the events recounted herein. My purpose at the time was to reveal the real Sherlock Holmes as corrective to the ridiculous fictional creation of John Watson. Holmes was my truest friend and my cousin, his mother, Violet Sherrinford, being my mother's sister. However, when in 1892 I showed Sherlock this account of our adventures in Paris, he asked me, quite sternly, not to publish it. Watson's writings he thought bad enough; far worse to have his true character revealed, his soul bared to the masses! He was also concerned about the privacy of others.

With regret I yielded to his wishes, and over the years, as yet another of Watson's foolish stories appeared, I gritted my teeth and tried to master patience. Now that Sherlock, God rest his soul, and John Watson are both dead, I can finally publish what was truly Holmes's strangest case. The devil's foot business cannot possibly compare with this.

Sherlock Holmes was a much more interesting, a much deeper, man than Watson rendered him. Watson had little imagination and was extremely conventional in the stuffiest British sense. His accounts transfer that same conventionality to my cousin, including the typical British imperialistic sentiments of the day. Nothing could be more false! Sherlock was also extremely cynical about contemporary religiosity. When Watson has him declaiming that the beauty of a rose reflects the Creator or lecturing a maimed woman against suicide, he was creating pure fiction. Sherlock was an agnostic, and he despised smugness and cant.

Watson could be quite obtuse about Holmes. For instance, he took my cousin's disdain for the fair sex at face value, never wondering if perhaps "the lady doth protest too much."

Watson was accurate in his physical description of Holmes, but Sydney Paget's drawings were highly idealized. My cousin was not so handsome, nor did he resemble the actor Basil Rathbone! His hawkish nose threw his face off balance; his hair began to recede in his late thirties; his lips were thin; and he had a weak chin. All in all, he had a certain grotesque quality, his skeletal frame, his blazing eyes, pale complexion, and large nose all contributing to the impression. My frankness here may seem unkind, but his heart and his mind were what made Sherlock Holmes great.

He could be a difficult man to live with. As even Watson notes, he alternated between periods of frantic activity and black depression. During the latter, thoughts of death, evil, and his own failings tormented him, but to his dying day, he was not one to confide in others. Watson and he were temperamentally poles apart, and their relationship was nowhere near so rosy as in the stories. In fact, a major row separated them for several years. Watson was so angry that he promptly invented Moriarty and killed off my cousin (much to Sherlock's relief) at Reichenbach Falls. The events I recount took place shortly after that falling out.

It is probably rather obvious by now that Watson and I never much cared for one another. I cannot forgive him for parading so distorted, so petty a rendering of my cousin before the public for all those years. Since I, too, was trained in medicine, I can state that his failings as a physician were even greater than those as a writer. I encountered several examples of his incompetence firsthand!

But I must be charitable to the dead. Even after all these years, Watson still warms my old blood! This book is about Sherlock Holmes, not John Watson, and I hope the reader will not be displeased to discover Holmes, "warts and all." Despite his faults, he was a great and generous man, the finest I have ever known. My wife and I named a son after him, and we who loved him still miss him deeply.

I have made few alterations in the manuscript, leaving my youthful enthusiasm intact. Those were gentler, more innocent times, when mankind could still look to the future with wonder and hope instead of despair. Often have I wished that I could leave this dark, wretched twentieth century and return to the 1890s to again walk the streets of Paris with Sherlock Holmes.

Doctor Henry Vernier
London, July 1939

# *Prologue*

S herlock Holmes stared at the goddess of death, the incarnation of
evil, while I, being of a less melancholic nature, mused upon the
young woman playing the piano.

Wales in January—the large hall of the ancient castle cold and empty,
a major blizzard raging outside. Susan Lowell's music, more than the
coal glowing in the fireplace, lightened the darkness and warmed us.
Her powers as a musician were extraordinary, but I lack my cousin's
technical understanding of music and his perfect pitch. Harmonic
theory, sonata allegro form, and fugues are mysteries to me. I enjoy
serious music, but it takes a clumsy player indeed to deviate so much
from the rhythm or pitch that my ear (clumsier still) can detect the
variance. The woman's physiognomy and her beauty were what drew
my attention.

Her face displayed both her Indian and her Anglo-Saxon heritage. She
had the large, almond-shaped eyes, the long, straight nose and narrow
face, the combination of delicacy and dignity, so often found in the
women of India. Sadly, the trachoma which had left her nearly blind had

thickened and disfigured her eyelids and cast a film over her stunning black eyes. The effects of the disease were only too familiar; I had seen them everywhere in the Orient. Her hair was not pure black, but had a brownish cast inherited from her father, and her skin, too, was paler than that of a pure-blooded Indian. Her dress, however, had nothing of the exotic: her hair was bound up in conventional British or French fashion, and she wore a dark skirt and a white shirtwaist made of silk. Her long brown fingers stretched with ease to strike Chopin's chords.

I could not help but reflect upon the two absurd blows fate had struck her. Still in her early thirties, Susan Lowell was beautiful, sensitive, intelligent, and wealthy; but no family of even modest pretense would allow their son to marry a half-caste. Some simpering blonde with the intelligence of a spaniel, gladly—but never one such as she! Nature had also treated her unkindly, afflicting her at an early age with a disease virtually nonexistent in the temperate climate of England. Had her father returned sooner to his native land, she would still possess her sight.

Although she was slender and of moderate stature, there was nothing meek or mild in the thunderous conclusion to Chopin's piece. She let the final chords fade slowly until silence had once again claimed the massive chamber. At last she sighed, and the flush on her cheeks also faded.

Sherlock turned from the statue. "Bravo." He clapped his hands. "Really most excellent, Miss Lowell. I have not heard Chopin played better."

"I am no music critic," I said, "but it was beautiful."

She smiled, turning her head toward me, but her eyes stared vacantly into space. "Thank you, gentlemen. It is vain, I know, but I enjoy having an audience. However, it is very late, and I am weary."

I stood. "It was boorish of us to let you continue for so long, but your playing was utterly captivating."

She smiled again. "You are very gracious, Doctor Vernier. Catherine."

Her maid took her arm, but she needed little guidance in so familiar a room. "Until tomorrow, and I hope, Mr. Holmes, that you will again join me on the violin."

"You have my promise, Miss Lowell. You know the *Kreutzer?*"

"Indeed, yes."

"I shall look forward to it."

Sherlock stood rather stiffly. I reached out and gave her arm a squeeze. It felt soft under the smooth silk. "Thank you again, Miss Lowell."

The smile she gave me made me wish briefly that my affections had not been pledged elsewhere. How I missed Michelle! Sherlock waited until she had left, then withdrew his pipe, lit it, and soon exhaled a cloud of smoke.

I coughed once, and he gave me a twisted, sardonic smile that seemed completely unrelated to Miss Lowell's radiant expression. He wore his customary black frock coat and gray striped trousers; his face was pale and tired. "A foul habit, Doctor, but one of a very fixed and determined nature. You seem rather taken with the young lady."

"She is not only beautiful, but has a quick mind and a generous nature."

"I see you have noticed her interior qualities as well."

I smiled. "It required no great powers of deduction."

"Indeed? Then it is surprising there is not a crowd of fine young fellows courting the lady."

"That is because the world is filled with fools."

"The same thought had occurred to me."

"I noticed you seemed more occupied with another lady, one of a more bloodthirsty disposition."

Holmes nodded. "She is indeed a woman of a different stripe." Slowly he approached the statue, then stood with folded arms, his pipe in one hand. "She is ghastly, is she not? Kali Ma, the Black Mother, the goddess of murderers and assassins, the goddess of blood and death."

"It is strangely beautiful."

"Do you think so?"

"Yes," I said, "in a perverse sort of way. Certainly Major Lowell must think so to have kept it all these years."

Sherlock gave me another brief, crooked smile, but his gray eyes had an odd glint. "I think she is the most truly ugly thing I have ever seen or am likely to see." He put the stem of his pipe between his lips.

The statue had been carved from black marble, and the smooth polish of the stone clashed with the roughness of execution and the hideousness of the subject. Kali, the Black Mother, stood nearly three feet tall. A corpse carved with exquisite detail hung from each earlobe. An equally elaborate necklace of skulls hung about her neck, falling below the pointed breasts, and at her waist was a girdle made up of a double row of severed hands. One of her four arms held the head of a giant, another a sword with a curved blade, another a terrified man. Her free hand was raised in an upright gesture. She stood upon the crouching form of another god, one leg raised and bent. Her tongue thrust grotesquely from her mouth, and her eyes were two blood-colored rubies. Unlike the dusky marble, the gems had the trick of catching any stray light so that they had a faint, disconcertingly life-like glow.

"The jewels are beautiful," I said. "They must be worth a fortune."

"In themselves they might be beautiful, if you could remove them from so polluted a context. However, I think they will always remain the eyes of the goddess of death."

"You are keeping something from me. In your best consulting detective manner."

"Nothing which should not be rather obvious. By the way, I received this note today forwarded from London. Read it."

My eyes widened. Written in French, it was a solicitation from

*L'Opéra de Paris,* signed by Messieurs Richard and Moncharmin, asking for his aid in clearing up the matter of an "opera ghost" who had been disrupting things. "This sounds like the very case for you. It appears to have everything."

"Would you care to accompany me, Henry? I shall want to be there in a fortnight. I could use your services."

"You're joking. You know I have absolutely no skill at detection."

"True, but your command of the language would be helpful."

"Sherlock, you speak excellent French."

"But I have had no practice for some time, and I do have an accent."

"A very slight one."

"Perhaps, but enough to give me away. That accent will limit where I can go and what I can discover. You would have no such limitations. Besides, we shall stay in an excellent hotel, dine like royalty, and no doubt attend several performances gratis. Only the French can do *Faust* justice, and there are rumors of some new sensation doing Marguerite."

I laughed. "You know I am no great opera enthusiast, but the hotel and the cuisine are very appealing. I would be glad to come. I have not been to Paris for two years now, and any excuse would suffice—not that I do not enjoy sharing your adventures. Michelle will cover our practice for me. Oh, she will not want me to rush away again so soon, but I shall persuade her. I shall have a week to shower her with my attentions."

Holmes nodded. "Good. It's settled then." He drew in deeply on his pipe, his eyes drawn again to the statue. "We are almost finished here."

"Almost? Have you not captured the last of the thugs? The threat to Major Lowell and his daughter is gone."

A cloud of white smoke drifted from his lips, but his eyes remained fixed. "Perhaps. There remain a few... details."

"That statue certainly fascinates you."

"Evil has always fascinated me, Henry, and I doubt I have ever seen a case of purer, more unrefined evil than this."

"But the thugs, in the end, did not amount to much. Life is very simple for them. Their mission is to strangle as many of their fellow creatures as possible for their goddess there. They were out of their sunny Indian element here in the cold wastes of Wales. I almost felt sorry for them, having to deal with the English winter and the net Sherlock Holmes had laid for them. Major Lowell should not have shot them, you know. Murderers many times over they may be, but they deserved their chance before a court of law and an English jury."

"Major Lowell had an excellent reason for shooting them."

"Indeed?" I said.

He took his pipe from between his lips, but said nothing.

"Sherlock, will you stop staring at that cursed statue and explain yourself."

Another cloud of smoke came from between his lips, then he turned to look at me. "You will understand soon enough."

"Ah, my friends, still admiring my statue, yes?"

Major Lowell was in excellent humor. He wore a crimson velvet dressing gown and held a large cigar, which my physician's instincts made me wish to pluck from his lips. From his accounts of his involvement in India during the thirties, I knew he must be well into his seventies. His color was never good, and I could tell from being around him for the past few days that he suffered from shortness of breath and angina. His hair was quite white, the bushy sideburns connected to a large white mustache, but his chin and jaw were smooth shaven. The style had been the rage decades ago. His face was flushed, probably from drink, but the skin about his eyes had a sickly grayish cast.

Holmes nodded. "In many ways I consider her the key to the entire case."

The hint of a frown clouded Lowell's brow. "You do?"

Sherlock stared at the statue. "You contacted me shortly after Colonels Davidson and Broderick were found dead. You recounted your shared experiences in India more than fifty years past when you were part of British efforts to suppress the 'thugs,' ritual murderers and assassins who killed thousands in the name of their goddess Kali. Both Davidson and Broderick appeared to have been strangled by thugs, intruders from the past seeking vengeance. You feared you were next."

Lowell's smile had returned. "Quite so, Mr. Holmes, and a good end we have seen to this troublesome business." Sherlock stared at him so long before replying that the old man began to fidget nervously with his cigar.

"A very convenient end, two of the men dead, including the priest who led them, and the other two in police custody. How fortunate, also, that those two speak not a word of English. It would be interesting to discuss their fierce goddess with them. Alas, I have studied most European languages, but not Hindustani."

The Major shook his head. "A barbaric and ugly tongue, Mr. Holmes, hardly worth your trouble."

"Ah, but as a near relative of Sanskrit, the mother tongue of all our Western languages, it would be fascinating. Anyway, Major, all your enemies are conveniently eliminated, and now you may dwell in peace during the remainder of your days."

"All thanks to you, Mr. Holmes."

Sherlock set down his pipe on the table next to the statue. "I fear that there is still one complication."

"Complication?" Lowell echoed.

"Yes, Major Lowell. The complication is that you yourself are a thug."

I have never seen a man so transformed as Lowell was at that moment. The cigar fell from his lips, and all the color went out of his face, his lips turning bluish. I would have been more concerned for his health had I not been so totally surprised myself. "Sherlock, what are you saying?"

"I am saying that Major Lowell is and has been a thug, and not in the quaint, colloquial usage of the word, but in its darker, original meaning. Instead of acting with Broderick and Davidson to suppress the thugs, he was secretly a devotee of the black goddess. As such he has betrayed everything: his compatriots and his commission as a British officer, his country and queen, even the Christian God."

Lowell put one hand on his chest, then turned and sank back into a massive oaken chair. The thick sturdy oak contrasted with his own frail and aged frame. "This is… a monstrous lie, some terrible joke."

Holmes shook his head grimly. "Not at all. Your devotion to your hideous goddess has blinded you, made you careless and stupid. Why would a man who had spent many years trying to stamp out murderous fanatics keep an image of their deity prominently displayed in his home?"

"A memento only," Lowell mumbled. Unconsciously he had begun to wring his hands.

"Surely it has some appeal as a work of art," I said. "This cannot be true."

"Yes, yes." Lowell nodded eagerly.

Holmes again shook his head. "Are you blind, Henry? Look at that thing, study her closely. She reeks of blood and death. You carry aesthetic detachment too far. Besides, I have further proof, even though it was the statue that first convinced me that Major Lowell was not the man he pretended to be."

"Proof?" Lowell whispered.

"Yes, proof. There were many small details which did not fit, and of course there was your obvious zeal to shoot the two men, one as elderly and infirm as yourself."

"He was dangerous! I knew his powers! I have seen his tongue mesmerize the masses, their black eyes fill with the love of blood and slaughter! No one would have been safe while he lived."

"Least of all you, Major Lowell."

"This is… preposterous, an outrageous insult!" Somehow the old man managed to stand up, but he clung desperately to the chair with both hands. "You have no proof—this is all supposition! Get out of my house—go, at once!"

Briefly I thought I saw pity in Sherlock's face, but it was gone almost at once. "I have all the proof I need, Major Lowell." He withdrew a folded paper from his coat pocket and opened it. A large reddish-brown splotch, clearly dried blood, marred one corner. "This is the letter you wrote the priest to entrap him and his friends. This explains their walking right into our hands. I found this on the dead man, despite your efforts to get rid of the body as quickly as possible. You were not so stupid as to sign this, and you made some attempt to disguise your writing. Not enough, however, to fool me or any other handwriting expert. You address the priest as an old friend and fellow believer, Major. I suspect, although I do not yet have proof, that you were an accomplice in the killings of Broderick and Davidson. One did die, after all, under your roof."

I felt a sickening dismay and could not bear looking at the frightened old man. "Can he be such a black traitor, such a… monster?"

Sherlock gave a curt nod. "Yes."

Lowell's hands tightened on the chair back, his knuckles white. He opened his mouth, a grimace baring his brown, worn teeth. "You are so smug, so condescending—the great Sherlock Holmes! What do you know of evil, real evil! Have you ever cut open a man, torn his heart from his chest and bathed your arms in blood? I have killed more men than you will ever save." He stared at the statue, a shuddering sigh slipping from between his bluish lips, then a dreadful energy animated him, filling his eyes with power.

"You yourself cannot be such a fool as to believe in the Christian God, that comical hodgepodge of banal goodness and petulant destructiveness—I am certain of it! But you are too weak to turn to the dark one, the Black Mother. Evil rules the world, Mr. Holmes, touching all things with her black fingers—even you and that youthful fool with you. Can you blame me for choosing the winning side? The goddess of death and destruction will reign long after this ridiculous empire of ours has fallen and only our absurd monuments remain. Can you blame me for choosing Kali? You understand—I know you do! You feel her power! You know she is no mere statue, but the true goddess who must be obeyed and worshiped! Look into her red eyes, into those bloody orbs, and then tell me I am wrong!"

Tears ran from his eyes, but he began to laugh. He was so old and sick that the sound was feeble, yet I heard such madness, such hatred and pain, that I wanted to clap my hands to my ears.

Sherlock wrenched the chair away from Lowell, then used both hands to raise and swing it. The blow sent the statue crashing to the floor. The oriental carpet did not go all the way to the wall, and the marble struck the stone of the castle floor and shattered. The impact broke off two of the black marble arms and the fearful head itself.

Lowell had slumped against the wall, but he screamed, *"No!"* Where he got the strength for such a cry I do not know. He staggered forward, but I seized his arm.

"It is finished—you will make yourself ill."

"My statue! My statue!" He began to weep, and if I had not held him up he would have collapsed. "You have killed her, you have killed her. She was so beautiful."

"Good Lord, Major—sit down. You are not well." I helped him

to another chair, the mate of the one lying on the floor. I turned to Sherlock. "Are you all right?"

He was fearfully pale, and I could see his large white hands quivering at his sides. The fury still showed in his eyes. He nodded. "Yes. I'm fine." He bent over to retrieve his pipe, then raised the chair. He was of such a tall and slight build that these occasional feats of strength always amazed me. I have seen him so weary from lack of proper sleep and diet that he could hardly stand up, and yet he could hurl an oak chair of a good five stone as easily as if it were a pillow.

"For God's sake, Mr. Holmes, spare me–spare me!"

"A moment ago you mocked the Deity, Major Lowell."

"Please, Mr. Holmes, if not for my sake, for my daughter's. It would destroy her to know. She has no inkling. She and her mother were the only good things that ever happened in my wretched life. Her mother was gentle–while she lived I turned from the black goddess. My fellow officers mocked me, and there was no longer a place for me in the regiment. What did I care? But when she died, when she left me, I grew weak again, and your wretched God–he blinded my little one when she was hardly more than a babe! Can you blame me for choosing Kali? Don't tell her, Mr. Holmes, I beg of you!"

Holmes and I stared at one another. "You need some brandy, Major," I said. "Calm yourself, please–as you say–for your daughter's sake." I walked to a nearby table and poured brandy from a heavy crystal decanter.

"Please, Mr. Holmes. What would be the harm? You are a gentleman, I know, and a reasonable man. Let us forget this disturbing business. They were only dirty Indians. We are white men, are we not? As a white man and an Englishman, I implore you…"

Sherlock's pipe toppled from his hands, and he stepped forward. I dropped the glass, spilling its contents onto the carpet, then lunged forward and grabbed his arm. "Sherlock, he is old and sick–you cannot strike him!" He turned, and for a moment I thought he would hit me instead.

"Tell him... to keep silent."

The old man was still weeping and blubbering about his daughter. "Major, please," I murmured. "I think we could all use some brandy. I know I could." I let go of Sherlock.

"I'm sorry, Henry," he whispered. "Yes, get me some brandy."

Soon we were all sipping silently at the Major's excellent Cognac and not tasting it. Outside we heard the icy, lonely howling of the wind. At night there is no more melancholy a sound. I remember as a boy cowering in my bed in the cold and dark of a winter night, listening to that unceasing moan. None of us said anything for a long while.

Finally the Major spoke, but the furor which had possessed him was gone. He sounded old, sick, and weary. "You are right, Mr. Holmes. I have betrayed every trust given me, save one. My daughter will tell you that I have been a loving father. I have cared for her. That is why... If only myself were involved, I could bear the disgrace, but she has done nothing—nothing at all. Some merciless god has already punished her enough. Why should...?" The old man's voice faded, and he began to weep in earnest.

Holmes and I stared at each other. He was tired and discouraged, his own energy spent. I stood and helped the old man up. "Go to bed, Major. You are weary. We shall continue this discussion in the morning when we have all rested."

The old man tottered in my grasp. He felt unbelievably light, the flesh and muscle wispy nothingness over the hard bone.

He took a few steps with my aid, then turned again to Sherlock. "Mr. Holmes, I have but one final thing to ask of you." Holmes raised his head, but his eyes were evasive. "Promise me, promise that you will look after my daughter."

"What?"

"Promise me you will look after her. I have no other living relations. She has little experience with men save her father. When the two of you played that German music yesterday, I could see that you understood her. She respects you. Her musical powers are a mystery to me, the more so because of her blindness. Whatever happens to me, howsoever I am punished for my sins, I beg of you to look after her. Will you promise me that? I beg of you, sir. Please."

The blood suffused Sherlock's face in a slow flush, and he looked away.

"Good God, Mr. Holmes—you have destroyed me! It is only fair. Promise me you will watch over her for me."

"Major Lowell, it is late, and…" I began.

Sherlock did not look up, but he spoke softly. "Very well. You have my promise."

The old man sagged in my arms, and again I thought he would collapse. "Thank you."

He let me lead him down the long corridor to his bedroom. The butler and I exchanged knowing looks. The Major shuffled along, taking very small steps and not saying a word. The cry of the wind was fainter here. We stopped before the doorway.

"I will look in upon you shortly, Major. I can give you something that will calm your nerves and help you sleep."

"You are very kind, Doctor Vernier." His eyes were red from weeping, but the bluish tinge had left his lips. I doubted he could live more than another six months.

He closed the door, and I started back down the hallway, a prey to the clash of conflicting emotions. The man was guilty of terrible bloody crimes, but I questioned his sanity. Moreover, he was old and sick, only a step away from the grave. What would be the benefit to anyone should he go to the gallows now? It would bring back none of his victims, and there was his daughter. She was as innocent as he was corrupt.

Sherlock had crossed his legs, the upper foot bobbing rhythmically. His pipe was relit, and the empty brandy glass sat on the table beside him. I shared his melancholy sentiments.

"What is to be done?" I asked.

He shrugged and shook his head.

"It was kind of you to promise to look after his daughter."

His sardonic smile returned briefly, even more harsh and humorless than usual. "He had cornered me. He left me no choice." He inhaled deeply from the pipe.

I poured myself more brandy, shivered, then took a deep swallow. "Lord, it's cold in here. This business has shaken me, I can tell you that. You may be used to it, but I... What's wrong, Sherlock?"

He shrugged. "What's right, Henry? Nothing. Nothing at all. The great Sherlock Holmes reduced to striking a sick old man in a rage. If you had not restrained me..."

"You were provoked."

He gazed at the statue on the floor. "At least that thing is destroyed. There was, Henry, a certain perspicuity in his ravings."

"No."

"Yes. Do you think one can stare into the face of evil as I have, the face of the Black Mother, follow her every manifestation, and still remain untouched? I struggle with my opponents at the edge of an abyss, and even if I win, they may pull me over. Hamlet has a line, which escapes me, about a virtuous man being caught up in the general censure. It is the greatest danger I face. I have seen too much that is sordid and wicked; it is hard not to despise the human race—including myself. Evil and hatred are powerful forces. Who indeed can face them without being corrupted? I was ready to kill that pathetic old man."

"You might have struck him, but you would never have killed him."

"No?"

"Of course not."

Holmes sighed. "This is one of the blackest cases I have ever seen; yet if I turn the Major over to the police, am I not killing him in a slower, more ruthless and brutal manner? Would it not be better if I struck him dead or put a bullet through his heart?"

I opened my mouth, then closed it.

We both remained silent, then he smiled. "Watson would no doubt have had a ready answer for me." I glared at him, which made him laugh. "Who am I punishing if I expose him? He cannot live much longer."

"Six months, at most."

"Exactly. One way or another, he is dead in a year's time, but his daughter will not be. She will have to live the rest of her life knowing her father, her only relation, was a great villain. Where is the justice in that, Henry?"

"There is none."

"Then you think I should remain silent?"

I hesitated, then finally said, "Yes."

He ran his hand back through the dark, oily hair over his broad forehead. He did not look particularly well himself. "I am glad to hear you say so."

We were both relieved. "Perhaps I will go tell him, Sherlock. He will sleep better, I am sure, if one can sleep with such crimes blackening one's soul. He seemed so distraught I…"

The same thought struck us both. I set down my glass, and Sherlock stood abruptly. "How could we—how could *I*—be so blasted stupid?" He turned and strode toward the hallway.

I followed. "Perhaps…" But I was too sick at heart to speak.

The wind was louder now, even in the corridor. The door was not locked, and when Sherlock opened it, the chill of the stormy night and a few snowflakes swirled about us. For some reason, Major Lowell had opened the shutters to his window. He hung in the center of the room, snowflakes shimmering about him in the gray-white light. His face and his bare, bony feet were bluish white, and he turned slightly with the wind. A piece of silk had been tied to a hook in the ceiling, the noose placed about his thin throat; now his weight stretched it tight; and in the dim light, I could barely make out that the silk was red, the color of blood.

I had seen many dead and dying men, but this was all too much for me. My own hands felt icy. I turned away and stepped back into the hallway.

Holmes's voice was steady and distant. "His goddess has claimed her final victim."

Holmes and Susan Lowell played well together; even I could hear that. With Watson's emphasis on the cerebral—the rational side of Sherlock's nature—the violin seemed another oddity, an eccentricity like revolver practice in the parlor of his rooms. However, anyone who ever heard him play, who heard him actually spinning out the long quivering lines of Beethoven's melodies, bringing the mere notes alive, filling the room with their power and sensual warmth, knew better than to consider him some mere brain, some unfeeling lump of intellect. Beneath all that ice was fire. Mastering any instrument requires intelligence, yes, but that which separates the mediocre from the inspired is a matter more of instinct and feelings.

Miss Lowell was equally inspired. They had been very good before, but today they outdid themselves. As she played, her unseeing eyes remained locked straight ahead, but she managed unerringly to make the leaps in the bass to the left of the keyboard. Although she had no real sight, seeing only shapeless gray light, she had total command of the instrument. She had related how, as a child, she had picked out melodies by feel alone and how she had begged her father for lessons. Finally he had relented. Within a few years, she could hear her teacher play a piece once or she could attend a concert, then play back the music without missing a note. Sherlock had remarked on both her perfect pitch and her incredible memory. He had never met her equal. All in all, seeing her play was like watching a miracle, some great mystery, manifest itself.

The last movement, the presto, went very quickly. The end was sudden: her hands struck the final chords even as Holmes's bow glided across the strings for the last time.

"Bravo," I cried, rising to my feet and applauding. "Bravo!"

Holmes lowered his violin, set down the bow, then took the white handkerchief off his shoulder and wiped his face. "Bravo, indeed, Miss Lowell. You are among the foremost musicians I have ever been honored to hear, let alone accompany."

"You are too generous, Mr. Holmes."

"Not in the least."

"Besides, I was the accompanist, not you. Your violin was the hero of the piece. I had no idea…. Your reputation as a detective preceded you, but I had never imagined you could be a musical genius as well."

Perhaps because she could not see him, Sherlock let his face briefly reveal his satisfaction. "Now it is you who are too generous."

She smiled so warmly, her face so radiant, that I wanted to whisper to him to squeeze her hand or at least touch her shoulder, but he stood rather stiffly and again wiped his brow with the handkerchief.

"I feel so happy, and yet…" The tears slipped down the dark skin of her cheeks. "It is wrong with father… But I know he would want me to—and after all, you are leaving tomorrow. Oh, blast it all." Abruptly she sat down on the piano bench and began to weep in earnest.

Since I had been expecting some such outburst of grief, I was not surprised. The night before last, after Holmes and I had cut down her father, we agreed, with the concurrence of the butler Russell, that the Major's bad heart was to be the cause of his death. My being a physician made the matter quite simple. We had broken the news to her yesterday morning, and she had born it courageously, shedding until now only a few tears.

Sherlock and I stared at each other, then I lay my hand gently on her shoulder. "We are very sorry, Miss Lowell."

"You have both been very kind to me." She dabbed at her eyes with a handkerchief. "I... I am being very selfish."

My brow wrinkled. "How so?"

"I loved father, and I shall miss him, but... I fear... I worry more for myself. The days—the years—seem so long at times, so very long. Sometimes I... I fear for my sanity, and I pray for death." Her voice was almost a whisper.

"You cannot mean that, Miss Lowell."

"Can I not? What have I to live for?"

I opened my mouth, then hesitated. I loathed physicians who mouthed Polonian platitudes and gave false reassurances, but nothing else came to mind. "You... you..."

"Tell me truly, Doctor Vernier, and you, Mr. Holmes, are we of Indian descent... repugnant? Let me know the truth, as you are my friends. Do you find me so very ugly?"

A pained laugh slipped from my lips. "Miss Lowell, you are far from ugly. Who has told you such lies?"

"Why, then, do so many shun my company? We have had few visitors and little mingling with our neighbors, but I could hear the coldness in their voices. My father claimed I was beautiful, but I knew he would do anything to shelter my feelings. I feared... I must be ugly compared to others, either my race or my features making me despicable. As you are my friends, I beg of you not to spare my feelings–I must know the truth."

I squeezed her shoulder gently. "In God's name, Miss Lowell, you are one of the most beautiful women I have ever known."

Her blind eyes stared into the shadowy part of the room, and you could see confusion writ upon her lovely face. She was silent, then said, "Mr. Holmes?"

Sherlock's fists were clenched, and his own eyes were filled with a strange passion. "Henry–Doctor Vernier–has spoken the truth. You are... beautiful."

Her astonishment seemed genuine. Over the years she must have pondered the matter deeply, seeking to comprehend her isolation. Since she could see neither herself nor others, she could not judge for herself. Little wonder she had come to consider herself ugly.

"Can this be true...?" she whispered.

"Yes, Miss Lowell."

She began to cry again. "I don't understand. I don't understand."

I hesitated, then asked, "What is it?" Sherlock's eyes blazed at me, and I could tell he wanted us to leave the room.

"Why am I so alone? If I am no freak, why must I be so alone? Why are the consolations, the affections, granted to other women, denied to me?"

"Prejudice and stupidity, Miss Lowell–they blind others to your attractions. Believe me, if..."

"I thought also that it might be my wickedness."

"Wickedness?"

"Yes. I... I have strange, morbid thoughts and... wicked longings.

Oh, why must life be so wretched–why?"

Again I could not bring myself to utter some hearty banality. I glanced at Holmes. His face was pale and pained. He motioned toward the door, but I could not leave her so desolate.

"Please, Miss Lowell. Don't... We have not known you for long, but we do consider ourselves your friends."

She drew in her breath, straightening her spine, then let out a final shaky sob. "Thank you, I am being very selfish, I know, but..."

"No." Sherlock's voice was very loud, and she turned her head in his direction.

"I shall be... fine," she said. "I have–there is my music, after all. When I play as we did, Mr. Holmes, I forget everything else. There is no suffering, no blindness, no time, only the music everywhere, washing over everything, even my troubled spirit. How foolish I must sound to you both. I am sorry if... Please leave me alone for a while. I feel such a fool, but the time which lies before me–the hours, days and years which stretch into the darkness of the future–it seems so vast and empty, such an abyss."

"Miss Lowell..."

"Please leave me, Doctor Vernier."

She regained her composure, and I felt I must honor her request. Sherlock's mouth twitched. He had grown more and more agitated as he had listened to her.

"Very well," I said. Sherlock and I started for the door.

Suddenly he stopped and turned. "Miss Lowell." His voice was so loud the words had a faint echo in the vast stone chamber.

She raised her head, held her handkerchief loosely in her right hand. "Yes?"

"We are indeed your friends. I–I am your friend. You can count on periodic visits, and if you ever require anything, you need only ask for it. My cases require much of my time, and often the fate of men or nations hang in the balance. All the same, if you summon me, I shall come as quickly as I possibly can. I hope you understand."

"Oh, Mr. Holmes—you offer me more than I have any right to expect."

"Also, once your period of mourning is at an end, you might consider moving to London. A musician such as yourself is wasted here. I know many in the London musical circles and could introduce you to those who could not fail to recognize your talent."

She began to cry again, but now her face was joyful. "I do not deserve such kindness. Oh thank you, thank you both."

Holmes clenched both hands into fists, took one step forward toward her, then stopped. "We will speak of this later… when your sorrow has abated." He whirled about, then strode toward the door without looking at me. I followed him. In the hallway he took out a cigarette and lit it, his hands trembling slightly.

"You seem greatly moved." My voice had a faint tinge of irony.

"Not really. I… human suffering always discomforts me, especially unnecessary suffering."

"To think that all these years she has considered herself some homely freak. Strange, is it not, when she is so beautiful?"

He exhaled a cloud of smoke. "Very."

"You seemed quite interested in Miss Lowell, and she in turn seemed particularly interested in what you had to say. You do not believe in 'tainted blood,' do you? The sins of the fathers being passed on to the children, and so on."

"Utter rubbish."

"Then you might be of more direct assistance to the lady."

"You know my views on the fair sex."

"Come now, I am not Watson. Do you think I, too, am blind? It did not require your fabulous powers of deduction to see something of your feelings just now."

"Don't be ridiculous, Henry. I have no need of an alienist to sort out my mental states. Kindly keep such counsels to yourself. Tomorrow we return to London, where I have some other business to finish. Can you be ready to leave for Paris in ten days time?"

"Yes."

"Good. The situation at the Opera sounds most interesting, and Paris will be a welcome change after this Welsh desolation." He dropped his cigarette, then with the toe of his boot crushed out the butt on the gray stone.

## One

Holmes and I paused before the portal to Le Palais Garnier, the Paris Opera House. The February sun illuminated the columns, arches, busts, friezes and reliefs, shone on marble, bronze, stone, and wood. Along the very top of the building was a row of masks, their grotesque faces with black O's for mouths and eyes gazing down upon the Place de l'Opéra. Their oddly abstract faces did not match the style of the conventional representations covering the facade. Just below the words ACADEMIE NATIONALE DE MUSIQUE was a row of busts, Mozart above our doorway, Beethoven to his left, Spontini to his right.

"Who was Spontini?" I muttered.

"A minor opera composer who was briefly court musician to Louis XVIII, two of his better known works being *La Vestale* and *Fernand Cortez.*"

I wondered briefly at Holmes's capacity for remembering trivia. The Opera was clearly a secular temple, another of the monuments Napoleon the Third wished to erect to himself and Paris. Determined that his capital should have the largest, most splendid theater in the world, he had chosen Jean-Louis Charles Garnier as architect and builder, then lavished huge sums on its construction. Ironically, although begun in 1861, it was not completed until 1875, some five years after the collapse of the Second Empire. All the same, it remained a monument to that period between 1850 and 1870 when Louis Napoleon had transformed Paris into the modern city of today. Even a person of socialist or republican leanings such as myself could not help but admire the results.

However, the Opera was another matter. It was not to my taste. The style was so ornate, there was such a surfeit of sculpture and design, that the eye soon grew weary. It was cloying in the same way as Saint Peter's in Rome, another example of excess and the determination to create the greatest specimen of its kind. Also, one need not see much of Paris before tiring of bronze female representations of la France, la Liberté, la Justice, la République, la Musique, la Poésie, all those sisters with the same formidably muscular bosoms and limbs, robes flowing, their stalwart faces uplifted to the heavens.

"I see you do not care for the grand style," Holmes said. "Think, however, of the many artists and masons kept gainfully employed for so long."

"Some of whom were second rate."

"Nevertheless, the Paris Opera will endure long after we have shuffled off this mortal coil." He opened his coat and withdrew his watch from his waistcoat. "Nine fifty-five, Henry. We shall judge something of the seriousness of this matter by the length of time we are kept waiting."

Holmes was dressed formally: black overcoat, top hat, and frock coat, gray striped waistcoat and trousers, gold watch in one gloved hand, a fine walking stick with a silver handle in the other. As he was already tall, the top hat further added to his stature and made his nose appear smaller—imposing, rather than merely large. Having decided to play a subordinate part, I wore more casual garb, a tailored suit of heavy gray tweed.

Sherlock placed one hand on the massive iron door handle. "Behold the fatal portal. '*Lasciate ogne speranza, voi ch'intrate.*'"

"Dante, at the gates of Hell?"

"Yes. Come, Henry; we have our own fearful specter with whom to do battle."

"'Into the valley of death rode the six hundred.'"

Holmes grimaced. "Quoting bad Tennyson will surely irritate both the shade of Dante and that of the Opera, our mysterious ghost."

Inside an attendant awaited us. "*Monsieur Holmes? Ah, Messieurs Richard et Moncharmin vous attendent. Suivez-moi, s'il vous plaît.*"

"*Merci bien,*" Holmes said.

Our footsteps echoed faintly as we went up that grandest of all grand stairways. Inside was the same abundance of sculpture, ornamentation and riches, with elaborate paintings on the dome high overhead. Again, the similarity to a church struck me. Once past the stairway, the interior had a certain labyrinthine quality; one could easily lose oneself in the Opera.

Messieurs Moncharmin and Richard awaited us in an office as grandiose as the rest of the edifice. Our interview was conducted in French and began with a round of facile introductions. Holmes had told me that Firmin Richard was a mediocre composer of martial airs. He was a large, burly man who seemed out of place in formal attire. Although his ruddy face was youthful, his hair and beard were white, his joviality forced. Armand Moncharmin was short and slight with a dandyish air. His frock coat, his cravat, his white cuffs were elegant and absolutely spotless. He wore a monocle in his left eye, and as he spoke, the waxed ends of his black mustache moved up and down.

"*Eh bien,* Monsieur Holmes, you have read our letter about this embarrassing business of the ghost." For ghost he used the word *revenant*. "My partner and I are not superstitious. When we took over the Opera last October and the former managers, Messieurs Poligny and Debienne, told us about an opera ghost, we assumed this was a good-natured jest on their part."

Richard smiled, but something cruel showed in the set of his mouth. "I enjoy a good trick myself, and I thought this was one."

"However," continued Moncharmin, "certain events have transpired which, while not completely convincing us that supernatural entities exist, do suggest some malevolent agency at work. Imagine our surprise when our predecessors showed us certain documents demanding payment of several thousand francs a month."

Richard nodded curtly. "You English have a word, 'blackmail,' I believe."

Holmes had sat drumming at the chair arm with the fingers of his right hand. "Documents? Where are these documents?"

Moncharmin handed him a thick stack of papers. "This is the complete contract between the Opera and the Government of France. On page thirty-seven is a list of four conditions which may cause the termination of the agreement."

I leaned over so I could see the paper Holmes held. At the bottom, scrawled in red, was a fifth condition: "Or if said management delay beyond a fortnight the monthly payment of twenty-thousand francs to the Opera Ghost." Here the word used was not *revenant* but *Fantôme*.

"Further on," noted Holmes, "certain boxes are reserved for the President of the Republic and various ministers. Notice the addition on page ninety-two."

In the same red scrawl had been added, "Box Five on the grand tier shall be reserved in perpetuity for the Opera Ghost."

"*Le Fantôme de l'Opéra,*" Holmes said. "What remarkably crude and childish handwriting. This could not have been done with a regular pen, and the source of the ink is a mystery to me."

I sat back in my chair. "Obviously it is meant to represent blood."

Holmes raised one hand. "The intent is clear, but actual blood would be brownish."

"I know that. I am a physician."

Moncharmin laughed nervously, a flowing sound which recalled a harp too tightly strung. "It is a relief to hear you say that it is not real blood. We could not help but wonder…"

"Are there other amendments, Monsieur Moncharmin? No. Well, thus far this does resemble the common garden variety of blackmail, although the request for a box is curious."

"As I said, Monsieur Holmes, we assumed this was a joke. However, since then, so many odd occurrences have happened that…"

"Such as?"

"Some are rather trivial. The principal white horse, César, has disappeared."

"A horse?" I said.

Richard nodded. "The opera has a stable of ten. This one starred recently in Meyerbeer's *Le Prophète.*

"There have been difficulties with Box Five. At first, the superstitious old woman who acted as box keeper, a Madame Giry, kept it vacant. When we discovered this, we dismissed her. She seemed to consider the ghost her employer rather than us. However, after several disturbances, we have again left Box Five vacant. Its occupants complained of mysterious voices and laughter, hardly conducive to watching a performance. Our patrons' well-being is always a major concern. And now, one of our employees, Monsieur Buquet, has been… been… deceased."

Holmes frowned, whether at the fact or the twisted syntax I was not sure. "How did he die?"

Moncharmin flinched at the word "die." Richard said, "We think he hanged himself. He was found in the third cellar near a scene from *Le Roi de Lahore.* Most people think the Phantom murdered him."

"Did the police not look into this matter?"

Richard and Moncharmin again eyed each other. Moncharmin managed a tepid smile. "Their determination was that it was suicide. The whole business was most embarrassing, and if not handled with great delicacy, could have affected box rentals very adversely. We understand, Monsieur Holmes, that you can be relied upon for discretion, and we hope…"

Holmes had been drumming at the chair arm again. "I do not speak with newspaper reporters, and I keep everything completely confidential. In return, I require the utmost frankness from my clients. I will tolerate nothing less than the absolute truth."

The managers regarded each other again, then Moncharmin laughed weakly. "Of course, Monsieur Holmes. That goes without saying. There have also been… letters."

Holmes sat up. "Let me see them."

Richard opened a desk drawer, took out some papers, and handed Holmes the top one. "This is the most recent one." I leaned over again; the handwriting and red ink were unmistakable.

Gentlemen,

So it is to be war between us? You have repeatedly ignored my requests that you honor our contract. You are now two months in arrears on your payments, and Madame Giry has left your services. This is insufferable. Here are my demands:

1. You will immediately reinstate Madame Giry and have her leave my full payment in Box Five.

2. You will never again attempt to avoid paying my

monthly fee, nor will you ever again rent out my box to usurpers.

3. You will cast Christine Daaé as Marguerite in the upcoming production of *Faust*. Madame Carlotta in her prime was never appropriate for this role. Now, when she has attempted to prolong her career by substituting loudness and vibrato for beauty of tone, she is an offense to your patrons who pay dearly for their seats. Madame Carlotta will therefore be indisposed on opening night.

If you refuse this, my final courteous and reasonable request, you will present *Faust* in a house with a curse upon it. You and you alone will be responsible for the ensuing catastrophe.

Regards:

Le Fantôme de l'Opéra

I shook my head. "I wonder if this person is quite sane."

Holmes gave me his brief, sardonic smile. "'Sanity' is a very odd and relative concept." He lifted the paper, and his nose twitched as he sniffed vigorously. "See what you think, Henri." He had been using the French variant of my name since we had arrived in Paris.

The paper was thick and smelled musty. "Mildew?" I asked.

"Exactly. An amusing touch, quite ghostly. And this paper…" He stood abruptly, walked over to a table by the window, took a piece of paper from a pile there, then held both up before the light from the window. "I assume, gentlemen, that the Opera stationery has come from the same manufacturer for many years."

Moncharmin seemed incapable of speech. Richard said, "I think so."

"One would certainly expect a Phantom of the Opera to use Opera stationery, which he has. Another clever touch. How long, I wonder, would it take to acquire so pronounced an odor of mildew?" He set down the paper, then clapped one hand over his chin as he reflected. "No matter. Now, gentlemen, who is Christine Daaé?"

The way the two managers stared at one another was becoming comical, but Sherlock was not amused. Finally Moncharmin spoke. "She is a singer."

Holmes gave a snort. "Any imbecile could have surmised that much. Next you will be telling me she is a soprano. I require more information than the obvious."

"She is... very young, rather a delicate little thing with blonde hair and blue-green eyes. Pretty actually, but in a sickly sort of way. Not very... robust. You would never guess she could fill a theater the size of the Opera the way she did."

Monsieur Richard nodded. "She sang some of the minor light, lyrical roles like Siebel in *Faust,* but no one ever took much notice of her until last month at the gala. Carlotta was ill, so Christine sang the final prison trio from *Faust.* She created quite a sensation, brought the house down. I've never heard anything like it myself, extraordinary really. I can tell you we're already getting pressure from our patrons to put her in *Faust.* The Viscount de Chagny worships the ground she walks on, and his brother the Count let me know he would be grateful for anything we could do for her."

"Let me see the other letters, please." Holmes took the entire stack. "I have not heard of the de Chagnys."

Moncharmin raised a gloved hand. "Ah, Monsieur Holmes, they are one of the first families, true French nobility. The Count is one of the wealthiest men in France, and his younger brother the Viscount is very dear to him."

"Then he can hardly relish the thought of his brother being snared by an opera singer."

Moncharmin's eye opened wide, the monocle popping out, and Richard grinned. "The Count wants to help his brother out, but there is certainly no question of marriage here. No more than with the Count and Sorelli."

"Sorelli?" Holmes asked. "The dancer?"

"Who else? You know our nobility." Richard was grinning again.

Holmes's upper lip curled disdainfully. "Only too well." He read the letters one by one, handing each to me for my perusal as he finished. All were in red ink on the same paper, done by the same clumsy hand. A total of five, they were requests for payment and for Box Five which grew increasingly threatening. "Your ghost seems singularly well informed about goings-on at the Opera."

"If he's an outsider," Richard said, "he must have a confidant within the Opera."

Moncharmin shook his head, sighing wearily. "Whoever could do such a thing?"

A sharp laugh escaped Holmes's lips, almost a bark. "Come, Monsieur Moncharmin, surely you must realize than an institution such as the Opera is a breeding ground for jealousy, dissension and egoism. Most members of the chorus or the corps de ballet are certain they deserve to be in the limelight, and they eagerly await failure of any sort, a cracked voice or a twisted ankle. Singers, dancers, poets, writers—no more envious and petty group of creatures exists. They have few rivals in their capacity for hatred and petty bickering."

Moncharmin put his monocle back over his eye. "What an extraordinarily cynical view, Monsieur Holmes."

Richard took a cigar out of a wooden box. "Ah, but an interesting theory. Cigar, gentlemen?"

I shook my head. Holmes's nostrils flared. "No."

Richard lit the cigar. "You think, then, that it might be an envious member of the chorus, one nurturing a grudge for many years?"

"It is certainly possible, but it is much too early for theories. There are too few facts. When can you arrange for me to tour the Opera? I wish to visit every floor, every corner."

Richard laughed. "Have you any idea how large the Opera is? Or how long such a tour would take?"

"Nevertheless, we shall attempt it. Surely in a day or two, I can see much of the Opera. I am interested in the cellars, especially this third one where Monsieur Buquet was found."

Moncharmin smiled warily. "We shall do our best to assist you. Finding persons willing to venture into the lower regions is… difficult. Perhaps Monsieur Gris… Our employees are naturally rather fearful of late."

"Are these cellars not considered the home of the Phantom?" Sherlock asked.

Moncharmin dabbed at his face with a handkerchief. Richard rolled the cigar about his mouth, then took it out. "Quite so, Monsieur Holmes."

"And what is this ghost supposed to look like?"

Moncharmin's eye seemed to swell behind the monocle. Richard hesitated. "Oh, there are various silly stories about a mysterious man dressed all in black, a mere shadow, with a bizarre face."

"Bizarre?"

"A death's head—a skull, Monsieur Holmes. What nonsense." He laughed, appearing in truth to find the idea amusing.

"Excellent, a death's head. Perhaps you can work on arranging for the start of our little tour for tomorrow. I have other inquiries to pursue today. Let Miss Daaé know I shall be visiting her."

Richard nodded. "I'll see to it."

Moncharmin stared at the surface of the desk. "There is one other minor matter to attend to, Monsieur Holmes."

"Yes?"

"There is… the question of your fee."

"My fee, gentlemen, as I told you in my letters, is one thousand francs a day, a sum which is not negotiable."

I stared in disbelief at Holmes. That was forty pounds a day, an extraordinary amount. Watson was correct in that Holmes sometimes took on a case for sheer interest, charging nothing at all.

Moncharmin nodded. "Quite so, Monsieur Holmes, quite so. All the same…" He gave Richard a desperate look.

"The President's brother-in-law told us of a case involving blackmail where you charged half that amount."

Holmes smiled. "Quite so, quite so."

"Well, then, Monsieur Holmes?" Moncharmin had not raised his eyes.

"Gentlemen, I tell you frankly that yours is the highest fee I have ever charged, although it is not double my usual rate. However, I can explain my reasoning if you would care to hear it."

Richard again took the cigar out of his mouth. "Gladly, sir."

"Never before have I had so distinguished a client. Is not Paris the virtual capital of the world, and is not this edifice its shrine, the greatest Opera House in the world? A first-class opera must pay first-class rates. For La Scala it might be different, but this is not Italy. The honor of France and your unrivaled stature demand such a fee. Besides, you would end up paying your Ghost much more in a few months."

Richard reddened. "We shall never pay the bastard!"

"Do not underestimate an unknown enemy, Monsieur Richard. I sense a worthy foe, regardless of his motives. I hope that you now understand the basis of my fee. It is a measure of my esteem for both *l'Opéra et la belle France.*"

Richard seemed wary, but Moncharmin was vastly relieved. "We do indeed understand, Monsieur Holmes, and there was no question about the sum. We merely wished for some… clarification, which we now have."

I saw that Holmes was ready to leave, but he and the managers made some polite conversation about musical matters. Not sharing his knowledge of the minutiae of contemporary singers and opera, a knowledge every bit as thorough as that of tobacco varieties, bloodstains and other matters of crime, I soon grew bored. When we at last stepped outside and joined the carriages and pedestrians crossing la Place de l'Opéra, I was relieved.

As we started down the Boulevard des Capucines toward the hotel, I asked him about his extraordinary fee. A sharp laugh slipped from his lips, making a frosty cloud in the cold Parisian air. "I thought you would remark on that. I was curious to see whether they would willingly pay such a sum. If they had a genuine need or were less arrogant and insufferable, I might have lowered the amount. You noticed how, when I related it to French honor, Moncharmin immediately swallowed the entire explanation. Really, if they can accept such nonsense, how can I refuse the money? The day may come, I hope, when Sherlock Holmes has less notoriety. As the thrifty squirrel hoards his acorns for winter, so now I must put something into my bank account."

I laughed. "Now you are testing my credulity, too. I shall not swallow such an explanation."

"Good. Actually, Monsieur Moncharmin was the person who needed persuading. A tightwad like Monsieur Richard is a hopeless case."

"What makes you think Richard is a tightwad?"

"I *think* nothing, Henry! Have you no eyes? Did you note the length of Richard's hair and its uneven cut? He is overdue for a visit with his inferior barber. His coat, trousers, and waistcoat were poorly made. Worse yet, his trousers had shiny spots at the knees; they should have been replaced long ago. That abomination of a cigar which he offered us was not even second rate; such tobacco reflects very poorly on the institution it represents." He shook his head grimly.

By then we had reached the entrance to the hotel, and he withdrew his watch. "How is your appetite? Myself, I am ravenous. The French cuisine is without equal, but breakfast is its weakness. Croissants and coffee do not hold one like eggs, bacon, and porridge."

"I am hungry."

"Excellent. We shall be having company for lunch."

A doorman in a uniform of navy and red which would have made a French general envious opened the door for us.

"Whom?" I asked.

"*Le Comte de Chagny*. He left a note for me at the desk last night inquiring if he might see me on a matter of some urgency."

Holmes stopped at the front desk, an ornate construction of carved oak with a marble top. "*Pardon, mais auriez-vous un message pour Monsieur Sherlock Holmes?*"

"*Ah, oui, Monsieur Holmes. Quelqu'un vous attend, ce Monsieur là-bas.*" He pointed at a man seated at one end of the scarlet sofa beside an enormous fern in a pot.

As we approached, the Count stood rather stiffly and withdrew the glove from his right hand. Under his left elbow were a top hat and a walking stick. His frock coat was a dark navy color, nearly black, and over it he wore a brown fur coat. A diamond stickpin went through the center of his cravat. Obviously, his tailor was among the best. He had black wavy hair, brown eyes, and a mustache with a bit of gray in it. His was an imposing presence, but with something chilly, rather impersonal, in his manner. After introducing us, Holmes asked if he wished to join us in the hotel restaurant.

"No, no—we can do much better. Please follow me. My carriage is waiting."

Barely were we settled in the carriage when it halted. The Count stepped out and waited for us to join him. "*Attendez*," he said to the coachman, then gestured with his hand toward the small building. Painted in gold above the plate glass window was CHEZ ARMAND. We had traveled all of two blocks. The proprietor fussed over us, and despite the small crowd waiting to be seated, immediately put us at a table before the window. The sterling settings on the white linen table-cloths appeared adequate for starting a small mint.

"The rabbit and the veal are both very good." The Count had a certain fashionably weary air, as if he needed a good nap. He smoothed the right corner of his mustache with his long white fingers.

"We are in your home territory," Sherlock said. "We shall trust your judgment. Choose what you will for us."

The Count gave a slight nod, then rattled off an order in rapid fire French. "And we will have a '79 Beaujolais as well."

The waiter clicked his heels together as he bowed. "*Oui, Monsieur le Comte.*" He wore his hair cut short and spoke French with a German accent.

"Well, Monsieur Holmes, it is tiresome I know, but we may as well discuss business before our meal arrives."

Sherlock nodded. "*Certainement.*"

The Count sat up and rallied enough energy to proceed. "I have, of course, heard about this affair of the ghost and the Opera. All of Paris is talking about it. They are also discussing my brother, Raoul, *le Vicomtede Chagny,* and the singer Christine Daaé."

The Count stopped talking to attend to the waiter, who had arrived with the wine. The man uncorked the bottle and poured some into a beautiful crystal glass. The Count sniffed twice, sipped, sloshed the liquid around his mouth, then spat it back into the glass. "Atrocious. Bring us another bottle, perhaps the '77."

The waiter reddened slightly about the ears, nodded, retreating with the bottle and the glass.

The Count continued. "My brother is twenty years younger than I, only twenty-one, and something of a child when it comes to women. Frankly, I was relieved when he became interested in this Daaé. An opera singer would be an amusing introduction to the sex, and there could, of course, be no consideration of marriage."

Sherlock's mouth drew into a straight line, but he said nothing.

"Ours is an old and honorable family, our arms dating back to the fourteenth century. In a few years finding a suitable match for Raoul will be simple. In the meantime, he has chosen a career in the navy. He has completed a voyage about the Mediterranean and was to leave in another month on a polar expedition."

"Was?" Sherlock said.

The Count nodded, then paused while the waiter poured from another bottle of wine. Behind hovered the wide-eyed proprietor, all the while rubbing his hands together. The Count sipped cautiously, then nodded. "Better. It is tolerable at any rate." Relieved, the waiter filled our glasses.

The Count took another sip. "I say 'was' because he is beginning to talk of remaining behind. Placing him on that expedition required a great deal of effort on my part, and he would be throwing away a tremendous opportunity."

Sherlock held his glass up to the light and slowly turned it. "For an opera singer."

"Exactly! Our mother died when he was born, and he was raised by my old aunt and my two sisters. I was not, I fear, as involved as I should have been, but I am trying now to make amends. As I said, at first this interest in Daaé seemed healthy enough, and I encouraged him."

Holmes nodded. "This no doubt explains your efforts on the lady's behalf with the opera management."

"You have heard of that, have you? Exactly so. Raoul requested it, and I was glad to assist him. Anything to make the lady more compliant." The Count made a dry sound which was apparently a laugh. "She does have a remarkable voice. Raoul and I heard her at the gala in October, and that is when I saw that he was smitten. I hoped to shake off the unhealthy female influence under which he was raised. It is not good for a young man to be too good, if you take my meaning. However, the lady is behaving rather... oddly. She has rebuffed all of Raoul's approaches."

I could not restrain a smile. "What, then, is the problem?"

The Count's eyes grew even colder. "The problem is that she plays upon Raoul like some puppet mistress. I suspect some grand stratagem with a single goal: she wishes to become the Viscountess de Chagny."

Already I sympathized with this unseen woman, but I said nothing.

"Has it not occurred to you," Sherlock asked, "that the lady may be genuinely uninterested?"

"Nonsense. I have had enough experience to know a scheming little baggage. She draws him in, even in her refusals, and for his part, he behaves as a very idiot, a love-sick puppy. I even..." He savagely buttered a slice of bread, putting it a quarter of an inch thick. "I tried to see this Daaé. I wished to probe her real intentions, but she refused to talk to me. Can you imagine such impudence? If it was money she wanted, I would willingly have paid her, but if it is the de Chagny name, then it is war between us."

The waiter arrived and set the plates before us. The smell of the veal and mushrooms made my mouth water. We waited silently until the waiter had left. A woman walking a small dog passed by, her face flushed and pretty. She wore a huge bustle, her posterior protruding behind her so that she resembled an abbreviated centaur with all four legs hidden beneath skirts. I noticed both Holmes and the Count watching her.

Sherlock raised his fork. "This is all very interesting, but what has it to do with me?"

"You will no doubt be in the middle of things at the Opera. I ask that you keep an eye on this Daaé and keep me informed. Perhaps you will have better luck fathoming her intentions. Again, if it is only money which she wants, there is no problem. I shall gladly pay her whatever she wishes. You may tell her so."

Sherlock set down his fork, his mouth twitching. Something in his eyes reminded me of the time he had almost struck Major Lowell. Not here, I thought, not when we are starving and about to eat. I shared something of his feelings, but did not think it was worth coming to blows.

"You seem to be suffering under some delusion, *Monsieur le Comte.* I am a consulting detective, not a pimp." The French word he used was almost more insulting than the English.

The Count dropped his fork. He and Holmes stared at each other for a very long time. I wanted to speak, but feared I would only make matters worse. At last the Count cut a piece of meat, chewed carefully, then dabbed at his mouth with his napkin. "There is no question of that, Monsieur Holmes. You may say nothing to the girl if you prefer. Mainly, keep my interests in mind and let me know what you find out."

Not to be outdone, Sherlock cut his meat and ate a morsel. "This is excellent, really very good."

It was indeed, but I had a hard time swallowing.

The Count took a sip of wine. "What fee do you charge for your services, Monsieur Holmes?"

"Two thousand francs a day."

Some wine escaped down my trachea, and I began to cough.

"Are you all right, Henry?" Sherlock asked.

I drank more wine, then nodded. It was the best I had ever tasted.

The Count raised his right hand, crooked his forefinger at the waiter. "*Une autre bouteille ici, la même vendange.*" He had regained his lassitude and ate slowly. "Monsieur Holmes, when we are finished eating, I shall write you a check for 25,000 francs. I think we understand one another."

Holmes raised his eyes from the plate. "Only too well. You realize, however, that I can promise nothing."

The Count shrugged. "*Eh, bien.* The veal is acceptable?"

"Oh, yes."

I am afraid the company we kept spoiled what should have been a memorable meal. A certain wariness, a certain tension, was in the air, although both men were good at dissembling. After coffee and dessert, the Count wrote out a check for 25,000 francs, then offered us a ride back to the hotel, but Sherlock assured him we would rather walk.

My cousin set off briskly, his head thrust forward such that his nose resembled a ship's prow. Clouds of vapor steamed from his lips, and his walking stick clacked on the pavement. After a block he finally slowed down, then gave me an ironic smile.

"That insufferable swine! So the great French aristocracy has sunk to this?" He opened his coat, took out the Count's check, and proceeded to tear it into tiny pieces. Several of our fellow pedestrians eyed him fearfully. "I am not a pimp, nor am I myself a whore."

"That was a great deal of money, but I think you have done the right thing."

"I feel much better. Even my digestion has improved."

"I must admit he left me with a touch of heartburn."

Sherlock inhaled deeply and turned his face toward the wintry sun. "This cold air and the light are cleansing. I take it you did not much care for his company either."

I shook my head. "No."

"The fourteenth century indeed! Five hundred years, and the culmination is a creature like him."

No sooner had we stepped inside the hotel lobby, than a young man rushed up to us. His face was pale and unhealthy, his watery blue eyes were bloodshot. His hair was reddish brown, and he wore a mustache so faint that one wondered whether it might not float away from his upper lip. His morning suit was of a fine cut, but both his clothes and his person had a wild dishevelment.

"Monsieur Holmes, Monsieur Sherlock Holmes? Ah, thank God! Monsieur Holmes, I beg of you—I must speak with you!" His voice was a high, piping tenor. "You are the one man in all of Paris who can possibly help me! Without you I am lost—ruined—damned! I shall pay you well. I am…"

"Yes, I know: you are Raoul, *le Vicomtede Chagny*."

De Chagny's eyes (and mine) opened wider. "But we have never met, Monsieur Holmes. How could you possibly…?"

"You resemble your brother about the eyes, and your carriage with the de Chagny coat of arms emblazoned on the side is parked across the street. Come, Monsieur, we can discuss your problem in my rooms."

# Two

The hotel room was enormous and luxuriously furnished with plush chairs and sofas of velvet, small and large tables of oak and cherry wood; it had a fireplace and a view of the carriage traffic on the Boulevard des Capucines three floors below. Sherlock and I sat while Raoul de Chagny paced, apparently attempting to wear a path in the thick carpet.

As a physician I would have prescribed rest and a stay in a warm climate for the Viscount. He seemed a likely candidate for consumption. His pale face had a reddish flush at either cheekbone, exactly as if he had a fever, and he was overwrought, his comments rambling and barely coherent.

"We were childhood sweethearts, Monsieur Holmes! She will not see me, and yet she must know my feelings! I have tried to write to her, to see her, and she turns me away. I worship her—she is an angel, a goddess—without her I am doomed! And yet I am prey to the most dreadful jealousies. This passion will... I told you—I heard her—I heard the voice say, 'Christine, you must love me,' and she replied, 'Tonight

I gave you my soul, and I am dead.' God in heaven!—the little harlot!—how shall I ever endure it?" He struck himself a blow on his forehead with the palm of his open hand. "I waited and waited, but she was the only one to leave, and the room, the room was empty, Monsieur Holmes! Who was that voice, who was that cad in there with her? I shall kill him, I swear to God!"

Sherlock sat back in his chair and pointed at the glass decanter on a silver tray. "*Monsieur le Vicomte*, I can do nothing for you unless you calm yourself. Pour some cognac, drink it, and if you must pace, do so in a more controlled and deliberate manner. I wish to question you about what you have told me, but you must think carefully and answer quietly. Do you understand?"

De Chagny gave a great sobbing sigh. "*Oui.*"

"Very well. Drink your cognac, and then let us begin with you seated."

De Chagny sat down, swallowed the brandy in a single gulp, then began to cough. At last he was still.

"Now, you said you knew Miss Daaé as a child."

"Yes, she and her father were staying at Perros Quignac on the coast of Brittany while I was with my aunt. The father was a Swedish peasant, but very good on the violin. Christine was a shy and serious child, but already she…"

"And you did not see her again for many years, not until you noticed her at the Opera? Very good. The first time you approached her was after the recent gala in October?"

"Yes. I hardly recognized her. That night of the gala her voice was heavenly. No one in the audience was unmoved. She sang as an angel, a true angel. It was enough to make the most unrelenting atheist believe in the Creator."

"Yes, I have heard that she was very good. And you went to see her after this performance?"

"She had fainted."

"You spoke with her, and she behaved strangely?"

"Exactly so! As if she were under some spell."

"She asked you to leave, and you did, but... then you stood listening at her door?"

De Chagny nodded. Holmes stared at him, but he seemed to consider his behavior perfectly normal.

"And then you heard a voice say, 'Christine, you must love me.'"

He leapt to his feet. "Yes, dear God—yes!"

"Please sit down, Monsieur. *Un peu plus de cognac.* Good, very good. Now then, you saw her leave the room?"

"Yes. I hid in a dark corner and watched her depart."

"And then?"

"I went in determined to discover the villain who had spoken to her. The room was... dark. I struck a match and cried for him to come face me. I turned up the gas and lit it, then searched the room. I thought he might be hiding behind the dressing screen, but there was no one. The room was empty, absolutely empty."

"Were there any windows? Perhaps..."

"None. The door I came through was the only way in or out."

Holmes took out his silver cigarette case. "Most interesting. And what do you make of all this, *Monsieur le Vicomte?*"

"I am at my wit's end." He gave a sob and covered his face with his hands.

"Yes, yes." Holmes lit the cigarette. "Do you believe in ghosts?"

De Chagny let his hands fall. "Of course not. I am a practicing Catholic, Monsieur."

"Indeed." Holmes gave him a rather frightful smile. "I suppose then you believe in the sanctity of women and the marriage vow?"

The Viscount leapt to his feet, a flush turning him crimson. "How dare you, Monsieur?"

"Oh, do sit down, *Monsieur le Vicomte.*"

"I will not be insulted!"

"I said sit down. Very well, so you do not believe in ghosts. Have you heard talk about *le Fantôme de l'Opéra?*"

"Yes, Monsieur Holmes."

"And you do not believe in this Phantom?"

He hesitated. "I do not believe in ghosts, but... something else may be at work here."

Holmes nodded. "Yes, I think we may be certain of that. Well, Monsieur, exactly what do you want of me?"

The Viscount took out a letter and handed it to Holmes. We both read it.

> Monsieur,
>
> I have not forgotten the little boy who rescued my scarf from the sea, but it would be best if we do not meet again. You are of noble birth, and I am the child of a peasant. This Saturday is, in fact, the anniversary of my dear father's death. He too was fond of you. A strange power pulls at me. I do not know myself, but I shall go to Perros for this anniversary and visit the graveyard near the village church. There he was buried along with his violin. Remember how as children we played near that church? And there we said farewell many years ago. Again I say farewell, dear friend, but be assured you will remain always in my thoughts and my prayers.
>
> Christine

The corners of Holmes's mouth twitched into a smile, then he resumed a grave air. "What do you intend to do?"

De Chagny folded his arms. "Is it not obvious? I, too, shall go to Perros."

"Yes, it is obvious."

"And I wish you to accompany me, Monsieur Holmes."

Holmes inhaled deeply on his cigarette. "That requires some thought."

"I suspect my unseen rival in this business. I shall pay you whatever you wish, Monsieur Holmes."

Sherlock raised one hand contemptuously. "We can worry about that later. There are some things you should know first, *Monsieur le Vicomte*. As a general rule, I do not engage my services in anything concerning love triangles or the like."

De Chagny covered his face with his hands again. They were white and soft with nary a blemish. "Then I am lost."

"Oh, do stop that!" Holmes snapped. The Viscount looked up at once. "Nor do I spy on young ladies." The flush again colored the Viscount's face. Partly because of his diminutive stature, partly because of his immaturity, he appeared younger than twenty-one, closer to seventeen or eighteen. "However, there are aspects of this case which interest me. I have no doubt that a connection exists between Christine Daaé and *le Fantôme de l'Opéra*. For that reason only, I may be willing to accompany you to Perros."

The Viscount clenched both hands into fists. "Oh, thank you, Monsieur Holmes—thank you!"

Holmes held the cigarette between two long fingers. "Before you thank me I wish to ask you one other question. Please think this over carefully and do not, I beg of you, fly into a huff. What, *Monsieur le Vicomte*, are your intentions toward Mademoiselle Daaé?"

The Viscount jumped up again. "Sit down!" Sherlock roared. De Chagny sat.

The young man's watery blue eyes stared out the window. "I... I am not certain. I... the de Chagny name is a very old and honored one."

"All the more reason not to sully it by disgracing some young woman."

"Surely, Monsieur..."

"If Miss Daaé were 'ruined,' as it is so nicely stated, the difference between a viscount and a common rogue would hardly matter." For once Raoul de Chagny was at a complete loss for words. Holmes kept his eyes fixed on him.

"I... I do not know exactly. I wish... I wish to do the right thing, but my brother..."

"Will survive, regardless of whom you marry. Please remember that." The Viscount nodded weakly. "Very well then. I shall let you know in a day or two whether we shall accompany you to Perros. Please consider my words carefully and remember that I do not employ my services in the seduction of young ladies."

"Monsieur Holmes, I love Christine!"

"Then you will, of course, wish to do what is best for her. You would not want all of Paris whispering about the mistress of the Viscount de Chagny whenever she passes by."

De Chagny grew so pale that I worried he might faint. He sank back into the chair.

"You may go now, Monsieur de Chagny. Please leave me your card. I shall be in touch with you."

The Viscount put his card on the table, picked up his hat and gloves, and went to the door. I opened it for him. "*Au revoir,*" I said. He did not seem to hear me.

Sherlock had crossed his legs, and he regarded the street below. "Were you not somewhat hard on him?" I asked.

Sherlock stared so intensely at me that I could not meet his gaze. "I do not believe so, Henry. Another twenty years and he will be the twin of his brother."

I walked over to the window. The Viscount soon appeared below crossing the boulevard. I was thinking of Michelle. I was not a viscount, I had not made false promises, but how long had I dallied, refusing to commit myself one way or another?

Sherlock took out his watch. "There is yet time before supper. We shall return to the Opera." He stood.

"What for?"

"Before I can begin my work on this puzzle, I must see the celebrated Christine Daaé."

Someone rapped on the door.

"*Entrez,*" Holmes said.

"*Ah, Monsieur Holmes, encore une communication pour vous.*" It was one of the hotel bellmen.

"*Merci, Monsieur.*" He closed the door, then opened the envelope and took out the paper. His brow furrowed, then he smiled. "Ah, excellent." He held the paper up to the light. "The same, of course. Have a look, Henry."

I felt a lurch in my bowels when I saw the red ink and the clumsy hand. The notes the managers had showed us were all written in French, but this was in English.

Dear Mr. Sherlock Holmes,

Your fame is nearly as great in Paris as in London. Truly it would be a tragedy if a genius such as yours were to meet its end at the Paris Opera, but such it must be if you choose to take the part of the managerial buffoons and meddle in my affairs. Do not trifle with the unknown and the unknowable. Return to your native land before it is too late.

With the profoundest respect,
the Phantom of the Opera

The note certainly unsettled me, but Sherlock was positively jubilant. "We are making genuine progress today, Henri. Come, let us go see if Mademoiselle Daaé is in. I absolutely must meet her."

The attendant at the Opera took us down two flights of stairs and along a dim hallway. I soon lost what little sense of direction I had. We passed a party of medieval warriors in armor carrying long spears. A few of the men were smoking cigarettes, and on the whole, they were distinctly unheroic close up. Christine Daaé's dressing room was at the end of a long dark corridor, a distant gas flame casting a feeble light.

The attendant paused. I thought I heard voices through the door. He knocked. "*Mademoiselle Daaé?*"

The voices stopped; then from behind the door a woman said, "*Oui?*"

"*Il ya deux gentilhommes ici qui voudraient vous parler.*"

"*Une minute, s'il vous plaît.*"

The door opened, flooding the dark hallway with light. Christine Daaé was left mostly in shadow. "May we speak with you?" Holmes asked. "I am Sherlock Holmes. I believe the managers let you know I would call."

"Yes. Please come in."

She was a rather fragile-looking young woman, a good foot shorter than Holmes and I, but she had the most extraordinary eyes, large and of a luminescent green, their white-hot intensity somehow reminding me of the flame of a Bunsen burner. Except for her eyes, she was young and pretty in a conventional way, with very fair skin. One could see the blue veins in her eyelids when she blinked. She had high cheekbones and a small, full mouth, a mouth which somehow called attention to itself. Her throat was long, white, and slender. She wore an inexpensive-looking green dress, which showed off her fashionably tiny waist to good advantage.

"You are alone, Mademoiselle?" Sherlock asked.

"But of course. I was merely… memorizing a new role. I practice the words alone, and… I know it is foolish, but I sometimes modify my voice and read both parts. Would you care to sit down? The room is small, the chairs not the best, but please make yourself comfortable."

She was so fair that I saw a slight flush spread about her ears and along her neck as she told about learning her lines. If the Viscount had not mentioned her Swedish father, I would never have noticed that she spoke French with a slight accent.

Sherlock took a wooden folding chair, twisted it about and sat down. He set his top hat and walking stick on the floor. I sat beside him. Before us a large mirror made up almost an entire wall of the small room. We could see Miss Daaé's back and our own faces. Her blonde hair was bound up, the pale skin of the nape of her neck showing above her collar. Jars and tubes of makeup were scattered across a small table before the mirror. The only light in the room came from a gas lamp.

"Mademoiselle Daaé, this is my cousin, Doctor Henri Vernier. We have been engaged by the management to investigate a ghost who has been plaguing the Opera. You have no doubt heard some talk of this Phantom."

She nodded. "Yes, Monsieur."

"Do you believe in ghosts, spirits of the dead and the like?"

She nodded again. "Of course. And I am surprised they have turned to you, Monsieur Holmes. I would think a priest would be the person to drive away a ghost."

Holmes smiled. "Perhaps. And have you seen this ghost?"

"No, but many of the dancers have, and Joseph Buquet did before the ghost killed him."

"Did you know Monsieur Buquet?"

Her lips briefly formed a small circle. "He was a vile man. None of the dancers—the decent ones—liked him. They warned me to watch out for him."

Holmes had crossed his legs, and his boot began to bob up and down. "So you believe that the spirits of the dead can return?"

Her green eyes grew even more intense, and she closed her small hand about a gold cross hanging from her neck. "*Oui, certainement.*"

"Have you ever met such a spirit?"

She hesitated only an instant. "No."

"That is a very pretty cross you have there. Are you a Catholic?"

"Oh yes, Monsieur."

"And what does your faith tell you about ghosts?"

"That the spirits of the dead are all about us, especially the souls of those who loved us and of the saints to whom we pray. Often I sense that my father is quite close, especially when I am singing. I know that there are other spirits very different from us, full of great powers. There are the wicked devils and the angels, many many beautiful angels. Archangels, seraphim, cherubim, and... others."

Normally I would have been inclined to smile at such a discourse, but the girl had such a hold on us with those eyes of hers, and the room was so dim and dreary, that she had me half seeing spirits floating about the ether. Holmes appeared rather grim. I saw his face and mine in the mirror. It is most distracting trying to carry on a conversation while staring at your reflection. I turned my chair slightly.

"Have you ever seen an angel?"

Again a faint hesitation. "No, Monsieur."

He stared at her, but she looked past him, the same faint rosy flush showing alongside her ear. "Very well. Do you have any idea why the Phantom would concern himself with your career as a singer?"

"What, Monsieur?" Her surprise was genuine.

"Do you know why the Phantom might take an interest in your singing?"

"No. I do not know what you are talking about."

"There are many who want you to sing Marguerite in *Faust*, the de Chagnys for instance."

This time there was nothing subtle about her blushing, but her eyes were angry. She made one hand into a fist. "They think themselves very grand, especially the Count. I wish to become a great singer through my own efforts. Perhaps the world of opera does not work that way, but I shall try my way first."

"And the younger de Chagny? I hear he is an admirer of yours."

She smiled. "He can be very sweet, but at times he is much like his brother. His brother is very cold, and everyone knows about him and Sorelli." She paused, her mouth twisting. "They deserve each other, those two."

Holmes gave a sharp laugh. "Indeed?"

"All that interests her are furs and dresses and jewels. Dancing means nothing to her anymore."

"And you? What interests you?"

"I want to be a great singer. I want people to think they have never heard such a voice before. I want to make sublime music, heavenly music, music that comes from the depths of my very soul." Her eyes had grown hot again. "I shall have the furs and jewels, too, but they are not important."

"We hear you are well on your way. Even the London papers mentioned something of your triumph at the gala."

"It all came together that night, Monsieur Holmes! I had worked hard for so long, and as I stood there and sang, the music filled me with such power and beauty. I felt that I truly had become Marguerite—that I had triumphed over vice and squalor, that the angels had come at last to carry me home. The very air tingled, and I could sense the golden blur of their wings. It was so wonderful."

Holmes nodded. "I wish I could have heard you."

"But afterwards—afterwards I was so weary, and I fainted. It was silly, really, and I…" Her smile was gone, her countenance earth-bound again.

"Yes?" Sherlock's gray eyes were fixed on her, something faintly predatory in his gaze.

"I was almost… afraid. I do not know. One must work so hard, and sometimes I am alone and afraid." She laughed nervously. "I felt something like a ghost myself after that night. I was absolutely spent. Perhaps it will be easier next time."

Holmes sighed. I noticed him briefly staring at himself in the mirror. "Perhaps. By the way, who is your teacher, Mademoiselle?"

Her face went pale, her mouth stiffening. "I received a degree from Le Conservatoire de Musique here in Paris."

"Ah, a first-rate institution, but with whom do you study now?"

"No one, Monsieur Holmes. No one."

"That is rather unusual."

She said nothing and would not return his gaze, but her eyes again reminded me of a white-hot flame. "Monsieur, it is late, and I must be leaving soon."

Holmes took out his watch with great show. "Ah yes, it is very late. We shall no doubt see you again, Mademoiselle, and I hope to hear you sing. Perhaps there is a chance we may have the pleasure of your Marguerite this season."

She smiled sadly. "I fear not. I shall be singing Siebel as usual."

"Ah, well, that is a nice part. What do you think of Madame

Carlotta's voice? I have heard…"

"She is an old cow, but she bleats like a billy goat!"

Even Miss Daaé seemed surprised by her own sudden vehemence. She blushed. "I am sorry, but it is true. She is a spiteful, wicked woman, and she has been at me ever since the gala. She never misses an opportunity to make me squirm. She is an insufferable tyrant, rude to everyone. And her voice—she screeches and wobbles. I do not understand how the public will spend good money to… Pardon me, Monsieur, but as you can tell I do not care for her."

"Yes, so I noticed. Frankly, Mademoiselle Daaé—and this must remain in your confidence—I never much cared for her either, even in her prime some fifteen years ago. She was all volume and technique, little else."

"You understand! Are you musical then, Monsieur?"

"I have some small talent with the violin."

"Well, some day I promise you shall hear me as Marguerite."

"I am certain of it, and perhaps it will happen sooner than you think."

"Oh, I hope so."

Holmes picked up his hat and gloves.

I stood. "Mademoiselle Daaé, I am, alas, not so musical as my cousin, but I, too, look forward to hearing you sing. *Faust* is at least one opera where I can follow the story."

She laughed, and I was pleased.

"Do you like the part of Marguerite?" Holmes asked.

"Oh, very much. She is a young girl, very innocent, very trusting, and Faust thinks he loves her, but he destroys her. In the end, though, she triumphs over Faust and the devil. The angels carry her off to heaven, and Mephistopheles pulls Faust down to hell. The music suits my voice perfectly, and it is so beautiful, especially at the end in the dungeon when the angels come."

Holmes had stood. "Yes, it is quite a role. You should sing some Mozart as well. I wager you have just the voice for Zerlina or Susanna."

She clapped her hands together. "I love Mozart!"

I noticed Holmes again staring at himself in the mirror. His eyes shifted, and he saw my reflection staring back at him. He turned, his mouth forming a smile. "That mirror is rather awkward. Do you not find it disconcerting, Mademoiselle Daaé, to have your reflection always following you about?"

"Yes, Monsieur Holmes, I do. I sing before the mirror. It helps me to position my mouth right and form the tones, but I do not like it. Sometimes… sometimes I almost want to throw something over the mirror or even shatter it. This is childish I know, but I fear–I fear…" She laughed nervously. "I think my image may move apart from me, do something that shows it is another… *thing,* and not me at all."

"Perhaps you should practice somewhere else, Mademoiselle Daaé, somewhere outside the Opera."

"Oh, no. I am used to my plain little dressing room and even my great mirror. Good evening, Monsieur Holmes, Doctor Vernier."

When we came out of the Opera, I was surprised to find it so dark. Carriages and pedestrians filled the Place de l'Opéra, people returning home from work or venturing forth for a night on the town. The gas streetlights had been lit, and the square was reassuringly bright after the dim interior of the Opera.

"A charming girl," I said.

Holmes laughed. "Henri–Henri! You cannot resist a fine pair of eyes."

"Well, she did seem quite… spirited. I liked her."

"Did you see her face light up when I mentioned Carlotta? *Une vieille vache.* She said it with such venom. An odd combination that–lyrical moonbeams and artistic venom."

"I am certain this Carlotta has treated her poorly."

"Oh, no doubt of it. Did you remark her one glaring falsehood?"

"Falsehood?"

"Yes, a rather blatant one. A twenty-year-old soprano is never without a teacher, especially a soprano of any talent, especially a soprano who has scored a great triumph. There is nothing natural about singing a high florid line with trills and octave leaps. The fact that she created such a sudden sensation argues strongly that she has been working with a new teacher, one who was spectacularly successful. Why would she not tell us his or her name?"

"Perhaps... the teacher does not want Carlotta to know of his involvement. Perhaps he, too, has a grudge against her."

Holmes stopped abruptly. A carriage passed before us, the horse's hooves clopping rhythmically on the street. "An interesting idea, although perhaps a variation... the Phantom also condemned Carlotta's singing."

I laughed. "Surely you do not believe a ghost would be giving her singing lessons?"

"She was certainly preoccupied with spirits, a most unusual obsession for a young singer. The notion of a musical ghost does seem absurd, and I am always skeptical of the supernatural. In my long career I have dealt with many cases where supernatural powers were supposedly at work. In every single case a human agent, usually a malevolent one, was at work. I doubt this business will turn out any differently."

# *Three*

E arly the next morning, there came a polite, gentle rap upon our door. Upon opening it, I saw an unctuous-looking gentleman whom I had taken for some permanent fixture behind the hotel front desk.

"Monsieur Holmes?"

I stood aside and gestured toward my cousin, who was finishing some correspondence. "How may I be of assistance?"

"There is a… person downstairs who wishes to see you. I regret to say that she does not appear of be of that class which frequents the Grand. Knowing your desire for privacy, I attempted to send her about her business, but she will have none of it. She vows loudly that wild horses cannot drag her away and that she will remain in the lobby until she can see you. I could, of course, have her removed, but it would create a most disagreeable scene. I thought I would inquire of you if…"

"And what is this imposing person's name?"

"Madame Giry."

"Ah, then I fear, sir, that you have completely misjudged the situation. Although she is a trifle eccentric, Madame Giry is an old and dear friend."

The blood drained slowly from the man's face. "Forgive me, Monsieur Holmes. If you wish, I shall bring her to you at once."

"Do so, Monsieur."

The man bowed stiffly, turned, and left.

I closed the door, then glanced at Holmes. "Who is this Madame Giry? I do not recall…"

"Were you daydreaming during our interview yesterday with the managers? She was the box keeper whom they dismissed. One of the Ghost's demands was that she be reinstated."

"Oh, yes. Her name had completely escaped me. Whatever can she want?"

A few minutes later we heard another knock, the twin of the earlier one. No sooner had I opened the door, than a large woman dressed in black swept into the room. Behind her stood the hotel man, his mouth agape.

"Monsieur Sherlock Holmes, I must speak with you!"

"And so you shall, Madame Giry." My cousin rose, and with a smile he gestured at an overstuffed chair.

Madame Giry was a most imposing presence. I could well understand her giving the hotel management some unquiet moments. Her face was flushed; and her large neck, her moon-shaped chin beneath another chin, was even broader than her head. A few gray ringlets showed beneath an enormous black hat, but her eyebrows and the hairs above either corner of her mouth were still black. She wore a bustle, an unfortunate choice, as it made her posterior appear even larger; one could imagine the formidable thews of a small bull beneath those copious sable skirts. Sitting in a bustle is something of a project; we heard swishing, shifting sounds, small groans, and a creak. She opened her mouth to sigh, and I noticed she was missing teeth. Those which remained were an unhealthy color.

"This is my cousin, Doctor Henri Vernier." Holmes nodded at me.

"What can I do for you, Madame Giry?"

"Is it true, Monsieur Holmes? Is it true?"

"Is what true?"

"Is it true that you have been hired to exorcise the Ghost?"

Holmes laughed once, then shook his head. "No, no, Madame. I am no exorcist. Who told you this?"

"Christine Daaé."

Holmes frowned. "She told you I was an exorcist?"

"Well, she said that you were hired to get rid of the Ghost and that you agreed only an exorcist could make a ghost go away."

"No, Madame, you suffer from a misapprehension. I have only been employed to look into the matter of the Opera Ghost. The managers have…"

"Managers—*hah!* They are not managers. They are—clowns, nothing but clowns! They could not manage boiling an egg. Now their predecessors, Messieurs Debienne and Poligny, they were real managers. We were all one great happy family. Every month I would leave the envelope for the Ghost with his twenty thousand francs, and the Ghost left me a tip of two hundred francs. I can tell you truthfully that every month I thanked the good Lord for that sum. A better, a more generous ghost never lived! I will not have you hounding him, Monsieur! All he wants is his paltry twenty thousand francs and his own box. The view from Box Five is one of the best, and I know he watches every performance. What harm is there in any of this, can you tell me that?"

"None, Madame, none whatsoever. Calm yourself. I have been employed by the managers, but that does not make me their tool. I hope to return your Ghost to his box and you to your employment."

Madame Giry's color had gradually returned to normal. "You do?"

"I do, Madame. I shall not be dictated to by the managers. If the Ghost is a good honest ghost…"

"He is, Monsieur—he *is*."

"Then he need not fear me, I promise you."

She gave a tremendous sigh, her huge bosom rising, then falling. "Oh, that is such a relief, Monsieur, such a great relief."

Holmes had sat on the wooden chair near the writing desk. He placed his hands on his knees and leaned forward. "You seem to know the Ghost quite well, Madame Giry. Had you been box keeper for long?"

"Since the day we opened in '75."

"Ah, so you have known the Ghost since then?"

"Yes. He appeared during the first season. That was when we began reserving Box Five and paying him for his good influence."

"And the managers were not skeptical?"

"Perhaps at first, but he convinced them."

"How did he convince them?"

"It has been so many years… Some odd things began to happen, but once they listened to him, things returned to normal."

"Odd things, you say? Do you mean accidents?"

"Accidents—yes, that is the very thing! A set collapsed, props would disappear, and then a weight nearly hit Madame Sponelli when she was doing *Norma*. That is what really convinced them. Of course, the Ghost would never have really injured Madame Sponelli. He only wished to frighten the managers."

"I see. However, what of Joseph Buquet? I hear that…"

Madame Giry's neck seemed to swell again, the scarlet color returning. "*Ce cochon,* that great fat greasy pig! Do you know what he did to Meg, to my daughter Meg?"

"No, Madame."

"He tried to seduce her! Can you believe that? This ugly old goat was always trying to seduce the young girls. It is one thing to be seduced by a fine young gentleman, but an old pig like him… He offered to pay my Meg a hundred francs. A hundred francs! Can you believe such a sum?"

Holmes shook his head. "Outrageous."

"If the Ghost killed Buquet—and I am not convinced he did—then he did all the girls of the Opera a service. My Meg is in the corps de ballet, did I tell you that?"

"No, Madame."

"Some day she will be a great dancer, and…" She broke off her sentence, then glanced warily at me. "The Ghost has predicted great things for her, Monsieur Holmes, great things. I cannot reveal the details, but she will be rich and famous, I can tell you that much. Some day hotel managers will beg for her business and for mine, if God should grant that I live to see the great day."

Holmes nodded. "I do not doubt it, Madame Giry, I do not doubt it."

She eyed him closely, but his whole attitude was so forthright, so respectful, that she gave another great sigh. "Oh, Monsieur Holmes, it is such a relief to me to know that you mean the Ghost no harm."

"Again, if he is an honest ghost—as I am sure he is after speaking with you—then I can promise you he need not fear Sherlock Holmes."

"Oh, thank you, Monsieur Holmes. Thank you!"

"I may wish to ask you a few questions another time, but this morning I have another engagement."

"Then I shan't trouble you no more."

She stood up, and Holmes and I rose as well.

"It has been a pleasure meeting you, Madame. You have been most helpful, and it is good for me to know that a person so knowledgeable of the Opera Ghost is readily at hand. I shall call upon you soon."

"Any time, Monsieur Holmes, any time. Ask my little Meg at the Opera or any of the girls. They all know me and my little house on the Rue des Infirmes."

"Good day, Madame Giry."

The old woman's face formed a smile which I would not have thought possible a few minutes earlier, then she left.

I closed the door behind her, then turned to Holmes. "You have certainly made a friend for life."

"I hope so. A good-hearted woman such as she can be invaluable in a case such as this. No doubt she knows every bit of gossip in the entire Opera."

"Ah, so that explains your behavior."

Holmes frowned. "Not in the least. I liked her. Come, we are late. If we are to join the Viscount on his trip on Saturday, only two days remain this week to explore the Opera."

For our first day, a Monsieur Bossuet was our guide. He was about my age, around thirty, but already he managed the Opera's technical facilities: the lighting, gas, stage machinery, etc. As a trained engineer, he hit it off immediately with Holmes.

We began on the stage, which at over one thousand feet in width was the largest in the world. The carpenters were taking a short break from assembling the village set, and as the three of us walked across the stage, our footsteps echoed faintly. Its sheer size overwhelmed me. Overhead, I could dimly see countless ropes and hanging horizontal rods, then an impenetrable darkness. Impossible to tell how high the roof was. Out before us was the auditorium, everything red and gold. Above the main floor were five balconies, each sweeping about in a U. The pillars rising toward the dome were gilded, and the box fronts were all velvet and gilding.

I stopped, then took a few tentative steps forward toward the footlights. Briefly I imagined people filling the balconies and ground floor, all of them staring at me. A singer would need to face the crowd, then manage somehow to open her mouth and fill that hall with sound. It seemed humanly impossible from where I stood, but I knew it could be done. Nevertheless, merely thinking about all those eyes watching made me uncomfortable. Something akin to a shiver worked its way up my spine.

"Fear not, Henry. You have not been cast in any of the upcoming performances."

"Thank heavens for that."

"Once more into the breach, dear friends!" Holmes declaimed loudly, his voice losing itself in the airy heights above us.

"Bravo, Monsieur Holmes!" Bossuet applauded. "You have the makings of a thespian, I see. I myself share your cousin's sentiments. It is a mystery to me how anyone can perform on such a stage before so many people. However, as I was saying, the lighting system still employs gas, but the time is coming when the electricity will reign supreme. For many years we have used the electric carbon-arc to supplement the limelights, but next year we will begin to replace all the regular gaslights with the electric filament bulbs. The float of the footlights there, and the battens to the side, will be among the first." The footlights were off, but the battens overhead were on. You could see the rubber hoses feeding them, the blue flames burning behind their protective metal screen.

Holmes pointed overhead out at the auditorium. "What of the chandelier?"

"It will be retrofitted as well. When the job is done, our patrons in the uppermost balcony will be much more comfortable. It gets devilishly hot up there, and the stale air is difficult to breathe. So many gas flames consume an enormous amount of oxygen."

I could see the chandelier, the faint glitter of crystal and gilded metal, but it hung in shadow like some shimmery creature from the depths of the sea. I looked forward to seeing it all alight. Above it was a painting on the dome which I could not make out, but which, no doubt, partook of the grand style everywhere in evidence and included more heroic female representations of Liberty, Art, Music, etc.

"The chandelier also is the largest in the world, is it not?"

"Yes, Monsieur Holmes."

"Venting it must require a large structure."

"Yes, the lantern, as we call it, has several windows and is quite spectacular. The auditorium dome is copper, but the lantern supports and its sculpted masks are golden. Garnier wished to gild nearly everything on the roof, but alas, the funds ran out. You will enjoy the tour of the roof, gentlemen. It will help you understand the layout of the Opera, and the view is remarkable."

My legs faltered; I stopped walking and took a slow deep breath.

"Are you ill, Doctor Vernier?" Bossuet was genuinely concerned. "You are so pale."

"I am afraid," Holmes said, "that my cousin will have to forgo the tour of the roof. He suffers from vertigo."

"Ah, that is a pity, but I understand. The flies on either side of the stage go up many levels, and at the very top, the actors below are like tiny ants. Even I feel a bit uncomfortable, so it will be best if he remains below."

"Yes," I nodded. "I shall remain below."

"Perhaps, though, we could persuade you to go up one or two levels. That is where the first limelights are situated. Have you ever seen a limelight close up, *Docteur*?"

"No, but…"

"Oh, but you must let me show you!" He started enthusiastically for the wings. "Pierre, Pierre, would you find old du Bœuf for us? Tell him we want a display of the limes for guests."

I gave Holmes a look of dismay, but he only smiled.

"One caution, gentlemen. Do not say a word about electric lights to du Bœuf. He is an old man and rather set in his ways. To him electric lights are a thing of the devil. To be fair, the limelights are unique, and certain effects cannot be duplicated. We shall not replace them all."

"It does seem sad," I said, "that gaslighting is to be vanquished. I do hope this is not a mere fad, a rush to embrace the fashionably modern."

Holmes turned to me abruptly. "Have you ever treated a victim suffering from massive burns?"

"Yes, I remember a small child…" I shuddered. "The pity of it is you can do almost nothing to save them, not if the burns cover most of their bodies. All you can do is give them morphine to relieve the pain, and even that does not always help much."

"Then you will understand," Holmes said, "why I am eager for the infernal era of gaslighting to end. Few theaters last ten years, and even if a general conflagration does not burn the building to the ground, many people are killed annually. I have seen a dancer with her costume aflame, and I shall never forget the sight. It will be a blessed day when the last gaslight in a theater is extinguished."

"I had not thought of that," I said weakly.

"There is also the heat and the fouling of the air," Bossuet said. "However, safety is our main reason for making the change. There was always much talk, but it was only after l'Opéra Comique burned down that the decision was finally made. We would not want anything to happen to our magnificent Palais Garnier."

"Have you ever visited d'Oyly Carte's Savoy Theatre in London?" Holmes asked Bossuet. "It was completed in '81 for performances of Gilbert and Sullivan and relies entirely upon electric lighting. The lighting is much brighter, but the theater is pleasantly cool."

"I attended one of the first performances, Monsieur Holmes, and I also saw the *Iolanthe* in which battery-powered electric lights were a part of the fairies' costumes. Ah, here you are, Monsieur du Bœuf. These two gentlemen would like to see one of your limes in action. Could you oblige us?"

"Gladly, sir."

Du Bœuf was stooped over, his face wrinkled, two folds of flesh descending from his chin into his shirt collar. He had long white hair neatly parted and an enormous white mustache. Despite his age, he seized the metal railing of the stairway and bounded up the steps. I hesitated, then warily grasped the cold metal and started upward.

"Courage," Holmes whispered behind me.

"Here we are, gentlemen."

We were only about ten feet above the stage, but the floor was a metal grillwork through which one could see. It made me think of walking on air. I looked up and saw a similar grillwork above, then another beyond the first. I shuddered. Lord knew how many levels there were! Ten feet I could endure so long as I stayed back from the rail, but I dared go no higher.

Du Bœuf pointed to a wooden box about a foot square which was clamped to the railing. It had two thin rubber hoses trailing from the back. "Here's a fine old lime. She's lined with metal on the inside, but made of wood so she doesn't get too hot to handle. The hole here in front is where the beam comes out, and these turncocks in back adjust the flow of oxygen and hydrogen. Shall we light her up, Monsieur Bossuet?" The elderly du Bœuf's voice had the enthusiasm of a small boy.

"By all means, Monsieur du Bœuf."

Du Bœuf withdrew a string with tiny white cylinders threaded upon it from his leather apron. "Here's the limes, gentlemen. They have to be drilled right through the center, or the light is uneven. They have wax on them to keep them from breaking up, but it's still best not to touch them. They can burn you." He used a pair of metal tongs to withdraw a cylinder from the string. The back of the box was open, and very carefully, he set the one-inch cylinder onto a spindle inside, near the front opening.

"Lime, common quicklime," Bossuet said, "as you two gentlemen surely know, is calcium oxide."

"I remember that from my university chemistry class," I replied.

Holmes's mouth twitched. "Yes, yes. It is derived generally from heating limestone, calcium carbonate."

Du Bœuf struck a match on the bottom of his boot, twisted one of the turncocks, then touched the match to the gas jet. The flame caught with a whoosh. "First we give it some hydrogen and let her warm up the lime for a minute or so, and we turn this here metal knob at the back, which turns the spindle round and round."

The burning lime at first gave off a yellowish light, but gradually changed color. "There she goes. You wait until she turns red."

"That happens when the calcium begins to be consumed," Holmes said.

"Look at that!" Du Bœuf smiled at the reddish light glowing off the metal inside the box. "Now watch what happens when we gives her some oxygen, just watch!"

He had stopped turning the lime cylinder. He twisted the turncock to the other hose, then tipped the box all the way back so we could see the lime disk through the projection hole. A thin metal pipe curved around in front of the spindle; from it came the gas jet. The character of the flame changed, and then upon the reddish cylinder appeared a luminescent white dot. It did not really grow much in size, but the intensity of the light made it appear to swell, the color a dazzling white. I blinked my eyes and stepped back. White light from the box shot upward, hurling a great beam into the darkness above.

"There she goes!" Du Bœuf tipped the box forward toward the stage, then turned the small metal knob. "We have to give her a turn once in a while. You want the lime disk to burn down evenly, little by little. In the old days you had to turn the lime by hand, and that was tricky, believe me. Gloves always get in your way, but you can burn yourself well without them. This knob and those gears really do a neat job. It's a pretty light, isn't it, gentlemen?"

We all nodded, and Holmes said, "Indeed it is." The box cast an oval of white light upon the stage floor.

"Yes sir, this is your basic limelight. You can put a lens in front and get an even tighter beam. We use them that way for a follow spot. Hand me one of the glass squares, Monsieur Bossuet."

"Which color?"

"How about a nice orange?" Du Bœuf continued to give the knob a tiny turn every so often; he must have done this for so long that it had become an unconscious reflex upon his part. "Here's what we do when Monsieur Mephistopheles makes his entrance."

The orange square of glass had a metal frame; he slid the square into a holder in front of the box. Immediately the light became a lurid red orange. A carpenter walking past gazed up at us, his blue jacket changed to black, his skin an impossible shade. He had a beard, and when he smiled up at us, he did appear rather diabolical.

Holmes gave an ironic smile. "I recall some music critic saying that it was his unfortunate fate to spend much of his life at mediocre performances of *Faust* gazing upon the devil bathed in reddish limelight."

Du Bœuf's white eyebrows sank down and inward, a ready crease appearing. "Nothing mediocre about our limes."

"No, of course not, Monsieur du Bœuf." Holmes glanced at Monsieur Bossuet. "Nor with your Mephistopheles either." Bossuet's amused expression made it clear he was not so quick to take offense.

"It certainly is bright," I said.

"It was first used for surveying," Holmes said. "A Lieutenant Thomas Drummond employed the first limelight in 1825 while the royal engineers were surveying Ireland. The light on a mountain top could be viewed from sixty miles away. Of course, as he was interested in portability, he used a spirit lamp rather than hydrogen. It is an acceptable substitute, but an inferior one. The oxyhydrogen flame is the hottest known to man."

Bossuet's brow grew more and more wrinkled during this disquisition, while du Bœuf's jaw gradually dropped. Finally the old lime man spoke. "You are very learned, sir. I never met anyone else besides an old limer or two like myself who had heard of Drummond." No minister citing chapter and verse ever received a more devoted gaze than Holmes received from the old man.

"Chemistry interests me, as do light and fire. Several orange limes are used to simulate great conflagrations on stage, are they not? I saw quite a spectacular display last year in which an entire house was on fire, the walls and floors giving way."

"Quite right, sir! I've done many a fire scene in my day. There's always a number of ladies that faint dead away and many gentlemen that come out in a sweat."

Holmes had found another friend, and he, du Bœuf, and Bossuet could no doubt have discussed stage lighting all day. However, Holmes at last reminded them of his schedule, and he and Bossuet ascended higher while I gladly returned to the stage floor.

When they came down an hour later, Holmes told me they had climbed all the way to the roof. At every level were lights, both limes and the electric carbon-arc variety. Some six levels up Holmes had come upon a row of gigantic bells; they were used for rousing climaxes, battles and triumphs, and church scenes. The view from the roof was spectacular, the copper dome weathered green, a statue of Apollo with a golden lyre situated at the highest point of the Opera.

During the afternoon Bossuet showed us the backstage area, which was as large as the stage itself. We saw completed sets for current productions. Three-dimensional building fronts, trees, etc., made of cardboard or papier-mâché had become the rage, supplementing the flat painted scenes. However, dozens of conventional backdrops hung high overhead, the building having been designed so they could be stored unfurled above the stage.

In a room nearby I saw several peculiar machines which resembled strange three-barreled weapons. These were the "magic lanterns" used to project various scenes from glass slides. Bossuet told us the lanterns employed the limelight because of its brilliance and intensity. Each machine actually had three lanterns stacked vertically; this allowed scenes from two slides to be combined, while the third could be used for a "dissolving" effect. The gas to one light was turned down while another was turned up; one scene, a blasted heath, say, would fade away even as another took its place.

At last we saw something more to my liking: the practice room of the corps de ballet. The girls were very young, lithe, and slender, and they leapt about with great energy. All wore white tights and white dresses with skirts of transparent gauze. I had not realized how much physical stamina dancing required. One could see powerful muscles in the girls' slim legs.

"Who is that man in the astrakhan hat?"

I was barely aware that Holmes had spoken. I turned my head and saw him staring at a man in the opposite corner of the room. He was wearing a fez made of black astrakhan wool, but what struck me was his villainous face. Although I, too, had been watching the dancers intently,

I hoped I had displayed no such leering lasciviousness as he.

"That is the Persian," Bossuet replied.

"Which Persian?"

"I do not know his name. He is only referred to as the Persian. He is a frequent spectator at the Opera. He is an acquaintance of Richard or Montcharmin, and they have given him ready access to the Palais Garnier."

"I do not much care for his face," I said. "Nor his hat."

At that moment the piano player came to the end of the piece. "Five minutes, girls," shouted the dance master. We strolled leisurely toward the door, but we were suddenly confronted by one of the dancers.

She was a short, slight thing with a pale face, large, luminous brown eyes, and black hair. Her hair was bound up in the same bun as the other dancers. Her forehead was damp with perspiration, and her nostrils flared as she tried to control her breathing.

"Monsieur Holmes? Monsieur Sherlock Holmes?" Her voice was little more than a whisper, and she spoke without hardly opening her mouth.

"Yes, Mademoiselle?"

"My mother... I am Meg Giry. My mother... You are not... angry?"

"Not in the least, Mademoiselle. We had a pleasant conversation this morning upon a subject of mutual interest, the Opera Ghost."

Mademoiselle Giry gave us a look of total incredulity. "She did not...? You are not...?"

"A charming woman. She does possess strong opinions, but I admire that in a woman."

Her incredulity changed to relief. "*Merci, Monsieur. Merci beaucoup.*" She gave us a brief smile that revealed brown, diseased teeth; then, instinctively, she closed her mouth. She nodded, mumbled, "*Merci,*" again, then turned and walked away. Her white dress came halfway up her back; the top of her shoulder blades were revealed and the slender white nape of her neck.

"I see, Henri, that I shall have to return you to Michelle quickly ere you run off with some youthful artistic denizen of the Opera."

My face grew hot. "I do not find that amusing."

"Do you not? Forgive me. I find the predictability of the sexes comical, but I should not have implied that your feelings for Michelle were less than genuine. What now, Monsieur Bossuet?"

Next was the main costume room, where dresses, suits, coats, doublets, capes, and other unusual garments hung from rack after rack. Each costume was neatly labeled as to size, and the characters and operas for which it was used. To the rear of the room were shelves stacked with shoes and boots of every size and variety. Next door was an incredible armory stocked with swords, lances, halberds, helmets, breastplates, and chain mail.

After that we visited several boxes, including the Phantom's Box Five. Holmes spent a good half hour minutely examining it. He rapped at the walls and the massive gold column to one side, then he went down on his knees and peered closely at the carpet. Bossuet gave me an odd look, but I had seen Holmes as bloodhound before. Afterward he refused, of course, to tell us anything, but he did murmur, "Excellent."

That evening I was exhausted, my legs aching. I took a long hot bath in a room whose marble and bronze splendor recalled the Opera; this was understandable since Garnier had designed the Grand Hôtel before going on to his chef d'oeuvre, the Palais Garnier, the Paris Opera. Before I fell asleep I saw great architectural vistas of marble, gold, and velvet, then ropes, scenery, and heavy canvases, all coming together in a vast maze.

Having visited the celestial realm, the next day we descended to the underworld, and worthy it would have been for any of the Stygian shades who confronted Virgil or Dante. Our main guide was an old-timer, a Monsieur Gris whose name seemed appropriate given the gray stubble of his beard. Gris was a silent, stoical type, but his youthful companion clearly grew more frightened as we went lower and lower. Holmes tried questioning Gris, but Gris told us one did not discuss *le Fantôme* in *his* domain.

Beneath the stage, supporting girders of steel were everywhere; despite the Opera's baroque, antiquated exterior, its "skeleton" was constructed of modern materials. Numerous ropes and winches were used to raise and lower platforms or other machinery. This level was well provided with gas lamps, and stagehands and carpenters bustled about.

The next level down was darker, the walls formed of stone blocks. In the electric room were the batteries which provided power for the electric carbon-arc lights. There too were the tanks used to store oxygen and hydrogen for the limelights. Because of the quantities of chemicals involved, including sulfuric acid, the room had an acrid smell.

In a large chamber next door, huge generators were being assembled which would provide electricity for the new bulb-lighting system. We also visited the "organ room." Up through the floor came thick black pipes filled with gas; they split and divided, then split again before radiating out to every corner of the Opera. Turncocks and levers were used to adjust the gas flow; here the head gas man could raise the light to the footlights or to the battens at the sides of the stage.

Gris had told us the Opera had five cellars, and the next ones lay mostly in darkness. A few scattered gas fixtures gave off a faintly bluish light, but they and our lanterns seemed feeble before such darkness. The air was cold and dank. Dust motes and gossamer webs floated gently in the beams of the lanterns. More than once when we entered a room, we heard the scurry of tiny feet. I have a horror of rats, and I asked Holmes if we need visit every filthy lower chamber of the Opera. Our two guides seemed to share my sentiments, but Holmes was resolute that he would go on. At that point Gris insisted that we keep one hand raised to the level of our eyes.

"What on earth for?" I asked.

Gris hesitated, his eyes glancing all about us. "The Punjab lasso," he finally whispered gruffly.

"The *what?*"

Holmes frowned. "Do as he says."

This soon grew quite fatiguing, but Gris and Holmes both reprimanded me sternly whenever I lowered my arm.

Gris had told us the Opera had twenty-five hundred doors; if so, I am certain the majority must have been below ground. We passed ancient pieces of scenery and piles of rolled-up canvas flats. One room was filled with replicas of pagan deities which were used in various operas; another was littered with armored dummies which represented fallen warriors in battle scenes.

As we went on and on, further and further down, I grew colder, wearier, and more heartsick. My mouth felt dry, and I found myself talking senselessly just to break that dreadful, weighty silence all around us. At last a stairway passed through a tall doorway, and the light from a single bluish lamp glimmered faintly on a vast expanse of dark water. We heard it lap softly at the mossy stones. Our breath formed clouds of white vapor.

"Good Lord," I murmured. "What is this? The sewer?"

"No, Monsieur. It is a lake," Gris said.

"A lake?" Holmes asked.

"*Oui, Monsieur.* When they were excavating for the Opera, they struck water. Pumps were used to remove it temporarily; then when all was finished, the water was put back, forming this lake."

"Let me see your lantern." Holmes shone the white light out across the black water. "How far does it go?"

Gris shrugged. "Who knows?"

"Some day I think I shall want to explore this lake."

"That, Monsieur Holmes, is a very bad idea."

Distantly I thought I heard a low sound like a moan. It raised the hair on the back of my neck and, along with the cold, set me convulsively shivering. "Did anyone hear that?" I asked.

Gris's youthful assistant appeared too frightened to speak, but the old man shrugged again. "Some say it is the sound of the traffic above on the Rue Scribe. Others tell stories about voices—*la sirène*—a woman calling."

"It is better not to speak of such things," the younger man said.

"Let us go, Sherlock," I said. "Please."

"Very well." We turned and started back up the stairs. "A lake. Who would ever have imagined…"

It took a five-course meal (one for each cellar), half a bottle of red wine, and some pastries with coffee to revive my spirits. The noisy, brightly lit restaurant seemed the most wonderful place on earth, but Holmes was quiet and subdued. I asked what was troubling him.

"It is too large, Henry, far too large, a world, a universe unto itself. We are outsiders, explorers, who have hardly touched its shores. Mapping it would take a year or two. A man—a phantom—who has dwelt there for many years would have countless hiding places and secret strongholds. You could employ an army down there for weeks looking for him. If we could lure him out… He need not be a spirit to rule over such a place, and if he were truly intelligent, an evil genius… Well, tomorrow we join the Viscount on his love-sick quest to Britanny. Perhaps we shall discover something there."

That night I took a much longer hot bath, but the cold and darkness of the underworld seemed to have seeped into my bones. My dreams were all of cobwebs, dim blue flames, dust, and death. Strange ghostly things floated over black waters, then pursued me as I fled through long stone tunnels and plodded up endless stairways, vainly seeking the surface of the earth and the wondrous light of the sun. I wanted to find Michelle, but I knew I had lost her forever.

*Four*

The next evening we left Paris from the Gare Montparnasse on the Brittany Express. We had hoped to depart that morning; but the Viscount was late because of a carriage accident; hence an annoying delay, which meant we would have to spend the night on the train.

We gazed out the windows of our first-class compartment at the brightly lit streets of Paris, aptly named the City of Light, but before long we were into the darkened countryside. The Viscount appeared even more unsettled than before, and he had a habit of biting his nails, which was difficult because their ragged edges had been nibbled to the quick. Holmes had brought along his pipe and soon filled the compartment with a thick smoke. A large false mustache hid his mouth and swallowed up the pipe stem.

Not wanting anyone to recognize us (especially Christine Daaé), Sherlock had purchased some secondhand clothing for us both, pasted a goatee onto my chin, then added some gray coloring to it and my mustache. I also wore a pair of spectacles with thick lenses of plain glass. We were two obtuse English men on an oddly timed winter holiday.

Despite my initial misgivings (I had not played dress-up games since my childhood), I found myself enjoying my role immensely, especially the opportunity to mutilate the French language when I spoke to the ticket collector. I doubt even Michelle would have recognized me.

The train hurtled forward into the night at a tremendous speed approaching fifty miles an hour, transporting us away from that greatest metropolis of nineteenth-century Europe toward remote Brittany, the westernmost part of France. Brittany's peninsula thrusts itself into the Atlantic like the face of some open-mouthed, big-nosed dragon. Our journey seemed to transport us through time as well as space: gas lighting, central heating, and modern plumbing were little known outside of Paris; and the people of Brittany were another race, an ancient one. The name of their country, Brittany, or "land of the Britons," said it all. They were Celts, not Gauls, and for much of their history had been closer in touch with Cornwall and Wales than Paris. Some years past, inspired by Flaubert's example, I had taken a walking tour of Brittany. Many of the inhabitants still spoke their Celtic language, which was close to Welsh, and the landscape itself recalled Wales, the same cold gray gloom on overcast days.

I slept fitfully that night. The young Viscount turned out to be a frightful snorer. His tonsils and adenoids must have been huge; that would also explain his frail, sickly appearance. Whenever I awoke, in the dim light of the swaying, rumbling car I saw Holmes's weary eyes staring at me. The Opera, especially its cellars, had made quite an impression on him, and for the past day he had been melancholy.

At one point I saw him staring out the window. I blinked my sleepy eyes, noticing that the gray-white light seemed somehow brighter, and then I recognized the white flecks blurring past the window.

"Snow?" I murmured.

"Yes. We are well past Normandy and into Brittany. Go back to sleep,

Henry. Dawn is still a long way away."

When I woke again, the light from the white sky filled our compartment. Snow covered the land, only a few trees and small farmhouses breaking the long white curves. I thought of our recent journey to Wales, of Susan Lowell and her father. This falling snow was another bond between Wales and Brittany, and I wondered if we would again encounter death. The memory of the Major's corpse twisting slightly in that dark room full of wind and snow filled me with apprehension. I drew a blanket about me. Holmes appeared wearier than ever, his eyes half open. The Viscount continued to snore with amazing gusto.

We reached Lannion shortly after dawn, and again I had the impression of having traveled backward in time, Paris miles and years away. The diligence which took us to Perros was the type that had prevailed throughout England and the Continent before the railroad; young David Copperfield would have ridden in such a vehicle. The driver mentioned that he had taken a young Parisienne to the inn the night before.

The Inn of the Setting Sun lay on a rise before a long beach, the sand hidden by an inch or two of snow, much less than at Lannion, which was further inland. The wind was very cold, but the snowflakes had ceased falling. The inn must have been a hundred years old. From the edge not covered by snow, I could tell that the roof was constructed of the blue-gray slate common to the region, and the walls were made of stone. Inside was an enormous fireplace with a good blaze going. Thick rafter beams spanned the room, hams hanging from hooks near the kitchen. The innkeeper had blue eyes and white hair and spoke French with a heavy accent. If I spoke any Gaelic or Welsh, he would no doubt have understood me.

As we had agreed between ourselves earlier, Sherlock and I

pretended not to know the Viscount. I was just asking the innkeeper about the local sights in very bad French, when I heard a woman exclaim, "Raoul!" then more softly, "*Monsieur le Vicomte.*"

It was Sunday morning; and Christine Daaé, having just come from Mass, still had her missal and rosary in hand. Her cheeks were flushed from the cold, her green eyes bright, and she was very pretty. She wore a blue dress, a coat with a fur collar, and a tiny hat. Her apparel was certainly more chic and expensive than the green dress she had worn at the Opera; it set her apart from the other women at the inn, Parisian high couture clearly unknown at Perros in the dead of winter. She and the Viscount spoke briefly. Finally she shook her head, touched his arm lightly, then swept past Holmes and me without appearing to see us. Our disguises were a success!

Holmes, the Viscount, and I stood before the fireplace warming ourselves. "She will see me late this afternoon," the Viscount said, "at dusk in the cemetery where her father is buried."

Holmes nodded. "We shall meet you here at four p.m."

We spent most of the day in our room, and after the Grand Hôtel the Inn of the Setting Sun seemed only slightly superior to a penitential establishment. The beds were plain and hard, the room sparsely furnished. The innovation of a large glass window did overlook the broad expanse of the beach, the sky, and the ocean, but it made the room even colder. The stove was much too small and feeble to heat the chamber. By midafternoon the sun came out, touching the breakers with highlights of white fire and setting the blue-green waters of the Atlantic all aglow. We heard the dull roar of the ocean, a very soothing music. Blankets wrapped about him, Holmes fell asleep in a chair near the window and slept for three or four hours. I finally had to wake him so we could go to meet the Viscount.

Soon the three of us were trudging along a snow-covered path. It was bitter cold outside, the wind sweeping in off the sea, biting. Holmes and I wore heavy overcoats, round-topped bowler hats, leather gloves, and woolen scarves. The Viscount was bareheaded, his overcoat cut with fashion more in mind than warmth. The sun was a red-gold brilliance to our left, far too bright to look at.

"I remember this path well." The Viscount seemed to speak more to himself than to us. "It was not so cold in summer. We came here at dusk. The hill above the cemetery is a good place to watch the sea, and there is the tree…"

Ahead of us on a hill was the black silhouette of an enormous oak, its gnarled barren limbs clawing at the yellow sky. Our breath formed clouds of vapor, and I thrust my hands into my pockets, clenching and unclenching my fingers. The path led uphill to the oak.

The trunk of the oak must have been a good six feet across. Downhill away from the sea was a graveyard and a small stone church. However, far more striking was the tree's companion, a giant menhir, the slab of granite some twenty feet tall. It stood just far enough downhill that you could not see it until you reached the hilltop. It must have dated back to Neolithic times thousands of years past, forming a part of the same mysterious lost culture that had built Stonehenge and the other megaliths scattered about Britain and Europe.

"That's one of the largest menhirs I have seen," I said. "If I did not know better, I would say the tree was equally old, but of course that is impossible. Still, this may have been the site of some ancient Celtic rituals."

The Viscount stared out at the sea. Earlier there had been white-caps, but now it was still, the blood-red orb of the sun hovering above its vast, flat expanse. "We came here to watch the korrigans dance in the moonlight."

"Korrigans?" I asked.

"The fairy people of the Bretons, small sprites. I could never see anything, but Christine claimed she saw them."

We walked downhill toward the church. One or two people had been here earlier, their solitary footprints in the snow winding about the graves. The small tombstones were made from the Breton granite, names and dates chiseled into the hard rock. A few graves had large crosses with ornamental flourishes. The site had an aura of great age and gloom, and I thought it must have been a graveyard for centuries. When I glanced at the church, my supposition was verified. At the back, on either side of the sacristy door, bones were piled in an ossuary typical of Brittany. Those earlier occupants had lost their places in the frozen ground.

Holmes walked toward the stacked skulls, femurs, ribs, and vertebrae, then reached out with his walking stick and scooped up a skull with the tip. He took the skull in his left hand. The mandible and many of the upper teeth were gone, the bone yellowish and brittle.

"'Alas, poor Yorick, I knew him, Horatio,'" Holmes said. "My favorite speech in *Hamlet*, Henry. It is wise not to forget that we all come to this end, even the great Sherlock Holmes." He raised the skull in his gloved hand and held it alongside his own head. It made his nose appear enormous. His lips twitched, then he hurled the skull away. It struck the stone wall of the church and shattered. He winced. "Sorry, old fellow, old Yorick." He stared at the pieces lying on the ground, then turned over a fragment with his stick.

The entire hillside, including much of the church, was in blue shadow, and I felt cold. "You are in a morbid mood."

He pointed with his stick at the bones. "Can you blame me? Could there be a more morbid setting than this ossuary? The frozen earth vomits forth its dead, and here the remnants lie neatly arranged. Note the small femur there, Henry. A child of approximately ten or eleven. Your medical background may allow you to trace past history, those afflictions and diseases which led to death. However, if someone there met a violent end, then I can determine how it happened."

I shook my head. "I am no pathologist, and my practice has been limited to the living. All the same..." I picked up a small skull, part of its right side gone. "This disintegration on one side was probably caused by mastitis, an infection of the middle ear spreading into the surrounding bone."

"Excellent, Henry. Excellent. Another child, too." His lips formed that characteristic smile, but his voice had such an undercurrent of despair that I seized his arm.

"Come away from here."

He slipped away from my grip, then shrugged. "Very well."

The sacristy door was clear of bones, and I noticed the beautiful carved design: long, straight tree trunks rose, their branches interweaving near the stone arch framing the top. "Look at this design, Sherlock. Those tree limbs are what you would expect of Celtic Druids, not Christians."

"The boundary between Druid and Christian is ephemeral in Brittany. Christianity rose out of the Celtic past, no doubt incorporating many of its traditions."

"I say—I've found it!" the Viscount cried. We walked through the snow to him. He pointed at a pathetically small tombstone. "It is the grave of Christine's father." Some red silk flowers had been placed there, the bright color jarring, vibrant, against the bleak whites, grays, blacks, and browns of the landscape.

Holmes took out his watch. "It is nearly four-thirty. Henry and I shall hide behind the menhir. The air is quite still, the hill sheltering us from the wind off the sea. We should be able to easily hear you. See if you can discover anything about her teacher and her recent success. And, Monsieur de Chagny..."

"Yes?"

"Be gentle with the girl. Curb your emotions and listen to her with an open heart. Jealousy is the most unpleasant of sentiments."

The Viscount nodded, but his lips drew back petulantly. Again it was difficult to believe he was so old as twenty-one.

We walked uphill, and Holmes and I stood behind the menhir. I stared up at the dark expanse set against the blue-white sky.

"I suppose," Sherlock said, "that as it has stood for a few thousand years, it will manage to stand for another hour or two."

I shivered and stamped my feet. "Did you really need to mention that? I wonder how many tons it weighs. Good Lord, it is cold. Once the sun is down…"

"Raoul!" a voice exclaimed.

Sherlock seized my arm and drew me back. "The lady is prompt," he whispered.

"Christine–ah, Christine!" The Viscount's tenor voice was piercing; we should have no difficulty hearing him.

"Are you waiting for the korrigans to come out? See where the last rays of the sun touch the water? It will not be long. Why did you come, Raoul? You should not have."

"You wished for me to come–admit you did. You sent me that note knowing full well that it would draw me to your side."

"I… I do not know what I meant. I remembered our childhood and our time together. I remembered… that we had been fond of one another."

"Then why did you send me away the night of the gala? Why have you refused to see me?"

A long silence followed. Holmes peered out from behind the granite, and I stepped beside him. The Viscount and Christine were just below the summit of the hill, and she was staring down at the graveyard.

"You do not answer me. Very well, I shall tell you why. You were hiding another man there! I heard you say, 'Tonight I gave you my soul, and I am dead!'"

"You heard that! You were listening at my door, Monsieur de Chagny? How dare you? How dare you!" Her voice rang with fury.

"I dared because—because I love you! I love you, Christine, with all my heart. I heard him—I heard what he said."

Christine drew back. "You heard…? What did you hear?" She spoke softly, but the icy air was clear and still, a vast primeval silence all around us.

"I heard him say, 'Christine, you must love me!'"

Her hand shot out and seized his arm. "You heard? You heard *that*?"

"Yes!"

"What else did you hear?" Her voice had grown strangely quiet.

"I heard you say, 'I sing for you alone.' *You alone.*" De Chagny's voice quavered.

Sherlock gave his head a brisk shake, and I heard him mutter, "Fool."

"Then he said, 'Your soul is a beautiful thing. The angels wept tonight.'"

She turned away from him. Holmes and I darted back behind the menhir. "You heard that? You heard him speak? *His* words?"

"Yes—yes!"

Again silence, then the soft sound of the wind swelling. The sky was darker, the cold worse. I wiggled my toes inside my boots.

"Very well, Monsieur. I shall tell you something very serious, but first I must have your promise you will never speak a word of this to anyone."

"You have my word of honor as a gentleman."

"Do you remember… the Angel of Music?"

"The *what*?"

"Surely you cannot have forgotten him? Remember the stories my dear father told us? Remember Little Lotte? 'Little Lotte thought of everything and nothing. Her hair was gold like the sun, her soul as clear as her blue eyes. She was kind to her dolly, but most of all she loved, when she went to sleep, to hear the Angel of Music.'"

"Christine, whatever has this to do with us—with our love?"

"You cannot have forgotten the Angel of Music?"

"No, of course not. I remember him well." He was sarcastic.

"All of father's stories involved the Angel of Music. He chooses a few special people and whispers into their ears. He gives them his great gift, the gift of music. Only his chosen ones have that genius, that magnificent fire, which moves men's souls, that fire which transforms and ennobles, making music divine—celestial."

"What on earth are you talking about? What is this nonsense?"

Again her hand reached out to seize his arm. "Can you not understand? Must I spell out everything! I have heard him—the Angel, the Angel of Music."

"*What?*"

"You heard me! The Angel has spoken to me—not once, but many times! He has taken me under his great golden wings and made me into what I am. Do you think that the poor little Christine Daaé you once knew could sing as I have sung? I have been melted away and re-forged in his sacred fire."

The Viscount appeared utterly perplexed. "Perhaps... You were inspired, Christine, your singing magnificent. Who... who else has heard him?"

"Why, you did. That was his voice in my room."

De Chagny stepped back, then laughed weakly.

"What are you laughing at! You thought... Now I begin to understand you, *Monsieur le Vicomte,* my old playmate, my father's trusted friend! How you have changed! I do not shut myself into rooms with strange men. If you had opened the door, you would have found no one there!"

He nodded. "That is true. After you left I searched, but no one was there."

"You *searched*? You went into my dressing room?"

"Yes, but…"

"So what now, Monsieur—what do you think of me now?"

He hesitated. "I think someone is playing you for a fool."

She pulled her glove free and slapped him hard with her bare white hand. The impact of the blow broke the stillness, the silence of that snowy hillside near the sea. She turned and swept past him, her dark silhouette briefly showing at the hill top, minute beside that of the great oak, and then she was gone.

"Christine," the Viscount moaned. He touched his face where she had slapped him.

Sherlock shook his head. "He is incorrigible, Henry. I wish we had not had to overhear this, although what she said was quite valuable. Come."

I was only too glad to be moving again. The snow had turned slightly crunchy under our feet. I stared out past the graveyard and the church at the bare, lonely fields in the distance. A huge full moon had just risen, the parting sun giving it an eerie yellow-orange hue.

"You heard, Monsieur Holmes—you heard what she said? An Angel of Music. How am I to take such nonsense?"

"Take it as you wish." Holmes strode past him.

The Viscount's youthful face was totally confused, the imprint of Christine Daaé's hand still a vivid red on his cheek. He was close to tears, and I actually felt sorry for him. "It was a very odd story," I said. "Come, *Monsieur le Vicomte,* we will freeze out here. I am ready for a hot supper and the fire."

However, when we returned to the inn, the Viscount would not join us for supper but stalked off to his room. He had missed lunch and breakfast as well. Sherlock had little to say as we ate stewed mutton and dark bread, peasant fare which tasted absolutely wonderful.

"What did you make of her story about the Angel of Music?" I asked him.

"She believes in him absolutely, and the appearances are on her side. How else can one explain her spectacular rise?"

"Surely you do not believe in angels?"

"I have met many an angel and a devil."

"You have?" I smiled. "You are speaking metaphorically."

"Perhaps."

He would comment no further. I left him sitting by the hearth watching the flames crackle about the pile of logs, his pipe in hand. He was ready for some serious thinking while I was ready for some serious sleeping. I lay down on the bed, still clothed, and fell asleep at once. The moon rose above a snowy graveyard, the wind howling in vain at the great black oak. Out over the waters, strange faery shapes gathered, their naked white limbs cold and faintly bluish. As the korrigans began to dance, a long row of yellow skulls leered at the show.

Someone shook me. "Henry—Henry."

I opened my eyes and had to think before I could recall why Holmes's face had a big mustache. He had on his overcoat, and behind him was the Viscount, pale and weary. "Christine Daaé has gone out, Henry. Do you wish to accompany us?"

I sat up. "What an absurd question. What time is it, two or three in the morning?"

"Eleven-thirty."

"I must have slept for an hour or two." I sighed. "Well, as Watson would no doubt come, I must not be outdone by him."

Holmes smiled. "You are a worthy companion." I put on my heavy coat and followed them. "I was sitting by the fire," Holmes said, "and I noticed her slip out a few minutes ago."

No one else was up, and the main door was not locked. Bretons tended to be abed early. Outside the full moon was brilliant, the blue-white light bathing the snow and casting shadows. I had never seen so bright and clear a night, nor so cold a one. I gazed at the bareheaded Viscount. "Good Lord, man—get a hat."

"There is no time for that. Where can she have gone?"

"To the graveyard, no doubt. Ah yes, here are her tracks." Holmes pointed with his walking stick. "The earlier tracks are partly frozen over and obscured, but these are sharp and distinct. The pointed toes are characteristic of the fashionable Parisienne boots which no other women at the inn are wearing."

Even a novice consulting detective like myself could have followed Christine Daaé's tracks that night. Their shape was unmistakable, and her feet were remarkably small. I had never much cared for fur coats, but by the time we reached the hill top with the black oak, I was wishing for one. Such clear cold weather was unusual here along the Breton coast, clouds, mist, and drizzle being the usual fare.

We gathered near the tree, sheltering ourselves from the wind. The moon was higher now, and the church, the menhir, the tombstones and crosses cast sharp blue-black shadows. Below us, Christine Daaé stood with her hands folded, her head bowed, before a small headstone. De Chagny stepped forward, but Sherlock seized his arm. "No," he whispered. "This is no affair of ours. We should leave her to her thoughts."

"But…" the Viscount began.

Christine moved, turning. Sherlock pulled the Viscount back against the tree and put his hand over the youth's mouth. I flattened myself against the rough bark. The wind moaned softly. The tree must have hidden us, for Christine turned away.

Sherlock was several inches taller than the Viscount, and the way he held him, one hand over his mouth, reminded me of a father restraining a spiteful child. "Will you keep silent, *Monsieur le Vicomte?*"

De Chagny's eyes were angry, but he nodded. Holmes released him. From the village a mile or two away, we heard the dim chime of the clock tower twelve times. As the sound faded into nothingness, another began, almost growing out of the other—music, the most incredible music I have ever heard—a violin, the melody beginning softly, sadly, but swelling, its power and intensity apparent. The strain was sorrowful, but romantically so, its beauty almost painful. The Viscount sprang forward, but Holmes grabbed him and again clamped a hand over his mouth.

The music lasted only a few minutes, but it seemed much longer, as if somehow time were frozen, as if the universe were centered on that moonlit graveyard and its magical harmony. Christine Daaé had sunk down onto her knees. Sherlock did not move. I could see that he was absolutely transfixed, his eyes revealing something of the passions at the core of him. Even the Viscount had stopped wriggling.

The music faded, finally drifting away on a long shimmering note even as a soul passes from this world into the next, and then there was only the faint murmur of the wind and the blue-white light of the moon on the snow all around us. Christine Daaé sobbed and buried her face in her hands. The Viscount jerked forward, but Holmes had him in his iron grasp. We stared at each other, and although we were in the shadow of the tree, I thought I saw tears in my cousin's eyes.

Christine stood at last. "*Merci,*" she said, then made the sign of the cross. She turned away and walked slowly across the graveyard, back toward the path to the inn. Again the Viscount tried in vain to escape. When Christine Daaé had gone, Holmes released him.

"This is outrageous, Monsieur Holmes—you will keep your hands off me or suffer the consequences!"

Holmes was still under the hold of the music. He sagged back against the tree. "Perhaps... perhaps there is an Angel of Music."

"Here—he is here?—I shall deal with him." De Chagny started down the hill.

I took a step after him, but Holmes grasped my arm. "Let him be."

"What was that music?" I asked.

"You felt it, too?"

"Yes. How could anyone resist it?"

"Ask the Viscount."

"Did you recognize the tune?"

"Yes. It was a simple folk ballad, 'The Resurrection of Lazarus.' Someone must have played that music, but what a genius! I have never heard his equal. Sarasate is good, but this... I would give my soul to play like that. Henry, you did hear it?"

"Of course I did."

"We had better follow the Viscount. Perhaps Paganini could have played that way, but he was full of tricks and mere virtuosity. Some did believe Paganini had sold his soul to the devil. It is, however, far harder to play a simple tune so expressively than some wild caprice." We had passed the menhir, its black shape blotting out the starry night.

"Come out and face me!" cried the Viscount. "I know you are there!" He stood in the shadow before the sacristy door and the heaps of bones. Something white flew at him. He shrieked and leapt, briefly dancing in the air. Another skull, and yet another flew at him, and then an entire pile of bones collapsed and tumbled toward him. A dark shape briefly showed itself, then vanished behind another pile of bones.

"I have you now!" de Chagny shouted. He lunged forward. The sacristy door was open, and he snatched at the shadow, then vanished into the dark entrance.

Holmes and I ran the last few feet. My boot struck a skull and kicked it aside as if it were a ball. A high shrill scream tore open the night's calm surface. I recognized the Viscount's voice.

Because my lungs were unsullied by tobacco smoke, I reached the arch of the stone doorway before Holmes. Inside, the moonlight came through a big stained glass window, flooding the dark granite altar with shards of strange light, ghostly hues which all tended toward gray, parodies only of color. The Viscount was on his knees. The black shape darted among the shadows at the far end of the church, then the front door opened, a brief burst of moonlight showing.

De Chagny stood and swayed wildly. I grabbed his shoulders with my hands. Mottled light from the window blotched his face, but I could see his terror. "He was dead—*dead*—his face a death's head!" He collapsed, slipping free of my hands.

I knelt on the cold ground. Like many old churches, this one had no real floor, only the dark Breton soil stamped smooth and hard by many feet. The Viscount's eyes were closed, his face and hands nearly as chill as the earth. Holmes stood beside me, a tall silent presence.

"He has fainted, and no wonder!" I said. "He has had nothing to eat the entire day, and it is very cold and late. He seems determined to contract pneumonia. He did have something of a shock. I wonder… Would you care to follow whoever went out the front of the church?"

"No, Henry."

"I cannot say I blame you. Something gave our friend here a good scare, and although I am not particularly superstitious, I would not relish chasing some dead fellow through the night."

"I am not afraid. I only… He gave us the gift of his music, something which I shall always treasure. I shall not go chasing after him as if he were some common thief. Besides, do you intend to carry the Viscount back by yourself?"

"He appears rather light."

Holmes laughed. "Come, Henry. You take his shoulders and stay to the rear while I grab his feet." We hoisted him up, Sherlock grasping his ankles on either side, the Viscount's legs straddling him from behind. "Let us proceed via the sacristy door." He swung about that way and I followed.

The moonlight was so bright that I blinked my eyes as we walked through the dazzling white snow between the granite tombstones. It was quiet now, the graveyard still and silent, the only sounds that of the snow crunching underfoot and of our labored breathing.

"You might have caught him, Sherlock—the Angel, that is—the Angel of Music with the death's head."

"I know, Henry. Another time I may be sorry for it, but tonight I am not. Not here, not now."

His voice was sad, and I shared his sadness. The music had been such a wonder, such a mystery, the night entirely transformed, but now all that was finished. We came to the end of the tombstones and left the graveyard behind us. The music and the moment were gone, only a dim echo of its beauty remaining in my mind, an echo which would grow fainter and fainter. I might hear that music again in my dreams, but during my waking hours it would only be a feeble memory of a beauty that could never be reclaimed.

With his usual exquisite sense of timing, the Viscount regained consciousness almost at the door of the inn. Once inside, I found a bottle of brandy and made him drink some. I also forced him to eat some bread and cheese, all the while lecturing him upon the dangers of consumption and pneumonia.

*Five*

Early the next morning, while I slept late, Holmes returned to the churchyard. From the tracks in the snow he could discern that the violin player had been hiding behind the ossuary by the sacristy door and had fled through the church, then walked a mile to a waiting carriage. At Lannion, the clerk at the ticket office recalled a woman in black purchasing a ticket for the early express train to Paris. "Ugly, she was very ugly, from what I could see of her face behind the black veil, and tall, very tall."

Sherlock smiled as he related this. "A clever disguise, Henry. I have done the same thing on occasion, but my height also makes such a charade difficult to pull off."

After the primeval gloom of Brittany, Paris with all its present-day splendors (especially modern plumbing and readily available hot water for bathing) was even more welcome. Although my family was not poor, neither were we wealthy; hence it was an unaccustomed pleasure to stay in one of the finest hotels and to sup at the best restaurants in a country where food was truly appreciated. The French and English have their strengths and weaknesses, but when it comes to cuisine, the tricolor utterly vanquishes the Union Jack.

We returned on Monday evening, the opening of *Faust* scheduled for the following Saturday. Early Tuesday morning Holmes went to the Opera and asked the managers if they possessed any architectural plans or writings about its construction. By way of reply, they took him to a large room which served as the Opera library. The original architectural drawings were there, along with photographs, books, and stacks of newspapers containing articles about the building, performances, and singers. Holmes went at once to Garnier's own memoirs, *Le Nouvel Opéra*. He lit his pipe, opened the first volume with his long thin fingers, and told me to go enjoy the city.

The winter sun being bright and cheery, I decided to visit La Tour Eiffel, which had been finished the year before for the exposition. I was not greatly impressed, but had a pleasurable time all the same. However, in my solitude, my thoughts often turned to Michelle.

Holmes spent a long day sequestered in the Opera library, then another day visiting old haunts about the city and questioning various people. He did not have so large a network as in London, but he had worked in Paris enough over the years to have contacts at the various social strata. Among them were a second-rate poet living in a garret in Montmartre who knew all the talk of the Bohemian world, an inspector of the French police whom Holmes had helped with several cases, an elderly nobleman whose daughter he had saved from a notorious rake, and a pickpocket who frequented all the markets and would do anything for a few francs. Holmes also called upon Madame Giry.

Sherlock told me about them all at dinner that night. He was frustrated with his interviews. "Everyone in Paris knows of the Viscount's sudden infatuation with Christine Daaé. Take your choice. She is either an innocent girl and brilliant artist being pursued by an aristocratic libertine, or she is a calculating little vixen skillfully reeling in the sweet but gullible Viscount. Everyone has heard something of *le Fantôme,* and there are a variety of ingenious tales involving him, Carlotta, Christine Daaé, and Joseph Buquet. Buquet's death is widely attributed to the Phantom." He wiped at his mouth with a napkin, then sat back and shook his head as the waiter approached his glass with the wine bottle.

"And what of all your reading in the library?"

"Ah, there things were rather more interesting. I remained at the library until two this morning. Garnier is something of an egoist, but his narrative constantly refers to a Monsieur Noir who was involved in every phase of the construction, a true jack of all trades, builder, designer, carpenter, contractor. Near the end of the memoirs Garnier finally acknowledges his dept to Monsieur Noir and mentions his '*affliction tragique.*'"

"And what was the nature of this tragic affliction?" I asked.

"He does not say, but he thought it almost a blessing that Monsieur Noir had died."

"And how did he die?"

"Garnier does not say, but it happened even as the construction was being finished."

"Oh, I forgot to tell you: de Chagny came to the hotel this afternoon looking for you. He has received a note from Christine Daaé saying he must not see her again, for his own safety."

"Indeed?" Holmes took out a cigarette. "If I missed the Viscount, then the day's travails were not totally in vain. Friday I shall meet with the managers, and they will demand an answer to their problem. Enjoy the wine, Henry; we may soon be forced to sample a cheaper vintage. I have a few threads, nothing more."

The next day Holmes wandered about the Opera while I tried

to keep up with him. In the morning we traipsed about the upper cellars, the two subfloors just below the mammoth main stage. What a labyrinth! Theseus himself would be confounded. At one point we watched men turn various wheels; ropes creaked; machinery ground in the distance; and overhead a trap door opened, Mephistopheles rising slowly upon a platform.

In the afternoon Holmes visited the upper regions over the stage. I let him talk me into accompanying him partway this time, and I was soon sorry. We went up the stairs past three or four of the metal catwalks. I gazed past the rail and saw the vertical lines of literally hundreds of ropes, some supporting long iron pipes to which flats could be attached. Dimly I heard voices from below and made the mistake of looking down. The vertigo was upon me at once. My chest seemed to constrict, my hands turned to ice, and I began to sweat profusely. Telling Sherlock I could endure no more, I started down, keeping my eyes always fixed straight ahead.

That night I had dreadful nightmares. Insubstantial catwalks quivered over great depths; instead of the stage being below, there was only darkness, eternal darkness. At last I fell, plummeting downward into the abyss. I woke up in a cold sweat and could not fall back to sleep for some time.

The next morning I was in poor spirits, and joining Holmes for his interview with Madame Carlotta did not help matters. A very disagreeable hour it was. If I had had any doubts about Christine Daaé's appraisal of her rival, Carlotta dispelled them. A large woman in her late fifties, she seemed a likelier Valkyrie than a Marguerite. Her hair was an incredible shade of red, her cheeks were heavily rouged, and she wore a white dressing gown with a silvery fur collar. Her companion was a surly little white cur who constantly barked or snarled; both his yellowish teeth and his diminutive size made him resemble a rodent more than a canine. The dressing room was at least three times the size of Christine's.

The mention of Miss Daaé's name was enough to launch a lengthy diatribe against the young singer. She was too small and too stupid to sing well; she had no high notes, a poor middle range, and weak low notes as well; she had returned Carlotta's kindness and generosity with malice; she and her supporters were capable of any villainy; the Phantom did not exist, but was only a device dreamed up by the increasingly desperate Daaé, etc., etc. I found myself growing rather warm at such a display of bile, but Holmes was at his most polite and charming. She showed us the threatening notes she had received. The clumsy hand and red ink we recognized at once.

"I agree, Monsieur Holmes, with Messieurs Moncharmin and Richard on this matter. One can never yield to petty threats. My admirers deserve better."

Holmes gave a rather noncommittal shrug. "I shall be discussing the situation with those gentlemen this afternoon."

He had made the mistake of introducing me as *Docteur* Vernier. Madame Carlotta begged that, as her own personal physician was indisposed, I might examine her throat. Despite the irritating letters and the ingratitude of Mademoiselle Daaé, she felt quite well, but one could never be too careful. I concealed my reluctance, placed her where the light was best, then peered down the gaping maw of her mouth. All was pink, moist, and healthy. I considered giving an ominous groan and diagnosing an incipient infection, but professional responsibility got the better of me.

When we left at last, I muttered, "A truly unpleasant woman."

Holmes laughed. "I am glad I did not have to look down her throat. Yes, unpleasant, but it is these great unfeeling brutes who manage a career of thirty or forty years. The romantic ones like Christine Daaé burn out like shooting stars, consumed by their own fires, while the oxen such as Madame Carlotta plod monotonously onward. It is one of the tragedies, the paradoxes, of music, of art. You will never see Madame Carlotta lose a good night's sleep over anything–or miss a meal, either."

Later that afternoon we visited the managers in their office.

Richard lit a cigar and folded his burly arms. "Well, Monsieur Holmes, what have you to tell us? Tomorrow night is the performance of *Faust,* and we have received yet another note."

Holmes glanced at it, grimaced horribly, then laughed and handed me the paper. "This Phantom is remarkably clever for a shade."

The note was briefer than the others: "Mr. Sherlock Holmes will not be of any assistance to you or Madame Carlotta should you defy my wishes. The curse remains. Ignore it at your peril."

"So what are we to do, Monsieur Holmes?" Moncharmin peered at him through his monocle, that eye appearing larger and resembling that of a fish in a glass aquarium.

Holmes walked to the window and leaned against the sill, his back to us. Richard scratched at his white beard and puffed his cigar. Finally Sherlock turned. "Gentlemen, I am afraid that I must counsel you to yield to the Phantom's demands."

Moncharmin's monocle popped out of his eye.

"What!" Richard roared.

"Please hear me out, gentlemen. Let me first dispel a common misconception: I am not, Doctor Watson's writings to the contrary, a magician. All of my cases are not miraculously resolved in a day or two. In this instance I require more time. I have been in Paris little more than a week."

"But we do not have all the time or the money in the world!" Richard exclaimed. "Have you discovered nothing? The best you can do is tell us to pay this blackmail? It's outrageous! I..."

Moncharmin placed his hand over his partner's wrist. "Let us listen to what he has to say."

Holmes nodded. "Thank you. Gentlemen, the difficulty with this case lies in the Opera itself, this incredible edifice surrounding us. You told me it was foolish to think I could tour it in a day or two. You were correct! This is a world unto itself, a miniature cosmos with its Heaven above and Hell below. The difficulty is compounded by the opponent we face. I sense a genius at work, one so far turned toward evil. This genius, I have no doubt, has spent many years in the Opera; most likely he has dwelt here since its completion in '75, some fifteen years ago. Many of your older employees have told me the Ghost has been here from the earliest days. The Phantom must know every corner of the Opera, above and below ground—every room, every attic, every closet—the lake underground and the mazes of rope and steel above and below the stage. This knowledge is the source of his power and the very real threat he presents. I will continue my efforts, but I urge you to comply with his demands until I can discover more. I know what your annual budget is; the sum he demands is a pittance, as your predecessors realized."

Moncharmin began to tap nervously at the desk. "This is unacceptable, Monsieur Holmes."

"Outrageous, as I said before!" Richard's face was even redder than usual. "We shall not pay this blackmailer one franc."

"Then, Messieurs, you and you alone will be responsible for the consequences." Holmes voice was cold and soft.

"Consequences be damned!" Richard exclaimed.

Moncharmin placed his monocle back over his eye. "To what consequences do you refer?"

Holmes placed his hands on the edge of the desk and leaned forward, causing Moncharmin to instinctively draw back. "Let me be frank, gentlemen. In all my years as a consulting detective I have never seen a greater disaster waiting to happen. Do you have any idea what even one clumsy saboteur could do during a performance? And I very much doubt the Phantom is clumsy."

"Surely you exaggerate, Monsieur Holmes." Moncharmin withdrew his handkerchief from the pocket of his frock coat.

"Do you wish me to spell things out? You have hundreds of meters of gas lines running everywhere; an accidental fire would be simple to arrange. Scenery could fall and injure one of your principals, such as Madame Carlotta, or a trap door could unexpectedly open, swallowing her up. You have many high balconies from which an accidental fall could occur. There are chandeliers and heavy statues everywhere...."

"Enough... enough..." Moncharmin moaned, wiping his forehead with his handkerchief.

Richard hit the desk with his right fist. "He's trying to frighten us! Just whose side are you on, Holmes?"

Sherlock stood up straight and stared back. "And what do you mean by that remark, Monsieur Richard?"

"You know damned well what I mean! It's bad enough charging us so ridiculous a fee, but then you stand there and practically threaten us!"

Holmes put on his gloves, tugging at each one fiercely, then picked up his overcoat, his top hat, and stick. "I can see my services are no longer desired. Gentlemen, I wish you the very best of luck in your endeavors at the Opera." His voice shook slightly.

"Please, Monsieur Holmes. You must understand our position!" While Richard had grown redder and redder, Moncharmin had grown paler. "There is Madame Carlotta to think of—and all that money..."

Richard shook his head. "We will not pay a franc, not a sou. The Ghost be damned!"

Holmes gave a ghastly smile and raised his hat. "Very well. Good day to you, gentlemen."

"Monsieur Holmes…" Moncharmin groaned, while Richard glared on.

Holmes strode off, his walking stick angrily tapping at the floor. We marched along the grand foyer beneath its painted vaults and crystal chandeliers, gilt surfaces glittering all around us, then we went down the grand stairway. The vast spaces, the gaudy splendor of all that marble, wood, bronze and gold, suddenly seemed ominous to me, cold and inhuman. I was relieved when we stepped outside into the open air.

I shook my head. "I think of myself as a fairly intelligent man, and I have followed you all about the Opera House. However, the idea of sabotage never even occurred to me until you mentioned it just now. How could I have failed to…?"

"Yours is not a deranged mind, Henry. Nor is mine, I hope, but I have long practiced thinking like my opponents."

"Dear God, they should have listened to you! The place is a powder keg, a disaster waiting to happen."

"Calm down, Henry."

"All those gas lines! What a fire it would… Do you think the Phantom would harm innocent people?"

"I do not know. I do not know. I would like to think that our Angel of Music could not, that a being capable of such music was beyond petty malice, but the honest truth is that I do not know. I have had more proofs of man's bottomless capacity for evil than I care to remember."

"But what can we *do*?"

Sherlock smiled wearily. "That was my problem—that was why I told them to humor their Ghost. The Opera is too large a territory to attempt to guard. How could they protect against every possible threat? They would need as many policeman as spectators. Of course, they expect the great Sherlock Holmes to know exactly where the Phantom will strike. Watson be damned! They all require a magician—a sorcerer! I must wrap up the case in a day or so with a few clever deductions, and…"

I smiled. "Calm yourself."

He shook his head angrily. "I will not calm myself. It is insufferable, intolerable!"

"Now you sound like Monsieur Richard. If it were not for Watson, you would not have received a thousand francs a day."

"Much good it does me if they are not willing to keep me on the case. Christine Daaé is the key, I am certain. If I had more time I would next turn my attention to her."

"What shall we do now?"

"Eat an especially fine meal, as it has been a strenuous week, attempt to get a good night's sleep, and attend the performance of *Faust* tomorrow evening. Wild horses could not drag me away from le Palais Garnier tomorrow. I doubt the managers will bar us from the box reserved for our use. We shall be on the grand tier and not too distant from Box Five."

"Do you think…? Will it not be dangerous?"

"Certainly."

I wished for some of his sangfroid.

When we arrived early the next evening, a great throng of humanity crowded the grand stairway. All the multicolored raiment, the movement, the rumble of that chorus of voices, transformed the stairway; the mood of the place was completely different. Gone was that ominous, brooding silence I had sensed the day before.

The spectators rivaled the Opera in their splendor, especially the women. The men wore one of two costumes. The usual formal wear included a black coat, top hat, trousers, and waistcoat with white shirt, gloves, and bow tie. The second type was a uniform with the gaudy ostentation at which the French excel: tight white or scarlet trousers, shiny black boots, and a jacket of bright blue or darker navy covered with gold buttons, braid, and epaulets. The women were allowed more variation: their dresses were of every color; and the blazing light from the gas lamps glittered upon the diamonds, rubies, emeralds, gold and silver of their jewelry. The gowns of the younger and more daring revealed white shoulders, throats, and décolletage, but all the women wore long white gloves rising midway between shoulder and elbow.

Along the stairway, members of the Republican Guard stood stiffly at attention, their silvery helmets polished mirror bright, gaudy red plumes sprouting from the tops. I passed one young guard whose neatly waxed black mustache had pointed ends at least two inches long.

Because most of the lamps had been extinguished on our former visits, I had never noticed their abundance; but that night gas flames flared everywhere, brilliant behind glass. A multitude of bronze sculptures held torches mounted with lamps, and when I looked overhead, I could see more lights as high as the fifth balcony, the last before the dome.

The main foyer was less crowded, and we made our way directly to our box. The floor underfoot was an elaborately designed mosaic of colored pieces. Holmes noticed me staring downward. "Venetian. The same Italian craftsmen worked on the ceiling mosaics in the advance foyer. And these doors, I believe, are cherry wood. Notice the glass windows shaped like portholes. The nautical effect is probably unintentional."

Holmes closed the door behind us and drew a curtain across the round window, hiding us from the foyer. The interior of our box was red velvet and gold, the same two colors predominant in the auditorium before us. My eyes followed the vertical lines of the tall gilded pillars converging upward at the dome high above. The great chandelier was aflame, all gold and sparkling crystal. Heroic figures were painted on the dome itself, various deities in the act of ascending into the heavens.

"It is a most imposing theater," I said. "Covent Garden does seem second rate in comparison."

Holmes pulled off a white glove. "Only if you put the emphasis in the wrong place—the architecture before the music. Great music does not depend upon the opulence of the auditorium and the spectators for its power. It should not surprise you that the most accomplished violinist I have ever heard played in a wintry graveyard. All this"—his upturned hand swept about in a curve—"is mere distraction. However, most of the spectators would willingly admit that they come here to see and be seen, rather than to listen. That is the real reason why the chandelier is not extinguished during the performance. One might be forced to regard the stage rather than one's neighbors. I hope some day they will follow Bayreuth's worthy example and leave the audience in darkness."

"Speaking of neighbors," I said, "do you see the de Chagnys?" Their box was on the first tier not far from ours. The Count sat back slightly from the railing, his expression cold. The Viscount's face showed only slightly more color than his white shirt, and his reddish brown hair was an unruly mass of curls. "The Viscount looks the part."

"Which part?" Holmes asked.

"The romantic lover alone and palely loitering."

"His brother plays a similar part."

"How so?" I inquired.

"Romantic pining and cynical debauchery are opposite sides of the same coin. One views women as impossibly good, the other as impossibly bad. It would also explain the Viscount's sudden turns of mood. One moment Christine Daaé is an angel, the next she is a harlot ready to run off with another man."

I nodded. "And you—how do you view women?"

"I fear I have seen more trollops than angels, but finding a worthy man is also a difficult quest. Diogenes was not the last to have a hard time of it. This topic interests you, Henry."

I hesitated. "I have been thinking of Michelle a good deal lately."

"Why do you not marry her and be done with it? She has twice the spirit and brains of any of the other women you have courted."

"Do you think so?"

"I do. You are nearly thirty, past the age when a man should still be looking at women with his eyes full of moonshine or calculation. If you like the lady and she will have you, then take her."

I smiled. "Strange words to be coming from you."

He gazed out at the crowd. "I have no time for the great chase. My work occupies me, and I would not wish my eccentricities upon any member of the fair sex."

"I know of at least one who would willingly tolerate them."

His face stiffened. "You approach forbidden ground, Henry."

I hesitated again. "Michelle may not... There have been other men before me."

"Given her age, that is hardly surprising. Have you avoided all women during the same interval?"

My face felt flushed. "That is... different."

He gave a short sharp laugh. "You know better. Youthful indiscretions of one kind or another are common; my business has made that all too clear. The question is whether she—and you yourself—will be faithful now. Trust your heart, Henry."

"I cannot believe that you of all people are telling me this."

"Forget who is speaking. Do, however, avoid the extremes of the two de Chagnys." He sat back and withdrew a pair of opera glasses from his coat pocket. "The orchestra is in the pit. The performance should be starting any moment now. It is rather amusing, I must admit, to hear me pontificating upon the subject of women. Be assured that I am your cousin and your friend."

"And a very good friend!" I exclaimed. "I only wish that you would not shut yourself away from that intimacy, that solace, which you counsel me to take."

The corners of his mouth twitched. A strand of oily black hair fell across his forehead, and he thrust it back. His gray eyes on either side of the great nose glowed. "Not for me, Henry. Not for me."

"Why? Miss Lowell…"

"Here is the conductor. You will see now that the audience at the Paris Opera is not capable of genuine silence; a low buzz is the best we can hope for."

That night, however, there was an expectant hush before the music began. The crowd might not be aware of the Phantom's threat, but they knew about the rivalry between Carlotta and Christine Daaé. And who knew what bizarre rumors had circulated involving the ghost? Holmes pointed to our right, and I saw Moncharmin and Richard alone in what must be Box Five. Richard seemed content, while Moncharmin obviously wished to be elsewhere.

*Faust* has its moments, the music occasionally rising above the treacly plot. Mephistopheles, the basso devil, is a far better part than those of the fatuous tenor hero or soprano heroine. Since Marguerite did not appear until well into the opera, we had a long wait before us. The first scene had only the two men, the aged Faust agreeing to trade his soul to the devil in return for youth and love (represented in this case by the not so alluring vision of Carlotta at her spinning wheel behind a scrim downstage right). Mephistopheles made a spectacular entrance amidst a burst of smoke illuminated by one of Monsieur du Bœuf's sinister orange limelights.

The second scene had several rousing choruses, Valentin's farewell aria, and Mephistopheles' 'Le Veau d'Or'. A murmur went through the crowd when Christine Daaé entered early in the scene. A few of the more zealous members of Carlotta's claque actually hissed, and you could see that Daaé was shaken.

Siebel is one of the so-called trouser roles, but any fool could tell that Christine Daaé was a small pretty girl in a man's costume. (I was also skeptical a man would wear powder blue tights and doublet.) Valentin was a good foot taller than Siebel, and his entrusting the safety of his absent sister Marguerite (the massive Carlotta) to Siebel (petite Christine) was inadvertently comical. Christine was the one who needed protection! Her singing was competent, but somewhat listless. She sounded tired.

At last the students and young village girls entered, including Marguerite. Carlotta's enthusiasts applauded wildly, and she gave them a gracious nod. Perhaps I lack some aesthetic faculty, but I simply could not get beyond Carlotta's appearance, age, and size. Such an assault on verisimilitude was too great for me. Who could be taken in by that bloated, rouged face framed on either side by a blonde braid of her wig?

Holmes seized my arm. "She has only two lines in this scene."

And she sang them without incident: "*Non, Monsieur! Je ne suis demoiselle, ni belle. Et je n'ai pas besoin qu'on me donne la main.*" Her claque again applauded loudly, and she gave them another smile and nod.

Holmes's eyes wandered about the auditorium. I felt apprehensive myself, but a minute or two passed, and still nothing had happened. I saw Richard grinning ferociously.

"It will most likely be during Act Two," Holmes whispered. "Marguerite has her first major aria then."

During the intermission Holmes paced about the grand foyer. I was rather edgy too. Ladies in their brilliant plumage and their male companions in somber black sipped pale yellow champagne from thin goblets. The din finally became too much for me. I made my way through the crowd to a doorway and stepped out onto one of the small balconies overlooking the Place de l'Opéra. Carriages of every size and shape were below. While the masters in their finery lounged about, their attendants sat and waited. Holmes soon joined me.

"The clear, cold air feels good," I said.

"Yes."

Someone cleared his throat behind us. I turned. The Count de Chagny stood with the dancer Sorelli at his arm. I recognized her from her photographs. She had the longest neck I have ever seen. She wore diamond earrings and a necklace worth a fortune, her jewelry competing for attention with the considerable amount of bosom revealed by her gown. Smoking was unknown amongst respectable women, but in keeping with her notoriety, she held a cigarette languidly between her long fingers. She had the same cold, predatory eyes as the Count.

"*Laisses-nous un instant, ma chère,*" the Count said. Sorelli turned and left. The Count placed one white gloved hand upon the stone railing, covered it with the other hand. "Monsieur Holmes, you have not cashed my check."

Sherlock stared out at the square. "No. I fear I have misplaced it."

"That can be remedied easily enough."

"Ah, but I am afraid, too, that I am rather busy. Perhaps at a later date."

"Very well." The Count took out a cigar, cut off the end and threw it onto the crowd below. A match flared, revealing the dark eyes, the mustache with its few gray hairs. "My brother's interests and mine are ultimately the same. Both of us must think first and foremost of the de Chagny name."

Holmes nodded. "Of course."

"My friends I reward. My enemies... I am not without influence, Monsieur Holmes."

"I am sure of it."

"If you would like another check, simply let me know. All I require is that Christine Daaé does not become the Viscountess de Chagny. Do we understand each other?"

"We do, Monsieur. We do."

The Count nodded, then eased a cloud of cigar smoke from between his lips. He turned and went back inside.

Holmes smiled at me, his eyes angry. "Perhaps the Viscount is not such a bad fellow after all."

"I prefer his side of the coin."

Sherlock laughed. "We had better return to our seats."

No sooner had we stepped inside, than we saw lurking before us the Persian (the fellow who had been ogling the dancers), a particularly foul-smelling cigarette in his mouth, his dark eyes filled with only faintly veiled malice. I must admit that he gave me a start. Obviously he had overheard our conversation with the Count.

Holmes smiled at him. "*Bonsoir, Monsieur le Perse.*"

His black eyebrows dipped inward, a crease appearing between them. "*Bonsoir,*" he muttered. He had an ugly scar along his right cheek, the red seam of a wound that had been very poorly stitched.

"What a villainous face," I said, making certain he was out of hearing. "Does he never take off that astrakhan hat? Perhaps it is bolted to his skull. Why was he listening to us?"

"Obviously he has some interest in this case. Were I still employed by the managers I would make it my business to find out why. Perhaps he has some connection with *le Fantôme.* Garnier mentions that his Monsieur Noir was very useful because of his mastery of languages, not merely the customary European tongues, but Egyptian, Turkish, and Persian."

"How do you remember such trivial details?" I asked.

"There are no trivial details."

The auditorium felt warm and stuffy after the cool air. I glanced upward; at the top of the columns, gilded angels with bare breasts blew upon long thin horns. Again there was a hush before the music started. Act Two began with Siebel (Christine Daaé) alone on stage. This time the antagonism of Carlotta's claque seemed to spur on Christine instead of unsettling her. Her voice was louder and more vibrant, the tone very clear and pure. She was a good actress, her passion very convincing and, I could not help but notice, somewhat directed toward the de Chagny box. The Viscount had leaned so far forward he seemed in danger of falling out. When Christine kissed Marguerite's flowers, some genuine color appeared in his cheek. She was loudly applauded.

"Not long now," Holmes whispered.

The tenor had his main aria, and then Mephistopheles set his trap for Marguerite, baiting it with a casket of jewels. Carlotta made her entrance to tremendous applause and many bravos, and again I reflected that there could be no more unlikely innocent young girl than this aging prima donna. She sat at her spinning wheel and sang. Whatever vocal problems she might have, lack of volume was not one of them. Those in the highest balcony would hear her perfectly.

Holmes leaned forward, his hands grasping the gilt railing. I thought of fire, flames and smoke, and tried to recall the fastest way out of the theater. The song seemed to last forever, but it ended without incident. While the audience applauded, I gave a long sigh.

"Curious," Sherlock murmured, sinking back into his seat. "Perhaps during the Jewel Song. Did you notice the small scoops she made while rising into the high notes? Her intonation has never been good." He raised the opera glasses and scanned the crowd below.

But the Jewel Song was equally uneventful. I could see that the managers were relieved. Moncharmin was actually smiling, albeit rather hesitantly. Before long Faust and Marguerite were alone together, singing of love. Fontana the tenor did not look his best in white tights;

Faust seemed to have been cheated, his restored youth limited to makeup, a corset, and wig. I was only too aware of two singers past fifty matching their formidable, if worn, voices. The effect was worse when I gazed through the opera glasses: their thick necks quavered, sweat seeping out from under their wigs onto their foreheads and beading on the greasepaint. I recalled Holmes's remarks about oxen plodding on for many years.

"*O silence! O bonheur! Ineffable mystère,*" Carlotta sang, and then came a tiny break in the music as the phrase ended and she drew in her breath. Out came a truly ghastly sound, something between the croak of a frog and the loud belch small boys will make as a prank. It was so unexpected, so loud and ugly, that the undercurrent of whispers and talking ceased at once. The audience was totally silent. Even the orchestra faltered, but the conductor kept them going.

Sherlock gave me a painful smile. "Of course," he murmured.

Carlotta was amazed and confused, unable to believe she could have made such a sound. Even I felt sorry for her. I remembered standing on that stage and gazing out at the vast, empty theater. If I had felt a qualm then, what must she be feeling now? To have stumbled before so many, before a full house. The Phantom knew how to wound her!

She rallied and tried to continue, but again came that croak, an animal sound which seemed impossible for the human larynx to make. Again it came, and again, beautiful French melody mixing with blaring discord. Finally she clutched at her throat with both hands, but the ghastly noise would not cease. She shook her head, and the orchestra stopped, the music fading away. Obviously shaken, Fontana had stepped back, perhaps afraid he, too, might be transformed into a croaking toad or lowing ox.

At that instant, while the shocked silence still held, a voice materialized out of the air in the vast empty space of the hall, a man's voice, the velvety, ringing baritone of a trained actor: "She is singing to bring down the chandelier."

Everyone heard him: all eyes rose to the apex of the dome overhead. A shudder seemed to pass through the chandelier, the dangling crystal quivering as if it, too, sensed what was about to happen.

Once during a visit to Southern Italy I had been reading a book when I noticed a strange rattle coming from the lamp. Puzzled, I reached out to touch it, felt it tremble under my hand, and then abruptly the whole room shook, a picture banging at the wall, a vase falling from the bureau and shattering. Something of the same terror that the earthquake had inspired came over me that night at the Opera.

Holmes and I both jumped to our feet. "Clear the floor!" he shouted in French. "Clear the floor!"

In a panic, the people on the ground floor fought for the exits. A tall fat man in a black frock coat large as a tent pushed aside an elderly lady; only the consideration of another man who supported her saved her from serious injury. No one wanted to remain beneath that awesome mass of crystal and metal, no one save a woman dressed in black who scowled ferociously and did not move from her seat.

The chandelier had begun to rock, swinging back and forth, then careening in an arc. Its lights went out, the gas extinguished, and then it fell. Enough other lamps still flamed that we could watch it plummet downward like some fallen angel, the splendor of its light gone forever. A tremendous chorus of screams arose, operatic in magnitude, Carlotta's voice rising above the others. The crash, the impact of all that weight plus so much crystal shattering at once, was incredible. Luckily there had been time for the crowd to get out of the way, but I recalled that one stubborn scowling woman. The chandelier was a good twenty feet across; it lay at an angle; but I could not see if anyone was trapped beneath its iron frame.

Holmes collapsed into his seat and ran his fingers back through his hair. "I tried to warn them. I said he was a genius." His mouth twisted. "A fallen angel."

"I must get down there. They will need all the medical help they can get. If no one has been killed, it will be a miracle. What a disaster!"

"Go on, Henry. Do what you can. I shall join you in a moment. Lord, where shall I search for clues? Up there?" He pointed at the center of the darkened dome. "Shall I fly thither and search for our angel! Go on, Henry—*hurry*."

Six

Although several people were injured in the press of the panic-stricken crowd, there was only one fatality: that somber, stubborn-looking woman dressed in black whom I had noticed. She was Monsieur Firmin Richard's concierge and the person whom the managers had chosen to replace Madame Giry as box keeper. We discovered this fact the next afternoon when the managers reemployed Sherlock Holmes at one thousand francs a day. Richard was subdued, if not exactly penitent. They had also decided to pay the Phantom, rehire Madame Giry, and replace Carlotta with Christine Daaé.

Holmes nodded his approval, then said this was already proving to be one of his most difficult cases; they must resolve to be patient. Richard bit at his tongue, while Moncharmin's head bobbed up and down. Moncharmin told us that Monsieur Mifroid, the Superintendant of Police, would be investigating the prior night's disaster.

Holmes's mouth twitched. "Monsieur Mifroid is an individual of minimal intellectual capabilities with an almost total lack of imagination. I could name you a half dozen better men, but Monsieur Mifroid does excel in self-promotion. He also has certain connections which allow him to choose his work. No doubt the notoriety provided by the falling chandelier has brought the Opera to his attention. You would do well to tell him as little as possible. Now, I have one or two requirements to bring to your attention."

Moncharmin's blue eye peered through the circular glass. "Yes?"

"I shall want to interview Mademoiselle Daaé again as soon as possible and..."

"Alas..." moaned Moncharmin.

"What is the matter?"

"The young lady has vanished," Richard said gruffly.

"However, she did assure us that she would be available for *La Juive* a week from this coming Saturday." Moncharmin wiped at his forehead with his handkerchief. "And for *Faust* the week after that. Thank God!"

Holmes tapped at his knee. "And when did she tell you this?"

"Last night," Moncharmin said. "After the catastrophe."

"You spoke to her *then*?" My surprise must have been evident.

"Oh yes, Doctor Vernier. Firmin dealt with the police and the crowd, but I went to find Miss Daaé. Carlotta was clearly indisposed, and we needed a singer to ensure the season's continued success."

"Of course," Holmes said rather dryly. "Tell me, sir, how did you find the young lady? How would you characterize her mood?"

"She was most distraught, Monsieur Holmes, most distraught. Her countenance was very pale, and I feared she might faint. She and Carlotta were not always on the best of terms, but that dreadful sound... Mademoiselle Daaé said she would not wish it on anyone, and then the chandelier's falling..." Moncharmin's voice quavered.

"Yes, yes, a veritable tragedy, all the more so since it might have been avoided." Neither of the managers would meet Sherlock's cold gaze. "But she did assure you that she would carry the rest of the season for you? Ah, I thought so. Well, how exactly do you know that she has vanished?"

"The Viscount was looking for her this morning," Richard said. "He assured us she was not at home. We sent one of our assistants with him, but they could not find her in her dressing room or any of her usual haunts."

"Where else might she have been?" Holmes asked.

"She likes to watch the stagehands at work on the sets and the young dancers, the children. Of course, since it is Sunday, very little is going on."

"You do not think"—Moncharmin's voice was still trembly—"she could not have disappeared for good? She would not miss *La Juive*!"

Holmes shook his head. "I am certain she will return before then. Rest assured, she will not miss her engagement."

Moncharmin gave a great sigh. "I never imagined that managing an Opera House could be such a wretched business."

Richard placed one paw of a hand over the other; his fingers were red and thick, the span of his knuckles enormous. "What were your other requirements, Monsieur Holmes?"

"I suppose speaking with Madame Carlotta would not be possible?"

Moncharmin shook his head quickly. "No, no, not at this time. She will not see anyone, not even us. Her manager says she has had a great shock and is under her physician's care."

"I also wish to spend more time wandering about the Opera."

Moncharmin held his head stiffly like a small bird. "You do not, of course, wish to explore the cellars beneath the Opera?"

"I intend to do just that."

"But it could be very dangerous! Everyone says… No one goes down there alone."

"Oh, I shall not be alone."

"No?"

"Doctor Vernier will accompany me."

With both of the managers regarding me, I managed a feeble smile, but a queasy sensation manifested itself directly below the center of my rib cage.

Holmes stood and pulled on his gloves. He took his hat, then hesitated. "Tell me, gentlemen, did anyone notice anything out of the ordinary last night?" A bark of laughter escaped from his lips, then he laughed in earnest while the managers stared at him as if he were mad. "Forgive me, but the absurdity of my question suddenly struck me. I mean other than Madame Carlotta's indisposition and the falling chandelier."

The two men regarded each other. Moncharmin said, "No, Monsieur Holmes, not that we are aware of."

"I doubt anyone would have noticed anything in such chaos. Good day, gentlemen." We started for the door.

"Oh, there was one thing, hardly very important." Moncharmin smiled warily. "The prompter was quite drunk, something which has never occurred before. He is usually most scrupulous, but last night…"

Holmes hunched slightly, his eyes bright. "Drunk?"

Richard nodded. "How else could you explain his sleeping in a corner amidst all that uproar? I could hardly wake him, and he smelled awful. I was ready to fire him, but Armand…"

"Really, Monsieur Holmes, it was the first time. I did speak to him severely and told him any reoccurrence would lead to his summary dismissal."

"And what was his reaction to your generosity?"

"He tried to deny it, but I would not hear any of his excuses."

"Most interesting. Please keep me informed of any developments."

Again a brooding, gloomy silence hung about the vast, empty edifice, the contrast striking after last night. The Phantom had given the Opera a sinister aura; for the first time I wondered if he might not be hiding close by, watching from the shadows; and even the gaudy opulence of the grand stairway seemed threatening. I was relieved to reach the open air outside.

"Were you serious," I asked, "about wandering the lower cellars?"

"Come, Henry, you know me well enough to answer your own question. If you are uneasy, you need not accompany me."

"Uneasy or not, I certainly cannot allow you to descend alone to that underworld. You heard Moncharmin."

"I have put myself in far greater danger."

"That hardly matters. If you think that I could loiter about the hotel while you are risking your neck down there, you are quite mistaken."

"Henry, I did not ask you to accompany me in the capacity of bodyguard."

"Nevertheless, I cannot let you go alone."

"The choice is entirely yours."

I muttered a curse under my breath. We had been in Paris nearly two weeks and had nothing to show for our time. Michelle had not asked me not to accompany Sherlock on this trip: she was far too clever for that! No doubt she foresaw that I would soon be missing her. Male companionship was fine for a short period of time, but I had begun to tire of its triviality. Already I had sensed with Michelle the possibility of a genuine intimacy. Not only was she witty and intelligent, but she was quite beautiful. I would have given anything to have her waiting for me back at the hotel.

"Perhaps you are thinking of Michelle," Holmes said.

I stopped walking abruptly and stared at him. "How the devil…? Have you now taken up mind reading? Is the privacy of my own thoughts to be denied me?"

He laughed. "No, no. It was not mind reading, nor any grand trick of logic. You have told me she is much on your mind, and I have noted your tendency to gaze into the middle distance, oblivious to the surroundings. The symptoms are all too common."

"Regardless, it is very annoying."

"You are discouraged," he said.

"Yes, I am. I was thinking we have precious little to show for our time here."

"To the contrary, I understand our opponent quite well. The problem now is to devise a stratagem to render him harmless."

A cab passed us in the street, the horse's iron shoes clopping evenly on the pavement. Late Sunday afternoon was among the quieter times in Paris.

"Do you mean you understand that mysterious business of last night? Even I am beginning to wonder if the Phantom does not have supernatural powers."

"Nothing occurred last night which would require supernatural powers."

"How then did the Phantom cause Carlotta to make such a dreadful sound? It did seem the manifestation of a curse."

Holmes smiled, his expression gentle, yet triumphant. "Carlotta did not make that sound."

"*What?*"

"You heard me. Be patient a while longer, but be assured that we are not dealing with any ghost. *Le Fantôme* is real enough, and he has dwelt in the Palais Garnier since its construction. Our difficulty lies in tracking him through such a vast maze. The Opera itself would be formidable enough with its seventeen floors, its hundreds of doors, its many rooms, attics, and closets, but I fear there are hidden passageways connecting everything, a labyrinth within a labyrinth."

I wanted to ask more questions, but he put me off. The next few days found us again exploring the Opera, especially its lower depths. The managers provided Monsieur Gris as our guide, much to his displeasure. He again offered a bit of "precious advice," holding up a calloused hand alongside his face. "Your hand at the level of your eyes, Messieurs, as you value your life." He looked about, then whispered, "The Punjab lasso."

"What foolishness!" I exclaimed, but again Holmes and he relentlessly pestered me. By the end of the day I was in a foul temper, both my arms sore.

We saw nothing but damp gray stone, dusty sets and props; we climbed up and down narrow stairways, trudged through dark corridors and vast rooms, and heard only the occasional scuttle of rats or roaches fleeing our approach. Soon I grew heartsore, then afraid, a vague, amorphous dread settling about me like a somber cloud. When we finally came above ground and stepped outside, I blinked at the bright light, even as some mole coming up from its hole.

The Viscount appeared at least twice a day and implored Holmes to search for Christine Daaé. Sherlock always refused, assuring him that she was well and that she would reappear in time for *La Juive* a week from Saturday. The Viscount responded with either rage or tearful despair, both of which were equally tiresome.

"How can you be so certain she will return?" I asked Holmes one day.

"The Angel of Music is her guardian angel. He did not bring Carlotta and the managers to their knees only to snatch Christine away forever. She will return for her night of triumph in the limelight."

And indeed, he was shortly proven right. On Friday, at the end of a long week of wanderings through the Palais Garnier, broken for me by Holmes's time spent perusing plans and documents in the Opera library, the Viscount appeared with a note that had been found on the street and delivered to him. Christine Daaé requested that he meet her at a masked ball that was to take place at the Opera the next day. He was to come dressed as a Pierrot. "As you value your life, dearest, make sure no one can recognize you."

Holmes told the Viscount we would accompany him. I could not help but notice a childish delight in my cousin, the explanation of which soon became clear. He dearly loved disguises!

The Opera Ball, which occurred shortly before Shrovetide and the beginning of Lent, was a Paris ritual, a bacchanalia that attracted both the youthful occupants of Bohemia, that subculture of painters, musicians, poets, and writers residing near Montmartre, and the upper classes, who came to watch the show and display the finery of their own costumes. As a result, I soon discovered that finding a costume to rent or buy was impossible. I spent Saturday morning vainly visiting shops. I was on my own, since Sherlock had devised something for himself that was a great secret.

When I returned dispirited to the hotel, there on my bed were a black robe, a long staff with a reaper's blade at the end, and a mask with the visage of a skull.

"Where on earth did you find them?" I asked Holmes.

"The Opera, of course. They have hundreds of costumes, as you no doubt recall. I managed to prevail upon the wardrobe master's generosity."

I felt extremely stupid not to have thought of this myself. A huge chamber had been filled with row after row of costumes. Holmes still refused to reveal his own costume.

We ate an early supper, and since the ball did not begin until late, I lay down briefly. I rarely sleep during the day, but as the past week and the morning's quest had been exhausting, I was soon fast asleep. I began to dream about the ball and the Opera, then remembered that I needed to wake up and dress. By some curious act of will, I managed to pluck myself from my dream, opening my eyes and discovering a frightful vision. With a cry, I staggered to my feet.

Before me stood a deformed hunchback, his red hair a tangled mess, broken teeth protruding from his swollen upper lip, his face horribly mangled and twisted, completely lacking in symmetry. A large mole covered one eye, rendering him half blind; and his smile was grotesque, hideous, his clothes completely black. The thought struck me that this must be the Phantom, come at last to pay us a visit. No wonder he hid himself in darkness!

"Good God," I murmured, but then the Phantom laughed.

"Sherlock!" I shouted. "This is impossible! You go too far!"

"Henry, I did not know you would choose to wake up at this particular moment. It was unintentional on my part, I assure you."

"Unintentional, my foot! I'll wager you have been lurking there for the past hour just waiting for me to open my eyes!"

"No, no."

"The truth, wretch!"

"Well, five minutes perhaps."

My fear had abated, and I knew I had been fairly bested. "I owe you one for this. I shall have my revenge."

"You had a most curious expression on your face."

"Villain! To think that the great Sherlock Holmes would stoop to frightening innocent sleepers. You look quite remarkable. No one would recognize you. I assume that is putty on your nose and cheeks."

"Correct." His voice was garbled, and he reached into his mouth and withdrew his front teeth. "That is better. Talking for any length of time is awkward."

"You are, I assume, Quasimodo, the Hunchback of Notre Dame."

"Very good. What better tribute to Hugo and the city of Paris?"

"There may be other hunchbacks at the Opera, but none will be half so frightful."

"Thank you, Henry."

Indeed, the Viscount stepped back when he saw Quasimodo-Holmes, murmuring, "My God."

"Pay him no attention," I said. "You are only flattering his vanity." The Viscount appeared ill at ease and somewhat ludicrous in his white clown suit with the black buttons, pointed white hat, and mask. The mask hid most of his face, curving over the mouth so that only his chin and lower lip showed. "Where on earth did you find your Pierrot costume, *Monsieur le Vicomte?*"

"I had it made," he replied coldly.

"It suits you remarkably well," Holmes said, his mouth distorted by the teeth.

The Viscount's mask hid his expression, but I could see in his eyes that the remark did not please him.

The evening was cool, not cold, late February giving us a preview of the Parisian spring to come, and the Place de l'Opéra teemed with people laughing or talking and dressed in outlandish costumes. The grand stairway itself was virtually impassable. Several clowns cried out to the Viscount, greeting him as an old friend, and the young ladies, some in scanty costumes (an Arabian princess with naked midriff, a Greek goddess whose flimsy robes left both shoulders uncovered, an Amazon warrior with bare legs), welcomed him. However, he behaved in a decidedly un-Pierrot-like fashion, forging coldly ahead. Holmes and I had a more sobering effect on the revellers; indeed, Holmes's face opened up the crowd before us even as Moses parted the Red Sea. One woman cried out, "Quasimodo!" but she kept her distance.

A young blonde in a black silk gown made way for Holmes, then seized my arm. She held a glass of champagne in her slim white hand.

"'Death, where is thy sting?'" she said in heavily accented English. Then in French, "What have you to show me under those robes?" She wore a black mask that revealed most of her pretty face, and her gown was scandalously low cut, the white curve of her breasts apparent as she leaned toward me, swaying slightly.

The desire I felt embarrassed me; I wished again that I could hold Michelle in my arms. "Bones," I replied.

"One bone only delights me." She gave a drunken laugh, and then a swarthy man in a turban with fierce black eyes and mustache pulled her away, cursing me.

"No one respects the Reaper nowadays," I said.

We finally reached the top of the stairs, where our Viscount Pierrot awaited us. "She was to meet me before Box Five." The Viscount shuddered involuntarily as he glanced at Holmes's face.

"Yes, I had not forgotten that."

"Grant me a few minutes with her alone. Then I shall try to divert her to a place where you can overhear our conversation."

"That will be difficult in this din," I said.

He shrugged and headed for Box Five. Behind us the crowd suddenly quieted, even the oaths of exclamation having a hushed quality. Turning, I saw ascending the marble stairs Death himself. The apparition was so frightful that it took me a moment to recognize this particular manifestation. "The Red Death," I whispered.

"Yes," Holmes said. "Of Edgar Allan Poe. 'No pestilence had ever been so fatal, or so hideous. Blood was its Avatar and its seal—the redness and horror of blood.'"

The specter advancing toward us wore a scarlet robe and hood, the cloth visibly decomposed in the manner of something long in the grave, but it was the face under the cowl that drew everyone's attention. At first I thought it must be a mask, but as he came closer, I decided it must be makeup applied in an extraordinarily realistic manner. Above the black sunken eyes, with their dreadful blend of rage and sorrow, was the yellow-white, hairless dome of the skull. The lack of a nose, an irregular black cavity in the center of the face, was a particularly gruesome touch. The thin lips were barely discernible, the tissue about the mouth very slight, so that the outline of the protruding upper and lower teeth showed. His color was of a particularly cadaverous hue, white but with hints of both green and yellow. Specks of red marred the face, the signs of Poe's pestilence. As a medical man I had seen the worst effects of death and disease and had grown somewhat inured to them, but this visage turned even my stomach. No wonder the masqueraders grew pale and quiet. The pretty girl in black on the stairs had spilled her champagne, and her companion's face now showed revulsion, not anger.

On the front of the crimson robe was pinned a sheet of paper: JE SUIS LA MORT ROUGE. NE ME TOUCHEZ POINT. A drunk near the point of unconsciousness decided to test this prohibition; he staggered forward and pawed at the robe.

That face turned upon him; a skeletal hand seized his wrist, crushed it. He screamed in pain and vainly attempted to free his arm. The hand pulled him skyward, the red sleeve slipping down to reveal a long, bony forearm, then the specter seized his shirt at the collar and hurled him away. The fellow collapsed in a heap, slid down a few stairs, then clutched at his forearm, whimpering and cursing simultaneously. No one else seemed inclined to touch the Red Death; space opened up about him as he approached us. I took a step back, then realized Holmes had not moved. Even under his makeup I recognized that pained, ironic smile of his.

When the Red Death reached the top of the steps, he stopped a pace away to stare at Holmes. He was very tall, taller even than Holmes or I. The two men regarded each other for a long while, neither gaze wavering. At last the Red Death spoke: "Oh, all that I ever loved." His voice was a vibrant baritone, something of a surprise for so hideous an apparition.

The words were so strange, so utterly incongruous, that they seemed to me to be utter nonsense, but Holmes recognized them at once. After a sharp laugh he replied: "'And Darkness and Decay and the Red Death held illimitable dominion over all.'"

Holmes had spoken English, and although I had not read Poe for years, the source of the quotation was obvious: it must be the last line of the story. The Red Death had spoken French; perhaps his words were also a quote; they must be from *Notre-Dame de Paris*. In a romantic period of my youth I had read Hugo. Had not Quasimodo said some such thing near the end of the novel when he viewed his beloved Esmeralda hanging from a gibbet?

"You would do well to ponder carefully the words you have just spoken," said the Red Death.

"And you would be wise to consider your own words. What did that poor broken creature have to show for his love in the end? He could protect neither his gypsy nor his own heart."

The Red Death's mouth drew back in a way which made it evident that he wore no mask. "What do you know of love or loneliness? That face of yours, its deformity, its pain, is but a mask."

Holmes shook his head. "No, my real face is the mask, this the reality, that the pretense."

The Red Death smiled, an expression that made him look even more ghastly. "You are amusing, Quasimodo, most amusing, but I do not believe you. Your face is mostly putty."

"Your own face blinds you. It is no more real than mine. No faces are real: they are all illusions, constantly changing, all masks. It is foolish to envy another his mask. A mask has no more permanence or reality than anything else in this life."

The Red Death stared at Holmes, his eyes aflame. "You would not find that so easy to say if you were to trade places with me, if you had a face even a mother would cringe before." A strange, pained smile pulled at his mouth.

"I know that. However, although it is something of a cliché, that which lies under the mask is what counts. Too many fools and villains have the visage of Jove or Adonis."

"All the more reason to hate this life, this face, which Fate has bestowed upon me! Some Pierrot with a title, youth, and mediocre looks can triumph over me. None can love one such as I, none can begin to share the anguish in my heart."

Holmes shook his head. "No, that is not true."

"You dare to lecture–to advise me!" shrieked the Red Death. "What can you know of me!"

"I know you," Holmes said. "I know you."

Again he and the Red Death stared at one another, locked in a combat of wills. At last the specter turned, wearying of the contest but not yielding. He drew in his breath, then stalked away.

I had been watching him closely and had realized there was no possible way to create that cavity where a nose should have been with makeup. "Good Lord," I whispered.

The relief of the crowd was audible; they threw themselves into their merrymaking with renewed energy. I grasped Sherlock's arm. "What on earth was that all about?"

"Life," he replied brusquely. "Come, we had better find the Viscount." While facing the Red Death he had straightened up to his full height; now he bent over again and assumed the hunchback's deformity, ambling forward in the most incredible way. Anyone watching would have sworn he was born malformed.

We reached the door to Box Five, but the Viscount was nowhere to be seen. "Where can he be?" I asked.

As if in reply, the door swung open, and two Pierrots came out of the box. "Christine!" the Viscount cried, seizing her arm. "Forgive me! I–I did not mean it."

She wrenched her arm free. Her Pierrot costume was made of a cloth with a pattern of black and white diamonds, and her white pointed hat hid most of her hair. However, the small white mask did not conceal much of her face; the turned up nose, the full, narrow mouth and the electric green eyes made her identity obvious.

"You have as much as called me a harlot, *Monsieur de Chagny*, and I grow weary of your insults. It was foolish of me to think I could rely upon your understanding. I shall not trouble you again."

"But, Christine…" The Viscount's voice had a familiar whine.

She wrenched her arm free again, then turned to walk away. "Bravo!" shouted a red devil with horns and a tail, and his two female demons also showed their approval. "That's telling him, honey!" one of them cried.

Holmes had stepped forward and grasped Christine Daaé's arm. Thinking it was the Viscount, she tried to free herself, then turned and received the full impact of Quasimodo's hideous face. She cried out, then saw me in my Reaper's garb.

"Mademoiselle…" Holmes and I both began. Our voices steadied her, confusion replacing fear. Holmes continued: "It is I, Sherlock Holmes, and Doctor Vernier there. May we please speak with you?"

"But whatever are you doing here?" She turned upon the Viscount. "You told them! No one was to know–how could you! Oh, this is insufferable! So you were in his employ all along, Monsieur Holmes. I thought…"

"I am no man's lackey, Mademoiselle, least of all his. I am only interested in one thing—unraveling the mystery of *le Fantôme de l'Opéra*."

She drew in her breath. "What has that to do with me?"

"Surely by now you must have realized that he and your Angel of Music are one and the same."

If she had not been wearing white makeup, we would have seen the blood drain from her face. Thinking she was about to faint, I seized her arm. My mask disturbed her, so I took it off. Weakly she said, "What can you know of him?"

"A great deal, Mademoiselle Daaé. That is why I wish to speak with you. Believe me when I say I have his interests and yours at heart."

"You speak as if they were one and the same," she whispered.

"Do you not wear his ring?"

On the finger of her left hand was a gold band that I did not recall, and knowing Holmes's eye for detail, the ring must have been a recent acquisition.

"Christine!" the Viscount howled, ripping off his white mask. "How could you? How could you! Now I understand—you have played me for the fool all along. Even as you spoke to me, you wore another man's ring. I was right! You are nothing but a dirty little whore!"

"*Monsieur de Chagny!*" I exclaimed, but he turned and strode away. Christine sobbed once, and I put my hand on her shoulder.

"It is not true, Monsieur Holmes—in the name of God it is not!"

"He is a fool," Sherlock said.

"You're lucky to be rid of him!" shouted one of the female demons, raising her champagne glass in a toast.

Christine wept. "Come," Sherlock said. "Let us find a quiet place where we can talk."

She nodded. We started for the stairway to the second tier. Suddenly a scream, a man's voice, rose above the crowd.

"Raoul!" Christine cried.

"That could not have been him," I said.

Holmes smiled at me, the left eye with the wart over it opening up. "Come on. We had better see what he is up to."

We had gone only a few feet when the Viscount ran up to us. "It was he! The death's head–the death's head from Perros! For God's sake, come help me, Monsieur Holmes!"

Sherlock sighed, then walked forward past de Chagny. Christine Daaé tore her arm free of my grasp, then stepped between the hunchback and the Pierrot. "No! You must not!"

The Viscount appeared ready to knock her down. "You will not stop me! I shall kill the villain with my bare hands!"

"No, Raoul!" She raised a tiny white hand. "In the name of our love you shall not pass!"

An angry Pierrot is a vaguely comical sight, but the fury quickly left the Viscount's face. "Christine!" He clasped her in his arms.

I stared in disbelief, then glanced at Holmes. He was not surprised, but his smile was more cynical than usual, his eyes weary.

"We must get away," Christine said. "Follow me."

"The Red Death!" a voice shouted, and behind us, silence advanced like a shadow over the crowd.

Christine Daaé quickly led us toward the stairs, her hand holding the Viscount's. We went up two levels, then halfway around the foyer. She took a key from the pocket of her Pierrot costume and opened the box door. "We shall be safe here." She closed the door behind us, locked it, then drew the velvet curtain across the circular window. The auditorium was mostly in darkness, but we heard the voices of some revelers below.

Christine sank down into a chair. "I am so weary, so very weary. Oh that this were finished, all finished, oh, everything."

"What do you mean, Christine?" The Viscount sat beside her and took her hand.

She sobbed once. The light was dim, but I saw a strange, feverish gleam in her eyes. "Oh Raoul, my dearest, if only you knew!" She touched his cheek, and he quickly drew in his breath. "Be thankful, be thankful for your face, and especially for... especially for your nose." And indeed, she touched the very tip of his nose with her forefinger.

"Christine, Christine, what are you saying?" The Viscount's voice, for once, was gentle, but I detected a certain histrionic note, an exaggeration, that I found distasteful. However, I freely admit that by then my feelings toward the man were so hostile that I was incapable of an unbiased view.

Christine was staring intently, not at the Viscount, but at Holmes. "There is an Angel of Music, Monsieur Holmes. In the name of God the Father and the Blessed Virgin Mary, I swear there is an Angel of Music."

"I know, Mademoiselle. I know."

"You do! You really understand?"

"Only an angel could have played as he did at Perros."

"You do understand!" She seized his long, thin fingers with her tiny hand. His first impulse, I saw, was to pull away from her, but he did not. "He is an angel, Monsieur Holmes. You have heard that divine music. His voice is the same, if not more celestial than the violin. Saint Michael the Archangel when he sang to the other angels could not have sounded more heavenly! And yet..." She began to cry again. "His face, oh, his face–his poor face. Oh, poor Erik! How could God do this to his own angel!"

The Viscount stiffened. "Who is Erik?"

"His face is that of a demon, a creature from Hell! How can that be, Monsieur Holmes? You must tell me–how can God have done his own angel such a wrong?"

Sherlock had dropped the guise of Quasimodo; both eyes were open, the false teeth held in his left hand. "I know not, Mademoiselle Daaé."

"Oh, I do not know what to believe anymore! I do not know whether he is an angel or devil, but when he sings to me his voice is an angel's. I…" She was crying so hard her words were difficult to make out.

"Christine," the Viscount said, "what is this? What are you talking about!"

"I am talking about a tragedy, a great and terrible tragedy!"

"But… You spoke of our love, and you know that I do love you—you must understand that you are my heart, my soul, my very being! And yet you speak of this… this Angel. Angels do not appear to mortals. Someone is deluding you, my darling. And that ring… You must understand… Whose ring is it?" The Viscount's voice had gradually taken on its familiar whine.

"It is *his* ring. Erik's ring."

"But who is this Erik!"

"He is the Angel of Music, my own special angel, the one whom God has sent to me. He is my inspiration and my trial. Oh, if only I am worthy of him!"

"This is madness, Christine. Madness!"

"So you think that I am mad?"

"No, no, of course not. I only…"

She stood abruptly. "I must go. He will… Raoul, we may not see one another again in this life. Believe me when I swear I… that I loved you. Try to understand. I must go—I must go now. If he should find me here… Promise me, all of you, that you will not follow me. *Promise.*"

"But, Christine…" the Viscount began.

"Silence! You are incapable of understanding—absolutely incapable! What a silly little fool I have been!" She turned to Sherlock. "Promise me, Monsieur Holmes, that none of you will follow me for at least five minutes."

"Is it really necessary that you depart?"

"Yes—yes."

"Are you certain that he will not harm you?"

"Yes. I shall be safe with him."

"Then you have my promise."

"And you, Doctor Vernier?"

I nodded.

"And you, Raoul?" Her voice quavered.

"But dearest, this is madness. I cannot…"

"Promise me!"

He sighed. "Oh, very well. I promise."

She touched his cheek with her fingertips, then rose, opened the door, flooding us briefly with light, and closed it behind her.

The Viscount promptly leapt to his feet. Holmes's hand shot out and seized his wrist. "Where do you think you are going?"

"I must follow her! I must find this Erik!"

"Need I remind you that you gave your word?"

"You impertinent dog—spare me your lectures!" He tried to break free of Holmes, an endeavor I could have told him would be futile. "Release me at once!"

"You are going to keep your word and your honor, *Monsieur le Vicomte,* whether you wish to or not."

"But she is mad—delirious."

"That does not matter. Please sit down."

"*Ow!*" the Viscount cried. "You are hurting me. Let go!"

"Only if you will sit down."

"Oh, very well—just release me."

Holmes did so, and the Viscount sat and rubbed angrily at his wrist, then glanced at the door handle.

"I shall certainly catch you if you try it."

The Viscount began to curse. I turned to my cousin. "Do you think she has lost her reason?"

"She is quite sane."

"She is behaving most strangely," the Viscount moaned.

"That is certainly an understatement," I muttered.

"She has been placed in a most difficult position." Sherlock's fingers began to drum at his right knee. "The choice is usually not so stark, so dramatic. The outcome is predictable, but I wish…" He sighed, then stared out at the dark dome of the auditorium overhead.

"What are you talking about!" the Viscount cried. "Has everyone gone mad but me?"

"Oh, be quiet for once!" Holmes snapped.

After a brief interlude, Sherlock stood. "We have waited long enough to honor our promise." He opened the door, and I blinked at the light. "It will no doubt be futile, but let us see if the Red Death is still about."

"We might have followed her to him if you had let me out earlier," the Viscount said.

"Yes, but then you would have shown yourself to be a filthy liar. Come." He twisted his body, metamorphosing again into Quasimodo, and started down the hallway.

We searched in vain for over an hour. Everyone recalled seeing the Red Death; some were so drunk they fancied he had just passed by; but the specter was nowhere to be found. We tried Box Five and discovered a man and woman earnestly assuming the roles of nymph and satyr, their earlier costumes discarded. An audience did not seem to disturb them, but Holmes quickly shut the door, his gray eyes showing a strange blend of repulsion and attraction. Again, I thought of Michelle, then was embarrassed at making such a connection. There was more to love than mere copulation, even if the most ethereal lovers and barnyard animals did share in the same biological act. My feelings for her were not merely carnal, nor, I hoped, did they have much in common with those of Christine Daaé and the Viscount!

We stepped out into the square before the Opera as the bells of Paris began to strike midnight. A cheer went up from the huge crowd. A Valkyrie with a spear seized my arm. "*Embrasses-moi, Mort!*" she cried, then pushed aside my mask and kissed me. Her lips were warm and moist, but her breath smelled of wine and tobacco. "*Au revoir, Mort!*" she cried as I nodded farewell.

An older woman in furs was willing to kiss Quasimodo, but Holmes held her at bay. Our Viscount Pierrot also rejected several amorous offers. "What about her dressing room?" I asked.

"Ah, let us try it!"

There were even more people on the grand stairway than before, and they had grown more quarrelsome or more amorous, no doubt because so many bottles of wine and champagne had been drunk. It took several minutes to reach the dim, quiet corridor leading to Christine Daaé's dressing room. We were almost to the door when we heard the voice begin. The Viscount wanted to cry out, but Holmes seized him at once and clapped a hand over his mouth. "Not now."

"Erik—*Erik*." I could hardly hear Christine over the music.

The voice was singing an aria. Usually I have a dreadful memory for melodies, but I had heard *Faust* only the week before. This was Faust's aria, "*Salut! demeure chaste et pure,*" sung, in effect, to Marguerite's house, that dwelling of "*une âme innocente et divine,*" a soul innocent and divine. Shortly thereafter, Faust ends up in his angel's bed, setting her on the path to dishonor, ruin, and madness. If you can forget the irony, the aria is beautiful, and I had never heard it sung so well.

Carlotta's tenor had a big worn voice with considerable vibrato. This singing was very clear and pure with minimal vibrato, full of genuine warmth and feeling, not mere acting. Christine's singing had something of the same quality, but one could tell this was the teacher, the maestro. He made it seem so easy. For someone like myself who had always been repelled by the artifice of opera, this was perfection, the beauty of the music with none of the usual defects.

Holmes glanced at me, and I could see he was similarly affected. "Our angel again," he murmured.

The final high C note of the aria was the best I have ever heard. Usually a high C is a trial for tenor and audience alike: the singer bellows like a bull to produce the proper pitch while the audience worries that his voice will crack or a vein in his head burst. This person made the note a part of the song, a culmination of love which made one ache from the beauty.

There was a brief silence, then Christine Daaé cried, "I come!"

Holmes had released the Viscount who shouted, "Christine!" He ran to the door and wrenched it open. Holmes and I followed slowly, unwilling to break the music's spell. The room was empty, the only sound the hiss of the low gas flame. A chair lay on its side before the full-length mirror, and we saw before us only Quasimodo, the grim reaper, and a befuddled Pierrot who had lost his mask.

"She walked into the mirror," the Viscount whispered. Then much louder, "My God, she went *into* the mirror!"

*Seven*

L ate in the afternoon of the next day, we spent an unpleasant hour with the Viscount. After our adventures at the Opera ball he had been stunned, but sleep and a few hours contemplation had been enough to work him into a state of genuine frenzy. He bitterly reproached Holmes for again laying hands upon him, threatening to challenge him to a duel if it happened one more time. He also blamed Holmes for Miss Daaé's relations with the mysterious Erik and finished by demanding that Holmes find her on the instant.

Although Sherlock was weary, having slept little that night, he showed the patience of a saint, albeit a somewhat sarcastic one. He assured the Viscount that Mademoiselle Daaé would soon reappear, noted that she had confessed her love for him, and told him that he was free to take his business elsewhere if so inclined. After having excreted a goodly amount of black bile, the Viscount left, somewhat placated.

"Promise me," I said to my cousin, "that if I ever begin to behave toward Michelle or any other female in a manner in any way similar to

Monsieur de Chagny, that you will apprise me of the situation."

"Fear not, Henry. You are not such an utter ass."

"Yet I see certain similarities. I fear that our general behavior toward the misnamed weaker sex is often reprehensible. They must tolerate a great deal of nonsense."

Holmes nodded. "The poor man beats his wife in a drunken stupor, the rich man treats her exactly as he treats his dog. Courtship is all clouds of perfumed sentiment while marriage has the stink of cynicism or indifference."

I laughed. "You might forge that into a pair of couplets worthy of Alexander Pope."

Holmes sighed. "You know, of course, that our Mademoiselle Daaé will end up with that sniveling wretch of a viscount."

"I cannot believe it."

"I have seen it happen too many times." He suppressed a yawn, covering his mouth with his hand. "I am tired. Fear not, Henry, your Michelle, like you, is made of sterner stuff, and with age—at least in her case—has come wisdom. And unlike Mademoiselle Daaé, she has an income and a livelihood of her own. Christine Daaé has hardly a penny, and the chances of her making and keeping a fortune on the stage are slim. At least she has spirit. I doubt she will ever be a meek slave to the Viscount."

"In spite of everything... life would be very lonely without women."

A brief smile passed over his lips. "I hope to return you to your Michelle in another fortnight."

"Are you serious? Can you see an end to this business?"

"Oh yes, but none that pleases me. That is the problem. However, one way or another, things are drawing to a climax."

I questioned him, but he would elaborate no further.

Monday morning when I joined him for breakfast, he had claimed two letters from the front desk. Upon one I recognized the familiar British postmark and stamps.

"Susan Lowell sends her regards."

I stared at him, but he sipped his coffee somewhat too loudly and regarded the tablecloth. "A lengthy letter?" I asked.

"Yes. She has some misgivings about leaving Wales to go to London. Perhaps she is right."

"All the same," I began, but an exclamation from Holmes cut me off.

"Have a look at this." He passed me the other letter. It was only three lines in which Christine Daaé pleaded for him to meet her at Notre Dame de Paris at eleven that morning. "I had foreseen something such as this. A rehearsal for *La Juive* is scheduled for this afternoon, and I expect her to be present. Eat your croissant, Henry, and then we shall take a cab to Notre Dame. No trip to Paris would be complete without a visit there."

Despite Baron Haussmann's many improvements to Paris during the reign of Napoleon the Third—the great wide boulevards, the many monuments, squares and parks—the cathedral remained the very heart of the city, as it had for centuries. My father had been French Catholic, my mother British Protestant, and I was not much of either. Still, I must confess to a certain thrill, a visceral shiver, as we stood across the street and stared up at the great facade of the church.

Hugo in his novel of the same name had immortalized Notre Dame de Paris forever. At one point he compares it to a monstrous, two-headed Sphinx, and despite its undeniable majesty, the edifice did possess a faintly sinister aura. Perhaps it was the dusky color the stone had taken on, a grayish black patina; and the sheer size of that immense front rising above us also contributed to its impact. The three portals with their pointed arches and elaborate sculptures were a good fifty feet high, the doors themselves some twenty-five feet tall. Next came the row of sculpted stone figures, each twice larger than life, then the gigantic, circular rose window, and finally those two towers, the Sphinx heads, each with two arches, their interiors black, the strange, rectangular eyes of the beast.

Perhaps the age of Notre Dame or my knowledge of that age affected me. Largely finished in the late thirteenth century, it was nearly two hundred years old in Hugo's novel, which was set in the fifteenth century; now over six hundred years had gone by. The Cathedral stood as a monument to the past, to a different age entirely, one more primitive than our own, one whose faith was both its glory and its terror. That faith drove men to create beautiful things such as the Cathedral, even as they committed the most dreadful atrocities in the name of their God. The witch trials and tortures carried out in Hugo's novel had their basis in fact, even if Quasimodo had never existed, had never crawled about that facade or pushed the evil priest Claude Frollo to his death.

The day was bright and sunny, the preview of spring continuing. How much more sinister would the dark facade have appeared against a stormy gray sky! I glanced at my cousin and saw in his face indications of reverie and contemplation similar to my own. He wore a top hat and frock coat, but because of the gentler weather, he had left behind his overcoat.

"It is imposing," I murmured.

"Quite. The carriages and pedestrians seem inconsequential. Curious that mortals could create something so much larger and more enduring than themselves. I wonder how much longer it will stand. One can almost feel the fundamental clash between it and our modern age. Perhaps it broods upon the folly of all notions of human progress."

"I wonder if it was truly an age of faith."

Sherlock shook his head. "I doubt it. The hearts of men remain the same. Only the surroundings, our monuments, change. This old Sphinx has had his day. A hundred years from now Eiffel's steel tower will probably be the emblem of Paris."

"That monstrosity?" I shook my head. "Never. There was a genuine outcry at its construction."

Holmes gave me his most ironic smile. "We shall have to settle this bet posthumously, I fear." He took his watch out of his vest pocket. "Come, we must not keep Mademoiselle Daaé waiting."

The interior of Notre Dame seems gloomier and darker than those of other famed cathedrals; one feels in walking through the great portal and under the vaulted stone walls high overhead that one is passing backward in time. Although other cathedrals may be more architecturally Gothic, Notre Dame is more Gothic in the sense of ominous atmosphere and mood.

We walked slowly down a side aisle and stared up at the soaring vertical lines all around us, the stone columns which became the graceful arches of the vault and the tall windows which curved at their tops into points. The sunlight passing through the colored glass was subdued, the air heavy and damp with the faint hint of incense. A match flared, and as an old woman in black lit a candle before a gray stone saint, I smelled burning wax. The ancient tombs we passed, complete with sculptured representations of the dead, added to the funereal aspect.

At the far end of the church, near a statue of the Virgin, Christine Daaé knelt praying. Her devotion seemed a trifle theatrical, her pious posture and the rosary held in her tiny gloved hands overdone. Of late her garments had become more fashionable and expensive; her hat, dress, and bodice were of brilliant purple, the fur at the collar and cuffs of the bodice a dark sable. Unlike the timeless old *dames* in black, that flock of aged crows, she seemed out of place, an incongruity. I reflected that the dye mauvine, a coal tar derivative, had only been discovered twenty or thirty years ago, a mere moment in time to the ancient stones about us.

Her blonde hair was bound up in back, the bun showing under the purple brim of the hat, and the nape of her slender neck was very pale. I remembered kissing Michelle on that very spot, a mere prelude to that which followed, and a physical ache of longing went through me.

Holmes slipped between the seats to join her, and she looked up at us. Her face was pale and weary, but she smiled, her lips parting slightly. She was like some small lavender flower set before a great gray tombstone; how many such flowers had these stones seen wither and die? She was so beautiful, so self-assured, that I tended to forget she was little more than a child. Remembering the awkwardness of my companions, male and female, at twenty years, I was glad to be past it all and near thirty. I recalled Holmes's comment that only the plodding oxen like Carlotta lasted as singers, and I wondered if she would tame her artistic genius or burn out young even as a flaming meteor.

She rose off her knees and sat down. "Monsieur Holmes, Doctor Vernier! I am so glad you could come." Still radiant, she laid one hand on Holmes's sleeve. Visibly he recoiled, but she did not notice. "I have been praying that you would come. I hope God will answer my other prayers." She pulled off her gloves and folded her hands on her lap. The golden band was still on her finger.

Holmes stared warily at her, his eyes tired. "You wanted to see us, Mademoiselle Daaé?"

"Yes. Erik... Erik has released me. I wept, and he said I could go if I promised to return. I promised, and yet... Oh, Monsieur Holmes, what am I to do?"

"You gave him your promise?"

She stared down at her hands, then put her right hand over the other so the ring was hidden. She nodded.

"Well, then."

She looked up at him, her face a mute appeal, but his face was stern and cold, like those of the stone saints all around us. I could not resist her. "A promise not freely given, a promise made under duress, may not be binding. Were you threatened or coerced?"

Her smile slowly faded, and I sensed how weary she was. "No. Yes. Oh, I don't know! If only—he is so mercilessly, so frightfully, ugly! If he were merely plain, but his face is hideous—*hideous*!" Her voice grew loud, echoing faintly overhead, and an old woman coughed once, then turned to give us a disapproving glance. Christine began to cry. She took a handkerchief out of her handbag and dabbed at her eyes. "Oh, I am sorry. I am... confused."

Holmes maintained his stony composure, but I could see in his eyes that he was troubled. My first impulse as a physician—and as a man— was to comfort her, but I held back.

"He lives beneath the earth, Monsieur Holmes. Deep underground. Did you know that?"

Holmes did not move, but I sensed the energy gathering within him, his attention caught at once. "I suspected as much. Beneath the Opera, yes?"

She nodded. "He took me part of the way on a horse, the white horse César, whom I knew so well. It was cold and dark down there. I was frightened, but his voice was so calm and gentle. He took me to the strangest little house all full of musical instruments, statues, and paintings. He told me how he had always loved me from the first time he saw me, how he worshiped me, how he would make me the greatest singer of all time. How could I resist that voice, so warm, so resonant, a sound like a caress, like the touch of a hand? No woman could resist. He was my Angel of Music. But that was before I saw his face." She covered her face with her hands.

Holmes pulled at his chin with his thumb and forefinger and inhaled slowly. "He was masked?"

"Yes, and that first day everything was wonderful. We were so happy together. It was as if we had been waiting all our lives to discover one another, as if fate had decreed our love, but I would not leave well enough alone. I had to see his face. Somehow I had managed to persuade myself that he was really handsome. Older perhaps, but handsome. He was playing the organ when I snatched the mask from his face." Her hands clenched into fists. "Merciful God," she whispered. "Why?" Another sob burst free, and again we received a disapproving gaze from the old woman.

Something in the last sob seemed forced, and I suddenly had the impression of someone playing a part. Not consciously—Christine Daaé was no transparent little hypocrite; all was deeply felt. Yet something was wrong.

"Removing masks is always a dangerous business," Holmes said.

"Believe me, Monsieur Holmes, I understand that now. God is testing me, I know." Her tiny hand closed about the gold cross she wore at her throat. "He has sent me my Angel of Music, but why has he given him the face of a devil? I told you how at times I have sensed the angels all about me, the shimmer of their golden wings, but now... they are gone. I sense demons—only demons. I smell the sweet sick smell of their rotting naked flesh, and I hear their laughter, a high-pitched chittering noise like that which rats make. I hear it at night; it creeps in and out of the silent darkness. Oh, they are terrible, these demons—they are black and damned! My father warns me, and I know that only my angel can save me. When I am with him, I am safe! Lucifer was the king of angels, the most beautiful, until he scorned God and was damned. His beauty was evil, a curse. Oh, if I abandon my angel I, too, am lost—am damned!"

"Please calm yourself, Mademoiselle," I said. "Such thoughts are morbid and unhealthy. These demons are fabrications of your mind. They are not real."

She bit at her lip, drew in her breath, and a change came over her face. "Do you think… do you think Monsieur de Chagny is fond of me?"

Holmes grimaced. "You know the answer to that question. You heard him declare his feelings for you."

"But is he to be believed?"

Holmes drew in his breath between his clenched teeth. "You must be the judge of that."

"But what do you think, Monsieur Holmes?"

"Mademoiselle Daaé, you put me in an impossible position! I have been assisting the Viscount, and he is my client. However, in good faith I must tell you that"—the anger had burst from him; he struggled to control it—"I… I am not an admirer of the Viscount. That is all I shall say." This sternness triggered more tears. Holmes gave me a grim smile which conveyed his wish that we could leave. I felt impatient with her myself.

In the midst of her tears she suddenly laughed. "What a silly little fool I am. He is a boy, such a boy, and yet… He is rather handsome, for a boy, and he says he loves me. Am I to be blamed for wanting a normal life? For wanting not to be poor? For wanting a husband who will take me places and buy me things and say sweet, stupid words? Do not all women want this? Who will blame me! Would you have me buried alive with a madman and genius? Would you blame me, Monsieur Holmes!"

He gave his head a swift shake. "No. Most women would not hesitate given the choice you face. The fact that you are troubled, that you hesitate, is to your credit."

She stared at him, her green eyes hard and bright, still frenzied, all the artifice gone. "Do you mean that, Monsieur Holmes?"

"Yes."

"But… but you know how it will end, how I shall choose?"

Holmes was briefly silent. "Yes, we both know how you will choose."

Christine struck the pew before us with her two fists so hard that it must have hurt. She stood abruptly. "We shall see, we shall see." She strode past us, hurling over her shoulder at the scowling old woman, "Go to the Devil, old cow."

Holmes and I sat stiffly, listening to her footsteps echo through the church, dimming as she went further from us. I sighed. "Good heavens."

Holmes gave an explosive laugh. "Exactly. I meant every word I said, Henry. I shall not blame her. She will make the Viscount sweat, I can tell you that." He looked around, then leapt to his feet. "Come—we have some unfinished business of our own."

"What business?" I turned to see him advance toward a man sitting a few rows behind us. His face with its dark skin and black mustache was only too familiar.

"*Monsieur le Perse*, let us have a chat."

"*Hsst!*" the old woman whispered loudly, one finger over her lips.

The Persian fled, with Holmes in pursuit. He crossed to the far side of the church, then ran down the aisle, nearly colliding with an aged priest in a long black cassock before darting out a side door. I strode after Holmes, nodding politely at the priest. He was pale and bald, his thick gray eyebrows furrowing his brow in disapproval.

The doorway Holmes and the Persian had taken led to a narrow stone spiral staircase. I started up, round and round, and before long my legs began to ache. I heard heavy breathing and came out onto a landing which opened onto the roof. Holmes stood with one hand against the wall, panting, his face pale.

"Henry, perhaps I should give up tobacco." The effort to speak even these few words made him breathe harder.

"Did he go out here?"

"No, blast it. I took a quick look, but I am certain he has gone higher. This must lead to the top of the tower. Let us go, but more slowly so my wretched lungs do not burst."

After a while we came to another doorway. Still panting heavily, Holmes leaned briefly on his stick, then raised his hand. "Let me go first." He held his stick like a club, a good foot beneath the heavy silver handle in the shape of a wolf. He stepped outside, and I followed.

The stairway had ended in a small stone enclosure only ten feet across that opened onto the roof of one of the majestic towers, those Sphinx heads of Notre Dame. A wall went all the way around the top of the tower, a wall of carved stone with a repeating pattern of ornate stone X's or lateral crosses. However, I was not so conscious of the wall as of the space, the openings, in it. The nearest section was only five or six feet away, and we were up a frightful height, all the roofs of Paris spread out before us. I took a few hesitant steps forward, got a glimpse of the Seine below, then shuddered and stepped back, clutching at the doorway's edge with my right hand, the vertigo overwhelming me.

"Oh, do come out, Henry. The view is marvelous." Holmes had gone straight to the wall, leaned upon it, and stared out. He was very tall, and the wall seemed a ridiculously trivial barrier, hardly going to his waist.

"For God's sake, Sherlock—take care!" My eyes briefly swept the tower top—no sign of the Persian—then fixed themselves on the dark stone at my feet.

"Fear not. I have a healthy respect for heights. Do you recall how Claude Frollo met his end?"

"Only too well."

"Quasimodo pushed him over, perhaps from this very tower. Frollo caught upon one of the gargoyles and hung for a while before falling to his death. You should have a look at the gargoyles. They are quite remarkable. Do you remember, too, how Quasimodo would climb all about the facade of the cathedral, totally unafraid of the heights? His bells must be directly beneath us."

"How interesting." I could not keep the weakness from my voice.

Holmes turned and raised his stick, the sunlight flashing off the bright silver wolf's head. "Please do come out from behind there, Monsieur. We mean you no harm. We only wish to discuss a mutual acquaintance."

To my left I saw the Persian appear. So long as I stayed within the doorway, one hand touching the stone, it was not so bad, but I dared not walk out onto the roof as Holmes had. I preferred admiring the gargoyles at a distance, from the solid ground below.

The Persian was sullen, his dark eyes hard. Instead of disguising him, the conventional morning suit and bowler hat only accentuated his foreign origins. Again I noticed that scar on his cheek which had been so poorly stitched. He must have been well into his forties, but his mustache was still solid black, only a light dusting of gray showing in his sideburns.

"What do you want of me?" His French had only a trace of an accent.

Holmes lowered his stick and leaned upon it. His breathing had finally slowed almost to normal. "Merely some conversation. We have, I believe, a mutual friend named Erik."

The Persian looked about nervously. "It is best not to mention that name."

Holmes leaned out over the edge, peering downward.

"For God's sake!" I exclaimed.

"I see neither he nor Quasimodo crawling about, so I believe we may speak freely."

"This is no joking matter," the Persian said.

Holmes's smile vanished. "No, it is not. Why did you follow us?"

He shrugged. "I wanted to discover what you were about. As you say, we have a mutual acquaintance."

"He followed us here?" I asked.

Holmes nodded. "It was done quite skillfully, as might be expected.

After all, we are not dealing with an amateur, but with the former head of the dreaded Persian secret police."

The Persian's mouth opened wide, then he clenched his fists. "How the devil…? Who has told you this? I shall deal with them."

"No one told me, *daroga,* so you need not add further to your already impressive list of victims."

"Then how did you discover my identity?"

"That shall remain my little secret. It detracts from my reputation when I reveal my methods. People such as you always interest me. I wonder how you can be so completely lacking in moral scruples, how you could have slaughtered your fellow-countrymen so easily. The book I have been reading numbers your victims in the thousands."

"I was only the tool of the Sultana."

"Ah, so that is your justification? Can you not do better than that?"

"You are rather insulting, Monsieur Holmes."

"The Sultana was supposed to have been equal in every way to the most corrupt and violent emperors of ancient Rome. Mere slaughter and torture did not suffice. She and her court had to watch, to be amused. You helped arrange these spectacles, I believe. Did you enjoy watching women and children being torn to pieces by wild beasts and other such sights?"

"The enemies of the state…" the Persian began.

"'The enemies of the state!' Ah, I like that! Such elevated language." Holmes's face had reddened, and he had that dangerous gleam in his eyes. "How good to know that in the late nineteenth century the most vile, primitive savagery can be justified with such lofty, vapid rhetoric. I am sure your motives were of the highest order. Tell me, the book says that the Sultana was a… peculiar woman, again implying some unnatural vice resembling that of the Roman emperors. Was this true?"

The Persian stared at Holmes as if he questioned his sanity. Perhaps his command of the French language was not so good as it seemed, or more likely, he may have wondered if any man would dare to speak to him so directly. At last a strange, furtive smiled pulled at his lips, revealing his teeth; he squinted slightly, lines radiating from the corners of his eyes. "It is true. She would copulate with anyone." The smile came and went again. "Except poor Erik."

The French word he used was not the equivalent of the English "copulate," nothing with the Gallic politeness of *accoupler,* but rather a very vulgar word, all the more shocking because French was usually so refined and lacked such blunt language. It was too much for Holmes. He could not maintain his sarcastic composure; genuine rage showed in his face; and the Persian took half a step back, a faint leer still twisting his lips.

I felt a disgust I did not quite understand. "Watch your tongue!" I exclaimed.

The Persian smiled again. "Come now, we are not schoolgirls. The Sultana had the soul of a whore, and everyone is glad she is dead, including me. That is all in the past. True, I followed you, but perhaps we can do business together. You want to know about Erik. Well, I can tell you all about him—for a price."

"Ah, yes, the price. Everything comes round to the price for your kind."

"May I smoke?" After Holmes nodded, the Persian took out a silver case, removed a cigarette, and lit it. I was not a tobacco expert like Holmes, but even I could tell these were Turkish, cheap, and very strong. "Yes, I know all about Erik, and I can tell you his secrets."

"And what is the price you had fixed upon?"

"For one hundred thousand francs I can lead you right to him."

Holmes laughed. "What a precise, round sum. How convenient."

The Persian frowned. "You need not mock me. I know how well paid you are. I know all his secrets, and you know *nothing,* great Monsieur Sherlock Holmes."

"Indeed? Very well, Monsieur. You tell me when I am mistaken. Erik lives deep under the Palais Garnier at the bottom of its cellars. He has dwelt there for some fifteen years, ever since the Opera was completed in '75. Before that he was one of the engineers, the contractors, who worked on the building, and before that he must have spent time in Persia, no doubt constructing fiendish and ingenious devices for the Sultana. He was also in India where he discovered the secrets of the Punjab lasso. Earlier still he was in the circus where he excelled as freak, ventriloquist, singer, and fiddler. He has always been deformed, his face a type of living skull. This explains why he usually wears a mask. Perhaps while in the Orient he developed a disease which further ravaged his poor face. No doubt he has always cultivated his voice and its powers because his face is so ugly. He has lurked under the Opera these many years, appearing above ground to view the performances from his box, Box Five. There he first noticed Christine Daaé. Who can explain how love happens, how it takes root in a man's soul? Suffice to say that he loves Christine Daaé. At least he thinks he does. That is why he is determined she shall succeed. She is also his pupil, the one to whom he has decided to pass on the secrets of his incredible vocal talents."

The Persian stared, his mouth open. "*Mon Dieu*—you know everything!"

I was equally impressed. "Why did you not tell me all this, Sherlock?"

"I just have."

"I mean…"

"I rarely guess, but a few of my suppositions were on shaky ground. Our friend here has just confirmed them. Now perhaps you would care to explain your past relations to Erik. I have no way of knowing much about his adventures in the Orient."

The Persian hesitated. "Why should I tell you anything?"

"Do you like music, *daroga*?"

"What?" The question obviously surprised him.

"You heard me. Do you like music? Violin playing, singing, the symphony, the opera?"

The Persian shrugged. "Not particularly."

"Thank God for that. I think perhaps you dislike Erik, yet you fear him even more. Some strange bond has kept you in Paris all these years. Tell me what you know."

"It will cost you. Perhaps not a 100,000, but 25,000."

Holmes laughed. "I shall not give you a sou. I should have realized I was mistaken. You can tell me nothing about such a man; you understand nothing; you know nothing—only facts, mere facts, and I have plenty of those. I am not certain I could believe much of what you say. Go to the Viscount de Chagny or his brother if all you want is money. The elder brother is rich and should enjoy the details of your exploits with the Sultana. Perhaps you can teach him a trick or two."

The Persian's eyes narrowed. "Beware, Monsieur. I am not a man to be trifled with. Few of my enemies remain alive."

"Really? And have your friends fared any better? You strike me as one who would sell his wife or mother for the right price."

"How dare you!" He slipped his hand into his coat, but Holmes stepped forward, his stick arcing through the air. The Persian cried out and grasped his hand. A small, double-barreled derringer clattered upon the stone. Without thinking, I stepped forward and seized it. "Damn you, damn you," the Persian muttered.

I looked about, saw the blue-green Seine and the rooftops, the tiles blue or red under the sunlight, then I retreated back to the doorway.

The Persian's face was red with hate, his eyes furious. "You and he are exactly the same with your damned arrogance, your damned smugness! You think you are better than everyone else, so refined, so intelligent, so sensitive. You are not—you are damned ugly freaks, dirty dogs. I shall make you pay for this, Sherlock Holmes—I swear to God I will!"

The corners of Holmes's mouth curved contemptuously. "Certainly. Good day to you, sir."

With further oaths and insults, the Persian swept past him and headed for the stairs. I gave him a wide berth, but he began cursing me as well. The sound of his voice gradually faded.

Holmes took the derringer from me. "American made. Not particularly accurate, but effective, if messy, at close range." He slipped it into the pocket of his frock coat. "Arrogant, greedy fool. A hundred thousand francs! What nerve. Did you see his face when I told him about Erik?"

"Yes. He was dismayed, but hardly more surprised than I."

Holmes removed his top hat, then wiped at his brow with a handkerchief. "This is certainly a splendid view, and it is a fine day. Do you see where they are building a basilica at the summit of Montmartre? We should also be able to see Eiffel's tower from up here."

"Please, Sherlock, can we go down now?"

"Yes, I suppose so, although after such a climb I would like to spend more time up here. I particularly like that contemplative gargoyle down a level, his chin in his hand, and the view of the spire is also excellent. Ah, but you have had trials enough for the day, and I saw how you seized the derringer, despite your phobia." He gave his stick a tap on the stone at his feet, then we started down the stairs.

Although going down was easier than coming up, we were both fatigued by the time we reached the bottom. The church seemed dark and cold after the warm sunlight above. We headed for the vestibule, the stone walls, arches and columns about us all part of some great gray presence. The sunlight had lit up the rose window, giving the colored glass a subdued glow, a kind of life; the window seemed the heart of the edifice or, perhaps its eye, a monstrous, intricate eye that saw all of Paris.

The elderly priest gave us a withering glance. Holmes smiled at him, then deposited a coin in the poor box. It made a loud, shimmery clang. This act improved the priest's disposition, but his smile was more frightful than his frown. He had pale, watery blue eyes which did not focus correctly. Although Claude Frollo died without issue and although he was a fictional character, this priest appeared to be a relative in spirit, if not in blood. What strange thoughts passed through his mind when he saw a pretty young girl?

It was a relief to step out of the church and return to the street and the sunshine of the late nineteenth century. "Hugo was wrong," I said.

"How so?"

"He wrote of the strange living bond between Notre Dame and Quasimodo and claimed that after the hunchback was gone, something was gone, too, from the edifice. However, the cathedral has a disquieting aura, something very old, ancient, something... half alive."

Holmes stroked his chin, then stared off into the distance. After a long while he said, "Yes, I remember that particular characterization. I shall need to think about it. He said Quasimodo was its... Come, Henry, we have earned a good lunch today and perhaps a fine burgundy. The morning has been strenuous, eventful, and as I am weary of this case, we shall take the afternoon off and stroll through the Louvre."

"Yes, but tomorrow you will finally tell me everything you know about Erik."

"So I shall. We shall be taking a brief boat ride, and we can discuss it then."

"This afternoon?"

"No, no—it is the Louvre today, the Opera tomorrow."

"But the boat ride?"

He gave that barking laugh of his, then started across the street. "No more questions. I am ravenous. Perhaps we should again try the restaurant where we dined with the Count de Chagny; however, this time we shall be able to give the food the attention which it deserves. Today it will be *le lapin,* not *le veau.*"

Our afternoon at the Louvre and an evening concert of French music by Saint-Saëns and Gounod provided a pleasant interlude, but the next morning we were back at the Opera. We were soon treated to the spectacle of the Viscount de Chagny and Christine Daaé billing and cooing at one another like two love doves. The Viscount wore a blue velvet frock coat and gray trousers, his usually pale face flushed a healthy pink, the ends of his airy red-brown mustache neatly waxed, and his fine white teeth showing more often than usual. Without his customary petulant scowl or the love-sick droop of his mouth, he was not unattractive. Christine Daaé wore a beautiful green dress and hung about his arm as if she drew sustenance from it. Between the two were all manner of smiles, laughs, and secret glances.

Sherlock gave me a look heavy with ironic disgust. "It has, I fear, begun."

"Whatever could have happened?" I asked.

Later that morning we had our answer directly from the Viscount. Christine was to be fitted for a costume. After giving her tiny white hand a final squeeze and flashing his teeth in a fierce smile, the Viscount parted from her. Even his voice had altered, the whiny tone gone.

"Ah, Monsieur Holmes, things are going splendidly. Erik is forgotten for the moment, and we are playing at being engaged."

"Playing?" I asked.

Something of his usual haughtiness returned. "It was her idea. There can, of course, be no question of real marriage. Some mysterious promise of hers and my position forbid it, but what is the harm in pretending to be engaged? It is a most delightful amusement."

I turned away, feeling the need to conceal my face. "It seems to agree with you both," Holmes said.

"It does. Yes, things have taken a turn for the better. You were right, Monsieur Holmes, and I regret my harsh words of yesterday."

"You are too kind, *Monsieur le Vicomte*."

"No, no—everything they say about your genius is true. You said she would reappear, and so she has."

"In that case, might I be so presumptuous as to remind you that I have not yet been paid?"

"Of course, Monsieur Holmes. You will have a check for 25,000 francs by the end of the day."

I jerked my head about. Holmes's smile was filled with irony. "You are most generous, *Monsieur le Vicomte*."

"You will discover that my gratitude is stronger even than my anger. You will have another check for the same amount when this Erik has been eliminated as a threat to me and my beloved Christine."

"I have high hopes that some such outcome will soon take place."

"Good, good." I had never seen the Viscount smile so much; it had begun to grate upon me. "I have told Christine that she will soon have her freedom."

"She seems free enough now," I said.

"No." For a moment the old scowl returned. "She has promised not to wander from the Opera House. She even has a cot in her dressing room. I like it not, but I cannot stay angry at her for long. Is she not beautiful, gentlemen? Ah, here she comes again, my heavenly vision—I must go. You shall have your payment, Monsieur Holmes."

The two of them greeted each other as if they had been separated from birth, not for a mere quarter of an hour, and again I had to turn away.

"You do not seem to enjoy the spectacle, Henry," Holmes said.

"No. I thought better of her."

"They make a handsome, if insipid, pair. Perhaps she thinks this way she can remain loyal to Erik while trifling with the Viscount. It will never work, but she wants to have her cake and eat it, too."

"This cake of hers," I said, "is too sweet and too rich by far. A surfeit of the Viscount would certainly turn my stomach."

Holmes laughed. "Rarely have I heard a metaphor so prolonged and so mangled. However, this nonsense has its benefits. I am to be paid, and if matters continue as they have, I shall be able to retire from the proceeds of this case."

"25,000 francs!" I shook my head in disbelief. "One thousand pounds is a healthy sum."

Holmes smiled. "I thought it best to mention the matter while he was in such a good mood. No doubt in a day or two he will be as churlish as ever. However, we have more important things to do than watch these young lovers. I believe I mentioned a boat ride to you."

"A boat ride?"

"Through one of the most scenic parts of Paris. Unfortunately, it will be a trifle cold and damp."

As I realized what he meant, I groaned. "Not the cellars again!" Familiarity had not made me any more eager to descend into that gloomy labyrinth below the Opera.

"Before we begin, however, we must don our special apparel. Come."
We were in the auditorium, but he led me downstairs to a deserted
room. Certain no one else was close by, he opened the satchel he had
been carrying and took out what seemed to be a thick leather belt.
"Unfasten your collar button."

"What on earth for?"

"I shall demonstrate." He unfastened his own collar, then placed the
belt about his neck, looping it through the buckle and fastening it.

"A dog collar!" I exclaimed.

"Exactly. I told them I had two particularly large and ferocious
mastiffs." He tightened his cravat, drawing the collar about the belt, but
refastening the button was clearly impossible. He took a wool scarf from
the bag, then wound it about his neck, hiding any sign of the dog collar.
I had wondered at his informal dress, a heavy tweed suit and bowler hat
instead of the usual frock coat and top hat. They were more suitable for
the cold dirty cellars, and I wished he had told me where we were going.
He withdrew another collar. "Here is yours, Henry."

"Why on earth are we wearing dog collars?"

"The Punjab lasso. I do not believe in magical devices, but these
collars will protect us from any unexpected ropes about the neck. Put it
on." With some distaste, I fastened it round my neck. "Oh, it must be
tighter than that!" Holmes drew it two notches tighter.

"I cannot breathe, Sherlock—*please*."

"I am sorry. I shall loosen it a notch, but it must be sufficiently tight
to protect your neck."

"Slow strangulation is not an appealing fate either."

He laughed. "There, that should do the trick." He withdrew another
wool scarf. "Put this on." He also gave me a small clasp knife. "If you
feel a rope about you, cut yourself loose at once."

I shuddered slightly, which was difficult because of the dog collar.

"You think it may come to that?"

"I hope not, but we must be prepared. After all, Joseph Buquet was found strangled."

"How pleasant of you to remind me."

We found our friend Monsieur Gris eating lunch with the gas men in the "organ" room. From there the black gas pipes branched out to every corner of the Opera. The men sat about eating baguettes and cheese, a few bottles of cheap red wine being passed about.

"Ah, Monsieur Holmes." Gris dabbed neatly at his mouth and bristly white stubble with a handkerchief which doubled as a napkin. "What project have you today?"

"Once more unto the cellars, Monsieur Gris. Henry and I wish to visit the lake and take a small boat ride, as I mentioned last week."

Gris shook his head gravely, and the other men were visibly disturbed. "Ah, Monsieur Holmes, I warned you then that I thought that idea extremely unwise. Wandering the lower cellars is bad enough, but the lake… There is *le Fantôme* to consider as well as *la sirène* who calls to men, then drowns them. I shall go to the lake with you and help you get started, but the devil himself could not entice me onto those infernal waters."

"I understand, Monsieur Gris, but my friend and I shall take the risk."

Gris swallowed the last of his wine from a dirty-looking glass, then shook his head again. "Very well, very well."

As we left I heard one of the men whisper, "*Ils sont fous ces anglais.*"

"Did you hear that?" I inquired in English. "They think we are crazy."

"Mere superstition, Henry. Nothing more."

Monsieur Gris took two dark lanterns from the storeroom, lit them, then gave one to Holmes, who in turn handed me the leather satchel. Soon we were trudging down the stone stairway toward the lowest depths of the Opera. The air grew colder and very damp as the strange, overwhelming silence of the underworld settled about us. The only sounds were our own footsteps and our breathing.

"Your hand at the level of your eyes," Monsieur Gris warned me. "You must not forget."

"But..." I was ready to tell him about our dog collars, but Holmes cut me off.

"Do just as he says, Henry."

"Oh, very well."

I was beginning to truly hate the cellars of the Paris Opera. They were a challenge to the rational structure which I had laid upon the world. Despite my education and my disdain for superstition and primitive religion, despite my convictions about the way the universe functioned, I was afraid down there—afraid, and slightly frustrated, slightly angry with myself for feeling that way. Each time I had returned to the surface, I had resolved it would be different the next time, but when we returned again to the darkness, I found myself quaking in my boots even as some medieval peasant might. The Punjab lasso made it even worse. The thought of a rope dropping out of the air and tightening about my throat kept me on edge.

We passed through a large chamber I remembered from before: bodies filled the room, dummies in suits of armor which were used for battle scenes. With only the feeble light from the two lanterns, it was difficult to believe this had not been the actual scene of some frightful carnage, these corpses left sprawling about grotesquely.

"Pile high the English dead," Holmes mumbled. "This would make a perfect hiding place. How are you faring, Henry?"

"Not well."

"Courage. Only another level to go. I think I am beginning to know these depths. Is not the stairway to our right, Monsieur Gris?"

"No, to the left."

"Are you certain of that?"

"Yes, of course."

And just as he said, the stairway was to our left. The stairs went down to a landing, then reversed, going in the opposite direction. We came out before the lake. A single gas fitting cast its feeble light across the dark waters. It was so cold we could see the white vapor of our breaths, but the water and the air were absolutely still. Holmes's glaring eyes, the rigid set of his mouth, revealed that he was angry with himself for not knowing in which direction the staircase lay. Since I possess almost no sense of direction, I was amazed that either he or Gris had any idea where we might be.

"The boat is here," Gris said. Behind us was a stone arch, the boat stowed beneath it. Holmes and I pulled it free, then pushed it into the water. Holmes looped the rope tied to the prow through a rusty iron ring set into the stone. "Very well, gentlemen. *Bonne chance.* I do not envy you. I shall return here in three hours, as we discussed, and I hope to see you again." He sounded skeptical we would be there. Lantern in hand, he turned and quickly started back up the stairs.

The water lapped faintly about the boat, still agitated from the disturbance we had made. Holmes shone the lantern about us. The walls were made of massive stones, the ceiling overhead of brick and mortar. We could not see the far shore, but every twenty feet or so a stone column rose from the black waters and curved up on either side into the ceiling. A musty, fetid smell permeated the chill air, and again I was aware of the awesome silence all about us. I reflected upon the many floors above, some seventeen or eighteen stories, those tons of steel, marble, stone, brick, and mortar. If the Opera were to collapse, we would be crushed like insects.

"Well," said Holmes, taking up the wooden pole which had lain beside the boat, "our voyage awaits us. You may sit, Henry, while I shall see if I have retained my technique with a punt."

I stepped warily into the boat, then sat while gripping both sides with my hands. Holmes gave me the dark lantern, then stepped in, freed the rope, and took the pole. Still standing, he raised the pole and used both arms to push. We swung gradually about.

"The water is not very deep, only about eight feet, but enough to drown anyone who could not swim. You do swim, do you not, Henry?"

"You know I do, but I am not so inclined today."

Holmes laughed. "I cannot blame you. I shall do my best to keep us afloat. Do you recall the names of the three rivers of Hell?"

"No."

"Lethe, Styx, and Acheron. Charon was the boatman upon the Acheron, but I hope you do not consider me that ugly rogue's counterpart. Yours is most assuredly not a damned soul, and..."

The sound made him cut off his words. Faintly it drifted through the empty darkness around us, more an impression than an actual noise: a woman's voice singing, the melody hauntingly sad and beautiful. "Good Lord," I whispered.

"Does it come from the right or left?"

"I cannot tell. Has it...? It has stopped. What on earth could it have been?"

"It was not, I fear, a beautiful young maiden or a watery nymph. Would you open the leather satchel? You will find a loaded revolver there. Handle it carefully. I believe you have on occasion used a revolver?"

"Yes, but I am a dreadful shot."

"Keep an eye open for sea serpents."

My laughter was strained. By then I was shivering slightly, both from cold and fear. "I say, are you keeping track of the way? I do not see the bank back there."

"Yes. We have passed some six stone arches like the one to our right, and we are proceeding in a straight line."

Another nervous laugh slipped between my lips. "I should not want to be lost down here."

"That is one worry you may dismiss. This seems an opportune time to thank you for accompanying me. This is a journey I did not wish to make alone." He poled with strong, rhythmic strokes, raising the pole high, then putting hand over hand.

"Wherever did you learn the mastery of a punt?"

"At Oxford." The water lapped gently at the boat, the pole cutting a neat straight line.

"You did?"

"You find that difficult to believe?"

"Not at all."

"Yes, you do. You assume, quite logically, that all my time was spent peering over the brittle pages of dusty, massive tomes or toiling over flasks and beakers in the chemistry lab. I certainly spent most of my time at such endeavors, but I had other interests as well, such as mastering a punt. Of course, a punt is nothing without a young lady."

"*What?*"

My voice was so incredulous that he laughed. "I, too, am a man, Henry, and I was frightfully young at the time. She was very beautiful, very beautiful indeed." A faint sadness could be heard rising over the prevailing irony, even as a curious overtone sometimes rises above a melody.

"What happened to the young lady?"

"The inevitable. She married a handsome future earl, a fellow whose stupidity had provided a never-ending font of amusement for me and my fellows."

"That must have been rather painful for you," I said. He did not reply but kept poling, his back to me. "That type of sadness can become almost like a physical illness, a disease, in its intensity. I have seen several patients who had literally made themselves sick over some misfortune in love. Women are more likely to see a physician, but men suffer no less. There is no drug to cure that affliction, but time does the trick."

"Ah yes, time," he said. "Healer and destroyer of all things. You need not fear, Henry. I am certain your Michelle has more sense than to run off with an earl."

I smiled. Her name was a hint of warmth amidst all the cold and darkness. "She tells me I am one of the few men she can tolerate."

"How perceptive on her part. I share her sentiments. Most people, male and female alike, are insufferable boors."

"She also thinks highly of you."

Holmes gave a strange laugh. "You are certainly jesting."

"Not in the least."

"I am… quite flattered. You must tell her that."

"I shall. I know another lady who shares her sentiments."

"A forbidden topic, Henry. Besides, this is hardly the best of times and places for such a discussion. The subject does have some bearing, however, upon our friend *le Fantôme*." He thrust the pole down, bracing himself and bringing the boat to a halt. "We have passed twelve arches."

I shone the light to either side, but saw only black water and a gray stone column with green moss growing in a two-inch band above the water. "Does this blasted lake go on forever?"

"It seems larger because of the darkness. To our right should be an exit, a channel which leads to an underground dungeon of great antiquity. The Communards of Paris used it in the uprising of 1871." He began to push the boat around to the right.

"However did you discover that?"

"Garnier mentions it briefly in his discussion of the artificial lake." He straightened the boat's course. "I am sorry you are so cold. I should have warned you to bring warmer clothes, but I was too busy being clever. Would you like to punt for a while? It keeps one warm and occupies the mind as well."

"You would not dare make such an offer if you had ever seen my efforts with a punt. I would capsize us at once. By the way, what exactly are we looking for?"

"*La maison du Fantôme.*"

"You think he dwells in this cold miserable place? He must be a specter indeed to survive down here without contracting pneumonia or some other equally severe respiratory disease."

"I did not mean to suggest that he was a fish or amphibian living in the waters. His dwelling is no doubt heated and lighted by gas from the Opera."

I rubbed my arms, trying to warm them. "Perhaps you will finally be good enough to elaborate upon what you told the Persian yesterday. How did you ever discover so much about the Phantom?"

"There was no single source, although Garnier's memoirs were again most helpful. I told you about a Monsieur Noir, whose name comes up frequently. Garnier mentions in passing that Noir was masked and that the man was a veritable genius. He relied upon Noir for the construction of some of the most crucial parts of the Opera. It was Noir who conceived the scheme for pumping out the ground water and constructing an artificial lake. The Opera rests upon a massive foundation of stone, a kind of immense bathtub. Noir also designed and placed the main columns supporting the auditorium, and his final task was to oversee the construction of the network of gas piping throughout the Opera."

"So you think he built himself a home down here?"

"Yes, a refuge from the world. He is hideously deformed. You remember what Miss Daaé said. Little wonder he hid himself away, but he knows every inch of the Opera—every attic, every corner of each basement, every door and trap door, as well as the aerie above the stage, the miles of rope, the flats, stairs, lime- and gaslights. Your mentioning the relationship between Quasimodo and Notre Dame helped me put our Phantom in his proper place. This grand and absurd edifice with all its splendor of marble, bronze, and gold, this gaudy baroque exterior built upon a skeleton of solid steel, has almost a life of its own, but it could not exist without its Phantom. His presence is everywhere; this is his universe, his world, his reflection. Hugo said Quasimodo was the very soul of Notre Dame; well, *le Fantôme* is the soul of *l'Opéra de Paris.*"

His words made me feel even more chill. "Hugo was only writing a novel. Quasimodo did not exist."

"But the Phantom does, and he is truly the soul of this place."

"You cannot be serious. A building, a place, cannot have a soul."

"I am serious. He is an unusual man, a true genius. In places I see the evidence of his presence, of his work, but certain other correspondences are so striking that I wonder if something larger is not at work."

"What are you saying?"

He turned and gave me that familiar ironic smile. "Must I spell out everything? Very well—some power, some god or deity, beyond our ken."

"You are serious." My hushed voice was quickly swallowed up by the silence around us.

"I shall give you an example. Have you noticed the two most familiar motifs in the Opera, the symbols repeated over and over?"

I tried to think, but I was cold and afraid. "There are statues everywhere, and columns…"

"No, no—not architecture. What lines the outer perimeter at the top of the building?"

I had to think, to mentally place myself before the entrance. Then it came to me, the image of green faces with black holes for eyes and mouths, faces all in a row. "Masks—*masks.*"

"Exactly! Masks. Everywhere you turn there are masks, the Greek representations of drama, of comedy and tragedy, repeated endlessly. There are more masks on the roof all around the lantern, there are the faces representing the Zodiac carved by Chibaud. Masks are one symbol, and the other golden symbol Apollo himself holds forth to the heavens at the highest point of the Opera."

I did not at first realize he was speaking concretely, not abstractly. "Apollo's lyre," I said. "Apollo holds a golden lyre."

"Yes. The lyre also appears everywhere, even in the fence before the Opera. They are the two key symbols, the mask and the lyre. Our Phantom wears a mask, and he has mastered music, the lyre, as has no other man. His powers on the violin and his singing are beyond belief. Do you now understand the strange correspondence I spoke of between him and the Opera?"

I shuddered. "Yes. It is uncanny. Is he... is he a man?" For the first time I was so shaken that I could almost believe he was a supernatural being, angel or demon.

"Is our Angel of Music a man?" He stopped poling, and the boat slowed, the turbulence radiating outward from the hull in great, dark circles. "Yes, he is a man, a poor weak mortal like ourselves."

"How can you be so certain?"

"Because he loves Christine Daaé."

Her name rippled through the air even as the waves upon the water, echoing throughout the vast cavern, and then the woman's voice began again, singing the same sad, beautiful melody. I hunched my shoulders, the chill seizing at the nape of my neck, and felt my body quake with a will of its own, a thing apart from me. The voice had an odd timbre, the pitch so high it must be a woman, and although it was miraculously beautiful, I could hear the singer's pain.

Holmes pulled the pole out of the water and laid it across the prow, then he took both the dark lantern and the revolver from my weak hands. Carefully he shone the light about us. "Erik!" he cried. "Erik!" The siren's voice ceased abruptly. "Erik, come speak with me. I shall not harm you, I give you my word. Come forth and speak to us, and I shall throw away the revolver. I would be your friend, not your enemy." His words died away, swallowed up by the vast silence of that subterranean lake.

"You cannot harm us, and we mean you no harm. I know who you are and how you suffer. Come speak to us. *Please.*" This time I heard the faint echo of that last word: "...*please...*" We waited, but there came not a sound, not a murmur. The boat had begun to turn slightly.

"Damnation," Holmes muttered. "*Damnation.*" He gave me the revolver and the dark lantern, then seized the pole and started us forward again.

"Was he really there?" I asked.

"Yes."

"But that was a woman's voice."

"Henry, can you fathom nothing for yourself?"

Cold and discouraged as I was, his anger cut at me. Why had I ever chosen to accompany my cousin? Perhaps he, like Erik, was beyond the comprehension of mortals like myself. "No," I replied.

"That was *his* voice. Man, woman, bass, tenor, soprano or contralto, he can do them all, and he can also project the voice far beyond himself. A toad, as well. Yes, he can most definitely do a toad."

"Carlotta. That was how he did it. She never made that sound."

"I told you so, did I not? He drugged the prompter and took his place in the prompter's box. That was also him saying, 'She is singing to bring down the chandelier.'"

"If that is true, then who released the chandelier? How did he make it fall?"

"I suspect an accomplice, but there is a problem with that supposition. It does not quite fit."

"What is the problem?"

"The problem is that he is alone." Holmes stopped poling, glanced all about us. Ahead I could see a black archway opening up in the stone wall. "Everything about him speaks of a being subject to a frightful loneliness, a profound separation from all other men. How can he be so alone and still have a companion who serves as accomplice? Yet someone cut off the gas to the chandelier and then released the chain holding it. I do not believe the Phantom could be in two places at the same time, regardless of his other powers. You do understand that we have met the Phantom; we have even seen his frightful face."

I thought for a moment. My brain felt sluggish, my body very weary. "The Red Death."

"Very good. There is yet hope that we may make a consulting detective of you." He said this not in disparagement, but with a certain warm amusement. I sensed he was sorry for his earlier display of anger.

We came closer to the wall, and the lantern illuminated enough of the archway that I could see the black water pass into it. "Are we going much further?" I asked.

"I think not. The dungeon is half a mile through that arch. Shine the lantern more to the right there. Look—look! Do you see the door?"

The yellow-white light showed a rusty rectangle set into the stone wall. As we came closer I saw that it was indeed a door, a formidable one, its face of solid metal. When we reached the stone landing, Holmes slipped the rope at the prow through an iron ring. He leapt ashore, setting the boat aquiver, then took the dark lantern from me.

"Wait a moment, Henry." He dropped down upon all fours and peered closely at the ground, the yellow light spilling before him. "Someone has been this way just now. There are footprints, wet footprints." He returned to the boat and extended a hand. "Come." His fingers felt like cold bone. "You are shivering. I think we are nearly finished here."

He turned, swinging the lantern about. "Let us have a look at this door." He raised his head, inhaling through his large nose, the bowler hat hiding part of his distinctive profile.

"Yes, our Erik is cautious. That lock is of English make, and even a very skilled burglar could not pick it. The frame is steel set into stone, and I would wager the door itself is solid steel. Perhaps it is only oak with a thick coating of metal. That would suffice. The hinges are on the inside, of course. You could not batter down this door without collapsing the entire wall, and it would require a mechanical ram. Your medieval soldiers with an oaken beam would hardly dent it. Yes, a formidable barrier, and were an assault made upon it, Erik would not loiter about."

"How could he get away?"

"Henry, do most homes have only a front door?"

I sighed. "I see why you think me hopelessly stupid. There must be a hidden passageway."

"Very good. I have no doubt that he took some liberties with the architectural plans while he served as contractor. Work crews have a way of asking no questions if the pay is sufficiently high. The Opera is something of a labyrinth, is it not?"

"*Yes.*" I gave an enthusiastic nod.

"Within this labyrinth lies another, a network of secret passages and hidden chambers which would take as long to master as the Opera itself."

"Would they not be interconnected so that if once you found one…?"

"I very much doubt it. He is far too clever for that. Sometime we shall try the one in Christine Daaé's dressing room."

"Behind the mirror."

"Exactly. Did you notice the eye in this door?" He pointed to what at first glance seemed an imperfection in the metal; on closer look it was an opaque piece of glass three-quarters of an inch across.

"What...?"

"It is a peephole with a lens which allows the person inside to examine all visitors."

My fear returned abruptly. "Do you think...?"

"I am certain he is peering at us at this very moment."

"Good Lord." I tipped my hat back and put my hand over my forehead.

"I do not think he will open up, so we shall soon depart." He turned to the door, smiling strangely. "You would not care to reconsider and let us in for a chat? We have much to discuss, and I would give anything to hear you play the violin again." Gradually his smile faded away. "The managers are buffoons, and the Viscount is a young puppy with less breeding than any of his dogs. I doubt you will believe me, but I would like to help you. I would not willingly bring harm to you. Perhaps a part of you is deformed, twisted, corrupted, and I do not refer only to your face. Still, there should be a place in this world for a man such as you. Your genius is wasted down here, wasted. Can the rats appreciate your music? Can even Christine Daaé? Please open the door."

But there was only silence, that cold, dark silence which had sunk its tendrils through the very stones and claimed the black waters for its own. We were further beneath the earth than most corpses; the tombs of Paris and their dead lay above us, nearer to the sun. I remembered Dante's Satan frozen in ice at the center of Hell, and the fear closed about my heart.

"For God's sake, Sherlock." I clutched at his arm. "Let us get away from here. *Now.*"

His eyes remained fixed on the door. "Very well."

Somehow I managed to stumble back into the boat. Falling into that icy water seemed the worst thing I could possibly imagine.

Holmes pulled off his tweed jacket and handed it to me. "Put this on."

"Are you not cold?" I stammered, putting it on only too gladly.

"Not particularly. The punting has warmed me. You have greater need of it than I." He stepped into the boat, then pulled free the rope and used the pole to shove us away from the landing. My hands made the lantern shake. I set it on my knees, but still it quivered. "There is food in the satchel, Henry."

"I have no appetite."

"It might warm you."

"No."

"Seven arches, then we turn to the left. It will seem faster returning."

The boat glided through the water, Holmes's breath forming a halo of white vapor about his head. His white shirt seemed very bright set against all the darkness. His vest, trousers, and the bowler hat appeared black.

"Henry, humor me. Close the shutter of that dark lantern for a moment. I wish to conduct an experiment."

"But it will be pitch black."

"For a moment only."

"Very well." I closed the shutter, plunging us into darkness. I should have guessed the effect it would have on me. Thoughts of the grave came to mind again and of the tons of stone overhead crashing down upon us. I bit down hard on my lower lip, then said, "Enough?"

"Do you see the light?"

"Light?" I blinked, then noticed a faint, liquid luminescence all about us, a cold blue. "What is it?"

"Some naturally occurring phosphorescence."

The longer we sat in darkness, the bluer it seemed. However, all was formless: dancing points of light and strange swirling colors similar to what you see when you close your eyes and stare at the inside of your eyelids. I could not tell what was real, what a trick of the mind. The silence was absolute, the faint murmur of Holmes's breathing all that I could hear.

"It is... strangely beautiful," he said.

At once I opened up the lantern, flooding the dark waters again with light. "Let us go! We must leave this place—you must leave it."

He turned toward me, and for an instant his eyes were angry. "Very well, Henry. You are correct, as usual." He began to pole, and the boat slowly gained speed.

I feared we might hear the siren's voice, but the rest of our journey was made in uninterrupted silence.

Christine Daaé caused a sensation in *La Juive*. Carlotta's partisans were out in force, determined to vanquish the usurper, but they were either overwhelmed or converted on the spot. Daaé's portrayal of the Jew Eleazar's fragile, persecuted daughter, Rachel, was everything one could wish for, both musically and dramatically. Her voice soared into the high registers, the tone incredibly beautiful, yet full and (so Holmes assured me) absolutely on pitch. At the final curtain call the crowd went berserk, applauding loudly and shouting bravos.

As a measure of our reconciliation, the Viscount had invited us to his box, and he, too, applauded enthusiastically. All the same, in his eyes I discerned a certain wary puzzlement. He had the type of leaden, petty soul which could never comprehend her art, and her singing was also a link to the despised Erik, her maestro. The Count's manner toward us was glacial, his fury barely contained. No doubt he did not care for his brother's game of feigned engagement and our part in it.

Holmes was weary. Our journey on the underground lake had made quite an impression on us both. I had caught a slight cold, and

Holmes seemed disappointed, discouraged.

After the performance on Saturday night, we did not return to the Opera House until the following Monday. The managers were in exceptionally good spirits. *La Juive* had sold out, and the papers were filled with rhapsodic praise for Christine Daaé, the critics for once unanimous in their verdict. Already the managers were receiving telegrams of inquiry from their counterparts throughout Europe. Tickets for *Faust*, scheduled for the following Saturday, were the most precious commodity in all of Paris.

Later that afternoon, Holmes and I were chatting in the foyer with Monsieur Bossuet when Christine Daaé and the Viscount walked by on their way to the auditorium. Bossuet was telling us about the new electrical light system which would be illuminating the exterior of the Opera on Saturday evening. Holmes brought our conversation to a close, then drew me away and led me upstairs. We went to the door on the grand tier marked Five. Holmes took out a key, unlocked the door, and gestured for me to enter. Once inside, I placed both hands on the golden railing and looked down.

The stalls were empty except for Christine and the Viscount. They sat in Row One, their backs to us. The high-pitched ripple of her laughter filled the empty hall. A few workmen on the stage were dismantling the set from *La Juive*. Holmes grasped my arm with one hand, and pointed with the other to our right near the back of the theater. Even had I not recognized the features, the astrakhan hat would have given him away.

"The Persian," I whispered. "Whatever is he doing here?"

Holmes shrugged. He turned, then stared intently at the gilded pillar to the left side of the box, the palm of one hand resting upon his waist. Suddenly he dropped down to his knees, bent over, and peered closely at the red carpet. "Open the door, please. I require more light."

I did as he asked. "What is it?" I said. He did not even seem to hear me.

"The box has not been visited since Saturday night, and Erik has large feet, unusually large." Finally he rose. "Come." He closed the door behind us and locked it. Before I could question him further, he said, "I do not like the Persian being here. Perhaps I am being premature in my judgment, but it does not bode well. We have problems enough. Erik has made too many enemies, far too many. His only other friend is Christine Daaé, and she cannot be trusted."

"And who is the other?"

He gave me a disapproving glance. "Sherlock Holmes."

"Are you serious?"

"Certainly." He started down the stairs.

"But we do not even know the fellow."

"Ah, Henry, you could not be more mistaken. I know him only too well."

Holmes went to the large dressing room of the men's chorus. It was deserted that afternoon. He opened a leather satchel and withdrew some dirty clothes. "Put these on." He removed his own frock coat and unbuttoned the buttons of his waistcoat.

"What for?"

He gave me that disapproving glance.

"I am sorry. Obviously we are to be disguised again."

"Exactly. I want to keep an eye on Christine Daaé, the Viscount, and the Persian. Especially the Persian."

He put on the blue workman's clothes, then took out his makeup box and sat before a mirror. He parted his hair in the middle, then began constructing a false mustache.

I sniffed at the shirt he had given me, then frowned. "Sometimes you carry verisimilitude too far."

"One can never carry verisimilitude too far."

"Where on earth did you get these?"

"From two gentlemen I spied on the street. In return I purchased them new suits and boots at a department store. We were all most satisfied with the arrangement."

I pulled on a worn boot. "At least the boots fit."

"I confirmed that before making the offer. They had the most curious expressions on their faces when I inquired about their shoe sizes. How does this look?"

I could not help but laugh. Remarkably dexterous and quick, he had transformed himself almost in an instant. His nose, that angular beak, had grown bulbous and assumed the blotchy red, characteristic of the Gaul too well acquainted with the fruit of the grape. Two teeth were blacked out; a large dark mustache had appeared; and he wore a black beret cocked to the left.

"No one will ever recognize you."

"Now it is your turn." He applied spirit gum along my jaw.

"Oh, no—not a false beard again! Taking the dreadful things off afterwards is such a nuisance."

"It hides the shape of your face. I shall also wax your mustache."

"You know that I loathe mustache wax. It is acceptable only for would-be emperors, cavalry officers, and circus strong men."

Before long I had a reddish beard of a different hue than my brown hair and mustache. Holmes applied a reddish wax to my mustache, curving each end to a point. He then blacked out a tooth, dirtied a few more, and jammed a blue cap similar to a French gendarme's on my head.

"Very good. You are an inspector from the gas company. We are examining the footlights and checking for leaks." He strapped a carpenter's leather tool belt about his waist. "I am your somewhat stupid assistant. Can you speak French gutturally, low and raspy in the throat."

"*Quelque chose comme ça?*"

"Perfect!"

"I hope I do not have to speak too much. My throat is still inflamed."

"We shall need you to do the talking because you have no accent. Remember, too, that you are a lower-class sort of person. Refinement and politeness are definitely to be avoided."

"I think I shall enjoy this."

"Good." He withdrew a packet of cheap Turkish cigarettes. "These would also help create the right impression."

"Not when I begin coughing and choking. Besides, would it be wise if we are checking the gas lines?"

Holmes began to laugh, gently at first, but soon with an unrestrained merriment that was rare. "Henry, Henry—you have me! How could I be so incredibly obtuse? This will make a nice bit of business. You will reprimand me and continually admonish me to put out my cigarettes." He lit a cigarette and let it dangle uncharacteristically from the corner of his mouth. "Here. Carry this." He gave me a large wrench from his belt. "And slouch."

"All the things my mother forbade."

"Exactly so."

Holmes might not have mastered the lower regions of the Palais Garnier, but the middle part he knew quite well. We went upstairs, down a corridor, and came out on the right wing of the vast stage.

"Let us attempt to get as near as possible to our two lovers. Remember, Henry, you are in charge. I know that you are at heart a thespian, bearing the histrionic French blood of our family in your veins, and I have complete confidence in you. Play the petty, smug official with an inflated view of his importance. Lead the way."

Swelling my chest and assuming what I hoped was the air of a minor tyrant, I started forth. Two men working at the set glanced briefly at us, then began hammering again.

"Begin with the footlights," I said imperiously. Holmes gave me a wary look, then advanced. No one would have ever believed this fearful, stupid workman was the world's foremost detective and one of the greatest minds in all of Europe. "Put out your cigarette, imbecile!" He complied fearfully, then we knelt before the float and peered down at the lamps at that end. Holmes unscrewed the fastenings which held the glass cover over a burner.

Christine and the Viscount sat a few feet away, and we heard them clearly. For the next two hours we endured the most trivial and insipid conversation imaginable while Sherlock "checked" each burner of the innumerable footlights on the gargantuan stage. In all fairness, even the discourse of the noblest and cleverest lovers must sound ridiculous to all but themselves. Nevertheless, the Viscount's constant flattery, lines such as, "You have the finest pair of eyes I have ever seen," or, "You know, my dear, you are quite, quite lovely," combined with Christine's high, rippling laughter soon grew tiresome.

Even seated, she hung upon his arm as if worried he might escape her, and he often clasped her shoulder and gave it a squeeze. In my experience, those couples most given to ostentatious displays of affection are most lacking in the genuine article. One sees a pair of love doves closely entwined for some six months or so, then mysteriously, they vanish, only to soon reappear, each joined to a new partner in devotion. Michelle is not given to these public displays, but in private I am certain no woman could equal her passion.

Later, the two lovers came on stage and wandered about, examining the sets going up for *Faust*. The Persian had left the main floor, and Holmes soon spotted him watching from the wings. At one point Christine came over and smiled at me.

"*Bonjour, Monsieur.* I have not seen you before." I scowled by way of reply. "What are you doing?"

"Checking for leaks." My voice croaked so I doubted even Michelle would have recognized me.

"Keep a civil tongue in your head, my good fellow!" The Viscount was put off by my truculence.

Christine only laughed and seized his arm. She wore a striking aquamarine dress which emphasized her tiny waist and slender hips. How good it was to have the wretched bustle out of fashion so you could once again discern something of a woman's true shape!

"He is only doing his job," she said.

I noticed Holmes staring somewhat lasciviously at her. For an instant I thought the look genuine, then realized he would never so willingly betray his true feelings. "Here now, beef head," I said. "Keep your eyes fixed on that there burner."

The Viscount frowned, but Christine laughed again. She disengaged herself from him, then raised her arms and spun about twice, her skirt opening up. She reached center stage, then slowly sang some scales, starting low and going up a full two octaves.

"What are you doing?" the Viscount asked.

"Singing." She sang the scales faster, then burst into song, her high lyric voice filling the vast empty auditorium of red and gold. I recognized the melody from the conclusion of *Faust*, Marguerite's triumphant outpouring as the angels come down to save her and carry her up to heaven.

The strangest expression came over the Viscount, one blending fear, admiration, and simple confusion. He seized her arm, and her music stopped. "You are hurting my ears," he said loudly.

For an instant the anger showed in her green eyes, then she laughed that same tiresome laugh. "What a compliment!"

"Come, my beloved, you know that I admire your singing, but..."

"It hurts your ears."

"You merely startled me. I have never heard you sing so close to me. I did not realize it was so… loud."

She gave him a hard, ironic glance which was truer than her earlier looks of loving idolatry. Rather bewildered, he turned and wandered toward the rear of the stage. "Oh, I say, Christine. Someone has left a trap door open. I wager a person might break his neck if he fell down there."

Holmes was working on a lamp, but I was watching Christine. Her expression of lively good humor vanished. She went white, her eyes and mouth widening with fear, then she rushed to the Viscount's side and seized his arm, not amorously this time. "For God's sake, be careful, Raoul—be careful!"

His smile was stiff and smug. "You have shown me all your empire above ground, Christine: this vast auditorium, the dressing rooms, the dance foyers, the wings and flies overhead there; but you have not taken me below ground. Strange tales are told of the lower parts of the Opera, tales every bit as bizarre as the fairy stories of the Bretons. Shall we descend together and explore the underworld?"

"Never—not on your life! It is nothing to joke about. The cellars and the lake are *his*—his alone." She drew him forcefully back from that black square gaping up at them like the grave.

"So he lives down there?"

Horror contorted her face, but by sheer will she managed a grotesque smile. "Of course not! Sometimes I wonder if you are quite sane." She pulled again at his arm, but he shook her off abruptly.

"If *I* am sane? Why then are you so fearful? Shall we have a look?"

"*No!*"

Her voice had hardly ceased when the trap door slammed shut with a loud bang. The noise made me and the workmen on the sets start. Christine put her fist over her open mouth, and the Viscount took a step back. His laughter was strained.

"Let us go somewhere else—somewhere higher. Soon it will be dark. Please, Raoul—*please*."

"Oh very well." He smiled as if he were only indulging a whim, but I could tell that he, too, was shaken. He let Christine draw him toward the wing.

Holmes stood up; his eyes briefly went out of character, revealing a strange fervor. "Time for a smoke, huh?" He jerked his head in the direction they had gone.

"Oh, I suppose so," I said.

The sounds of the Viscount's and Christine's feet on the metal staircase echoed softly across the huge stage. Holmes lit his cigarette, but his eyes remained fixed on the shadows above us. Suddenly his arm jerked up, his long, bony finger pointing.

"*There,* Henry—do you see him?"

It was so dark offstage that I saw mostly shadows above us, the faint shapes of innumerable ropes and the metal stairways fading into the gloom. "Whom?"

"A shadow—*there.*" He pointed again.

I laughed. "The whole blasted place is nothing but shadow."

He slipped a wrench back into the leather tool belt, then unfastened the buckle and set the belt down on the floor. "We must follow them."

My steps were tentative, and I faltered before the metal stairway leading up into the blackness. "I saw nothing. It is too dark. You must be mistaken."

Holmes dropped his cigarette and crushed it under foot. "I shall go alone." He started up at a brisk pace.

I took a deep breath and tried to quell the fear clutching for my heart. "Wait—I shall come, too." I seized the cold iron of the rail, then took a step.

"Do not look down, Henry. Only do not look down and you will be fine."

"Yes," I whispered. "I shall not look down."

He stopped abruptly and whispered, "Hush."

Above us the Viscount said, "Slower, my dearest—why hurry so?"

"We must go higher, as high as we can."

Holmes turned to me, his face a white oval in the shadow, comical looking with the black beret, red nose, and enormous mustache. "They are going to the roof," he said softly.

"Oh, damnation," I groaned.

We passed one of the ephemeral metal landings which one can see through. Round and round we went, my right hand always clinging to the railing. My hand was damp, clammy, and I held my head so rigidly straight that my neck soon felt stiff. Pondering how far below the stage was, I occasionally considered looking down; a wave of fear would wash over me, making me vow to abstain from such foolish reveries. This resolution never held for more than a minute or two; before long the same lunatic thoughts recommenced.

We passed the higher levels where banks of lights sat, including the spectacular limelights, and at last we came to the bells I had heard about, huge, curving shapes of brass all in a row, glistening faintly in the darkness. What if someone were to ring them? This close my hearing would be damaged, but worse yet, in the confusion I might clap my hands over my ears, stagger about, hit the rail, and plunge over.

"Are you all right, Henry?" Holmes whispered.

"No."

"You are a brave man. I know how fearful and irrational a phobia can be, and you…"

A reddish-yellow light suddenly burst through the darkness above us, a black silhouette blotting out part of the light. "Oh, Raoul, let us go outside. We shall be king and queen with all of Paris at our feet."

I nearly bumped into Holmes. His hand seized my arm. "Steady,

Henry." As we stood silently in the darkness, I became aware that my legs were shaking. Holmes was laboring to breathe silently in spite of being winded. "They have gone outside. Only two or three levels remain. Try to…"

Abruptly a black shape passed before the light, eclipsing it for an instant like some moon. "Dear Lord," I murmured.

"My shadow, the one I saw earlier," Holmes said, his tone faintly ironic. "Courage, Henry. It will not be long now. You will feel better once we are on the roof."

"The *roof.*" My voice gave me away.

"You will have solid ground, or at least something akin to it, up there, not this flimsy metal. It makes even me somewhat edgy. Come on.

We climbed two more flights and stepped out onto the landing near the open doorway. "Wait," Holmes said. I complied, flattening my back against the wall near the door and keeping as far from the railing as possible. Holmes glanced outside, then said, "Follow me." He slipped past the open door and continued along the catwalk. I attempted to go forward while at the same time keeping my back against the wall, the result being more a sidestep than a walk. The catwalk turned, passing over the front of the stage far above the proscenium arch. Some light came from the depths below, but above was only darkness; the stairway had led higher, the stage roof being taller than the auditorium dome.

"Where are we going?" I asked.

"There should be another door at the opposite end which also provides access to the roof."

It was dark enough that I would have had to lean over the rail to see the ground below; thus I tried to pretend that I was not very high.

"Ah, here we are." Holmes slowly opened the door, the brilliant reddish-yellow light making us both blink. "Remain here for a moment." He stepped outside.

I stood there, back to the wall, the cool evening breeze wafting across my face. My hands were still sweaty, but the light and the air were comforting.

Holmes reappeared. Although the bulbous red nose and the big mustache remained, the character of the loutish workman was gone, replaced by Holmes's usual intensity. "Come along, Henry, but keep very still."

The air was wondrously cool and fresh, the clouds overhead a brilliant pink from the setting sun. I was so happy to be outside, away from the darkness and skeletal metal stairways, that seeing the roofs of Paris below did not have the usual terrifying effect upon me. If the lake and Erik's abode were the underworld, then this truly was the celestial realm, the summit of what the Viscount had called Christine Daaé's kingdom.

Distantly I heard her voice. Holmes headed for the auditorium dome. The copper hemisphere and its ornamental ridges had weathered green, but the "lantern," a small structure at the summit with openings for venting the gas chandelier, was gilded, the gold dazzling under the fiery sky. A row of grotesque masks topped the lantern, the black holes of their gaping mouths contrasting with their golden faces. Other faces, women carved in stone, ringed the bottom of the dome, and below them was a stone wall interspersed with windows, a golden lyre set in each casement. Holmes stopped before a window, then started around the dome. Behind us the stage roof rose to its triangular peak some thirty feet higher; and there, at the summit of the Opera, stood the greenish statue of a naked Apollo crowned with a laurel wreath and holding his gilded lyre to the heavens. Beside him crouched two muses, Music and Poetry, if my memory served me.

We crept forward. The voices of Christine and the Viscount grew louder. Before the dome was the rectangular roof covered with lead tiles which was above the grand stairway. The two lovers stood near the outer perimeter wall, their backs to us.

"But you must go!" Christine's voice was shrill.

"I shall not. I have already told the Commodore to find another man for his Arctic voyage. You must have known a pretended engagement would not be enough to satisfy me."

"Your brother... He will be furious."

"Most assuredly, but why should we care? My inheritance is no longer under his control. Let Philippe sulk, if he will. Christine, I can take you away from here. You can be free of this Erik once and for all."

"Is it possible?" Her voice was full of anguish.

"Yes, of course, if only we love one another."

She began to cry. "Oh, I cannot bear to go back, but I promised him. It is so dark and cold under the earth. I am too young to be buried alive. I pity him, truly I do, with all my heart and soul, and yet he is so horrible, so deformed. The most awful thing was when he wept, the tears in the dark eyes of that ghastly, tortured face. Without reason, without justice, he is damned, and so am I, Raoul–so am I!"

"What utter nonsense! You must know that I love you, that I adore you. Do not cry, my Christine. I am no genius, nor a musician, but I do love you. I know I can make you happy. I can give you anything you want, anything at all."

"Can you, Raoul?"

"You know I can. Run away with me–now, this very night."

"I–I cannot. I gave him my promise."

"But he forced you–he forced you!"

The Viscount clenched his fists. The warm, rosy light was fading, the sky all awash with a sinister crimson, as if it were dying, bleeding into night. A strong, sultry wind blew upon the couple, carrying their words back to us.

"Who is this monster who has such a hold over you?"

Her reply was faint, hardly more than a whispered breath carried by the wind. "Erik."

"Who is this damned Erik! For God's sake, Christine, you owe me some explanations! Tell me, he does live underground, does he not?"

"Yes."

"Tell me!"

Christine nodded wearily. "He was my Angel of Music. Wait—you shall hear all. You are right, I owe you, my dearest, that much at least. I heard his voice many weeks ago, many months even. I cannot remember when I did not hear that voice. I asked him if he was the Angel of Music whom Papa had told me about, and he said he was. He taught me to sing, Raoul. Oh, how he taught me! My voice was weak, silly, and stupid, but he made it burn with beauty like a pure, hot flame. Every day he worked with me, but it was our secret until the gala. 'You are ready now,' he said. 'Show them,' and I did, but then, then…" Her voice grew hushed. "You came, and everything began to change. 'Come to Perros,' he told me, 'And you will hear me play 'The Resurrection of Lazarus' even as your father did, at the very stroke of midnight.' And he did—I heard him.

"I have not told you how beautiful his real voice is, how melodious, how gentle and warm. Who can blame me for believing it was the voice of an angel? I honestly think that when I die and hear the real angels, their voices will be no sweeter, no more majestic, than his. Can you now understand my fury when you told me someone was tricking me? I believed absolutely in my angel, more even than in God, for God was not real to me as my Angel of Music was real."

"But in the end he was a false angel." The Viscount's voice had an undercurrent of cruelty, restrained, but obvious enough.

"Remember the night the chandelier fell?" Christine asked. "I was terribly upset. I had hated Carlotta, but what happened to her was the worst nightmare of every singer. During the uproar I fled to my room and begged for the Angel to come to me. He did not answer, and I began to weep. At last I fell asleep, but music woke me, 'The Resurrection of Lazarus' again. This time the voice sang the words along with the violin: 'Come! And believe in me! Who believes in me shall live! Walk! Whoso hath believed in me shall never die!' I was half awake, half asleep, and somehow... I went to him through the mirror."

The Viscount started. "The mirror!"

"Yes. A tall man dressed all in black with a black mask waited for me. 'Come,' he said, and it was the voice. I followed him down into the darkness; his lantern gave almost no light. Nearby was César, the white horse from *Le Prophète*. The man helped me mount, and we continued our descent deeper and deeper, further underground than I had ever been before. At last we came to a great blue lake, which we crossed in a black barque. By then I was weary and felt strange, almost as if I had been drugged. He carried me into his curious little house filled with beautiful and terrible things: canvases of far-off places, Persian carpets from the *Arabian Nights*, beautiful vases and bronze statues, an organ that covered an entire wall, and the ebony coffin with a red pillow where he sleeps.

"'Who are you?' I asked. 'You are no angel.'

"He must have heard the sadness in my voice. 'It is true, Christine. I am not an angel, nor a ghost, nor a phantom. I am only Erik, and I love you.'

"At that he left me, and I must have slept until well into the next morning. When I awoke and saw where I was, when I saw that the strange house and its dark occupant still existed, it was as if the dreams of the night continued unabated. He led me to a table where the most wonderful breakfast was laid out, but he ate nothing. Indeed, I never saw him eat. Afterward we sang while he played the organ. He has the most incredible voice; he can reach the high notes of a lyric tenor or plunge so low in the bass that he would make a perfect Mephistopheles. We were both rather shy and quiet, but happy, I believe. The first day I worried about missing rehearsals and what my friends might be fearing, but the second day such thoughts came hardly at all. It was so… peaceful. But then came the third day." A moan escaped from her lips, its intensity catching me by surprise.

"Go on." The Viscount's voice was hard.

Christine bowed her head. Only a faint pink coloring remained in the western sky, and her bright blue dress was turning dark gray. "He wore a black mask, and I wondered what lay beneath it. He was tall, thin, and angular, but neither his body nor voice suggested any illness, any blot, which might mar his countenance. Oh, I considered that he might be scarred or pockmarked, but I convinced myself that his face must correspond to the sweetness of his voice and the gentleness of his manner." A sharp laugh escaped her. "Dear God, what a silly, stupid little fool I was! I knew nothing–*nothing*. He was playing the organ, part of his composition, an opera entitled *Don Juan Triomphant.* I should have suspected from his music. It was beautiful but terrible, full of strange dissonances, cries of anguish and dread mixed with its glory. As he played, I crept nearer and nearer. He was so caught up in his music that my stealth was wasted, a gratuitous insult. I snatched away the mask, and before he could turn away I saw his face."

Christine wept. She clutched at the stone wall with both hands, swaying slightly. The Viscount seized her arm to steady her. It was odd to witness such a scene, but to have their faces turned away, hidden. To us, they were masked, even as Erik, only their voices revealed.

"I have seen him," the Viscount said coldly. "Both at Perros and at the Opera as the Red Death. You need not describe him to me."

"No? Well, then may I describe his pain to you? He gave a cry as though I had stabbed him through the heart. Over and over he repeated, 'Why? Why? Why?' I tried to answer, to justify my folly, to somehow explain away his appearance, but nothing could soothe him. He writhed about the floor, moaning and clutching at his poor hideous face. At last he regained some measure of his senses. He stood and advanced toward me, and for the first time I feared him.

"He is a good foot and a half taller than I, taller even than the Englishman Holmes or his cousin. I could not take my eyes off his horrible face. It was incomprehensible that his beautiful dark eyes could have such a setting. 'Now you are damned,' he said. 'We are both damned. You must rot here beneath the earth with me. I can never let you go now.' Then he took my tiny hand in his and raised it to his face. I was truly frightened; I did not know what he could be doing. He pressed my fingernails into his ravaged cheek, pressed until I felt his flesh give way and tear open, then pulled my fingers downward.

"'What are you doing?' I cried. In vain I attempted to pull my hand away; my nails left four bloody scratches on each cheek before he released me." She sobbed once.

The sky was dark except for the reflected glow of the lights of Paris. The black form of the Viscount seemed to swell up, his hands clenching into fists. "The monster! Oh, how I hate him! You must hate him, too—you do hate him, do you not, Christine?"

"No," she said.

"No, of course not—why, you love him! Your fear, your terror, these are all part of love, love of the most exquisite kind, the kind people do not admit even to themselves, the kind that gives one a thrill even to consider. Think of it, a madman in a romantic underground palace." His voice had grown steadily more sarcastic.

"Then you want me to return to him?" Christine's voice quivered with anger. "Have a care, Raoul. He lays a great and tragic love at my feet. If I return to him, you will not see me again."

The wind swelled, suddenly colder and more intense. "Finish your story. He released you at last?"

"Yes, although I stayed with him until the masked ball."

"And you went back to him even then? For God's sake, Christine— why did you not flee him? I would have helped you to escape, even had you spurned me. Even now I can give you money to do with as you please."

"I gave my word."

"Your word." The sarcasm had returned.

"And does your word mean so little to you, to a member of the vaunted French nobility always prating about honor! Do you keep your word only so long as it is convenient? How then should I take all your vows of love?"

Holmes turned to me. I could not see his face very well in the darkness, but I could imagine his glee.

"It is not the same thing."

"Is it not?" Her sarcasm was more cutting than his.

They were both silent, the wind moaning about them, sweeping across the dark, empty roof of the Palais Garnier. The sound was plaintive, and for an instant I fancied I actually heard a man moaning, too. However, the wind died away into silence, and I knew I must have imagined it.

"For a day after I had exposed his face, he left the mask off. I think he wished to punish me. I tried to pretend his horrible face no longer frightened me, but all my resolutions melted away when that gruesome death's head with the sad eyes stared at me. I could not meet those eyes. Neither of us succeeded at our charade, and he put his mask back on. Too late, however, because I had ruined everything. Even our singing was lifeless and sad. After three days of silence, I pleaded with him to release me, if only for a little while. He told me he had planned to let me return for *La Juive* and *Faust,* especially for *Faust,* but he made me promise I would return to him afterward. Then, he said, he would decide my fate and his own. And he told me... he told me that he loved me still, that he could not bear for me to love... to love another man."

"I'll wager the dog did! If you are foolish enough to return to him, do you think that you will ever see the light of day again? He will keep you as his slave and his toy forever!" The wind hurled the Viscount's shrill, angry words back at us.

"Perhaps he will," she replied softly.

"Perhaps! Christine, Christine, you cannot do such a thing—I cannot let you!" He seized her hand. "Oh, Christine, must you torture us both? As God is my witness, I love you! I know I can be arrogant and unkind, but that does not mean I cannot love you. My voice may not be the voice of an angel, but this face is, at least, not that of a demon. Your angel is a madman. Let me take you away from him. Christine, my dearest, will you marry me?"

I would not have thought the Viscount could surprise me, but he had. Christine was stunned. "What?"

"You heard me. I want you to be my wife, the Viscountess de Chagny."

"Oh, Raoul, you cannot mean it. Your brother..."

"Be damned! He can marry whomever he wants, and I shall do the same. We can be married tomorrow if you wish—tonight even."

Christine laughed, but it was joyful rather than derisive. "You cannot mean it."

"You think not? You are wrong." He reached into his pocket: "I have only been waiting for the right moment. I have bought you a ring, a genuine engagement ring, and a fine one. Can you see it?"

"Not very well, but…"

"The diamond was the largest they had."

"Oh, I am sure it is beautiful. Oh, Raoul, I shall marry you, and we shall go away together and be happy, but first… It must be on Sunday, the day after *Faust*. It is best, anyway, to be married on Sunday."

The wind had picked up again, the air turbulent, but Raoul was still and silent. To our right, over the city, I saw yellow-white lightning leap across the clouds, illuminating the sky. A few seconds later came the dull rumble of thunder.

"You are still thinking of him," Raoul said. "Even now."

"I have my career, my singing, to consider as well. Will anyone ever trust me again if I run off? The performance is sold out. Let me do *Faust,* and then we shall go off together that very night."

"As Viscountess de Chagny you need not sing for your living. You will be well provided for."

"But I *want* to sing, Raoul. I must sing, even as I must breathe or walk or love you! I shall still love you and be a good wife, I swear to you on my heart."

Another silence, interrupted by the rumble of the thunder, closer now. "Oh, very well, Christine, but it must be Saturday night after the performance. I shall have my coach ready. We shall surprise everyone, especially Philippe. He will come around eventually. He will no more be able to resist your charms than I."

"Oh, Raoul, I am so happy."

Holmes turned and whispered softly, "We should go. This is becoming mere intrusion on our part."

"You are right," I replied. The whole thing had left a sour taste in my mouth. Perhaps the Viscount would be a good husband, but I disliked him intensely. He seemed such a child, and so too, ultimately, did Christine Daaé. A diamond ring and a proposal had conquered all.

"Put on the ring–go ahead."

"Very well."

"Christine–you must remove his ring first."

"Why?" The question did sound remarkably obtuse.

"You cannot wear the rings of two men! It must be one or the other."

"But… so long as I wear his ring, he promised to protect me, to watch over me. 'Lose this ring and you shall know my wrath,' he said. It is no marriage ring."

"Christine!" the Viscount shouted. "Must I yield to you on everything–on every point? I was a fool to think you loved me!" He turned away in our direction, but she seized his arm. Holmes and I flattened ourselves against the dome wall and held very still.

"Wait!" she cried. The wind swept past us, and I felt a few wet drops on my face. The rain would be cool, that of spring rather than winter. "See, I take off his ring and put on yours. Oh, my betrothed of only a moment's time, if I did not love you, I would never offer you my lips!"

The two black shapes came together in a violent embrace, and if I could not actually see their lips meet, I could certainly imagine it. I heard a tinkle as something hit the roof and rolled a small way. Erik's ring, I reflected sadly. Holmes squeezed my arm, and we had taken a step or two when a terrible, pained scream filled the night. So completely unexpected, it would have startled anyone, but it was of such intensity and conveyed such anguish, that my immediate thought was that someone had been killed or mortally wounded. However, the cry had come from above, which made no sense. The only thing higher was the stage roof with its statue of Apollo.

Just then a river of lightning flowed down, flooding the roof with brilliant white light. I saw the Viscount and Christine, arms still about each other, faces raised, then turning my head I saw the green Apollo with some black form clinging to him like a monstrous growth. One hand grasped the golden lyre, while a black arm and skeletal fingers clasped the god's chest, a great black cloak flapping about their shoulders in the wind. But the worst was that face alongside the god's, a white oval with black holes for eyes, a smaller hole for a nose, and the gaping black mouth with all its teeth bared, the mouth howling in agony, but all sound eclipsed by the cataclysmic bang of the thunder.

Then the darkness returned, and Holmes pulled me back to the dome. Christine Daaé was screaming.

"Stop it!" someone shouted. "Stop it!" Then another voice shouted, "Follow me!"

"Let them pass," Holmes whispered.

The rain striking my face was cold. The Viscount and Christine swept by, a tall figure behind them whose astrakhan hat was recognizable even in the dark. Christine wept loudly. "He heard everything—he knows. Oh God, I am so ashamed."

"Hush, dearest," the Viscount said.

"We must hurry," the Persian said. "I know a way to lose him."

They went through the door. Holmes at last released his iron grip on my arm. Another flash of lightning, thankfully more distant this time, lit up the roof. Apollo was alone now except for his two lady friends, Poetry and Music. The rain fell in earnest.

"Wait a moment." Holmes walked over to the perimeter wall, knelt down and felt about.

Walking over to him, I received a gust of wet wind full in the face.

"What are you looking for?"

"This." He held up something. "Christine Daaé's ring. Let us get inside. The roof is no place to be during a thunderstorm."

We stepped through the door, and I felt a familiar, but weary, fear—my vertigo. So much had happened, and luckily it was too dark to see much, the only light coming from the stage far below. Holmes took out a box of matches, lit one, then looked about. If he had seemed comical before in his disguise, now he appeared sinister with that ugly nose and black mustache. The black beret was lost somewhere on the roof.

"Ah, here we are." He had found a gas fixture. He lifted the glass cover, turned the cock, then lit it. "It should not be long." He took out a cigarette.

I was rather rattled. "What should not be long?"

"Erik must have taken these stairs to an outlet on the stage roof near Apollo. He will have to return the same way. This is the only way down. I think we shall meet him quite soon."

The logic of this made my mouth go dry. "Is that wise? He is… hardly in the best of moods, I fear."

Holmes gave a brusque, weary laugh. "Comic understatement suits you, Henry. I should think he is in a very black mood indeed." He glanced at the narrow metal catwalk above, the twin of the one upon which we stood. I had my back against the wall and was reflecting that meeting the Phantom up here might well prove dangerous. "Erik!" he shouted. "Please come down. We are unarmed and mean you no harm."

His voice had a faint echoey quality, and afterward I heard the dim sound of the storm outside. "Sherlock, are you certain…?"

"I know not. Erik, *please*—we can wait all night if need be!" He drew in on his cigarette, and I had the bizarre thought of spending the night trying to sleep on this narrow platform suspended high above the Opera.

It remained quiet for a long while. I began to relax, thinking the Phantom must have found another way down, when I heard the faint clang of a footstep above us. My heart seemed to stop beating. I raised my eyes and saw a dark, shadowy form through the metal grill above us.

"Ah, welcome, sir. Please come down." The shadow was still, then it moved, and I heard another footstep, then another; the sound changed when he reached the spiral staircase and started down.

He wore a long black cloak with a cowl and a black mask which covered his entire face. The mask blended into the darkness all about us, making it appear as if the cowl were empty. The eyes blazing at us from the holes in the mask had a blurry, liquid quality. He had been weeping, and I thought about how he must have felt watching that charming scene between Christine and the Viscount. If it had made me despondent, what had it done to him? He and Holmes locked eyes, and neither of them moved for a long time. I grew uneasy and again reflected upon our height from the ground.

At last the Phantom spoke: "Your meddling in my affairs grows tiresome." His voice was a remarkably warm and resonant baritone, the tone characteristic of a trained actor, and he spoke English with only the faintest hint of a French accent.

"I am sorry for that." Holmes's voice sounded thin and faintly nasal in comparison. "My intentions are not malicious; quite the contrary."

The Phantom laughed, the sound pitched higher than his speaking voice. "You will forgive me if I doubt you. My enemies' friends are my enemies."

"I do not consider those two buffoons who manage the Opera my friends, and the Viscount de Chagny is among the most disagreeable persons I have ever met."

"Yet you have your pay of them, your thousand francs a day, your thirty pieces of silver."

Holmes's thin lips formed a bitter smile. "You take their money as well. It has made you rich."

"Not that of the de Chagnys—*never*!"

Holmes sighed. "Let us not argue about trifles. I have longed to meet you since I first set foot in this theater, and the more I have discovered about you, the more curious I have grown."

The Phantom's laughter was cold. "Well, are you satisfied?"

"It is too early to tell. I shall let you know as soon as my opinion has formed."

"You have a sense of the comical, do you?"

"Yes. It is, no doubt, the best response to the tragic aspect of life. If we could not laugh, the pain might destroy us."

The Phantom drew back, then he and Holmes again stared at each other. "Perhaps there is more to you than I suspected."

Holmes gave one of his rare smiles where warmth prevailed over the ironic. "I hope so. I know there is a very great deal to you indeed. Your musical talent is phenomenal, your playing the best I have ever heard in the course of many years listening all across Europe."

"You know all that from hearing 'The Resurrection of Lazarus'? Perhaps that imposing setting, the Breton cemetery at midnight, had something to do with it."

Holmes shook his head. "Not at all. Your intonation was perfect, your command of the instrument total. Your violin had a familiar timbre. I suspect that it came from the same workshop as my own, that of master Antonio Stradivari in the early eighteenth century."

Erik was silent for a few seconds. "I have underestimated you. This makes things more… complicated."

"How so?"

The Phantom lowered his gaze, staring down below at the stage. "This is a war now. To the death. They would destroy me utterly, and the Viscount has taken…" A sudden swell of grief, quite unexpected, twisted that beautiful voice, and he looked away.

"I do not mean to be cruel," Holmes said. "I know there is no other pain like that which you feel, no other sadness which cuts quite so deep. Yet…"

"This is not some mere, silly infatuation from afar. I have watched

Christine through the mirror for weeks, drinking in her beauty even as I worked with her. I have seen her laugh and smile, heard her voice, her song. She is so beautiful, so terribly, utterly beautiful: the way she holds her hand, her palm so pink; the curve of her lips; the white expanse of her throat. Could any man, even a monster, withstand such beauty? You—you who have just met her—what can you know of it? You know nothing!" Rage swelled the dark figure, his arms spreading outward, the long fingers opening up.

"I know because I, too, have felt the same desperate love for a woman."

The two men regarded each other, and I felt stupid and rather shallow. I had fluttered about from woman to woman, always keeping my heart in reserve, always holding back. Even now when Michelle offered me her love, I rationalized, I equivocated, I found excuses. Perhaps I had never suffered as these two had, but I had never loved in the same way either. I had never, until recently, gone past the flirtatious stage; always I had fled before things became too serious. My cousin was the famed misogynist, yet he understood women and the human heart far better than I.

"It could not have been the same—you do not understand."

"I understand only too well. I also know the dangers of considering oneself unknowable, alien to all other men. You are not such a monster or phantom. You are only a man, as I am a man or as Henry is. We are all the same weak, pathetic creatures, and our only hope lies in trying to comprehend one another."

"You dare say that to me!" Erik screamed. "*To me!*"

"Yes, and I also dare to tell you that she is unworthy of you. She is only a child. There are other, better women."

The Phantom began to laugh, weakly at first, but then with more and more gusto. His laughter had the same power, the same cutting edge, as his voice. The sound rose into the darkness, echoing throughout the vast edifice about us. If any persons were below on the stage, they would hear it. Involuntarily my lips drew back into a smile, but there was nothing amusing in his laughter.

"Other men are not Erik—they do not have faces like this!" He wrenched away his mask, hurling it from him. The harsh gaslight emphasized the pallor of his death's head. The Red Death had prepared me, as had my work as a physician, but I still could not keep from drawing in my breath through clenched teeth. Sherlock, on the other hand, did not move a muscle. He stared at that hideous face as if it were absolutely unremarkable, as if the majority of mankind looked no worse. Dimly we heard the sound of the mask shattering on the floor below.

I tried to regain some of my physician's detachment and to render an accurate diagnosis. Something had eaten away his nose as leprosy might, and his skin had a clammy, sickly white appearance. Part of his upper lip was gone, so that the protruding teeth showed, and one cheekbone was higher than another. Four dark marks, scabs of dried blood, scored each cheek, and I remembered Christine telling how he had dug her nails into his flesh.

"Most unfortunate," Holmes said. He raised his right hand, tore the bulbous putty off his nose, threw it aside, then pointed at his nose. "This proboscis is hardly attractive either. Sometimes I wonder if I, too, might be better off without it!"

"How dare you!" the Phantom exclaimed, but then a laugh slipped from his twisted, maimed mouth, and soon he was laughing again, tears coming from his eyes. At last he whispered, "It is not the same."

"Why will you not let me be your friend?" Sherlock said.

"I can have no friends—I am the Phantom, the Ghost of the Opera, and you would do well to remember it! If you side with my enemies you will leave me no choice—I shall destroy you as well!"

"Why? For telling the truth? Christine and the Viscount are not worthy of your revenge. Leave them be. She will punish him far worse than you ever could."

The Phantom swayed, one hand shot out and gripped the rail. "She kissed him. Their lips touched. He will undress her and hold her white, beautiful body. He will kiss her bosom, her throat, her shoulders, and possess her utterly. He will have her." His voice broke, and Holmes took half a step back, his own face shaken.

"He will not have her!" I cried. "It is not the same. It will be her flesh only and nothing more, nothing that matters. It will bring them no closer."

"Silence!" The Phantom raised his right hand while the other gripped the rail. "I have warned you! Stay out of my way or I shall destroy you along with my other enemies, along with those silly fools. I, Erik, *le Fantôme de l'Opéra*, have spoken!"

What happened next went so quickly and was so unexpected that Holmes and I only watched like dumb children. The Phantom leapt over the rail, hurling himself out into the darkness.

"No!" Holmes cried.

I shuddered and turned away, but Holmes grabbed my arm. "Good Lord–look, Henry–*look*!"

I opened my eyes, then seized the rail with both hands. Several of the ropes out past us swayed, and below was the Phantom climbing down a rope, hand under hand, his black cape swirled about him, a dark stain against the pale brown of the stage floor. The vertigo overwhelmed me; I closed my eyes and clenched the metal pipe of the rail as hard as I could.

"How can he?" I murmured. "Perhaps he is not human after all."

"Do not be foolish, Henry. He is quite human, although completely unafraid of heights. I wonder if he ever did a turn as a sailor. See how quickly and skillfully he moves. If not human, he is an orangutan or other ape, not a specter. Blast it! Damnation!"

I opened my eyes, taking care not to look down. "What is wrong?"

"Everything—everything! How shall I ever track him through this cosmos of his? The lower part is a labyrinth that would baffle Theseus; this upper a jungle he can traverse like some monkey. He knows every corner; he has an uncanny strength and intelligence! His is a genius greater than my own."

"No," I said.

"Yes! This is hopeless."

"You told him yourself that you are both men, mortal men."

"I could perhaps trap him or destroy him, but I cannot and shall not! He is a far better man than... Damnation, Henry—it is hopeless, hopeless. I should go back to London and leave his wretched Opera to him. He is its spirit, its soul, and I imagined I could best him, he who was involved in every phase of its design and construction, he who has dwelt here for fifteen long years. Blast it, Henry, it *is* hopeless."

# Ten

Holmes left the Opera that night in a funk, while I was simply exhausted. Running up and down staircases and being frightened half out of my mind was quite fatiguing, and I slept a good ten hours. My dreams were troubled, but nothing could have awakened me that night.

When I went to see Holmes the next morning, it was immediately apparent that he had not slept a wink. He sat deep in thought before the fireplace, still wearing the clothes from the night before. We had changed out of our workmen's garb before leaving the Opera; otherwise, we would never have made it past the front lobby of the Grand Hôtel.

When I urged Sherlock to join me for breakfast, he dismissed me with a wave of his hand. "I must think. Go see Paris and do not bother me."

Restraining my tongue, I left abruptly. Although it was rather warm outside, the rain from the night before had continued. I spent the day wandering the Louvre and doing some thinking of my own. My vacillations toward Michelle now seemed childish to me, and I wondered if my concern about her previous suitors and her virginity was not really a manifestation of fear. With Michelle, I had neither the advantage of my worldly, male experience nor the excuse of her innocence. If our relationship floundered, I could not blame her inexperience or her failings (I knew her to be the most passionate of women); I could only blame myself. This explained the ambivalence I had felt toward her, an ambivalence my cousin could not comprehend.

Michelle was beautiful, intelligent, and full of life; why would any reasonable man not want her as his wife? Only one uncertain about love and the married state could reject such a woman, one who did not know his own heart, one who secretly feared such a woman.

I thought of the fervor of her kisses and of her touch, and my longing for her became an ache in my throat. No longer able to bear the naked nymphs all about me in bronze or marble, or the voluptuous nudes on canvas, I fled the Louvre and paced the streets of Paris, umbrella in hand. When it grew dark I returned to the hotel.

I knocked on Sherlock's door. "Are you there?"

"Yes, and still thinking."

"Will you not join me for dinner?"

"*No.*"

"Stubborn fool," I muttered.

In my current mood, eating alone in a splendid restaurant was a form of self-torture. I was angry with myself and my cousin, and of course I longed for Michelle's company. I had rather too much to drink and went to bed early.

The next morning I knocked on Sherlock's door again and received another hostile reception. I stalked away and wondered if I should simply pack up and leave. I could be in London—with Michelle—before nightfall. The familiar ache returned, and I cursed. I could not abandon my cousin, not now. I would wait at least until Sunday, until after *Faust*.

Not knowing what to do with myself, I took the familiar way to the Opera. Whom should I first see but Christine and the Viscount, arm in arm! Close by lurked the Persian and a small man in a dark suit. The Viscount said he wished to speak with my cousin, and I told him, truthfully enough, that I had not seen him that day. Christine hung upon the Viscount's arm, smiling radiantly, but her green eyes were curiously vacant, even fearful.

I returned to the hotel in the afternoon and spent two hours trying to write Michelle a letter. Not surprisingly, I found myself proposing marriage. However, I tore up letter after letter because my efforts seemed banal, or worse yet, they reminded me of something the Viscount had said to Christine Daaé! I had never been much for sweet talk, but the Viscount had ruined certain words and phrases for me forever. When I at last gave up in disgust, it was around seven and almost dark.

With a sigh, I rose and went again to Sherlock's door. When I knocked, he said, "Go away, Henry. I…"

Raining blows upon the wood, I roared, "Open this door at once!" in a voice which frightened an elderly couple walking down the hallway. The old woman murmured, "*Quelles bêtes, ces anglaises,*" and in truth, I felt like a savage.

Holmes opened the door. He was pale, his eyes bloodshot and angry, and his long face appeared even thinner, his nose even larger. Two days' worth of beard left a dark shadow across the lower half of his face. "Come in if you must."

"You look terrible," I said. The air was thick with tobacco smoke. "You have not eaten or slept for two days, I suppose. You have not even changed your clothes. This is disgusting—and quite simply childish. You will do no one any good by making yourself ill."

"I shall be the judge of that. I know what is best for me. Eating or sleeping are annoying distractions which cloud the brain."

"That is sheer nonsense," I said warmly.

"Henry, I will not be lectured to like a small boy."

"Nor will I. You asked me to come to Paris as your companion on this case. For two days you have not even spoken to me. Perhaps I should leave."

"Perhaps you should."

We stared at one another, and his face grew even paler. "Very well," I said. I whirled about and grasped the doorknob.

"Wait!"

I turned. He walked over to the chair by the fire, collapsed into it, and raised his feet, placing them on the ottoman. At that point the silence between us was healthy, forcing each of us to reflect upon the situation and his own shortcomings. At last Sherlock placed the fingertips of his right hand against his forehead. "You are right, Henry. Perhaps I am being childish. My mind does seem to be in something of a fog. Two days have been wasted. I am absolutely baffled."

"You need to sleep and eat. Why not join me for dinner? Sometimes the mind works best when not pushed too hard; in the midst of some diversion, the answer may come to you unsought for. You have struggled long enough."

"Yes. Sit down for a moment." I sat at the other chair near the fire. A large piece of coal did not flame, but glowed, throwing off great heat. "What am I to do with our poor Phantom? Perhaps you and I should leave Paris, but he undoubtedly plans to abduct Christine Daaé. I do think she would be better off underground with Erik than she would be married to the Viscount."

Sarcasm had crept into his voice, and I smiled. "I agree. By the way, I saw the Persian hanging about the Opera again."

"Hovering over our two lovebirds, no doubt. Did you also happen to notice a small, slight man of a pale, mottled complexion with a pencil-thin mustache? He would have been wearing a dark morning suit and a gray bowler."

"Why, yes. The man has something of the air of a ferret about him."

"Damnation. Another dismal turn of events. That is Mifroid of the Paris police. Anyway, Christine, the Viscount, or someone else might be hurt in the process of her abduction. Erik does not seem a bad man; yet he has killed at least two people, Joseph Buquet and the woman under the chandelier."

"He did, however, try to warn the audience. The voice said, 'She is singing to bring down the chandelier.' If not for that, several score people would have been killed or injured."

He sighed. "Yes, yes, Henry, that is quite true, but he is upset now and unbalanced. Conceivably he could go berserk and kill many innocent people. This time there may be no warning."

I opened my mouth, then closed it. "I wonder what he will do."

"Nor does he have the right to force himself upon Christine Daaé. She must be allowed to make her own choice, foolish as it may be. Yet I cannot bring myself to harm Erik. He could conceivably be captured, but that would surely destroy him. If only I could meet with him, talk to him, but the Opera is his maze, his lair. I shall never find him there."

"Oh, come now," I said. "You have already found his house."

"Little good that does. Forcing an entry would require hours and demolish it in the process." He slumped forward, resting his elbows on his knees, and stared at the red glow of the coal. "Meanwhile he would vanish into the Opera. He probably has another dwelling there, perhaps several. He could elude a small army for years. You would have to tear down the edifice layer by layer, peel it open like an onion, to find him."

"Yet you will do it, I know. You shall find him."

"No, no. It is hopeless, as I said. Two days of thought have only convinced me of the fact. My initial appraisal was correct."

"Sooner or later you will sniff him out."

Holmes shook his head, opened his mouth, then underwent a strange transformation. His jaw went slack; his mouth dropped open; his two fists simultaneously struck his knees. "Yes!" he cried. He leapt to his feet, walked about his chair and mine in a half circle. "Just the thing, the very thing." I watched warily, wondering whether his long fast and wakefulness had made him delirious. At last he gave me one of the most unrestrained smiles I had ever seen. "You have done it, Henry! By God, you have."

"What have I done?"

"Made me see the way out." He went to the desk, took a piece of paper, dipped the pen in the ink, then wrote furiously.

"Does this mean we can go eat dinner now? I am quite famished."

"Yes, of course, but this note must go to the telegraph office at once. In this case I can rely upon Watson. He will do it for old time's sake."

"Do what?"

"Contact that individual who will help us, as you so cleverly put it, to sniff out the Phantom in his lair. You will meet my master in this business, Henry, one who possesses a greater nose for crime than I."

"Are you... quite well?"

"Of course I am." He stuffed the paper into the envelope, then handed it to me. "Would you be so good as to send this out? I am somewhat tired. Then we shall eat." He went back to the large overstuffed chair, again putting his feet up on the ottoman.

"You are certain you are well?"

"Never better." His eyelids seemed to have grown quite heavy; he could not keep his eyes open all the way. His head swayed sideways, rested upon the high, curving chair arm; his eyes closed; and he was asleep.

I smiled and put an afghan throw over him. He was breathing heavily and even in sleep appeared pale and exhausted. I did as he requested and took his note to the telegraph office. The mysterious message made little sense to me. I also sent a brief note to Michelle, telling her that I loved her and wished to speak with her as soon as I returned to London.

The next morning I kept the officious hotel maids from Holmes's room. He did not awake until around noon, at which time he joined me for lunch. He had bathed, shaved, and put on clean clothes, and he looked better than he had in some weeks. His appetite at lunch impressed me and the waiter, but after all, he was making up for two days' fast. After he had devoured several small French pastries by way of dessert, we departed for the Palais Garnier.

The final rehearsals for *Faust* were taking place, and Christine Daaé was on stage as Marguerite. She wore a peasant costume: crisscrossed lacing drawing tight the scarlet bodice, a copious skirt, and a blonde wig with two long plaits. Carlos Fontana was Faust; he must have enjoyed, for once, having a soprano shorter than himself. The orchestra played in the pit. The Viscount sat at the rear of the auditorium, no doubt wishing to protect his sensitive ears. A few seats away sat the Persian, then off to the side was the small pale man Holmes had asked me about.

The Viscount rose to greet us. "Ah, Monsieur Holmes, how good to see you! Let us go outside where we can talk in peace."

We went out to a landing of the great stairway. With no other people present, one could see the pale hues of all the marble: cream, gray, pink, yellowish or brown. Our voices echoed faintly as we spoke, drifting upward to the murals five stories above.

"Monsieur Holmes, you have been most helpful, but I shall no longer need your assistance. Christine has agreed to be my wife, and we shall be leaving Paris shortly after Saturday's performance."

"Let me offer you my congratulations, *Monsieur le Vicomte*." Although faint, I heard the irony in Holmes's voice.

"Thank you." The Viscount's smile was smug. "You have received your check, have you not?"

"I have. Most generous."

"As I said, I always reward my friends. Very well, then…"

I knew a dismissal when I heard one, but Holmes continued to smile. "Are you not the least bit apprehensive about Saturday's performance? I do not mean to worry you, but Carlotta also challenged the Phantom with, as we know, tragic results."

"You need not concern yourself, Monsieur Holmes. Precautions are being taken."

"No doubt, Monsieur. I am sure the Persian and the police will do an admirable job."

The Viscount's smile vanished, and he took half a step back. "How the devil do you know about that?"

"Come now, Monsieur. One need not be the world's greatest consulting detective to discern the obvious. Well, I wish you luck. You have chosen your allies, and now the consequences of that choice must rest upon you and you alone. Come, Henry, we must see the managers."

The Viscount's smooth, youthful brow was furrowed with lines of worry, his eyes following us as we went up the stairs.

"That insufferable ass," I murmured when we were out of hearing. "Who was that small man seated in the stalls near the Persian?"

"That was Mifroid, Superintendant of the French police, and a worthy accomplice for the Viscount and the Persian. My friend François le Villard, another member of the police force, has told me all about him. Mifroid is all cunning and ambition, with minimal intelligence."

We had come to the managers' office, and Holmes knocked at the door. Richard's gruff voice beckoned us to enter. The two men were behind the desk; as usual Moncharmin was seated while Richard stood. Moncharmin's large round eye peered at us through the monocle lens.

"Cigar?" Richard asked. We shook our heads. Richard lit his cigar while we sat. Holmes's nostrils flared disdainfully at the odor.

"Monsieur Holmes, we are grateful for your assistance in this matter of the ghost, but…" Moncharmin's voice grew weak, and he glanced at Richard, beseeching aid. Richard exhaled cigar smoke and made ready to speak, but Holmes was first.

"You feel that my distinguished services are no longer required."

Moncharmin went very pale; one would have thought he had actually seen the Ghost, while Richard's front of boisterous good humor fell away.

"You know?" Moncharmin whispered.

"Come now, it is hardly mysterious. A thousand francs a day is a considerable sum, and your patience has worn thin. Rely on Monsieur Mifroid, if you wish. I hear he is rather obtuse, but it is not my way to argue the worth of my services. I shall send you my final bill, and we shall, I trust, part on good terms."

Moncharmin nodded eagerly. "Even so, even so."

"Would you be so kind as to humor one final request? Henry and I would like to be backstage during the performance of *Faust*. If you would write us a letter of admission…"

Moncharmin fumbled for a piece of paper. "Yes, yes, of course."

Richard eyed us suspiciously. He took the cigar from his mouth. "It is likely to be rather… crowded on opening night."

"Swarming with visitors and policemen, I suppose?" Moncharmin's monocle popped from his eye. Holmes continued: "We shall stay out of the way, I promise you. Having followed Mademoiselle Daaé's career thus far, we are anxious to see her Marguerite firsthand."

Richard stared at Moncharmin, who said weakly, "I see no harm." Moncharmin scribbled furiously, blew on the ink, then folded the paper and handed it to Holmes. "Once again, Monsieur Holmes, let me thank you on behalf of the entire Opera management and staff for your invaluable assistance in this unpleasant business. We may have had our disagreements, but..."

"Yes, yes—a pleasure, gentlemen, a pleasure. I am sorry to rush off, but I have other important business." He whirled about, hat in hand, then paused. "One last question, gentlemen, if you please. Are all your conferences held in this room?"

Moncharmin and Richard eyed each other. "Yes," Richard said.

"Including your discussions with Mifroid and his friends?"

Richard frowned, but Moncharmin nodded. "These are our offices. All our business is conducted here."

Holmes smiled. "I am glad to hear it. Good day."

Once we were outside, he shook his head. "These people are such fools, such utter buffoons. They are dealing with a specter who calls himself the Phantom of the Opera and who appears to know their every thought, and it never occurs to them..."

We were walking along the grand foyer, the Opera opulence all about us, when we heard footsteps behind us, their clatter loud in the vast hallway.

We turned and saw Madame Giry advancing toward us, her face quite red. "Monsieur Holmes!" she cried. "Monsieur Holmes!" She wore the usual black dress and a ghastly bonnet which appeared to have been constructed of crow remnants. I reflected again that the bustle was the worst possible style for a heavy, matronly woman such as she.

Holmes smiled, obviously happier to see her than the Viscount or the managers. "*Bonjour, Madame Giry.* How are you today?"

"Monsieur Holmes, it is an outrage—a disgrace! They are scheming, all of them, to capture him, our Ghost! Of course, it is foolish because one can never catch a ghost, but it is so—so *rude* to attempt it! Those nasty little worms—the Viscount and the policeman—and that filthy Persian! Have you noticed how dark and sinister his face—and that scar? You can never trust a foreigner, I always say, except perhaps the English, and of course you speak French so well that you are not truly a foreigner. Anyway, one of the carpenters overheard them. They are planning to trap the Phantom. He will come for Christine, and then… Oh, Monsieur Holmes, what is to be done? What is to be done?"

"Calm yourself, Madame, please calm yourself. As you yourself said, how can one catch a ghost, a specter? I know all about this little enterprise, and believe me, it is doomed to fail."

Madame Giry opened her mouth, then froze for a few seconds. "You know all about it?"

"Yes. Besides, you forget one thing, Madame. The Ghost, being bodiless, can go anywhere and hear anything. I am certain he, too, knows all the details of this ill-conceived conspiracy."

Madame Giry nodded thoughtfully. "True. That had not occurred to me. The Ghost must know."

"The Ghost is much wiser and cleverer than these men. Do not worry, Madame Giry. Everything will turn out fine. The Ghost will not be trapped."

Puffing out her cheeks, she gave a great sigh. "I am so glad. The Ghost has been very good to me, Monsieur Holmes. Didn't I tell you that he always leaves me a tip in his box?"

"You did, Madame."

"I would not want anything bad to happen to him."

"Nor would I. Rest assured, I have his interests and yours at heart."

She gave another massive sigh, and her face was less red. "Oh, I am relieved, Monsieur. I was so worried. Ever since they dismissed me and refused to pay the Ghost—things were different under the old managers, I can tell you. They were not so pompous as Monsieur Moncharmin or so haughty as Monsieur Richard. They appreciated my services, and they knew better than to trifle with the Ghost. They respected him."

"That was wise. Tell me one thing, do you think Christine Daaé knows about this plan to catch the Ghost?"

"Oh no, Monsieur Holmes! She would never be a party to such mischief."

"She was not present during the meeting the carpenter mentioned?"

"No, no—he did not see her. In fact he mentioned that it was odd for the Viscount to be by himself without Mademoiselle Daaé clinging to him. He laughed when he said that, and I warned him to watch his tongue or I'd give him a good cuff on the head, the dirty lout."

Holmes gently put his hand on her shoulder. "Do not worry, Madame Giry. I have matters well in hand. No one will harm the Ghost."

"*Merci beaucoup, Monsieur Holmes!* You are such a gentleman. Everything they say about you in the papers is true!"

Holmes laughed. "*Merci à vous aussi, Madame.*"

With a final coquettish smile, she turned and lumbered off, that awesome black, bustled posterior like the stern of a formidable dreadnought.

"Very well," I said. "Will you explain exactly what is going on?"

Holmes resumed walking. "Surely by now you must know. The Viscount, the Persian, and Monsieur Mifroid plan to capture the Phantom during the performance. They know he will try to abduct Christine, and they will be waiting for him. Scores of policemen will be backstage, a fruitless approach which presumes that sufficient force, mere brute numbers, can overcome cunning and intelligence. There are already so many people backstage during a performance that a few more will make little difference. Mifroid is clever enough to post guards at the prompter's box, the organ and battery rooms, but it will not matter. Erik knows their plans and will be ready for them."

"How can you be so certain? Surely that nonsense about a bodiless, omniscient ghost…"

"You are quite right; it is nonsense. I reassured Madame Giry in a way which I knew she would understand. Come now, Henry, have you not noticed that the Phantom seemed singularly well informed of our activities? Remember the note waiting for us at the hotel after our first interview with the managers?"

"Baffling."

"No, no, Henry! Do not be obtuse. Remember the maze within the maze?"

I frowned. "You are correct. I am stupid. There must be a secret passageway ending at the managers' office, a listening post for Erik."

"Very good, and the column in Box Five is hollow. Also, I said 'obtuse,' not 'stupid.'"

"Either term is equally unflattering."

"Not to my mind."

My face felt warm. "These sneaky wretches! The Viscount is truly contemptible. It is not enough to have Christine, to take Erik's one great love, but he must also capture and destroy his rival."

"He thinks that is the only sure way to have Christine."

"At least she is not a party to this scheme."

Holmes shook his head. "No. Her spirits are flighty; she resembles a will-o'-the-wisp; but she would not willingly harm Erik. Madame Giry spoke the truth."

"We must tell Christine."

"No. I wish this business of theirs to proceed exactly as planned. Once Erik has Christine, we shall be able to track them down and speak with Erik."

"But how?"

"Fear not, our extraordinary help is on the way! In fact we must return to the hotel. Watson has had more than enough time. By the way, it was unplanned, but I fear I am responsible for this turn of events. During our pleasant meeting with the Persian at Notre Dame, I told him to go to the Viscount or his brother if he wanted money. He has done just that."

"Madame Giry was right. He is a treacherous devil."

"And as I told her, do not fret, Henry. It should be delightful to see the conspirators' plans upset."

When we returned to the hotel, a telegram was waiting. Holmes eagerly ripped open the envelope, read the contents, then smiled. "Even as I said! Help will arrive shortly."

"Toby, you mean?"

He gave me a curious look, then laughed. "You no doubt read my note before sending it out. And have you never heard of good Toby, who is quite my master at sniffing out criminals, as you so cleverly put it?"

"Never," I said. "Should I have?"

"Watson recounts the assistance Toby gave us in the case of *The Sign of Four*. Much in the narrative is fiction or sensationalism, but Toby is real enough."

"Knowing your contempt for Watson's efforts I have scrupulously avoided his writings. Is this Toby truly so clever?"

"'Clever' is perhaps the wrong word. 'Tenacious' might be more apt. With the aid of this formidable detective we may at last follow the Phantom through the Opera."

I frowned. "How can this be possible? I find it hard to believe anyone could best your efforts unless he had some preternatural powers."

"Toby's senses are far beyond yours or mine. By the way, Toby is a she. That particular detail Watson did not get correct, although his confusion is understandable, given her name."

"A woman? Toby, this master sleuth, is a woman?"

"She is indeed female, but enough of these questions. You will meet her early tomorrow morning when she arrives in Paris." By then we were nearly back to the hotel. "I believe they are serving dinner already, and my appetite has fully returned. A bottle of champagne is in order, and perhaps today some frogs' legs, a delicacy sadly absent in London. As if our British frogs were not every bit the equal of their French counterparts! This will also be the last meal we shall directly charge to the Paris Opera, so it must be a fitting Gallic finale."

Our meal was truly an extravaganza, and when we saw the amount scrawled on the check, we were both happy that Messieurs Moncharmin and Richard would, albeit indirectly, be paying so formidable a sum. By that point, my general outlook toward life had been greatly improved. Champagne has always been a weakness of mine, and upon that occasion I overdid it. Sherlock did not drink so much as I, but he certainly did not abstain.

The next morning at five, the Herculean task of rousing me from bed fell to Sherlock. Cajoling did not work, but the threat of pouring a pitcher of water upon me finally did the trick. I sat, a weary lump of lead, while Holmes gazed eagerly out the cab window at the dark streets of Paris. The horse's hooves seemed to clop upon my skull rather than the pavement.

On a Sunday afternoon, no place on earth is busier than a Paris train station; it teems with humanity, every class and occupation being represented. However, at five thirty in the morning, things are rather peaceful; one can (if one's head is not wretched) take time to admire the architecture of the monumental interior of the Gare du Nord.

Holmes glanced at the schedule overhead, then headed toward the exit to the tracks. It had rained the previous night, and a white mist hung about the ground despite the shelter of the roof high above. Ornamental gas lights on iron poles shone all along the platform. We heard the distant whistle of a train. Soon the ground rumbled slightly, and the engine came steaming up, an old one that banged and clanged, its wheels slowing gradually. Holmes immediately started for the rear of the train, his walking stick tapping regularly, the rhythm another annoyance for my poor head.

"What class could Miss Toby have taken?" I asked.

"Last class," Sherlock replied.

"What?"

The cars seemed to go on forever, but at last we saw the end of the train and a car near it without windows. Holmes rapped upon the wooden door with his stick. The door slid open, revealing a man with a blue hat and a blue jacket with brass buttons. "*Eh bien, que voulez-vous?*"

"*Vous avez, je crois, une chienne pour moi,*" Holmes said. "*Une chienne de Londres.*"

"*Ah, oui, Monsieur! Attendez.*"

"*Une chienne?*" I said. "Did he say *une chienne?*"

Holmes's mouth twisted, and he gave a sharp laugh. "Yes, Henry, he did."

"Do you want the crate, Monsieur?"

"No, and you need not fear. The dog is quite gentle."

"You are certain of that, Monsieur?"

"Quite certain."

"Yes, you are probably right. It is the little dogs, the tiny yappy ones of the rich ladies, that bite. The wound in my calf has not completely healed. I'd gladly have made sausages of the filthy little cur."

Soon he reappeared with a great, slobbery beast, all brown and white, its pink, wet tongue lolling from its mouth. At the sight of Holmes, the dog gave a loud bark, then leapt from the train. The baggage man was nearly pulled out, but he managed to get the leash off his hand. The dog reared up, its paws clawing at Holmes's fine striped trousers and black overcoat.

He knelt and ruffled the dog's fur behind its ears. "Ah, Toby, I am glad to see you, too." He smiled at me. "Meet Toby, Henry, a wise old girl indeed. She may seem an ordinary mongrel, but she has a nose of incredible power. If anyone can track our Phantom through the Opera, it is she."

# Eleven

There were some difficulties in persuading the hotel management to accommodate Toby, her size being the main obstacle, but Holmes, employing both stern threats and honeyed flattery, at last prevailed. Indeed, as many ladies were allowed their small, yappy dogs (as the baggage man on the train had so aptly called them), why should Toby not be granted equal status? Holmes was required to sign a waiver promising to pay for any damage or requisite cleaning of carpets or furniture.

Watson describes Toby as half spaniel, half lurcher, this latter a breed with which I am not familiar, but he never explains how he came by this precise information. Being something of a cat fancier myself, I cannot speculate. Certainly the impression Toby gave was of a large, good-natured mongrel with none of the temperamental behavior of an overbred lineage. She was remarkably affectionate in a clumsy, slobbery way; and once I grew familiar with her pungent dog breath, we became, if not the best of friends, at least sociable acquaintances. I must also credit her with being so well trained that Holmes did not have to pay an extra franc for cleaning. She always announced her urges by staring at the doorknob and whining softly; as such displays were infrequent, she must have possessed a bladder of copious capacity.

Holmes remained in fine spirits, and we spent Friday strolling about Paris with Toby on leash. April was almost upon us, and signs of spring were everywhere. The temperature climbed into the sixties, the sun shone warm and yellow upon the bronze statues and the bubbling waters of the fountains, and sometimes an entire hour would pass without my thinking of Michelle. However, Saturday was a gray and misty day, the fickle weather returning again to winter. Holmes paced about the hotel room, clearly in a nervous state. After a light meal, we walked to the Opera, Toby accompanying us.

We were nearly two hours early, but already a row of carriages stood before the Opera. The façade was even more impressive with Bossuet's new electric lights illuminating it. Holmes raised his walking stick and pointed at a large barouche with two magnificent steeds, the coachman standing beside them smoking a cigarette.

"Do you recognize the coat of arms there on the side?"

"No," I said. "Should I?"

"It is that of the de Chagnys."

He stopped before a flower stand and selected a bouquet of daffodils, carnations, and tulips, the blossoms no doubt brought in from southern France by train.

"For whom are the flowers?" I asked.

"Christine Daaé. We shall visit her first."

The guard at one of the rear entrances perused Moncharmin's note, then let us by. He was not so sure about Toby, but Holmes said we were only delivering flowers and that the dog would not, of course, accompany us backstage to the performance. Soon we were walking along the dim corridor which led to Christine Daaé's dressing room.

I could not help reflecting upon all that had transpired since we first visited her. It seemed as if an eternity had passed, not a mere five weeks.

"Are you certain she will be in that same dressing room?" I asked. "Surely as the prima donna she deserves something more spacious."

"Yes, but she will have refused any offers of other rooms."

"Why?"

He paused before the door. "Because here she first heard her Angel of Music. Here he taught her to sing, and here she may yet hear his voice." He knocked. "Mademoiselle Daaé?"

"*Entrez.*"

Christine Daaé sat in the chair before her dressing table. Hanging before a screen were her costumes. The blonde wig with the plaits lay on the table, one plait drooping over the edge. She wore a gray dress, much less splendid than her recent finery. Her face was pale, her green eyes weary and troubled; one tiny white hand rubbed at the other. She smiled, genuinely glad to see us, and I reflected again on how very young she was.

"Oh, Monsieur Holmes, it is good to see you. Oh, how beautiful!" She took the flowers, raised them to her face and inhaled deeply. "They smell wonderful, and they remind me of spring." Turning to Toby, she laughed. "And who is this?"

"Permit me to introduce Mademoiselle Toby. She is Henry's faithful dog. He missed her terribly, so at last he sent to London for her."

She was so pleased with Toby that she did not see the black look I gave my cousin. "*Bonjour, Toh-bee, bonjour! Ah, que tu es belle!*" She sat down and scratched Toby behind the ears; she was rewarded with that look of fawning idolatry characteristic of the canine species.

Holmes dropped his stick, then half turned as he bent to pick it up, his black overcoat sweeping about. "We came to wish you our very best, Mademoiselle, and to say farewell."

Her smile did not entirely vanish, but quite changed character, complementing the sadness of her eyes. She nodded.

"We shall, of course, be attending the performance."

"I am sure it will be a great triumph," I said.

She nodded absentmindedly, then turned again to Sherlock. "I would like to thank you, Monsieur Holmes."

"For the flowers, Mademoiselle?"

"No, for more than that. For… for being so kind to me, and for looking out for me and for *him*. I think you understand him better than anyone, Monsieur Holmes." Her smile was pained, and she lowered her gaze, petting Toby again.

"I was glad to be of some service." Holmes's voice had a certain hesitance, none of its usual bite.

A brief silence followed, and then she said faintly, "Are you angry with me?"

Holmes frowned. "Why should I be angry?"

"For choosing… for my choice."

Holmes shook his head. "No, I am not angry."

"But disappointed perhaps?" Holmes did not reply, and I could see her green eyes assume a liquid quality as they filled with tears.

"I would have been most astonished if things had turned out differently. I shall not fault you for your choice. In real life, ugliness and disease are not so desirable as in romance."

She sighed, took her lower lip between her teeth, then flicked it out. "Real life is quite wretched." She looked up at us, a mocking quality in her eyes. "Do you think, gentlemen, that people ever truly change?"

Holmes shook his head. "No. A person's character is fixed at quite an early age."

"Come now," I said, "is that not rather hard? I should hate to think I have learned nothing in the last ten years, that I am still the same foolish youth that I was at nineteen."

"Maturation does occur," Holmes said, "but the core, the essence, remains the same."

I shook my head. "You are too harsh. Men are not rocks made of some stony and impervious matter."

"True, we are not rocks; the essence of our person is not matter; however, the personality, or the spirit, or whatever you wish to call it, is equally resistant to change."

"I do not agree," I said warmly.

Christine was staring at Toby. "Raoul seems different. We have not quarreled so much. He swears he loves me and will treasure me, and yet he still seems... a child, somehow, a mere boy."

Holmes and I said nothing, but the silence at last made me uneasy. "I am looking forward to the performance. I did not have the opportunity to tell you how remarkable you were in *La Juive*."

Holmes nodded. "Quite remarkable."

She smiled up at us. "Thank you, gentlemen. You are very kind. Have you heard? Carlotta will be attending tonight."

"Yes," Holmes said. "I did hear something of that. You will no doubt show her what a true artist, as opposed to a mere singer, can do with the role of Marguerite."

"Oh, Monsieur Holmes, you really are very sweet. May I ask you an impertinent question?"

"You may." His eyes had a wariness which contradicted his reply.

"Are you married? Is there a Madame Holmes?"

"No, Mademoiselle."

"Ah, that is a very great pity."

I was tempted to voice my agreement, but her words had such a sorrowful earnestness that I remained silent. Holmes reddened slightly about the ears.

"Well, Mademoiselle, it is time to say *adieu*. When you are singing in London someday, please look me up. Here is my card."

"Oh, I shall, Monsieur Holmes—I promise I shall."

"I am certain you will be magnificent tonight."

"So am I," I agreed.

"You are most kind, Doctor Vernier, and your dog here is a great sweetheart. I wish I could steal her from you."

"Well…" I began.

"No, no." Holmes shook his head. "It would break his heart."

We turned to go, and I was out the door when she said, "Monsieur Holmes, they will not—no one will hurt him, will they? Raoul hates him I know, and the managers… Oh, promise me…"

Holmes had put on his top hat, and he was very tall and imposing in black evening dress. "I can promise you that much, Mademoiselle. No one will harm him. I believe he can take care of himself, but he is also assured of my protection."

"*Oh, merci, Monsieur!*" Her voice broke, and she turned away. "*Merci.*"

We started down the corridor. Holmes lit a cigarette, and I let out a great sigh. "What an odd girl she is," I murmured.

"She is not so very odd. She is a representative sample of her sex. If she had chosen Erik, then she would be odd."

I stared at him. "You told her you were not angry with her."

"I am not."

"Are you certain of that?"

"Yes. It is life which frequently annoys me, but not being Jehovah, I cannot alter one wretched thing. I cannot turn the Viscount into a frog or Erik into a prince." He inhaled deeply through his cigarette, then hurled it down and crushed out the butt with the toe of his boot. "At any rate, I have purloined what I came for." He reached into his overcoat and withdrew a shoe.

Somehow I could not imagine it really to be what it appeared to be. "What is that?"

"What do you think, Henry?"

"A shoe."

"Very good. Go on."

The diminutive size and the style, laces, pointed toes, and a high square heel made the sex of its owner obvious. "A woman's shoe."

"Exactly."

I gave him such a strange look that he began to laugh. "Fear not—I am not one of those men with a perverse fondness for certain articles of feminine apparel. I took this shoe for Toby's benefit."

"You did? Just now?"

"Yes. Remember when I bent over to fetch my stick? Mademoiselle Daaé was in her stocking feet, and I had noticed her shoes under the dressing table. I seized the shoe while she was busy with Toby and the flowers."

Obtuse to the last, I continued to stare. "For Toby, you say? Is she one of those dogs with a taste for leather? That does seem rather cruel to Miss Daaé."

This speech brought a great outburst of laughter. My cousin was given to frequent harsh, staccato laughs which functioned more as exclamations than as signs of amusement. Only rarely did something strike him as truly amusing, but my words had done the trick. He laughed until he began to wheeze, and I ended up grabbing his arm and clapping him on the back. "Are you well?" I asked.

"Yes, yes. If only you could have seen the expression on your face just now. The shoe is not a delectable morsel for Toby's dinner, but is instead intended for her formidable nose. One whiff, and she will be able to track Miss Daaé wherever Erik should take her."

I opened my mouth, then closed it. "Perhaps if I were more familiar with dogs… Oh, it is hopeless. I shall never make a consulting detective."

"There is much to be said for a good laugh, Henry, and as I am already the world's foremost consulting detective, there is no need for amateur efforts on your part."

"I like that!" I said hotly. "Who gave you the idea of employing Toby in the first place?"

"Frankly, Henry, the idea had been brewing for some time, and your comment merely brought it to the surface."

"Now you are the one mixing metaphors most dreadfully."

"True, and I am sorry for my callous remarks. You appeared so utterly perplexed, yet I must admit no one of my acquaintance has ever absconded with a young lady's shoe. Perhaps the idea came to me because of a case involving a savage hound and a gentleman's missing boot, but that is a lengthy story which I shall relate another time. We had better go backstage and reserve a place. Tonight a veritable mob will be present."

Holmes was correct. The stairways were crowded enough, but on stage were dozens of people, many of them policemen in their blue jackets or firemen wearing their distinctive helmets. Carpenters were doing some last minute work on the sets, and overhead in the flies I could see men crowded about the lights. The gas jets in the battens suddenly went on full, illuminating the side where we were standing and also throwing out considerable heat. I was glad I had not worn my overcoat. Toby surveyed the people rushing about us with the same good-natured, if slightly imbecilic, countenance. A few of the workmen smiled; others regarded her curiously.

"Ah, Monsieur Holmes."

I turned and saw the man I had noticed in the auditorium, Mifroid of the Sûreté. At his side were two burly policemen of similar short stature, no doubt chosen because they did not make him appear small.

Unlike his men, he wore no blue uniform but a dark suit of expensive cut. His mustache was trimmed very close to his straight, thin upper lip. All in all, he recalled a head waiter, one with a very inflated sense of his own importance.

"We have not met before, but I have heard of your exploits." Although he was speaking to us, his eyes were fixed on Toby.

"And I, too, have heard of you, Monsieur Mifroid. I am sure the Opera management need have no fears tonight. The formidable presence of you and your men guarantees that we will be spared any further incidents."

Mifroid's eyes narrowed, and I could almost see the small wheels turning as he attempted to decide whether to take this compliment at face value. "When this Erik appears, my men and I shall take him at once."

"But have you considered where he might strike? If not a specter, he has shown a diabolical cleverness."

"You think I am not aware of that? I have my men everywhere. I suspect that he may try to interfere with the lighting again. I have several men in the battery room and others at each of the gas mains. There are others atop the dome itself, watching the chains which support the new chandelier, and two men are at each level of the flies. I have also employed twice the usual number of firemen. There will be no 'accidents' tonight."

"Indeed, you have thought of everything," Holmes said.

Mifroid smiled, then his eyes were drawn again to Toby. "Tell me, Monsieur Holmes, that dog there…?"

"Ah, yes, he is the faithful companion of my cousin, Henry Vernier." Mifroid and I nodded at one another. "Henry's eyesight is… diminished, and especially in the dark the dog helps him get about."

Mifroid bent over and scratched Toby between the ears. "He seems an amicable beast."

I gave a weary sigh, resigning myself to the inevitable. "Cataracts, you know. Once the lights go dim I can see hardly anything."

"A pity. I never heard of cataracts in one so young."

Neither had I, but I said, "Oh, it is a rare affliction, but I seem to have been frightfully unlucky. There are some promising surgical techniques, but in my case things have not progressed so far that…"

Holmes's smile bared his teeth. "Now, now, Henry, I am sure the inspector has more important business to attend to."

Mifroid nodded. "Regretfully, that is true, Monsieur Holmes." He clicked his heels together in a manner more befitting a Prussian than a Gaul. "The Phantom would think twice about striking again tonight if he knew Sherlock Holmes were present. I must see to my men."

After he was gone, I said, "He seems a harmless enough sort."

"You forget your *Hamlet*, Henry. One may smile and smile and be a villain. Mifroid has risen by trampling others underfoot, including my friend le Villard. Somehow whenever Mifroid is involved, the credit always goes exclusively to him."

"He has been methodical. Perhaps the Phantom will not appear."

Holmes gave that peculiar laugh which resembled a snort. "As if sheer numbers could ever intimidate our Erik! He is desperate, Henry— absolutely desperate. Nothing could persuade him to stay away tonight."

"Why?"

"Because he is in love." His shook his head, then raised his walking stick. "One simply cannot protect every gas line, every turncock, in this vast complex. Do you see those rubber hoses fueling the battens with gas? He could cut any of the dozens of similar hoses about the house, then light a match."

"But surely he would not harm Christine?"

Holmes sighed, weariness showing in his eyes. "I think not, but who can tell? Clearly his mind is unbalanced, and yet…"

"Yet what?"

"His music was so utterly beautiful. Ah, if only he were the Angel of Music! Unfortunately, the Deity rarely seems to send his intermediaries to assist in the affairs of men."

"What do you think Erik has planned?"

"Something truly spectacular." The battens overhead went out, plunging us into shadow. Carlos Fontana walked by clad in the brown robes of the medieval scholar Faust. As he had not yet sold his soul to the devil, he wore a white beard and wig. With him were his attendant and the stage director, Monsieur Gérard.

"*Silence–silence,*" came the sibilant hiss in French.

Holmes spoke so softly I could barely hear him. "Something as spectacular as the Opera House itself, something equally grand, foolish and magnificent. Above all, something theatrical."

All the lights were dimming now, and then we heard the applause from behind the curtain which greeted the conductor. Soon the low, melancholy music of the overture began. A few carpenters and attendants in black were still scurrying about; one nearly tripped, recovering with a whispered curse. Enough light remained that I could see Toby. She was panting slightly, but her tail still shook. I had the impression she was having the time of her life.

The curtain rose, the lighting in the auditorium spilling backstage, and then the battens and the footlights went on. The latter were dazzling; they made it difficult to stare out at the red and gold splendor of the auditorium. We were quite near the front of the stage; we had to turn downstage to see Faust seated at a massive table, with the backdrop showing his study and the German countryside beyond.

The first word he sang was "*Rien*"–"nothing," all that he had to show for a life of solitary scholastic pursuits. Fontana was in good voice, and we could hear him perfectly. Perhaps I had been wrong to equate him and Carlotta. True, he was short, stout, and plain, but every man would choose to be a young and beautiful Adonis if such a choice were possible.

The arrival of Mephistopheles was spectacular, although we could see how it was done. First a mist poured out from some vents, hiding the stage, then up through the floor came the Devil; simultaneously a limelight on the opposite side from us was opened up, bathing him in a brilliant reddish-orange light. We could hear the exclamations of surprise and fear from the audience.

This was a different Mephistopheles from the one who had sung with Carlotta, a much finer one, a (pardon me!) handsome Devil indeed, quite tall, and with a wonderfully deep bass voice. His diction was perfect. Unlike Carlotta and Fontana, he was obviously a native French speaker; the words were not mauled, the vowels not mangled and italianized. He held up the parchment for Faust to sign, then gestured with his hand; the wall behind him seemed to dissolve. Christine Daaé sat at the spinning wheel pretending to spin.

She seemed so small and vulnerable, so lovely, that a murmur went through the audience. The effect had been comical with Carlotta, but I could understand why someone would sell his soul for such a vision. I recalled the Phantom telling us he had watched Christine for weeks. How he must have savored her beauty, drinking it in like a man dying of thirst in the desert! I knew how he felt. Life seemed cruel and senseless at times, but one would be a brute indeed not to revere the beauty of a woman. I smiled in the dark, amused by my own pompous reflections. How I missed Michelle, how I longed to see her, to touch her! I had taken her beauty for granted; I had been a skeptic; but now it– *she*–seemed the most precious thing in my silly, trivial life.

After the curtain had fallen on the first scene, a horde of men rushed about. The backdrop was hoisted up, another displaying the interior of an inn lowered, the heavy canvas swaying like a sail. The exteriors of the village dwellings were pushed on stage, and next came the tables and benches. Short, sharp commands and muted curses filled the air, then came the faint tread, the whispers, of a great mass of people, the students, burghers, and soldiers preparing for their entrance. After all the wild motion came a brief stillness, then up went the curtain, the orchestra playing the boisterous music of the second scene.

Except for those few occasions when I had attended an opera or concert with Sherlock, I had sat in the celestial regions, the highest and cheapest balconies where one could admire the architecture of the dome, but where binoculars were required to discern whether the singers were smiling or frowning. I had never been so close to the performance, and I was enjoying it immensely. True, the sound was peculiar, the chorus being louder than the orchestra, but the vividness, the sense of being part of the events on stage, more than made up for that.

At one point Holmes gripped my arm. In his other hand were his opera glasses. "Do you see?" he whispered, pointing past Mephistopheles at a group of male villagers. They wore the hats and brownish jackets supposedly characteristic of rustic peasants (at least we were spared lederhosen), and they all sang loudly. One tall thin fellow had his mouth open in a huge oval. I was so caught up in the performance that Holmes's interruption annoyed me, and I did not reply.

Mephistopheles struck a small cask with his sword, and wine the color of blood poured out, the liquid all alight, glowing. The devil burst into loud and threatening laughter, and I quite forgot Holmes had said anything. I only remembered it at the intermission, and at that point I was outside with Toby, who was relieving herself against a spectacular bronze lamppost straddled by a sculptured nymph. When we were back inside, I asked Holmes about his remark.

"A mere triviality, nothing you need worry about. Did you notice how cool the audience seemed to Christine Daaé?"

"Stuffy, pretentious French swine—they have no…"

"Calm yourself, Henry. Carlotta was present. I saw her." He raised the opera glasses with his left hand. "Her expression was not pleasant. Nor was that of the Count de Chagny."

"The only good thing about Christine Daaé running off to marry the Viscount is what it will do to the Count. The articles in every cheap newspaper cannot have pleased him."

"No. Mademoiselle Daaé had only her one line. She will show them in the second act if I am not mistaken."

"I hope so."

Christine seemed rather nervous and weary when she came on, but once she began singing, her attitude changed. By the end of the Jewel Song she had completely won over the audience. Toward Faust she showed the proper blend of innocence and longing, and when the curtain went down, the crowd went wild. She and Fontana stood near us before going out for their curtain call.

"You were wonderful," I said, but she did not appear to even see me.

"Let her be," Holmes whispered. "She is that rare artist who so totally immerses herself in the part that she becomes the character. The transition back to real life is wrenching."

"This has been a remarkable evening. I am enjoying myself, but I wonder when the Phantom… when he will show himself."

"Not until the end. He may be angry with Miss Daaé, but he wants her to have her triumph, to show her worth to Carlotta and the managers."

"Good," I said. "The final scene is my favorite."

Holmes smiled. "Mine also."

The last act opened with Marguerite trying to pray in the cathedral. A chorus of awes came from the audience as the curtain went up. There were realistic pews and an elaborate altar, but all eyes were drawn to the magnificent window. Earlier I had seen them lower a plain white canvas backdrop; I could distinguish no lights shining upon it, yet a luminous rose window had appeared, the pattern brilliant with red, blue, green, and yellow.

"How on earth did they do that?" I muttered.

"It is a magic lantern projecting from the rear, quite an effective technique," Holmes said. "The limelight employed makes the projection very bright."

Marguerite sang her prayer accompanied by a sonorous organ, then abruptly Mephistopheles appeared before her, bathed again in red light. At the same instant the window changed color, the bright hues reddening; it was as if the window were drowned in blood. "Lord," I murmured.

As Marguerite tried to pray, the Devil and his infernal choir taunted her. Her pleas to God grew increasingly desperate. Christine's voice was so beautiful it made me ache inside, yet she conveyed such anguish. At the end Mephistopheles roared, "*Sois maudite! A toi l'enfer!*" his voice heavy with malice, totally evil. The rose window swelled, covering Christine with its bloody shadow. She gave a dreadful cry, shrieking more than singing the note. There was a brief silence after the curtain fell, then the applause began slowly, hesitantly.

"Is she only acting?" I asked.

Toby whimpered softly, and Holmes stroked her head. "I think not."

Christine walked past us, and she had the look on her face of one who truly believed she was damned. Mephistopheles appeared troubled, as if disturbed by his own villainy.

In the next scene, after the rather silly Soldiers' Chorus, Mephistopheles helped Faust kill Marguerite's brother Valentine. As Valentine died he cursed her with words similar to the Devil's: "*Marguerite, sois maudite!*" Christine Daaé had only two lines to sing, yet somehow she managed to totally dominate the stage. I borrowed Holmes's opera glasses and stared at her. Her eyes were open wide, her pretty mouth contorted with terror. No, whatever she was doing, it was not mere "acting."

After the scene was ended, I turned to Holmes. "How can she keep it up? She must be exhausted."

"The remarkable thing is that she sings so beautifully. There is no audible straining or forcing of the voice. I do not think we shall ever see a performance to equal this one. She does have a rest now during the Walpurgis Night."

Walpurgis Nights and witches' sabbaths were supposed to be frightening, the culmination of Satan's power as all the evil spirits cavorted, but I had always found them slightly comical, more of a devilish music hall show with competing acts and costumes. This one was better than most, the forest setting and various lighting tricks effectively done; yet with Christine absent, the scene was uninspiring and hardly frightening.

For the first time that evening I was almost bored. Holmes was methodically searching the stage with his binoculars. Suddenly he stiffened and restrained a laugh.

"What is it?" I whispered.

"Do you see that tall devil just behind Mephistopheles? Here, have a look."

The devil in question was even taller than Mephistopheles, tiny black horns affixed to his forehead, great dark wings on his back. Something about his face was peculiar, vaguely sinister. Many of the chorus members were spectators in costume, completely uninvolved in the action, but this man was demonstrating the old adage about there being no small parts, only small actors. His eyes were genuinely demonic.

"He is quite good," I said.

"That is Erik."

I actually dropped the opera glasses, but Holmes's hand shot out and caught them. "He was a villager in Act One."

"Good Lord, should we not do something?"

"No."

The curtain fell, the gaslights overhead brightened, and the stagehands swarmed about. Up went one vast backdrop, down came another much further forward. Several women and children angels dressed in white gowns and carrying golden harps trooped behind it; stagehands followed, pushing an enormous platform with a ladder attached. The thing slid along on rails beneath the stage, a small trench opened for it. We heard sounds of furious activity, whispered exclamations and commands, from behind the canvas. Meanwhile, in the foreground a prison cell had been constructed, the frame of iron bars set up, straw laid down inside. Christine walked on stage and went into the cell. A stagehand did something behind her back.

"What is he doing?" I asked.

"It will spoil the effect if I tell you," Holmes said.

"Christine looks rather cold."

She wore a white shift which left her white shoulders and slender arms bare. (Carlotta had worn a gown with long sleeves, no doubt to hide brawny arms worthy of a stevedore.) Her feet were also bare. Gone was the wig with its two plaits; her own long blonde hair spilled onto her shoulders. I had never seen her with her hair down; it made her seem somehow vulnerable. She was made up to appear frail and desperate with dark circles under her eyes, but I doubted she needed the false coloring. She was so small, delicate, and beautiful that any decent man would have wanted to throw his arms about her and offer his protection.

Suddenly upon the backdrop appeared the black silhouette of the scaffold and the hangman's noose. "The magic lantern again?" I asked, and Holmes nodded.

The music began, Faust and the Devil appearing on the opposite side of the huge stage from us. They had come to steal away Marguerite, who had gone insane with despair and killed her own illegitimate child. Christine had lain down, feigning sleep, and when she heard Faust's voice and sat up, I could almost hear a shudder of dismay from the audience. Truly she appeared mad. When she sang of happier days, her voice was so utterly beautiful that my eyes filled with tears. Mephistopheles rushed back in singing, "*Alerte! Alerte!*"

Christine tore herself free of Faust, retreating to the corner of the cell and cringed in horror. "*Le démon! Le démon!—Le vois-tu?—Là dans l'ombre...*" The back of my neck felt cold. Her voice was piercing. This terror was not feigned; she made you see the demon there in the shadow. Toby whimpered softly, but Holmes knelt and stroked her head.

Christine clasped her hands and raised them in desperation above her head. "*Mon Dieu, protégez-moi! Mon Dieu, je vous implore!*" Then she fell to her knees and sang first to angels: "*Anges purs, anges radieux!*"; then again to God: "*Dieu bon, je suis à toi!—Pardonnes!*" "Merciful God, I am yours—Pardon me!" Then again she prayed for the angels to carry her away to heaven. Only dimly was I aware that the tears had spilled from my eyes and run down my cheeks. Her voice soared over the orchestra, over everything.

Faust and the Devil implored her to follow, but she turned to Faust with horror, with loathing. "*Pourquoi ces mains rouges de sang?*" "*Va! Tu me fais horreur!*" she shrieked.

The Devil howled back, "*Jugée!*"—"judged," damned!

All the lights, both in the house and on stage, dimmed, and the backdrop of the prison shot upwards. Behind it, floating in the air against a blue-black sky sparkling with stars, was the host of angels with their harps. Many limelights were opened up and bathed the angels in brilliant white light. "*Sauvée!*" they cried, "Saved!" The Devil fell back, dragging Faust away with him into the shadows. The heavenly choir suspended over that vast stage sang of Christ's resurrection, of *paix et félicité,* peace and felicity. The organ accompanied them, booming out triumph. Christine turned and stepped toward the angels. The audience could not see her face, her rapture, but we could. She raised her arms to the angels, then lowered them, and slowly she began to rise as the orchestra built to a great crescendo.

A muffled laugh slipped from my lips. The whole thing was so preposterous, so conventional, so ridiculously sentimental, and yet I was crying and absolutely filled with emotion. I wiped at my eyes. Christine Daaé through her art had made the whole absurd business work.

She was some thirty feet above the stage, no doubt suspended from a dark wire, when every gas or electric light in the house went dead. The limes did not go out immediately. The lime spindles themselves briefly continued to burn even after their hydrogen and oxygen supply was cut off, but their light was greatly diminished. The angels hung not in radiance but in shadow. The audience may have wondered if this was part of the performance, but those backstage knew it was not. "Damnation—the Phantom!" someone cried behind us, and for the first time Toby barked, even as the music dwindled away.

Enough light remained that we could see a great black creature with leathery wings climb down from the darkness overhead and snatch Christine Daaé. She screamed once. The demon hurled her white form over his shoulder, then climbed rapidly back into the shadows. By then half the audience was screaming, and soon we were in total darkness.

"Henry!" Holmes exclaimed. He pulled me back against a wall at the rear of the stage. We heard the big curtain come down close by.

"Good God, did you see that!" I had to shout to be heard.

"Yes. Quiet, Toby!" The dog stopped barking. "We must wait for some light. It will be dangerous on stage until then. We could be injured in the pandemonium."

And indeed, the stage abounded with cries, oaths, footsteps, crashes, quarrels, and commands. Soon lights appeared, some few of Mifroid's men being provided with police dark lanterns.

"*Silence!*" someone shouted in French, then louder, "*Silence!*" his voice rising above the screaming angels. A light shone on the face of Monsieur Gérard, the stage manager. "Will you damned angels keep quiet! *Please!*" The din about us subsided, but we could hear women and children weeping.

"Did you see that thing snatch her!" someone sobbed.

"Hold your tongue, Madame! I shall fire the next person who goes into hysterics!" More lanterns had gone on. "Everything is under control. Please remain calm, and we shall get you all down as soon as possible. There is no danger. Everyone keep still. The audience is making noise enough." He was correct: beyond the thick barrier of the curtain we could hear the panic of the crowd.

Mifroid swept past us, accompanied by the same two of his men, each carrying a lantern. "This is impossible—impossible!"

"Come, Henry," Holmes said softly. "We can make our way out to the rear."

"Where is Christine Daaé!" Mifroid exclaimed.

"Keep your voice down!" Gerard shouted. Then he said in a breathy whisper, "The Devil carried her off. Did you not see? There are hundreds of witnesses. And how did all the lights come to be extinguished? You said it could not happen!"

"It is impossible!" Mifroid moaned. "My men were everywhere. It could not have happened."

"Do not tell me it was impossible! We all saw it. The gas was extinguished, and now all the pilots are out! Have you any idea how long it will take to relight everything?"

"Come," Holmes said. "We have seen enough."

We made our way to the rear of the stage. Abruptly Holmes pulled me back into the shadows. The Viscount rushed past us, still in evening dress, the Persian behind him holding a lantern. I reflected that evening dress and an astrakhan hat were not a pleasing combination.

"Christine!" the Viscount cried. "Christine!"

"Damnation!" Gérard roared. "Keep your voice down, you fool! You'll set everyone off again."

Holmes urged me forward. He had wrapped Toby's leash about his hand so she was next to him.

"Where are we going?" I asked.

"Down," Holmes said. "Down beneath where we are now."

Fear came out of the shadows, briefly clasping me in its icy arms. I had known what Holmes's answer must be. "But he went *up* with her."

"Yes, he did, and that should keep Mifroid and those other buffoons occupied for a while. They do not know about the house on the lake. I doubt the Persian would have told them about that. We may have to deal with the Viscount and the Persian, but they will not be able to actually follow Erik."

"But how…?"

"The shoe, Henry—the shoe. Now is when we employ our secret weapon, Toby's miraculous nose."

I sighed and kept silent, even as dread settled heavily about my heart. I had no wish to visit the Phantom's underworld again, with or without Toby. "It is his and his alone," Christine had warned the Viscount as they stood before the trap door, and now she had been swallowed up by the darkness. I could not see how the night could end but in death, and on Erik's home ground I knew only too well where the odds lay.

# Twelve

Holmes had a dark lantern in his leather satchel, and he stopped to light it so we could make our way through the darkened theater. As neither of us wished to wander the filthy cellars in evening dress, we went to an abandoned dressing room and changed our clothes. Remembering our previous chilling voyage upon the lake, I put on a heavy woolen sweater, trousers, and overcoat.

After he had finished changing, Holmes withdrew a familiar leather collar from the bag. "Put this on."

I sighed. "Dog collars again. Is this really necessary?"

"No, not if you prefer strangulation."

"Nothing happened the last time. It is so uncomfortable."

"Having a rope drawn tightly about one's throat is also uncomfortable. You forget Joseph Buquet's fate. The stories about the Phantom employing the Punjab lasso must have some basis in fact. Put it on."

I sighed a second time. "Very well."

Holmes had fastened the leather band about his own throat. He rebuttoned his shirt collar and took his bowler hat.

All was pandemonium on the first and second floors beneath the stage. The gas had come back on, and the stagehands were relighting the lamps. Policemen in their blue uniforms rushed about, and numerous small groups of men had gathered to hear the news from those witnesses who had seen Christine Daaé's abduction.

As we passed the battery room, a loud, angry voice exclaimed, "I tell you it is not possible! The current was not cut off."

"But the lights went out," said another voice.

"And I tell you everything was fine down here! It was not our fault."

Holmes laughed softly, then started down the stairs.

"How ever did he manage it?" I said. "It does seem supernatural."

"Not in the least."

"Then how do you explain it? There are three gas mains into the Opera House, separate piping of oxygen and hydrogen for the limes, as well as the electric wiring. If that in itself were not challenging enough, there is also the fact that we saw Erik climbing down from a rope an instant later."

"Do you think, then, that we have a very technical ghost with powers over gas pipes and electrical wires?"

We had reached the third cellar down, where cavernous stone archways replaced iron girders, and I was hardly in the mood for mockery. "You need not be sarcastic."

"Oh, very well, Henry. Do you recall my postulating an accomplice after the incident with the chandelier? On that occasion Erik was in the prompter's box while his accomplice overhead released the chandelier. Tonight Erik waited for this other person to extinguish the lights, then he struck."

"But how did this accomplice know the precise instant to act? And how could anyone shut off everything simultaneously?"

"Your first question is the more puzzling, but the problem with the electrical lines suggests to me a means of signaling across a distance. The Phantom knows every inch of the Opera and was an engineer. No doubt he has kept abreast of various technological developments. Such a man could easily add some wiring of his own. I suspect a simple switch high above the stage. When thrown by the Phantom, it set off a light or buzzer, which alerted his accomplice that the moment had come."

"But the second question remains. How could that accomplice shut off everything?"

"I think Erik constructed his own sort of organ room below ground. He has tapped into the gas line even before it splits into the mains, adding an extraneous loop which is normally kept open. From under the Opera he could easily reach any of the pipes which supply this great metropolis. He did the same thing with the main electrical line from the battery room. These hidden shunts would not be detectable until they were all closed, as they were tonight."

"Do you truly think he is so clever?"

"Without a doubt, Henry. It is amusing to think of his confederate in some hidden room tripping the various switches and levers which plunged the entire Opera into darkness. However, my theory still has one flaw."

"What flaw?"

"The Phantom's desperate, lonely nature. He is a man who considers himself utterly alone, totally cut off from normal human society."

Holmes took Christine's shoe from his pocket and knelt before the dog. "Smell this, Toby. Good! Sniff it well, remember that scent. Find her, Toby—find her. Mind you have a good hold on that leash, Henry. She…"

The warning was too late: as Toby bounded forward she nearly tore my arm from its socket. She sniffed briefly at the stone floor, bounded, sniffed, bounded, and so on, each time starting off again when I least expected it.

"I have found a way, Henry, to reconcile the Phantom's solitary nature and this necessary accomplice. This person must be someone of very limited mental powers, perhaps one of the feebleminded."

"Come now, could a feebleminded person be so adept at throwing switches and closing valves?"

"Yes. I recall a certain gang of thieves whose safe breaker could literally not speak a word, and yet he had a remarkable aptitude for locks, gears, and all things mechanical. The so called idiot savant is not uncommon, as a physician should know; one faculty is extraordinarily developed while others are almost totally lacking. Besides, pulling levers when a light goes on does not really require much intelligence."

Holmes had hold of the lantern and satchel while I attempted to rein in the eager Toby, whose nose busily examined every dusty nook. Pieces of sets were all about us. Here was a scaffold used for an execution scene, the thick rope dangling from the crossarm. Close by stood the ornate wooden head piece of a bed. "What on earth?" I whispered.

"*Lohengrin*, the second act," Holmes replied.

Toby led us into another room which I recalled from our last visit, the resting place for a variety of gods. On one side, gigantic Egyptian deities with animal heads lay on their backs, while their shorter brethren stood upright. Holmes did not need to help me this time. *Aida*, I thought, and there, *Samson et Delilah*. A golden calf ten feet tall stood by other graven images, the brilliant paint sullied by dust.

Holmes shone the light on the calves' legs, revealing a pair of glowing yellow eyes. They so startled me that I let go of the leash. With a bark, Toby leapt away. The eyes vanished, and we heard the cat yowl as it scurried away."

"Toby!" Holmes shouted. "No! Bad dog! Toby!" He glanced angrily at me. "Can you not even keep hold of the leash?"

"You hold the blasted leash!"

"I have my hands full."

"Give me the lantern and the satchel then," I said.

He did so, then went after Toby. I could still feel my heart beating from the shock, but the ridiculousness of the situation soon prevailed. I went around the calf and shone the light on a deity with a ram's horns.

"Holmes," I called softly. I heard a loud voice from the other room and turned, swinging the lantern about.

Holmes slipped beside me and said softly, "Put out the light— quickly."

I slid shut the cover, plunging us into the darkness, but soon another beam of light shot into the room, illuminating the silent gods.

"Christine!" It was the Viscount de Chagny.

"How many times must I tell you to keep silent! And keep your hand up to the level of your eyes. This is no joking matter." I recognized the Persian's voice.

"Christine may be close by."

"But you need not alert Erik and everyone else of our presence. Damnation! Will you keep your hand up!"

"But it grows weary," the Viscount whined.

"Then raise the other hand!"

"Oh, very well."

We were hiding behind the golden calf, but we could see them through its legs. Holmes had knelt and managed to keep Toby silent. The two men still wore evening dress, and the astrakhan hat was all too familiar.

"You are certain it would not be simpler to go by way of the lake?" the Viscount asked.

"That way is death. The siren's voice lures you close, then Erik's hand grabs you by the throat. He uses the reed to breath under the water, a trick he learned in his travels. We will try the secret entrance near where Buquet died. Wait a moment. I could use a cigarette. There is no rush."

"No rush, you say! Christine in that monster's hands, and you dare to tell me there is no rush!"

"He will not hurt her." A match flared, and I smelled the foul odor of cheap Turkish tobacco.

"How can you be so certain?"

"Because he loves her, because the fool loves her."

"Love—what does he know of love!"

The Persian sighed. "Calm yourself."

"If anything happens to Christine, you will not get a solitary franc from me! I should never have listened to you and that buffoon Mifroid. 'She will be safe, *Monsieur le Vicomte.*' It was a passable imitation of the policeman's voice. "'I shall throw a ring of steel about her. One move, and my men will seize him.' And you—'Trust the police,' you said."

"Mifroid took every precaution. Even I did not think Erik could pull off such an abduction."

"It is natural, I suppose, for a former policeman to stand by another policeman. Finish your cigarette."

After a brief silence, the Persian spoke. "I do not much care for your tone of voice, Monsieur. And I was not a mere policeman. I was the chief, and it was no ordinary force. My enemies could tell you—if any were still alive—that it is unwise to annoy me. If you wish to see Mademoiselle Daaé again, keep a civil tongue in your head."

"Oh, very well, but could you please hurry? And what if we cannot find him, or what if he finds us first and wrings our necks with this lasso you mentioned? My Christine will be his forever!"

The end of the Persian's cigarette glowed red. "No, Monsieur. One way or another, Erik is finished. At half past midnight, one of my servants will tell Mifroid about the house on the lake. Another will tell all the stagehands and the carpenters about the house and Christine's peril. Alcohol and concern for their favorite should do the trick. The cellars and the lake will be swarming with men. Erik will be under siege. He will never escape."

"How could you do such a thing without consulting me first!"

"I like to take precautions, Monsieur. If Erik should turn the tables on us and wring our necks, as you so nicely put it, then we will soon have the pleasure of his company in hell."

"Speak for yourself—I shall be in the other place!"

The Persian laughed in earnest. "Oh, no doubt, Monsieur, no doubt."

"Let's go."

"Very well, but your hand, Monsieur—at the level of your eyes."

The light swung about, danced upon the jackal head of Anubis and his fellow gods, then began to recede. "Damn that coward and his treacherous lasso!" The Viscount's voice was more distant.

Holmes stood, and Toby began to pant loudly. "Admirable dog!" he exclaimed. "What a pair they make, Henry. If ever two scoundrels deserved one another... And to think they consider themselves capable of challenging a mind as formidable as Erik's. The Persian is a mere thug. Yes, and Mifroid makes a worthy third. The police may find the house on the lake, but entering it is another matter."

"You heard what they said—we have at best an hour and a half to find Erik."

"Then we must get to work." He held out the shoe to the dog. "Remember, Toby. Find her."

Toby bounded forward again, but now Holmes held the leash securely. I shined the lantern on the gray stone floor before us. "That cat certainly startled me. I wonder how it survives down here."

"Come, Henry, is that not obvious even to you? The Opera employs many cats; their function is to limit the rat population."

"Lord, if there is one creature I cannot abide, it is a rat. When I think of the swarms of them lurking down here in this wretched, infernal darkness…" I shuddered.

"Although there are, as you so aptly put it, swarms of them down here, at least they have the good taste to keep themselves hidden."

A pained laugh escaped from my lips. "I do not find that reassuring."

Toby sniffed the toes of some goddess, then crossed over to a bas-relief of some Assyrian gods, the false stone slab tipped against the wall.

"Verdi's *Nabucco*." Holmes nodded at the slab. "Or perhaps Rossini's *Semiramide*. I suppose you would not relish the idea of the Phantom also lurking about somewhere in the darkness."

"No."

"I had hoped to find him before he made his way back to his house. We came down here quickly, and it must have taken him some time to descend from the heights of the stage."

"What if Toby does not pick up the scent?"

Holmes did not reply for a moment. "Then I shall have truly failed. Mifroid, the police and the mob may fill the cellars and surround the house on the lake, but they will never capture Erik. You saw the door to his house. Before they can break through, he will have fled to some other hiding place. He has had more than fifteen years to explore and to build secure nests. The fools might as well attempt to eliminate all the rats down here. Erik will laugh at them from the shadows."

We came upon long tubes of heavy canvas piled upon each other, rolled up scenery; between these canvas walls were narrow corridors. As Toby traversed them, I felt as if I were a pencil wielded by some giant hand trying to trace a way out of the maze.

Toby turned at the end of a row, halted, then thrust her nose even lower. She gave a loud bark which shattered the unnatural stillness, then she followed the trail between the gray stone wall on one side and the canvas on the other.

"Good dog, Toby!" Holmes exclaimed. "Remarkable creature! I'd gladly trade any number of Lestrades or Mifroids for an honest beast with a nose such as yours."

Toby led us to the stairway at the end of the room, then down the stone steps. The fourth level was much less cluttered. We were in a vast, empty cavern of brick and stone, and our footsteps gave a faint echo. We came to what appeared to be a great heap of corpses in armor, but I remembered that they were only dummies used to represent the fallen in battle. My light caught a vacant, cracked wooden face under a metal visor, the end of the nose broken off. Toby went round the pile, then stopped before the wall, sat back on her haunches, and barked loudly.

Holmes frowned. "As I thought. Somewhere in this wall is the entrance to a secret passageway."

"Then we are stymied," I said.

Holmes's black eyebrows dipped toward his formidable nose. "Not at all. I know a thing or two about secret passages. Once I have opened the door, Toby will follow the scent. Hold the light on the wall before me."

"We have less than an hour now before the Persian's servants act."

"It should suffice."

The wall was constructed of stone blocks some twelve inches square, and Holmes began to trace the outline of one with his fingertips. Fifteen minutes later he was down on his knees still examining the wall. Keeping up with Toby had kept me warm, but now, in spite of my wool sweater, pants, and overcoat, I felt cold. Toby whimpered softly.

"Perhaps we should try the place where Buquet was found," I said. "That was where the Persian and the Viscount were headed."

"We shall use the same route as the Phantom himself. The fact that Buquet was found hanging at that very spot does not auger well. If the Viscount does not heed the Persian's advice about keeping his hand raised, a similar fate may await him." Toby whimpered again. "Quiet," Holmes said sternly.

The cavernous cellar was so still that every sound seemed amplified: the scrape of Holmes's boots on stone as he stood up, his sharp quick intake of breath, Toby's rhythmic breathing. Behind us, from that heap of false dead, came a quiet scratching sound which made the hair at the back of my neck rise. A large rat, I thought. Toby heard, for she rose at once.

"Sit, Toby—*sit*," Holmes said.

She gave him a mournful glance, then obeyed. I was beginning to shiver; the silence weighed heavily upon my heart; and I had to struggle against a sudden urge to run away. "Any luck?" I said, although I knew the answer.

"*No.*"

The silence settled again about us, but soon I thought I heard music, someone humming. At first I suspected I was delirious, but then Toby rose and turned her head. "Holmes..."

"I hear it."

Across the vast chamber we saw a yellow-white light bobbing along. The humming changed to a whistling, and I recognized the tune. Sure enough, our visitor soon began to sing:

*Alouette, gentille alouette. Alouette, je te plumerai. Je te plumerai la tête, je te plumerai la tête. Et le bec, et le bec. Alouette, gentille alouette...*

"Who the devil can it be?" I asked.

"Someone of a strangely jolly disposition."

I swung the light about, and soon we saw an old man approaching us, lantern in one hand, the other hand holding a bag thrown over his shoulder. He wore a black beret and black woolen jacket. His face was lined and very pale except for a drunkard's bulbous red nose, similar to the one Holmes had sported as part of his workman's disguise. His gait was wobbly, probably from drink and age. For an instant I thought of Father Christmas with his bag of goodies, but this was clearly a darker, more sinister variant.

"*Bonsoir, bonsoir, mes bons Messieurs,*" he said with a silly laugh. Several of his teeth were gone, the remaining few brown and twisted. "*Bonsoir, ma jolie chienne,*" he said to Toby, at least getting her gender right.

She had shrunk back, and when he spoke to her, she began to bark furiously.

"Toby!" both Holmes and I exclaimed. She stopped barking, but a low growl came from her throat. I was quite surprised. She had always seemed to like everyone she met.

"How are you gentlemen this lovely evening?" the old man said. "We have not met before, have we? My memory is not what it used to be."

"No, we have not met," Holmes said, "and we are quite well. And you?"

"Oh, fairly well, although at my age the rheumatism or the liver is always a problem. It is tiresome to grow old, but I cannot complain. I have my work to keep bread and wine on the table and to entertain me. My old legs do get stiff." With a sigh, he lowered his bag; its shape shifted. The canvas material was filthy. Toby growled again.

"Your liver bothers you, does it?" I asked. Normally I found the French preoccupation with the liver comical; however, from the look of that nose, the old man was a good candidate for cirrhosis.

"Yes. The pain is right here." He pressed at his left side where his stomach would be.

Holmes's smile was rather frightful, and his fingers twitched impatiently. "What would your job be, Monsieur?"

"You do not know me? I thought everyone in the Opera knew old Jacob the rat catcher. Would you like to see the fine big ones I have just caught? They think they are smart, the rats of the Opera; they stay awake at night trying to figure a way to escape me; but I know the bait they like best. They cannot resist me, all save that old devil, the king of rats. He is as big as a cat, I tell you. I have seen him many times. He hurls taunts at me, but before I die I shall catch him. Then I shall really be famous. However, I have one here that is a good foot and a half long if you stretch his tail out all the way. Let me show you."

My mouth opened, but nothing came out. I could not tear my eyes from the bag. My hands were icy. The old man fumbled at the rope holding the bag closed. Toby rose, then barked madly, the sound echoing off the walls, filling the dark cellar.

"Toby!" Holmes shouted. "Toby! I am sorry, Monsieur, but you had better keep your bag closed. And now, will you pardon us? We have important work to do. We are inspecting the walls to make certain they are sound. We have heard of some... cracks."

"There is a fine big crack by the stairs near the lake. Would you like me to show you?"

"Another time. *Bonsoir.*"

"*Bonsoir*, Monsieur. Do you have the hour?"

Holmes withdrew his watch and grimaced. "Two minutes after midnight."

"Time to quit, I suppose. Time for a warm fire and a bit of drink. Hope to see you again. *Au revoir, ma bonne chienne.*" He hoisted the bag over his shoulder, and I could visualize the stiffening rat corpses shifting about inside. "*Alouette, gentille alouette...*" He strolled off, and soon we saw only the beam of his light bobbing upon the floor.

I eased my breath out between my teeth. Toby was still agitated. "What a dreadful little man."

"He seems quite good at his work, Henry, and quite pleased with himself. But how, I wonder, shall we ever get this blasted door open? We have wasted nearly half an hour. It must be something simple, a stone you press which activates a hidden mechanism. He has designed this for himself and does not want strangers or madmen like our rat catcher wandering in unexpectedly. The key must be his height. Only someone as tall as he can reach it, and yet I have examined all the stones along the ceiling."

I was shivering now and glanced overhead at the dark bricks set in dirty mortar. "Have you tried the ceiling itself?"

"I have not. Shine the light overhead. Ah, see that one brick, how the mortar about it is partially gone? You have redeemed yourself utterly, Henry. If ever I slight your abilities again, you need only remind me of this." He stretched out his arm and stood on his toes, but still could not reach the brick. "I did not think he was so much taller than I; however, his arms and fingers were quite long as well. This can be remedied easily enough."

Holmes seized one of the armored dummies by the leg and pulled it free. The others rattled about, and I heard a high pitched squeal which set my teeth on edge. Toby barked once, then leapt onto the dummies.

"Toby!" Holmes shouted.

I grabbed the leash and drew her back. Holmes stepped on the dummy's chest and pushed at the brick with his fingertips. "It gave way, Henry—it gave way!"

After a few seconds we heard a low, grinding noise; then a doorway in the wall appeared as a slab of stone slowly receded. On the left side was a black gap of about an inch. Holmes put his hand on the door and pushed; it swung open slowly. He took the lantern and briefly shone it through the doorway.

Curious, I took a step forward. Hard fingers sank into my arm, yanking me back even as some faintly hairy, slithery thing danced across my face, then leapt away.

"What in God's name…?"

Holmes shone the light upward on the thick hemp rope; its perfect hangman's noose still quivered faintly. "The Punjab lasso—one of them. When you stepped on that stone, the noose dropped; no doubt the heavy spring mechanism was meant to yank you up into the air and leave you dangling there."

I swallowed once, and a nervous cough slipped from between my lips.

"Fear not, Henry. The collar would have protected your neck, and I would have cut you down at once. We must waste no more time admiring these ingenious devices."

He gave the lantern back to me, then took Toby's leash. She lowered her head, her nose twitching eagerly, then started down the passageway. The stone walls were some three feet apart, but the outer wall against the earth was covered with a brownish moss or lichen. We had gone only a short way when we heard a grinding noise behind us, then a rumble: the door behind us seemed to have closed of its own will. My mouth still felt very dry, and I licked at my lips.

The passageway curved downward, the beam of yellow light jouncing along the outer wall. Toby panted heavily. Briefly I recalled one of Poe's tales where a character is bricked in alive, a recollection I could have done without.

We had walked for a good fifteen minutes when Holmes stopped so abruptly that I nearly bumped into him. Toby howled, the sound choked off abruptly.

"Good Lord!" I cried.

The floor had opened up before us, and Toby would have been lost if Holmes had not had a good hold of the leash. He bent over and seized her collar, then hoisted her up. He knelt down and stroked her head. His bowler hat was gone.

"Good dog, good Toby. Don't worry."

I stepped forward to the edge where the floor had given way and shone the lantern down. The light glistened off black water, circles radiating outward, some ten feet below. How cold it must be! A lone man would have fallen, his light extinguished, and be left floating–if he could swim–in utter darkness. Perhaps there was a way out. More likely, the poor wretch would swim about until cold, darkness, and fear took their toll; then the black waters would swallow their victim.

"What a sneaky trap! I–I almost knocked you over, Sherlock! Instead of just your hat, all three of us could be down there!" My hands shook, and the panic seized me.

"But you did not knock me over, and we are not down there," Holmes said quietly. "Thanks to Toby. I shall reward her for this. If we survive the night, I shall retire her to the country." He let out a great sigh. "A clever trap. One walks along at a good pace, and the floor abruptly gives way. It relies on the simple fact that a person walks in the middle of any path. The walls are some three feet apart, the opening two feet wide and exactly centered, a passage some six inches wide remaining on either side. I wonder. Have a hold of my arm, Henry."

With his back to the wall, he placed his right foot upon the narrow strip of stone; that section of the floor collapsed, swinging downward. All that remained was the narrow passage on the left side.

"Villain," I muttered. "Treacherous villain."

Holmes gave a sharp laugh. "Another clever touch. Most people, being right-handed, would take the passage on the right. This one seems solid."

He walked carefully across the narrow ledge. "Come, Toby." She barked once, then crossed.

I admired her equanimity, the quickness with which her good spirits had returned. My hands were still shaking, my fear gradually giving way to anger. I threw the satchel across, then followed Toby.

Holmes opened the satchel and took out a revolver. "We must be quite near the house on the lake. The long corridor behind us was designed to lull the senses into a misplaced confidence. I doubt Erik would try the same trick twice, but it is no longer safe to assume that the ground underfoot is solid. We must tread gingerly."

"Who—who will go first?"

He smiled. "Toby. And then I. Come."

Toby would gladly have resumed her earlier pace, but Holmes hesitated briefly with each step, testing the ground with his foot. The downward pitch of the passageway gradually leveled, and soon the light showed before us what seemed an ordinary oaken door with a brass knob. Holmes moved slower and slower, gradually wrapping the leather leash about his right hand and drawing Toby closer. He stopped some ten feet from the door, the dog at his side.

"Hush, Toby, hush."

"What is it?" I asked.

"I am not quite so willing to thrust my head into the noose a third time. This must be the very entrance to Erik's dwelling, and doubtlessly another booby trap remains."

"The floor again? Or the noose?"

"No, as I said, he would not use the same trick twice. Let me ponder this for a moment." He ran his long fingers through his black oily hair, his brow furrowing. His breath formed misty white vapor.

I could not understand his calmness. I was far too frightened to think clearly. Toby whimpered softly. "I wish I had a stick," he murmured, "a long one." I tried to slow my breathing down, but my nervous system would not be placated. I had to struggle with the urge to turn and run the other way.

"Hold the leash," he said. I did so, and he raised the lantern, shining the light slowly about us and peering sharply. "Do not move, Henry." Cautiously, he proceeded forward until he was only five feet from the door.

My lips formed a curse, but no sound came out. I thought of Michelle, and the thought completely unmanned me, bringing tears to my eyes.

"How does one usually open a door?" Holmes asked.

"By... by turning the doorknob."

"Exactly. So we shall at all cost avoid touching it." He took a step forward, raised his revolver, then gave the door a good solid kick. It swung open; he stepped back; a woman screamed. The room before us was dark.

"Monsieur Holmes—do not touch the doorknob!"

"Stay here," Holmes said, then rushed forward.

"Certainly not!" I cried. Toby bounded after him, and I followed, satchel in one hand, leash in the other.

The beam of Holmes's lantern darted about, revealing violins and organ pipes, then came an absolutely blinding light—as if the sun itself had suddenly appeared in that very room! I jerked shut my eyes, dropped the satchel, and tried to shield them with my hands. Toby howled, and Christine screamed again. I blinked, but all I could see was a kind of red fog, the afterimage of that terrible brightness. I lowered my hand. The light had dimmed, but I could not see right. I rubbed at my eyes, and finally they began to function normally.

We were in an oddly furnished room, one as baroque and outlandish as the Opera itself. Christine Daaé stood with her hand clutching at her head. She wore the white shift from the prison scene, her arms and feet still bare. A small man held her arm. He had a full black beard, brown skin, and black eyes, but something was peculiar about his expression.

"*Bonsoir*, Mr. Holmes, Doctor Vernier. How kind of you to come calling. Please make no sudden movements."

The voice came from behind us. I turned. The Phantom had had time to change out of his devil costume. He wore evening dress, the black cloak an archaic touch, and a black mask which hid his face but not his two blazing eyes. He held two revolvers. Holmes was half blinded like myself, his eyes blinking spasmodically, but he managed a smile. Both his hands were empty, and one of the Phantom's revolvers looked familiar.

Along the wall was a row of electric light bulbs, only about a third of them now illuminated, the filaments under the clear glass white hot. Just glancing at them made my eyes hurt.

"You have done very well, gentlemen. You made it past the noose, the trap door, and you did not touch the doorknob. If you had, the ceiling overhead and a ton or two of rock would have fallen upon you. Your eyes will recover soon. Electric light can be dazzling, and I like to show off the unusual features of my home."

Christine let her hand drop. "Oh, Monsieur Holmes, you should not have come. I am doomed, but I did not want you to be harmed."

We heard a muffled banging noise, then a faint voice. "Christine—Christine! What are you saying! For God's sake—get us out of here! We are burning up!" It was the Viscount de Chagny.

The Phantom's eyes smoldered behind the vapid mask. "My Christine is right—you should not have come. However, you are here; we are all here; and we must make the best of it. Please be seated, and then the final act will begin. I fear that the ending will not please you, not if you are enamored of happy endings."

*Thirteen*

꙰

Holmes and I sat on a purple velvet sofa with curved legs of elaborately carved wood. The parlor of the Phantom's house resembled something from the *Arabian Nights*, perhaps Ali Baba's cave, but he had the most modern conveniences, such as the electric light. The bluish orange flame within the stone fireplace was not from coal or wood, but from gas jets.

A spectacular Persian carpet covered the stone floor, the design minute and intricate, beautiful reds, golds, and blues on a beige background. Paintings in gilded frames hung from the walls: strange, haunted landscapes, and Botticelli's slender nymphs in gossamer veils. There was also a variety of musical instruments: violins, flutes, horns, and recorders. The organ pipes formed one entire wall, and on either side of its keyboards were a harpsichord and an ebony grand piano. Statues, busts, and vases were also abundant. Rising over the piano was Apollo holding forth his lyre, a miniature of the statue on the Opera roof; in a corner was a goddess, her smooth marble limbs nearly as enticing as those of a real woman.

Christine had collapsed into a purple chair which matched the sofa, and the Phantom handed the small bearded man one of the two revolvers. "If either of those two men tries anything, you will shoot him. *Comprenez-vous?*"

The man hesitated so long I thought he did not understand. His stare was vacant, his eyes curiously focused, but at last he nodded.

Two gas lamps hung upon brackets over the organ manuals. Eric turned up the flames, then threw a switch which extinguished the brilliant electric bulbs. The gas lamps were of colored glass and cast a warm yellow light, the effect much less stark. The room would have seemed cozy and relaxing if not for the two pistols leveled at us.

"You may remove your coats, gentlemen. I think you will find it rather warm otherwise."

After the damp chill of the cellars, the warmth was welcome, but we took off our overcoats slowly, not wishing to alarm the Phantom's armed companion. Toby sat at our feet, panting, her tongue lolling from her mouth, her tail brushing back and forth along the carpet, the very picture of contentment.

"Stupid dog," I muttered.

Erik sat on the bench before the organ and crossed his legs. His black mask was made of porcelain, its surface smooth and glossy. The long fingers of his left hand drummed out some pattern upon his knee, while the other hand held the revolver. Even the smallest of his movements showed a fluid gracefulness, and we knew he was physically strong. Weak men do not rapidly clamber up ropes with ninety-pound women tossed over their shoulders. All in all, he had the bearing of a natural aristocrat. The Viscount might have the title and the fortune, but not this man's genius or his sheer physical presence. With the mask hiding his face, it was easy to understand why Christine had imagined him beautiful; his horrible face seemed an impossible blemish.

"It is a great pleasure to have visitors in my modest dwelling, especially ones so distinguished as the diva Christine Daaé and the detective Sherlock Holmes. I know of Toby from *The Sign of the Four*, and you are also welcome, Doctor Vernier."

Again we heard the muffled voice of the Viscount. "For God's sake, Christine! Help us!"

She covered her eyes with the palms of her small white hands. "Please, Erik—*please.*"

The Phantom laughed, the sound as melodic as his voice. "Can I be blamed, gentlemen, if the Viscount and his friend the Persian are so stupid as to drop into my torture chamber? Did I invite them here? My chamber, unlike the one built for the Sultana, was not constructed to roast people alive. The temperature is no worse than that of a warm summer afternoon in Africa. He has been in there hardly an hour; yet the Viscount behaves as if he had been lost in the desert for days. The chamber is rather amusing, an arrangement of mirrors constructed to give the impression of a vast wasteland. We shall have a look later. It should interest you, Monsieur Holmes."

"No doubt. Mazes and puzzles have always interested me."

"I have not introduced my servant, Victor. He has been with me some twenty years, ever since Persia. The *daroga*'s men murdered his parents and cut out his tongue. He was only a boy then, and his mind has never recovered from the shock.

"But he is probably quite knowledgeable about gas and electric systems."

The Phantom stared at Holmes. The black mask hid his entire face; when he stopped speaking it was difficult to know anything of his true feelings. His eyes were expressive, but they could only tell you so much. At last he laughed.

"Monsieur Holmes, you are one of the few men I have ever met who more than lived up to his reputation."

Holmes's mouth twitched into a smile. "I might say exactly the same thing of you."

"What a pity you have left me no choice but to destroy you. Your death, however, will be brief and relatively painless." I sat up rather stiffly. "I am sorry, Doctor Vernier, but you must have realized that this was a dangerous business."

"My cousin is no threat to you," Holmes said. "You may let him go."

"I cannot take that risk."

"If you harm Sherlock, I swear I shall hunt you down if it is the last thing I ever do." As soon as the words were out of my mouth, I regretted my rashness.

"Please, Doctor—spare me the melodramatic clichés. You see, Mr. Holmes, that I have no choice."

Christine was pale, but her eyes were angry. "And what will you do with Raoul?"

The Phantom was briefly silent. "He and his companion will remain exactly where they are."

She clenched her fists. "You cannot do such a thing!"

"Oh, no? Tonight your lover and that human scum with him set a trap for me. He, the Persian, and Monsieur Mifroid thought they could capture me."

Christine drew in her breath. "No, you are lying!"

The Phantom turned to us. "Monsieur Holmes."

Sherlock nodded. "He speaks the truth."

"But why? We were going to run off together, yes, but it was not necessary to harm you! I did not know."

"I believe you, Christine." Erik's voice was soft as a caress. "I believe you, but that does not change matters. He must be punished, and the simple fact remains that I will never be safe so long as the Viscount or the Persian remain alive."

"You are not God, Monsieur! Only He can judge, only He can punish."

"You are wrong, Christine." The beautiful voice changed, a quaver shaking it, a quake which threatened to destroy everything. "Here in my domain, in my kingdom, I am God, I am the law. I make the rules. I punish, I reward, and those creatures shall die."

"And do you think I shall care to live on after all these deaths?"

"Yes. You are not the type of person to kill yourself. You could not commit such a sin." The last word was faintly ironic.

She closed her hand about the cross she wore. "We shall see—we shall see."

The two of them stared at one another, neither flinching. At last the Phantom turned away and set down his revolver. "Enough of such morbid talk. I thought we would have a musical interlude. I have at last completed my opera, *Don Juan Triomphant*, and I hoped it would interest you, Monsieur Holmes. Perhaps, too, we could play a duet on the violin."

Holmes crossed his legs. "May I smoke? Thank you." He withdrew his cigarette case from his coat pocket. "Nothing would be more agreeable, but I do not think we shall have the time."

"And why not? We have all the time in the world."

"Alas, I fear not. Monsieur Mifroid by now knows the whereabouts of this house on the lake, as do the stagehands and carpenters. They will all soon be knocking at your door."

Eric stared at him, then he stood. "I shall drown them! I shall drown them both like the rats they are!"

He started across the room, but Christine stepped before him. She was more than a foot shorter than he and seemed ludicrously small confronting him. "You shall not! I forbid it! Or will you destroy me as well? Am I not a vermin—a rat—as well?"

"No, Christine." His voice was quiet.

"But I am! I have promised to be the wife of that little vermin. I too must be an insect. I, too, must die."

Erik drew himself up to his full height and raised his hands; when they began to shake, he let them drop. "*No*." His voice was pained.

"Why not? You must murder everyone else—why not me?"

"You have not betrayed me—not yet, not as he has. You would not take even my home from me, my refuge, my universe. Please sit down. I must think about this."

"You must kill me, Monsieur. You must drown me or roast me or..."

"Sit down!"

Toby had risen. She whimpered, but Holmes bent over and petted her. Christine, her face flushed, returned to the chair.

The Phantom sat again on the bench. "It was the Viscount, was it not? I cannot believe you would..."

"It was the Persian."

"That vile maggot. I should have disposed of him long ago."

"Why did you not?"

"The Sultana grew bored with us both at the same time. His warning saved my life, but he could never have escaped on his own. We were even, he and I. He has troubled me before here in Paris, and I warned him the next time he invaded my domain would be the last. Mercy is foolish with such as he. Humanity will be well served by his death. He has slaughtered literally hundreds. My crimes are nothing compared to his."

Holmes exhaled a cloud of smoke. "No? How much blood is on your hands?"

Erik was silent, motionless, and I wished again that a mask did not hide his face. "The Sultana left me no choice. If I had not built the torture chambers, someone else would have—and I would be dead."

"And Joseph Buquet?"

"He was another vermin. Ask any of the dancers. He came seeking trouble, and he found it. I did not directly kill him. He had an unfortunate encounter with one of my traps, a certain lasso."

Holmes smiled faintly. "We know about your traps."

"They are barbaric!" I exclaimed. "You are no better than the squire who sets a steel leg trap for poachers. A man can be maimed for life, an innocent man, or even a child."

"Innocent men and children do not frequent the lower cellars of the Paris Opera." His voice was heavy with irony. "If vermin, filthy vermin or rats, invade a man's sanctuary, may he not trap and kill them? But it is not I who am on trial. Here in my kingdom I need not justify myself to any man."

"As Mademoiselle Daaé has noted, you are not God," I said. "Your genius does not raise you above common human decency. With your talents come greater obligations toward those less fortunate."

"What utter nonsense! All my life your common humanity has mocked and reviled me. My own mother could not bear to see my face. She made me wear a mask and sold me even as a child to a circus. My earliest memories are of people peering at me, their bloated white faces nearly as grotesque as my own. Fear and loathing, or contempt and amusement, are all my fellow men have ever offered me. Saints may return hatred with love, but I am no saint. Save your grand speeches for someone else, Doctor. My sins are not the issue here."

"But…"

Abruptly he stood. "Silence!"

Toby sat up and barked, but Holmes quieted her, then put his hand on my arm. "Leave him be, Henry."

Christine smiled coldly. "You see, Doctor. He does consider himself a god, the giver of life and death."

The Phantom stared at her, then he whirled about and sat before the organ. His fingers touched the keys; the majestic swell of the organ pipes filled the small room. He played a few scales with his fingers, then he used his feet. After a pause he began to play Bach, one of the toccatas and fugues. His playing was remarkable, the instrument a fine one, but I was hardly in the mood to appreciate the music. Christine Daaé shared my sentiments. Holmes, however, had closed his eyes and lost himself to everything but the music. His right hand tapped lightly at his knee, following the rhythm.

When the Bach ended, with no transition, Erik played the strangest music I have ever heard, its rhythms and harmonies completely alien. Some of the dissonant chords set my teeth on edge, but in spite of everything, it was beautiful—very sad—but beautiful. He made you feel his pain, the pain of being alone, of being born, and then he began to sing. No other man could have sung those melodies. Christine had said that his voice could encompass the range of tenor, baritone, and bass, and she had not exaggerated. One moment he would hit a low E or F, the bottom notes of the bass; then he would soar above high C, that bane of tenors. I do not think he was using falsetto; yet he sang impossibly high. The words were difficult to distinguish, something about the triumph of love, the triumph of Don Juan. At the end, the organ boomed out low notes while his voice became a cry at a still higher pitch, a shriek of agony. Not even a lyric soprano like Christine Daaé could have reached that height.

The silence after he was finished was overwhelming. Here, far underground, it seemed to emanate from deep within the dark earth. I heard Christine Daaé breathing and the ticking of the massive pendulum clock in the corner of the room. It was twelve-forty.

"Bravo." Holmes clapped. "Bravo." His face was flushed. Christine and I stared at him.

Erik turned. "You approve, do you?" He was wary.

"Yes," Holmes said,

"Christine—Christine, what was that din! Are you unharmed?" It was the Viscount.

Holmes laughed. "The Viscount does not appreciate the fine arts."

Christine clenched her fists. "You are burning him up, I know it."

"Nonsense!" The Phantom raised one hand and clutched at his forehead. When he felt the mask, his hand jerked away. "Enough of this. As Mr. Holmes pointed out, we have little time left."

A loud bang, only partially muffled, came from behind the wall to the torture chamber. Victor stood up and gazed at his master, but his revolver remained aimed at us.

"That fool." The Phantom laughed. "Does he think he can shoot his way out? My torture chambers have thick walls, as the *daroga* surely knows. He brought along his antique dueling pistols, which are each good for one shot, hardly a match for a revolver such as this."

"Erik—please." Christine rose, took a hesitant step, then rushed forward, fell on her knees, and grasped his legs. "I beg of you—let them go. In God's name, let them go." She wept.

The Phantom did not move. "Damnation," he whispered. "Oh God, how I am weary of life." He pointed with the revolver. "Would you like to have a look, gentlemen? You can see them through that small window. Do not forget that Victor or I shall surely shoot you if you try any trickery."

Holmes and I went to the window. Holmes looked first. "Very ingenious."

The floor of the torture chamber appeared to be an octagon. Mirrors lined the walls, casting the same desert scene all about. One of the sides must have been the original of the image, but I could not tell which one. A brilliant yellow-white light flooded the chamber, no doubt provided by hidden electric bulbs. The Persian and the Viscount had removed their coats and opened their shirts, to no avail; they were drenched with sweat. The Persian was down on his knees, feeling at the wooden planks, his astrakhan hat beside him. The Viscount appeared half delirious; he wandered about, striking at the walls and howling. I raised my hand to touch the glass; it felt very warm.

"Please sit down again, gentlemen. I assume the Persian is still searching the floor while the Viscount stumbles about?"

Holmes nodded. "And will the Persian find the mechanism he seeks?"

Erik laughed. "Perhaps. Your dog is making me nervous, Monsieur Holmes. Please take him to my bedroom there, Doctor Vernier." Toby gave us a desolate look. I grasped her collar and led her to the door. I saw red drapery hanging from the walls and an ebony coffin with red lining and a red pillow.

"You need go no further, Doctor, merely close the door. Thank you. Please sit down. Now, Christine, you may let go of my leg. This theatrical display is trite and annoys me." She stood and clenched her fists. "Ah, that is much better. Now you show me your true self, the flame of your anger. You are no whimpering, sobbing baby like your Viscount."

"Insults are cheap, Monsieur."

He crossed his legs, then pointed with the pistol barrel at the mantel over the fireplace. "I have a proposition for you. Do you see those two small black caskets? Open them up and tell me what you find."

Christine ran her hands up along her face, brushing her long blonde hair off her shoulders. Her eyes were swollen from weeping, and one could see how exhausted she was. She had, after all, sung an entire opera, then been hauled about the Opera House over Erik's shoulder. Still, she was very beautiful, her arms white and slender, her feet and hands delicate. If Erik had been a decent man, he would have given her a coat or blanket; the prison shift resembled a flimsy nightgown. She went to the mantel and opened one of the small black boxes.

"In the left one is a golden grasshopper; in the other, a black scorpion."

"Very good. Now tell me, would you do anything to save your precious Viscount?"

Her eyes opened wide, and she raised her hands. "Anything!"

He was silent for a moment. "Would you consent to become my wife?"

Her face twisted, and she slowly lowered her hands.

The Phantom gave a laugh which reminded me of Holmes's short staccato sounds. "I see that 'anything' does not really mean 'anything.'"

"You are cruel," she whispered.

"I give you a simple choice. Turn the grasshopper on the left, and you will become my bride. I shall release the Viscount and these two men. Only the Persian need die. Turn the scorpion on the right, and we shall all perish, quickly and painlessly. The choice is yours."

"You are bluffing!" I exclaimed. "How could you kill us all so quickly?"

Christine smiled at me, but Holmes shook his head. "He is not bluffing, Henry."

Silently I cursed the Phantom's mask for hiding him, for hiding everything but those desolate, unwavering eyes.

"Monsieur Holmes is correct, Christine. I do not bluff. Do not think that Mifroid or the others will save you. No one can enter or leave this room without my consent. The choice is yours—the grasshopper means life, the scorpion universal death."

Christine stared at the two caskets. "This is no *choice*. You offer me true death or, far worse, a living death."

"All the same, the choice is yours. Turn one and you will see."

Christine stared at the caskets, her eyes moving back and forth. Tears seeped from her eyes. She swallowed, and the muscles along her slender throat rippled. "I am so tired."

"Are you?" the Phantom murmured. "Ah, Christine, if only you knew how much I love you—how much I would treasure you." His voice spun her about as if she were a marionette on a string, and they stared at each other, neither one moving.

At last we heard a cry from the torture chamber, then the jarring voice of the Viscount. "Christine, there is black powder below us, barrels and barrels full, enough to blow us all to kingdom come!"

"My God," I whispered. Again I thought of Michelle, and although I was an agnostic, I prayed that somehow we might be spared.

"The Persian has found the trap door in the floor," the Phantom said. "The Viscount is correct. There is more than enough powder to end our miserable lives and to destroy Garnier's wonderful palace. Choose, Christine."

She stared at the two boxes, then raised one trembling hand and brought it closer and closer to the box on the right, the one containing the black scorpion. I bit at my lips to keep from crying out, then clasped Holmes by the arm. "Good-bye."

"I am sorry, Henry."

Christine had her hand in the box, but she jerked it away as if she had been burned. "Oh, I cannot—I will not! It is not fair! You are indeed a monster. I shall not choose." She went to the chair and collapsed into it, hiding her face from him

"Shall I choose for you?" Erik asked.

Holmes gave a sharp laugh. "Then it would hardly be much of a choice, would it? I am always amazed at how men of great ability can be reduced to idiocy by women."

The Phantom turned his smooth black mask toward us. The mask itself had a placid expression upon it, a thin slit in the insipid smile of the mouth. "What do you mean?"

"Do you actually believe you can force a woman like Christine Daaé to be your bride? Earlier you spoke of melodramatic clichés. How long do you think you could keep her? Coercion and threats are not a stable foundation for a marriage, no more than riches and handsome features. Would you make her your slave? For bondage is what you offer. Marry me or die—what a choice! Give her a real choice, once and for all."

"What would you have me do?"

"Release the Viscount. Put him alongside yourself, then let her choose."

Christine stared at Holmes in horror. "*No*."

"This ridiculous business has gone on long enough. You are too brilliant a man to wallow forever in the mire of love. Finish this thing, for her sake as well as your own. You say that you love her?"

"I do!"

"Then give her the choice and live with the results. None of us in this room wishes you dead. I can take care of the Viscount and the Persian. You will be safe from them."

The Phantom laughed. "They are the least of my worries."

"I guessed as much. Mifroid and his men will be here in a moment. Let us finish this scene. It is late, and we are all fatigued."

"Very well. Victor, you may open the door to the torture chamber."

Christine's eyes were wide open, fixed upon the Phantom. "What are you saying?"

"Open the door, Victor."

Victor must have been well past thirty, yet his face had a certain childish aura, a disturbing innocence blended as it was with madness. He shook his head and went "*Uhh*." That sharp, garbled vowel was very far from the mellifluous voice of his master.

"Open it."

Christine was up on her feet. "Raoul, he has spared you!"

Victor turned the doorknob, and we heard the grinding of hidden gears. A few seconds later, the oaken door swung open. A loud boom made me want to clap my hands to my ears. Christine screamed, while Victor whirled about, red blood spouting from a hole in his throat. He threw open his arms, dropping the revolver, and staggered toward Erik. The acrid smell of powder filled the room.

"Pick up the revolver," Holmes said to me, then he crossed the room in three strides and took the other revolver from Erik's hand. Erik hardly noticed. Victor had clasped his arms about him. He would have fallen, but the Phantom supported him. Toby barked loudly from the other room.

"You have killed him!" Christine shrieked.

"At last!" cried the Viscount.

I picked up the revolver and thrust it in my coat pocket. "For God's sake, try to stop the bleeding!"

Erik and I laid Victor on the sofa. His face was yellowish white, his eyes nearly empty of life. Although I knew it was hopeless, I put a handkerchief over the wound. Almost at once it was soaked through with blood. Victor choked, then closed his eyes. For a few seconds still I felt the faint pulse under my palm, then it stopped. His eyes opened again, but nothing was there. I closed them.

"He is gone," I said. "The bullet pierced the jugular. He had no chance." His black suit was wet with blood, as were my hands and the handkerchief. I stood up. The Phantom stood beside me, his white shirt and cravat stained bright scarlet, bloody hand prints on his coat. He did not move. I turned to the Viscount. "You damned murderer."

The Viscount let the dueling pistol drop from his hand. "It was an accident."

Erik sat down on the sofa beside the dead man and turned toward the wall, no doubt wishing to hide his grief from us. Christine took a step toward him, but the Viscount seized her wrist. "Who is that fellow?"

"His servant," she said.

The Viscount sighed, then fumbled at a button on his shirt. He was a mess, his shirt damp with sweat, the collar gone, his reddish-brown hair in his eyes. The Persian was equally disheveled, but he appeared pleased.

Holmes watched us all, revolver in hand, that bitter, ironic smile twisting at his lips. His face seemed grotesque, gargoylish, with its great nose, sloping forehead, oily black hair, and those furious eyes.

"Monsieur Holmes, you have saved the day," said the Viscount. "You will be well rewarded. The Phantom's reign has ended at last. He will not find it so easy to play tricks behind prison bars."

Holmes shook his head. "No, my dear Viscount." He aimed the pistol at de Chagny's breast. "If you or the Persian make any sudden movements, I shall, with very little regret, shoot you."

The Viscount was genuinely amazed. "You are jesting."

"I assure you I have never been more serious in my life." He backed over toward the organ bench, then sat down. "Henry, the other revolver." I walked over and handed it to him.

"This is an outrage! You will be sorry for this, I swear it!"

"No doubt, Monsieur. Kindly release Mademoiselle Daaé and go stand before the sofa. You, *daroga*, will stay where you are and not move a muscle. Both of you would be wise not to give me an excuse to shoot you. If I had not urged Erik to free you, that poor fellow would not be lying there dead."

Christine Daaé's smooth brow wrinkled, her small mouth forming a *moue*. "Monsieur Holmes..." Her green eyes were confused.

"Please remain silent, Mademoiselle. Erik, you have my sincere condolences. I blame myself for this death. I should have known the Viscount was capable of criminal stupidity."

"Monsieur Holmes!" Flushing, the Viscount took a step forward. Sherlock aimed the revolver at him and glared. After a few seconds the Viscount retreated a step. "By God, I shall pay you for this."

"Erik, would you please stand."

The Phantom drew in his breath unevenly because of the small slit in the mouth of the mask, then rose. His posture was very straight. His big white hands hung loosely at his side, half hidden in the blackness of the cloak. His eyes, staring out from the holes in the mask, were red rimmed.

Holmes crossed his legs. "Very well. Now, Mademoiselle Daaé, you may choose between them."

"What?" said Christine and the Viscount simultaneously.

"You heard me, Mademoiselle. Make your choice."

The Viscount smiled broadly and raised his hands. "Christine, my darling!" When she did not move, his smile slowly faded away.

She put her lower lip between her teeth, stared at first one man, then the other.

"Christine!"

"Please keep silent, Monsieur. If she loves you, she should not require prompting."

I watched her green eyes shift between the two men. She was very pale. Worried now, the Viscount could not keep silent. Perhaps he realized how small and immature he appeared alongside Erik. Moreover, having suffered in the desert of the torture chamber for over an hour, he certainly did not look his best.

"This is unfair. Make him remove his mask—then let her choose."

Holmes shook his head. "No."

Christine clenched her fists. She seemed as perturbed as earlier when choosing between the grasshopper and the scorpion. Tired as she was, her arms and the shift soiled from her journey through the Opera, she was still remarkably beautiful. I realized that her spirit had always appealed to me–a certain fire–a wildness which augmented her beauty.

She turned to Holmes and me. "What am I to do?"

"Christine!" moaned the Viscount.

I glanced at Holmes. "Surely…"

He put down the pistol in his left hand, then grasped my arm and shook his head. "*No*, Henry. She is not a child. She is a woman. She and she alone must choose. She knows them only too well. We need not comment upon their merits and demerits. Much as we would like to choose for her, we cannot."

Christine stared at him without moving, her face very pale. I could not bear to look at her and glanced instead at the statue of Apollo.

"Mademoiselle Daaé, you have dallied long enough. Put an end to this farce." Holmes's voice had an edge to it. Although I understood his anger, a part of me still wanted to protect Christine.

Finally she lowered her eyes and went to the Viscount. He embraced her, but she hardly responded. "You will never regret it, Christine–I swear it!"

Holmes reached inside his coat for his cigarette case. "A happy ending at last." He did not bother to hide his sarcasm. He thrust a cigarette between his lips, then dropped a box of matches on the bench beside him. "Would you light my cigarette, Henry?"

Erik turned away slowly; hence he could not see Christine's anguished look.

I struck the match. Holmes inhaled, then took the cigarette in his left hand. "Erik, how much time shall we have to make our escape? We can let these three out by the lake, and then Henry and I shall help carry away your most precious belongings."

"I do not wish to live. This is my home, my world, and I prefer to die here."

Holmes drew in on his cigarette. "Blast it all," he muttered. "I wish I had never come to the wretched Paris Opera, never heard of its wretched Ghost, never…"

The Persian eyed him uneasily. "Mifroid is late, but he must be here soon. Perhaps he is busy commandeering boats. Set us free."

Holmes stood up. "Gladly."

Erik whirled about, his black cape billowing out, then drew himself up to his full height, his eyes raging. "No, do not bother—you may as well die here with me."

We all stared at him. "What are you saying?" I asked.

"I mean that I am not so easily vanquished. This is my kingdom, and here I rule. It is not absolutely necessary that one turns the scorpion." He raised his long arm and pointed at the mantel.

"No, indeed." The high little voice came from one of the ebony caskets.

"We may turn ourselves," said a different voice from the other casket.

"Good Lord!" I exclaimed, and the Viscount crossed himself.

Holmes gave an impatient frown. "Henry, need I remind you that he is a skilled ventriloquist? Small scorpions and grasshoppers cannot talk."

"Can we not?" said the tiny voice.

"No. Your tricks will not put me off my guard."

The Phantom laughed. "My friends may not be real, but a few minutes ago, as a precaution, I started a timer connected to the detonator for the barrels of powder. Even without Christine turning the scorpion, we shall all be blown to pieces. You can run, if you wish, but you will never reach the surface in time. Tons of falling bricks and stone will crush you. Here it should be more immediate and painless, a brief black roar, then nothing. We have perhaps five minutes left."

His remarkable calm frightened me more than anything. I glanced at the clock. It was twenty-five past one.

"You are lying!" shouted the Viscount.

Holmes laughed. "How stupid of me not to realize it was all too easy."

I leaned against the piano, thinking again of Michelle and wishing I had not been so slow, so cautious, about my love for her.

"I do not want to die!" the Viscount said. "Christine, I…"

"Oh, keep silent for once," she said.

She stared at Erik. The Persian and the Viscount were terrified, but not she. She took a step forward, then another. She was so pale in the white smock that she seemed a ghost already. At last she reached Erik. His sad eyes stared down at her. Slowly she raised her hand, then pushed aside the mask. The black porcelain broke when it struck the floor.

She sobbed but did not look away. At that instant, I think all of us felt the cruelty, the injustice, of fate: that such a man should be afflicted with that face, that white, noseless, rotting visage! But was not that face also a mask? Its ugliness hid the true man, the splendid inner man, even more than the porcelain mask had. All of us were similarly trapped behind our masks. Mask that face might be, but one made of living flesh. I saw his pain in the grimace that bared his yellow teeth and in the shadows beneath those lonely eyes.

She put her hand on his shoulder, then slipped it around behind his neck and drew him down to her. Her face was hidden from us, his partly so, but I could see one of his eyes. As she kissed him, his eye closed, and he put his arms about her and lifted her up off the ground as if she were a child. The kiss went on, and I looked away.

The Viscount stared. "Christine!"

"Oh, Christine." The Phantom almost sang her name. He held her in his arms, clasped her to him, but she had gone limp. Her arms hung loosely, her head and blonde tresses sagging to the side.

"What have you done to her!" cried the Viscount.

Holmes put out his cigarette in a large crystal ashtray. "She has only fainted."

Erik picked up Christine, cradling her in his arms, then set her down in the purple velvet chair. "I could never have hurt her, do you understand? I do love her. How could I possibly harm her?"

He ran his fingers along her cheek, his horrible face showing a pathetic tenderness. She opened her eyes, saw him, and moaned. She whispered, "No." He stroked her cheek a last time, then walked over to the keyboard of the organ. His back was to us, the black cloak hiding him, then he turned.

"Take her and go. I have reset the detonator. You will have just time enough before the Palais Garnier tumbles down, its foundation blown away. Go to the closet in my room there. Inside the closet is a door opening upon a passageway. It leads to the surface near the Rue Scribe. Hurry now."

The Viscount and the Persian were only too eager to follow this suggested course of action. Christine slowly stood, and the Viscount pulled at her arm. "Come on." She was staring at Erik, a faint flush on her cheek, and she did not move.

He unfastened his cloak, whirled it about and threw it to her. The black cloth undulated like a sea creature swimming through dark waters. "The passageway is very cold, and you are hardly dressed. My cape will keep you warm." Even as he spoke he kept his face turned from her.

"Hurry, Christine!"

She wrapped the cloak about herself, hiding her lovely white shoulders in its black folds. "Good-bye. Good-bye, my Angel of Music. *Adieu.*" She could not bring herself to look at him, but her voice broke on the last word.

"Christine!" She let the Viscount pull her away, but I saw the tears glisten in her eyes. The Persian had opened the bedroom door, and Toby bounded happily into the room with a loud bark. Sherlock had sat in the purple velvet chair, and she went to him.

"Come," I said to Holmes.

He had set down both revolvers on the end table. He petted Toby and shook his head. "No, I prefer to stay. You go with them."

"But you will be killed!"

He shrugged. "I wish to speak with Erik."

The Phantom sat on the organ bench, the bottom of his black frock coat nearly touching the floor. Again he began to play that strange, disturbing music, his back swaying in time to the rhythm. Toby whimpered softly.

"Sherlock, this is madness!"

A loud rapping was heard at the door to the lake, the clang of metal upon metal. "Open up!" a voice cried.

Erik slumped, the organ music dying away, and he sighed. "Deal with them, would you?" he said over his shoulder.

Again came the high, jarring clang of metal upon metal. "Open up, I say!"

Holmes stood and went to the door. "This is Sherlock Holmes. Is Monsieur Mifroid at hand?"

"He is. *Un instant.*"

I gazed at the clock, watching the pendulum behind the glass swing back and forth. "Sherlock…"

"Monsieur Holmes?"

"*Oui, Monsieur Mifroid. Le Fantôme* has set a timer which will trigger a tremendous explosion. You and your men must return to the surface at once. Clear everyone out of the Opera House."

"My God—are you serious?"

"Yes. Go. There is not a second to waste. Christine Daaé is safe. She and the Viscount de Chagny have already departed."

"But you, Monsieur Holmes—can you not come out?"

"Never mind me. I have other business, but I may yet escape. Leave a boat, please, one with oars. Go at once."

"Very well. You are a brave man, Monsieur Holmes. *Adieu.*"

I grabbed Holmes's arm and squeezed it hard. "Now can we go?"

He gave me a withering glance, and I released him. "I wish to speak to the Phantom. Take Toby and go. Use the same route as the Viscount."

I hesitated; swallowing was difficult with so dry a mouth. "I cannot leave you."

"I command you to go."

"No."

"The doctor is quite rational in wishing to leave," Erik said. "I suggest you both depart."

Holmes returned to the purple chair, sat down, and crossed his legs. "This is a remarkably comfortable chair, one constructed in Versailles during the early eighteenth century. Pardon the digression. I have been wishing to chat with you for some time. You will not frighten me away now."

"I am not bluffing."

"I realize that. You need not hide your face from me. I do not find it particularly frightful."

Erik played a quick scale, then turned upon the bench to face us. His eyes probed ours and saw that we were not repulsed. I had observed cases of leprosy in the Orient which caused far worse afflictions. At least his limbs, his hands and feet, had been spared. The disturbing thing was the incongruity between his face and the rest of him, especially that remarkable voice.

Holmes lit a cigarette. "The Palais Garnier is a remarkable edifice, perhaps a trifle ostentatious, but remarkable all the same. The paintings and the sculpture suffer from a general sameness and an overblown grandeur, but a structure such as the grand stairway is truly magnificent. I have always had a fondness for marble. It seems almost alive, rather like living skin, the same delicate flushes and subtle variations of color. Would you destroy all of this? Would you deprive future generations of so splendid a monument? I appeal to you as an artist. Even if you must kill yourself, spare the Opera House."

The Phantom was silent for a long while. "Very well. As you say, what would be the point? Things of beauty are rare." He turned his back to us, again working some hidden mechanism. "There. The powder chamber is divided into separate compartments. Half the barrels will be flooded with water. Those remaining will only annihilate the cellars directly above us. The Palais Garnier itself will be spared. This also gives you additional time to make your escape." He glanced at the clock, which showed a quarter to two. "If you leave within the next five minutes, you will still live. The police have left you a boat, and you know the way to the landing by the staircase. That is far enough away that you will be safe from the explosion."

The torture chamber door was still open, and even as he finished speaking, we heard the roar of the flooding waters. I wiped the sweat from my brow and collapsed into an empty chair, immensely relieved. Perhaps I would yet live to see Michelle.

Holmes absentmindedly stroked Toby. "Tell me, Erik, have you read Hugo's *Notre-Dame de Paris*?"

"Yes, of course."

"And have you consciously modeled yourself after Quasimodo?"

The Phantom grimaced. "*No*."

"Perhaps it was unconscious. Quasimodo was the very soul of the

Cathedral even as you are the soul of the Opera. It will be a far poorer place without you."

"Monsieur Holmes, I have quite decided to end my life, and you will not persuade me otherwise."

"Why must you die?"

"What have I to live for?"

"Your art—your music."

The Phantom laughed. "One cannot hold one's art. I would trade it all for another kiss from Christine Daaé."

"As I told you once before, she is only a child. She was unworthy of you. By the way, I have the ring you gave her."

Erik stood. "I shall not allow you to insult her!"

Holmes smiled. "Now you sound like the Viscount."

The Phantom stared at him. His mouth twisted. "I do, don't I? How wretched of you to point out the resemblance."

"Do sit down. I also told you that there were other women."

Erik laughed, but we heard only pain. "Please do not say such things. Do not try to make me hope. My face condemns me to perpetual solitude."

Holmes hesitated. "You will always have one friend so long as you live."

"Forgive me if I am amused. I do not mock your friendship, but only some seventeen minutes remain of my miserable existence. I would greatly value your friendship, but it would not suffice. There are men who can live alone without the society, the intimacy, of women, but I am not such a man. Knowing Christine has made it far worse. I thought, I truly thought, that she might love me. I can bear my dreadful solitude no longer. Even Victor, poor, dumb Victor, has been taken from me. The need is like a pain, a hunger. Perhaps I have committed many grave sins, perhaps I am damned, but was I not born that way? Did some monstrous God form me with this face as a jest? Why should a mere child be tortured so? Ah, but God only laughs at my questions and my pain. One thing I do know, men and women were made for one another, to love, to cherish each other, and I… But you cannot understand. I only want to die."

Holmes stubbed out his cigarette. "I understand only too well."

The two men stared silently at each other, the same terrible intensity in their eyes, their faces. For an instant I sensed that all-consuming loneliness, something dark and sorrowful at the very core of their being. I felt suddenly cold: I struggled to recall Michelle's face, the touch of her hand, her lips. I glanced again at the clock.

"Sherlock, we must go."

"No."

The Phantom shook his head. "Why must you be so stubborn? I do not want yet another death on my conscience."

"I shall not leave you alone, not now. Besides, I am not finished with you. I believe I can offer you a new beginning, a new life."

"Sherlock…" I moaned.

"Take Toby and go—at once."

I could not speak. It was torture to keep still when every muscle in my body cried out for me to flee.

"I shall not answer to Michelle for your death. Go. You owe it to her."

I leapt to my feet, tears in my eyes. "That is unfair of you—unworthy! How dare you use my affection for her?"

Holmes also stood. "Will you be quiet and go! I do not want you to die with me."

"Both of you go," Erik said.

Holmes let out a great sigh. "Oh, very well. Come on, then." He turned, went abruptly to the massive metal door and began throwing the huge bolts.

I stared dumbly at him. "We are going?"

"Yes! Now come on. Take the dark lantern and these matches." He turned the latch, then used both hands to pull open the door.

Relief washed over me. I stared at the Phantom. "Good-bye." I put on my overcoat while walking to the doorway.

"After you," Sherlock said.

I started forward, but something struck me between the shoulder blades, square in the back. I staggered out onto the slippery stones and fell to my knees, nearly dropping the dark lantern. Behind me, the door closed with a great clang that echoed across the subterranean lake. The gas lamp on the wall cast enough light that I could see the dark waters and the dreary stone of the vault. I rose at once, struck the door with my fist, then winced with pain.

"Sherlock, come out here at once!"

"No. Be gone. Remember, take the boat down seven arches' distance, then turn to the left and continue on until you come to the stairway."

"I shall not leave!"

"Will you stop behaving like a fool? I do not want your ridiculous sacrifice. I may yet persuade Erik, but you are only in my way. I cannot think clearly or speak freely while I am worrying about you. Wait for me by the steps. You and Michelle need one another, and you owe her far more than you owe me. I shall not speak to you again."

"Open this door!"

There was no answer, only the vast, haunting silence of the black lake deep beneath the streets of Paris. With a final, futile blow that made me moan, I turned away. I managed to light the dark lantern and stepped warily into the boat. No doubt recalling my clumsiness with a punt, Holmes had asked for a boat with oars; he had known even then! Utterly alone, I wept as I rowed. The long night's adventures had overwhelmed and exhausted me. I remembered Victor dying, red blood spouting from his throat; I wondered how beautiful Christine Daaé could have ever chosen so petty and vicious a man as the Viscount; and I thought about the senseless waste of two such geniuses as Erik and my cousin. What for? What for?

I managed to quell my tears by the time I reached the stairway. I paced about the small stone landing, occasionally pausing to shine my light across the black waters. "Do come—please come, Sherlock."

I was still pacing when the great thunderclap came. The stones beneath me trembled, the very walls groaning in agony, and I thought Erik had miscalculated. I would be buried under tons of gray stone, my body lost forever. Then it was over, and the awesome silence returned.

I went to the steps and collapsed, burying my face in my hands. At last I sat up. There was no use staying any longer, but I was so tired, so heartsick, I could not move. An immense wave of water swept with a roar up over the stone floor, wetting my feet and legs, then withdrawing almost as quickly as it had come.

A few minutes later, I heard a regular splashing sound. I wondered what it might be, but I still could not bring myself to move. A figure clambered up out of the water, the top half white, the bottom black. I seized the lantern and raised it. His hair was wet and plastered back, but there was no mistaking the large nose, the ironic smile.

"Sherlock!" I cried, and I embraced my cousin as I had not done for many years.

"Why so surprised, Henry? I told you to wait for me."

Something else came out of the lake, then shook itself wildly, sending water flying everywhere.

"Toby!" I cried.

"You did not think I would abandon Toby?"

"And Erik?"

The joy went out of his eyes. "I have failed. Come on, let us get to the surface. I am freezing. The waters are cold and rather dirty."

"Take my overcoat."

"You are cold, too."

"Not now, and I have my sweater."

"Very well. Thank you Henry."

It was a good thing he had appeared, for I doubt I could have ever found my way alone through that maze of the cellars. The Opera House was empty. We walked alone down the grand staircase. The gas lights burned brightly, and the marble seemed warm and alive after the dead gray stone of the depths. When we stepped out into the night air and I saw the stars overhead, my heart swelled with exultation. I felt as Aeneas must have after returning from the underworld. I was alive, Michelle and all my life still before me.

A cry came from the crowd that had formed, then Mifroid and his men rushed toward us.

"Monsieur Holmes, we felt the explosion, and yet..."

"You need not worry, Monsieur Mifroid. This business has ended."

The streetlights of the Place de l'Opéra provided abundant light. I recognized most of the faces in the crowd: the managers, Montcharmin with the monocle swelling one eye, red-faced Richard towering over him; Monsieur Gris in his soiled work clothes, a cigarette drooping from his lips; stout Madame Giry with her little Meg—Meg who resolutely kept her mouth shut, hiding her bad teeth; Christine and the Viscount, her face pale and troubled, his arm wrapped protectively about her; the Persian, his astrakhan hat gone forever, buried in the rubble of Erik's home; the youthful Bossuet in evening dress; the aged du Bœuf wearing his soiled leather apron, the precious limes in the pocket; and all the other carpenters, stagehands, gas men, and dancers whom Holmes and I had come to know during the weeks spent exploring the Palais Garnier.

"But *le Fantôme*..." Mifroid began.

"*Le Fantôme n'est plus,*" Holmes said. "He will trouble you no more."

Christine's face twisted, but the Viscount, relieved and triumphant, led her away. The crowd murmured, then grew strangely silent.

Madame Giry began to cry. As usual, she was dressed all in black, an outlandish black feathered thing on her head. "Poor Ghost, poor Ghost. He was a good fellow and always looked after me and my Meg." She blew her nose loudly, then drew in her breath, her great bosom swelling. "I do not believe you, Monsieur Holmes! How can a ghost die? *Le Fantôme* lives, I know it. Even as the Opera lives on, so does the Phantom. He may hide for a time, but he can never die!"

# Afterword

The breeze coming through the tall stone windows was a spring wind, warm and fragrant. The light of the longer, clearer days had transformed the castle in Wales. It was difficult to believe this was the same gloomy chamber where Holmes had confronted Major Lowell only a few weeks before. Gone was the statue of Kali, the Black Mother, which had so dominated the room.

The violinist played at a tempo which was simply impossible; it seemed beyond the bounds of a mere mortal. Surely the great virtuosi like Paganini and Liszt had no greater technical skill. The final movement of the *Kreuzer* was supposed to be presto, but this was a presto to end all prestos. Somehow Miss Lowell managed to keep up with him, her own playing clearly inspired by the challenge.

I sat with my hands clutching the chair arms, absorbed in the music to an extent which was rare for me. Unlike my cousin I am easily distracted. During concerts my mind inevitably wanders, losing itself amidst the oddest reveries. I end up reflecting upon the pudding I had for dinner or the peculiar sensation in my big toe. However, even the dullest clod must have been moved by this performance.

The bow made the final, lightning dance across the strings, and Susan Lowell's fingers struck the closing chord. For an instant the music was there, the majestic echo of Beethoven's living genius, holding us fixed in our seats, and then there was only silence, or rather, the lazy murmur of the afternoon breeze wafting in through the windows along with golden light.

"Bravo!" I cried. "Bravo." I had leapt to my feet.

"Bravo indeed!" Michelle stood beside me, applauding.

My cousin sat in his chair, his mouth half open, his eyes still closed. Our bravos made him wince. Slowly, unwillingly, he opened his eyes. He took out his handkerchief and wiped his face with it.

Susan Lowell stood up, groped at where she knew the violinist to be. Her hand found his shoulder, slid down and gripped his wrist. "Oh, thank you, Monsieur Noir. Thank you."

The eyes in the white mask seemed strangely lost, hovering somewhere between the celestial realm of the music and this corporeal chamber in Wales. One could see the pull between the two worlds, but at last he gave a great sigh, the sound muffled by his mask. His eyes settled upon Miss Lowell and did not move.

"You did not tell me you were a genius, Monsieur. Dear God, I have never heard such music! I did not think it was possible."

"You were very good, Miss Lowell." His voice, that full baritone, was tremulous.

"Will you not call me, Susan, Monsieur. You have been here for over a week now, and after *that* I feel I know you to the depths of your soul."

"Very well." He spoke so softly his voice was difficult to distinguish behind the mask.

"And will you do me one other favor?"

"Anything you wish."

Her face was still flushed. "Would you remove your mask?"

Erik stiffened, then did not move.

"Forgive me, I am being terribly presumptuous. It is only that... You do not sound... right... through that mask. Your voice is so resonant. Someone who could see might not notice, but every time you speak I am aware of that mask between us. I sense its presence—I can *hear* that it is there. I do not think... Oh, forget my foolish request."

Holmes's fingers drummed at the arm of his chair, playing out some unheard, inner rhythm. "It seems a reasonable enough request to me."

The mask hid Erik's face, but now his eyes showed confusion and fear. He glanced at me, then at Michelle.

"I am a physician, Monsieur Noir." Michelle's voice relished the irony as she spoke his name. "I have seen many distressing sights, many grave wounds, injuries, and sicknesses. While in India I visited a leprosarium and saw even children afflicted. Lepers, mercifully, feel little pain, physical pain anyway, and they can hurt themselves dreadfully without even realizing it. Remove your mask, if you wish. It will certainly not disturb me. The weather is ideal, the touch of the breeze on one's face warm and comforting."

"You need not hide yourself from us," Susan Lowell said. She let go of his wrist.

Erik said nothing. He and Sherlock stared at each other. At last he raised his hands, slipped off his mask, then held it very tightly, as if he were afraid he might lose it. I glanced at Michelle, but true to her word, her face showed no trace of dismay. I was not surprised. I knew from experience that she was less squeamish than I. She would have made an excellent army surgeon. Perhaps it was familiarity, perhaps the altered setting, but Erik's face no longer seemed so frightful to me. Again he and Holmes regarded one another, then he turned to Susan Lowell.

"You have removed it." Her voice was hushed. She smiled at him, her face radiant. I wondered again that such a beautiful woman could have led so solitary a life. Her dark skin and black hair added to her beauty, making her exotic and exceptional here in Wales. Erik must have reached a similar conclusion. He took a step forward.

Susan Lowell raised her hand, and it touched his face. He twisted away from her, and she took a step back. "I am sorry. I only... I can see nothing but light, no shapes or forms or faces. I was only curious. I... You are not angry with me?"

"I am not angry with you."

"Oh, good. I only... I would not hurt you."

They stood motionless, as if paralyzed, and we watched them silently. Finally Michelle strode past me, her skirts rustling. She grasped Erik's arm, then raised Susan's hand and set it against his cheek. This time he did not flinch. Michelle waited a minute, then stepped back.

Susan's fingertips explored Erik's face, tracing a line along his cheek down to his jaw. She came to the cavity where his nose should have been. "You are hurt," she murmured. At last she let her hand fall and lowered her head. "Forgive me, Monsieur, if I have... It is only because I... I like you that... Your music has unsettled me! I had no right to force my wishes upon you, to intrude upon your secrets. I have behaved most rudely. Please forgive me."

"There is nothing to forgive."

"Are you certain of that? You are not merely being polite?"

"No."

She smiled again. "Oh, I am glad to hear that. You do understand, do you not? Your face means nothing to us in this room, nothing at all. I think–I hope–that even if I had my sight I would feel the same way, but obviously I cannot be certain."

"I can." Michelle stood beside me again. "It would not matter to you, Susan. You are too noble a person to be constrained by appearances."

Erik stared at Michelle, then exhaled slowly. He breathed more freely without the mask.

"Michelle, you are a very good sort of person yourself," Susan Lowell said.

Michelle smiled. "It is time Henry and I took our afternoon stroll. The music was wonderful, but most invigorating indeed. Perhaps walking will calm my spirits and return me to the earthly plain." She glanced at me, and I saw the conspiratorial gleam in her eyes.

I stood up. "Yes, a walk is the very thing."

Holmes rose and took out his cigarette case. His face was pale, and he appeared weary. He glanced at Erik, then turned and started for the hallway.

He had not gone five paces when Miss Lowell turned to him, no doubt locating him by his footsteps. "Mr. Holmes?"

"Yes?"

"Thank you, Mr. Holmes."

He shrugged. "For what?"

"You must play again with me soon."

"I fear that I am hardly in Erik's league."

"Neither am I. It would be better to have a more equal partner. That presto has nearly finished me. Besides, you are too modest. You are a very good violinist. Your *Kreutzer* was also inspired; I remember it well."

"I am competent on the violin, Miss Lowell, little more. My playing is cerebral rather than passionate." He lit his cigarette, then resumed walking.

"Sherlock," Erik said.

Holmes glanced briefly at him, said nothing, then continued walking.

Michelle squeezed my hand, and we left Erik and Susan Lowell alone together. Soon we were outside following the mossy stone path across the grounds. The grass had that heavy, dark green lushness of spring, the blades still wet from an earlier shower. These spring days when the sun shone between the rains, cutting through the gray clouds, the light had a special brilliance, a unique clarity. A bank of daffodils glowed with yellow fire, and everything was sharp and fresh. A hot summer day could not compare.

"I can hardly believe it," I said.

Michelle's hands were clasped loosely about my left arm just above the elbow. Her skin was very fair, and already our walks had given her a few freckles across her nose and cheeks. Four tiny creases radiated out from the corner of her eye. "Believe what?" she asked.

"Any of this. That the world is so beautiful, those daffodils so yellow. That we are truly married; that we are here together. It was only some three weeks ago that Sherlock and I were wandering about in those cold, dark cellars beneath the Opera. I thought I should never see you again. How I cursed my foolish hesitations. I have told you what a debt we owe to Erik and my cousin. They made me understand my own stupidity."

"You would have come round eventually, Henry."

"All the same, I feel somehow rather… stupid, or ashamed, or… It took me so *long*. I cannot help but fault my character, pompous as that sounds."

"You have more character than most men, and you were worth the wait, my dearest. Ours may not be the first wild infatuation of youth, but it is real enough all the same." She stopped walking and touched my cheek with her fingertips.

We were still at that stage of love when we longed for each other continually, when the day dragged on until night finally came, when her every touch made me desire her. I kissed her. Her lips were very warm. She slipped her arms about me and drew me close. She was a tall woman and very strong.

"Oh, Henry—I do love you."

I kissed her again, and she responded vigorously. At last she drew away. "This will never do. We are only getting ourselves all hot and bothered."

"Very hot and bothered."

She caressed my cheek again. "Yes, extremely so." She sighed. "That rhododendron there is quite spectacular. Besides hiding us from any watchers in the house, it shares its beauty with us."

The plant in question was a good ten feet tall, more tree than bush. The sunlight glistened on the large, glossy green leaves, and the iridescent flowers were pale pink with streaks of orange and bronze in their centers.

"I have not seen blooms of that shade before," I said. "Perhaps the Major brought it back from India. The Himalayas are home to many unusual varieties."

"A pity he could not have limited himself to rhododendrons and left blood cults and dark goddesses behind. He must not have been completely bad, or Susan would not have turned out so well. Of course, we are all of us a mixture of good and bad."

"Except for you," I said. "You are quite perfect."

She laughed and squeezed my arm with both her hands. "You know better, you who have so nobly eaten my cooking."

"I did not marry you for your cooking, it is true. However, one may hire a cook to remedy deficits in that skill, but there are those wifely duties which cannot be contracted out, not if one wishes to remain within the bounds of propriety."

She stared at me, then laughed. "We had best continue our walk. This bush does not provide an ideal spot for those wifely duties of which you speak." We began to stroll again. "I wish Sherlock could provide for himself as well as he has provided for Erik."

"Yes," I replied. "I never before realized his talents as a matchmaker. I am not certain when the idea of bringing Erik here first occurred to him, but it must have been early on. He was sly about this business.

I was convinced for an entire week that Erik was dead, buried under tons of rubble. Imagine my surprise when I went one day to Baker Street and discovered Erik seated on the sofa in the parlor. He had fled the Opera via one of his secret passages, taking little more than his precious violin. He came to London alone, disguised again as a tall old woman in black. Naturally this was all done with Sherlock's help."

"I wonder how Sherlock convinced him to flee. You said he seemed most determined to end his life."

"He did indeed. That is why the thought he might still be alive never crossed my mind. When I saw him in London, I actually wondered for an instant if he were a specter. The nature of Sherlock's persuasion is obvious: he must have told him about Susan Lowell."

"She does seem perfect for him."

"Yes. That concert they gave us was extraordinary. It would have been a tragedy for such a genius to have snuffed out his life. Sherlock understood him from the first, even as he understood that I would see the light about you. Watson may have made him perhaps the most famous misogynist in England; yet he knows much about the secrets of the human heart."

Michelle shook her head. "He is no misogynist; he is a good actor, but not that good. I have seen how he looks at Susan. Bringing Erik here was no small sacrifice on his part."

"Perhaps someday he will look to his own needs."

"Perhaps, but..." She sighed. "Men are curious creatures, so self-important and so resolute; yet they know almost nothing of their inner lives, their inner thoughts and feelings. They mean only to protect themselves, but they do harm instead. They are like plants raised in the dark out of the light. They grow gangly and stunted, deformed. They deny themselves the greatest happiness our sad little lives can offer us. I have seen so much self-inflicted misery, so much sorrow that might have been avoided. Loving is not so very difficult, is it?"

"No. You are not only beautiful, Michelle." My words caught in my throat.

She squeezed my arm and gave me a glance that made me want to kiss her again. She gazed off into the distance back at the castle. "Here comes Sherlock. Let us walk with him."

"Perhaps he wishes to be alone."

"I do not think so; I think he needs comforting."

"'Comforting'? Never let him hear you say such a thing."

She smiled. "Come on, Henry."

We started back along the mossy path. He was strolling along at a good clip, walking stick in hand. He had changed clothes, trading his frock coat and top hat for a tweed Norfolk jacket and a felt hat.

He smiled at us, yet his face still seemed drawn and tired. "And how do you find the grounds today? The light appears most remarkable, the temperature perfect."

Michelle circled about him, then put her hand on his left arm. "It is indeed, and now we shall enjoy the fine view in your company."

"I fancy Henry, selfish knave that he is, would rather have you to himself."

"No matter. I shall have to endure him for many long and wearisome years to come, while you will no doubt be rushing off in another day or two." She took my right arm with her free hand, then the three of us started down the path.

"Sherlock," I said, "I must compliment you. You have done a very noble thing in bringing Erik to Susan Lowell."

Holmes's mouth stiffened, and he gave a slight shrug.

"I had not realized to what depths you would go to preserve your bachelorhood. Perhaps though, you will some day meet your Waterloo in female form."

Holmes frowned. "Figurative language is not your strong point, Henry. You have taken one of the few worthy members of the female species. I must therefore resign myself to the solitary life."

Michelle smiled sweetly at him. "Oh, is that all? I shall gladly abandon Henry to become your wife. I have, after all, put up with him for an entire week."

I shook my head. "Worse and worse."

Michelle was watching Sherlock closely. "All the same, I shall not rest until I see you married."

"I fear you will have a very long wait." Holmes glanced at the dark oaks along the distant ridge. "I am not the marrying kind. I lack patience. I would not inflict all my annoying habits and peccadillos on some poor woman. Besides, no woman could tolerate my slovenly habits and strange hours. She would attempt to reform me, and then the wars would begin."

Michelle laughed. "Do you honestly believe there are no slovenly women who keep odd hours? I can assure you that you are wrong, for I am such a woman. I know there are others."

I nodded. "I can vouch for the slovenliness."

"I wish to be serious now," Michelle said. "We have been jesting, but I have a request, Sherlock."

"Anything you wish."

"Do not be so accommodating, not before you know what I would ask." She and my cousin stared at one another. "Promise that you will not close off your heart and attempt to live in isolation."

"I cannot promise such a thing."

Although the sun still shone, it began to rain lightly, so lightly it was difficult to know if the drops were real or imagined.

"And why not?"

"Because it goes against my nature."

"Your nature." Michelle's voice was faintly ironic. "Can you understand Erik, can you save him, but not yourself? He built a complete world for himself, but one which cut him off entirely from everyone else. He considered himself a freak, a monster. At least he finally understood that his isolation was unbearable. Will you not learn from his example?"

Holmes did not reply; all traces of amusement were gone from his face. I agreed with Michelle, but I wondered if she had gone too far.

At last my cousin spoke. "I understand the parallels you speak of only too well."

"Then will you promise me that you will never become a phantom and hide yourself behind a mask?"

"Definitely not. Life would be unbearable without our masks."

"I am serious, Sherlock Holmes. Do not hide yourself from us, do not construct a Palais Garnier about your heart."

Sherlock laughed. "You are a formidable foe, Michelle, but you ask too much. I promise you one thing only: from you and Henry I shall never hide myself, not completely. You will be my friends always, and you may remind me of my vow when I become curt and prickly. That must suffice."

A few creases wrinkled Michelle's brow. "I suppose that will have to do for now." She stopped walking, slipped her hand about Holmes's neck, then kissed him lightly on the mouth. They stared at one another; then we resumed walking.

"I envy you, Henry." Sherlock's face was flushed.

"If an unexceptional person like myself can be graced with such a partner, surely there is hope for Sherlock Holmes."

Michelle smiled at me. I put my hand on the small of her back, just above the swell of her hips. Again I was grateful that the bustle had fallen out of fashion. Very softly, Sherlock began to hum the melody from the presto of the *Kreutzer* sonata.

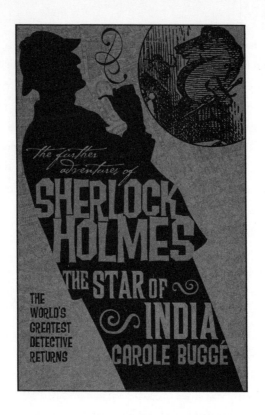

## THE FURTHER ADVENTURES
## OF SHERLOCK HOLMES

# THE STAR OF INDIA

*Carole Buggé*

Holmes and Watson find themselves caught up in a complex chess board
of a problem, involving a clandestine love affair and the disappearance of a
priceless sapphire. Professor James Moriarty leads the duo on a chase through
the dark and dangerous back streets of London and beyond.

ISBN: 9780857681218

## AVAILABLE AUGUST 2011

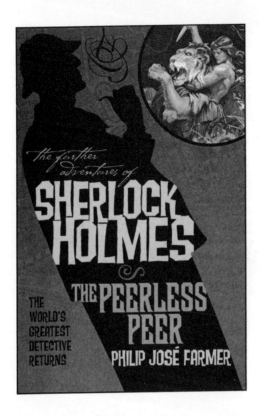

# THE FURTHER ADVENTURES
## OF SHERLOCK HOLMES

# THE PEERLESS PEER

*Philip José Farmer*

During the Second World War, Mycroft Holmes dispatches his brother
Sherlock and Dr. Watson to recover a stolen formula. During their perilous
journey, they are captured by a German zeppelin. Subsequently forced to
abandon ship, the pair parachute into the dark African jungle where they
encounter the lord of the jungle himself...

ISBN: 9780857681201

## AVAILABLE JUNE 2011

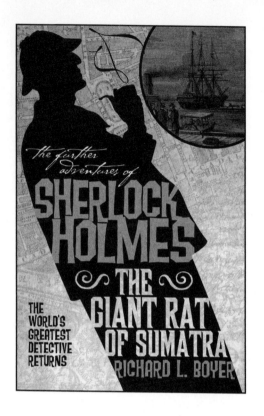

THE FURTHER ADVENTURES
OF SHERLOCK HOLMES

# THE GIANT RAT OF SUMATRA

*Richard L. Boyer*

For many years, Dr. Watson kept the tale of The Giant Rat of Sumatra a secret.
However, before he died, he arranged that the strange story of the giant rat should
be held in the vaults of a London bank until all the protagonists were dead...
ISBN: 9781848568600

## AVAILABLE NOW!

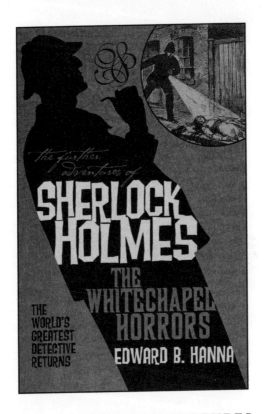

THE FURTHER ADVENTURES
OF SHERLOCK HOLMES

# THE WHITECHAPEL HORRORS

*Edward B. Hanna*

Grotesque murders are being committed on the streets of Whitechapel.
Sherlock Holmes believes he knows the identity of the killer—Jack the
Ripper. But as he delves deeper, Holmes realizes that revealing the
murderer puts much more at stake than just catching a killer…
ISBN: 9781848567498

## AVAILABLE NOW!

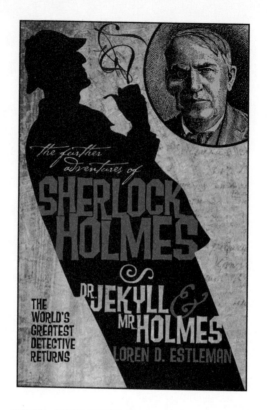

## THE FURTHER ADVENTURES OF SHERLOCK HOLMES

# DR. JEKYLL AND MR. HOLMES

*Loren D. Estleman*

When Sir Danvers Carew is brutally murdered, the Queen herself calls on Sherlock Holmes to investigate. In the course of his enquiries, the esteemed detective is struck by the strange link between the highly respectable Dr. Henry Jekyll and the immoral, debauched Edward Hyde...
ISBN: 9781848567474

# AVAILABLE NOW!

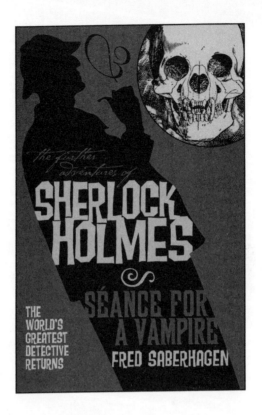

## THE FURTHER ADVENTURES
### OF SHERLOCK HOLMES

# SÉANCE FOR A VAMPIRE

*Fred Saberhagen*

Wealthy British aristocrat Ambrose Altamont hires Sherlock Holmes to
expose two suspect psychics. During the ensuing séance, Altamont's
deceased daughter reappears as a vampire—and Holmes vanishes.
Watson has no choice but to summon the only one who might be able to
help — Holmes's vampire cousin, Prince Dracula.

ISBN: 9781848566774

## AVAILABLE NOW!

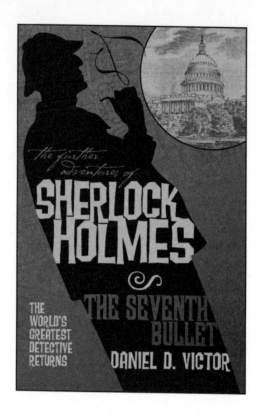

## THE FURTHER ADVENTURES
## OF SHERLOCK HOLMES
# THE SEVENTH BULLET

*Daniel D. Victor*

Sherlock Holmes and Dr. Watson travel to New York City to
investigate the assassination of true-life muckraker and author
David Graham Phillips is assassinated. They soon find themselves
caught in a web of deceit, violence and political intrigue, which
only the great Sherlock Holmes can unravel.
ISBN: 9781848566767

# AVAILABLE NOW!

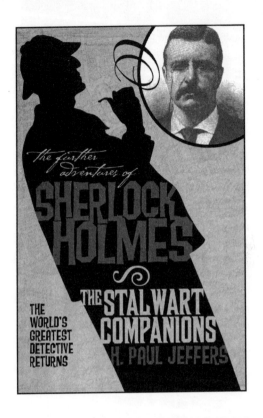

## THE FURTHER ADVENTURES
## OF SHERLOCK HOLMES

# THE STALWART COMPANIONS

*H. Paul Jeffers*

Written by future President Theodore Roosevelt long before The
Great Detective's first encounter with Dr. Watson, Holmes visits
America to solve a most violent and despicable crime. A crime
that was to prove the most taxing of his brilliant career.
ISBN: 9781848565098

# AVAILABLE NOW!

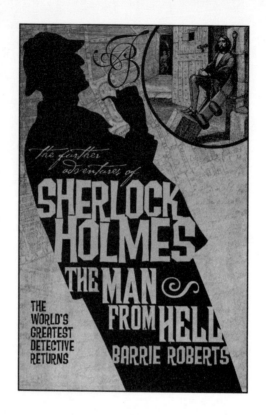

## THE FURTHER ADVENTURES
## OF SHERLOCK HOLMES

# THE MAN FROM HELL

*Barrie Roberts*

In 1886, wealthy philanthropist Lord Backwater is found
beaten to death on the grounds of his estate. Sherlock
Holmes and Dr. Watson must pit their wits against a ruthless
new enemy...
ISBN: 9781848565081

# AVAILABLE NOW!

## THE FURTHER ADVENTURES OF SHERLOCK HOLMES

# THE WAR OF THE WORLDS

*Manley W. Wellman & Wade Wellman*

Sherlock Holmes, Professor Challenger and Dr. Watson meet their match when the streets of London are left decimated by a prolonged alien attack. Who could be responsible for such destruction? Sherlock Holmes is about to find out...
ISBN: 9781848564916

## AVAILABLE NOW!

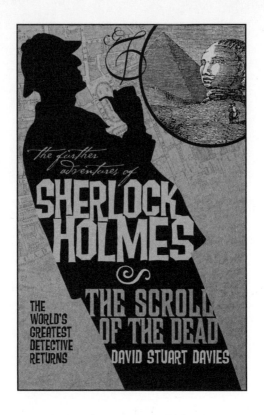

## THE FURTHER ADVENTURES
## OF SHERLOCK HOLMES

# THE SCROLL OF THE DEAD

*David Stuart Davies*

Sherlock Holmes attends a séance to unmask an impostor posing
as a medium, Sebastian Melmoth, a man hell-bent on obtaining
immortality after the discovery of an ancient Egyptian papyrus. It
is up to Holmes and Watson to stop him and avert disaster.
ISBN: 9781848564930

# AVAILABLE NOW!